THE PENGUIN CLASSICS
FOUNDER EDITOR (1944–64): E. V. RIEU

Paul A. Chilton was born in 1944 and educated at Magdalen College, Oxford, where he read modern languages (French and German) and undertook doctoral research in sixteenth- and seventeenth-century French literature. From 1970 until 1973 he was a lecturer at the University of Nottingham, since then he has been lecturer in the Department of French Studies at the University of Warwick where he teaches and does research in Renaissance literature and linguistics. His other publications are *The Poetry of Jean de La Ceppède* (1977) and articles on literature and language.

Marguerite de Navarre

THE HEPTAMERON

Translated with an introduction by
P. A. Chilton

PENGUIN BOOKS

Penguin Books Ltd, Harmondsworth, Middlesex, England
Penguin Books, 40 West 23rd Street, New York, New York 10010, U.S.A.
Penguin Books Australia Ltd, Ringwood, Victoria, Australia
Penguin Books Canada Ltd, 2801 John Street, Markham, Ontario, Canada L3R 1B4
Penguin Books (N.Z.) Ltd, 182–190 Wairau Road, Auckland 10, New Zealand

This translation first published 1984

Made and printed in Great Britain by
Hazell Watson & Viney Ltd, Aylesbury, Bucks
Set in Linotron Bembo

CONTENTS

INTRODUCTION

I. THE TEXT

The *Heptaméron* is a collection of some seventy stories. It has no definitive form: the order of the stories, the stories actually included and the textual details vary considerably from manuscript to manuscript and from printed edition to printed edition. As for the author, the scholarly consensus confidently attributes the collection to Marguerite de Navarre (1492–1549), sister of François I, patron of Rabelais, Marot and Des Périers, protector of reforming churchmen, and writer of intense mystical verse. However, this attribution is based on evidence which is at best circumstantial, and which needs to be interpreted with moderation.

Marguerite died in 1549, but the collection did not appear in print until 1558. It bore the title *Histoires des Amans fortunez*, and was edited by the humanist scholar Pierre Boaistuau. This first edition had only sixty-seven stories, arranged in an order not found in any of the other versions, and omitted the linking discussion passages found in the fullest manuscripts. Moreover, in his dedication (to the Duchess of Nevers) Boaistuau makes no explicit mention of Marguerite de Navarre as the author. Perhaps this was because Boaistuau had made a botch of her work. Perhaps it was because Marguerite was not the real author of the collection, or at least not the original author of all the tales and all the dialogues.

One year later in 1559 a new edition came out which claimed to restore the stories to their 'true' arrangement and to give credit for authorship where it was due – namely, to the late Queen of Navarre. Pierre Gruget, the new editor, also gave the collection a title it has had ever since, though it never had it in the manuscripts: *L'Heptaméron des Nouvelles*. In a dedication to Marguerite's daughter, Jeanne d'Albret, Gruget grumbles about Boaistuau's 'omission or concealment' of the author's name, and claims to have restored her work to its pristine state by collating all the available manuscript versions. Gruget certainly ordered the tales differently, distributed them into 'Days' of ten stories, and brought in fuller prologues and dialogues. But he still remains close to his predecessor. Both of them disguise proper names and suppress passages which might have been suspect to conservative theologians or which might have offended the religious orders. This did not become plain until the nineteenth-century editors returned to the extant manuscripts. At the same time it emerged that Gruget had removed three whole stories (stories 11, 44 and 46 in the manuscripts), presumably because they represent the Franciscans as gluttons, parasites and rapists, and had substituted three which were less disturbing.

So Gruget, who appeared to be establishing the *Heptaméron* canon, ends up raising questions about it. Where did his three stories come from? Are they by Marguerite? Are there any mislaid stories which still might turn up and make the *Heptaméron* the French *Decameron* its editors wanted it to be? Twentieth-century researchers have believed this to be the case. They have given attention to one particular version – an elegant manuscript dated 1553 prepared by the scholar Adrien de Thou. This manuscript calls itself *Le Décaméron* of Marguerite, and seems to leave empty pages for missing tales to complete the hundred implied in the title. It needs emphasizing, however, that this text, although it is consistent, readable and bristling with variants, appears to be a heavily edited version of other, earlier, manuscripts which are often incomplete or obscure. Its main interest, therefore, is as a guide to alternative readings and as an indication of how a careful sixteenth-century reader could make sense of faulty copy.

The expectations aroused by de Thou's blank pages have hardly been fulfilled. Apart from Gruget's three substitutes, only two further candidates have been discovered, a short story which occurs in three idiosyncratic manuscripts and a fragment of dialogue in another manuscript of de Thou's. So there are four more possible tales that one could add to the canon. While in style and content they are more or less compatible with the main corpus, there is no direct evidence as to authorship, and it remains largely a matter of taste whether or not one includes them. They have been left out of the present translation.

Much more research into the manuscripts needs to be done before we can have a complete picture of the *Heptaméron*'s evolution. There are seventeen existing manuscripts of differing degrees of completeness. They can be divided into two groups, although it has not so far been the custom to look at them in this fashion. The first group, whether or not they have the full seventy-two tales of Gruget or the full linking dialogues, all agree with his arrangement. The clearest and most complete of these (manuscript Fr. 1512 in the Bibliothèque Nationale) has been used as the basis of Michel François's edition, which is nowadays the most widely used version, and which has been adopted as the basis for this translation. But even here François has had to amend (using de Thou), and the resulting text still contains words, phrases and whole sentences which either do not make sense or require acrobatic interpretation. The second group of manuscripts has the stories in an order different from both Gruget and Boaistuau. It has no discussions between the storytellers, but instead an 'argument' preceding each tale and a 'conclusion', whose function is primarily to draw out moral and pious lessons. One of the stories in two of these manuscripts is the fourth 'find' which has been mentioned above. The best of this group is in the Pierpont Morgan library in New York. Besides offering seventy tales, it includes the Prologue and a delicate contemporary pen drawing of the storytellers. What is the status of this second group of manuscripts? In so far as it is mentioned at all by scholars it is usually assumed to represent later anthologies à la Boaistuau. Strictly speaking, however, it still remains to determine whether these manuscripts do not represent a proto-*Heptaméron* with a logic and intention of its own.

There is thus no definitive or generally agreed text. The variety of manuscripts suggests considerable scribal and editorial freedom, with at least three ways of organizing the material. If Marguerite was the sole author it appears that she did not set a personal prescription on the form of her work. And the same would be true of any other proposed author. In fact there is one definite proposal which should be mentioned, if only to save it from oblivion, and that is a proposal first put forward in 1839 by Charles Nodier, who claimed that the author of all or most of the *Heptaméron* was Bonaventure des Périers. Des Périers was the probable author of the satirical *Cymbalum mundi* (1537) and of much of a collection of stories called *Nouvelles récréations* published in the same year as Boaistuau's *Histoires des Amans fortunez*. He was also Marguerite's *valet de chambre* from at least 1536. Nodier's proposal should not be taken too seriously, but what it points to should – that just as it is difficult to pin down a single authoritative text, so it is impossible to pin down a single author. The reason is that the *Heptaméron* was a collective enterprise. The stories themselves may have been contributed by a number of different people, probably high-ranking noblemen and noblewomen in Marguerite's entourage. In all likelihood Marguerite was herself a contributor, and may also have edited them and added the story-telling framework in which they are embedded. The court gossip-monger Brantôme says in his memoirs that his grandmother, who was a lady-in-waiting to Marguerite, told him that the Queen 'composed' her tales as she was carried about the country in her litter. As Nodier pointed out, however, the tales could have been described as 'hers' by sovereign right, since their contributors were her servants. The fact is that the *Heptaméron* itself represents itself as produced by a group of individuals at the court of François I who really did, so the text claims, undertake to tell one another a collection of stories.

2. THE STORYTELLERS

The Prologue of the *Heptaméron* introduces the five men and five women who after various adventures involving bandits, floods and bears, find refuge in a Pyrenean abbey, where they agree to pass their time telling edifying stories until it is safe for them to return home. In so doing they are following an ancient tradition of fictional characters who find themselves in dangerous or unusual situations – a tradition that includes the *Thousand and One Nights*, the *Canterbury Tales* and Boccaccio's *Decameron*. The origins of the French *nouvelle* or short story are medieval: the *lais* of Marie de France, moral tales or *exempla* used by preachers, the *fabliaux*. But it was the fifteenth and sixteenth centuries that saw the rise of the short story as an important genre, and it was primarily Boccaccio's *Decameron* that served as the model. The first French translation of the *Decameron*, by Laurent Premierfait, appeared in 1414, inspiring the *Cent Nouvelles Nouvelles* composed in or before 1462. A new translation of Boccaccio is referred to in the *Heptaméron*'s Prologue. It was commissioned by Marguerite herself, was undertaken by one of François I's royal councillors, Antoine Le Maçon, and came out in 1545. This is a period of French history in which the kings sought to annex Italian territory by means of ambitious military expenditions and to assimilate and surpass Italian literary and artistic culture as well.

The *Heptaméron*'s Prologue tells us how much the royal family admired Boccaccio, and how Marguerite and the Dauphine (Catherine de Médicis) joined with other persons of the court to produce a French *Decameron*. There was, however, to be an important difference: all the tales were to be true, and on the insistence of the Dauphin (the future Henri II) there were to be no scholars or men of letters amongst the storytellers, since rhetoric was felt to be incompatible with historical truth. These stipulations appear to have left their mark on the *Heptaméron* we know. All the storytellers claim that their tales are true, and about twenty tales have been verified by modern research. There is only one from a literary source (number 70) and the storytellers permit this one only after discussion. But more important is the constant concern with the problem of truth and language. Rhetoric, lying, parody, blasphemy and obscenity – the treachery of human language is a theme that is subtly interwoven in the stories and discussions, counterbalanced by the theme of the search for verbal purity and security in the Word of God.

However, it is one of the puzzles of the *Heptaméron* that the text we now have is not, according to the Prologue, the same thing as this original royal project, which, we are told, was interrupted by more pressing affairs of state (like the invasion of France in 1544) and completely forgotten. This assertion provides the opportunity for the fictional, or rather semi-fictional, storytellers to make good the loss.

A lot of scholarly effort has been expended in trying to establish the historical identities of the storytellers on the basis of the various clues to be found in the text. It certainly seems to be the case that the names of the storytellers refer to some historical individuals, and that the Prologue and the discussion passages are meant to represent some historical story-telling enterprise. But each storyteller becomes a distinct character in the fictional world of the *Heptaméron*, relating to the others in a consistent manner, speaking in an idiosyncratic style, and telling stories to reflect his or her personality. There are antagonisms within the group, the most fundamental of which is between the male and female members.

The names of these characters are bizarre at first sight. The general principle behind them, however, appears to be this: a historical individual's name is rearranged to form an anagram, not a meaningless anagram, but one which suggests the personal attributes of the character to whom it is applied. In some cases oral and scribal transmission may have obscured the original; in others it may even have introduced new meanings and associations. The oldest and most authoritative storyteller is Oisille. The name could be derived anagrammatically from 'Loise' (a possible spelling of 'Louise'). This character may, it is thought, stand for Louise de Savoie, Marguerite's mother, or more plausibly for Louise de Daillon, Brantôme's grandmother and a lady-in-waiting to Marguerite at about the right period. It is Oisille who is the group's spiritual leader, and this within the setting of a monastery, that is, within an exclusively male community. She is imbued with the spirit of evangelical reform, and her name (which suggests *oiselle*, 'female bird') can be taken to reflect her longing for spiritual flights. Parlamente, also an authoritative figure, may represent Marguerite herself, since the name can be derived from *perle amante*, 'loving pearl', which would be a pun on *marguerite*, another word for 'pearl'. There would also be symbolic associations of purity and perfection. Incidentally, if Marguerite is taken to be the author of the Prologue, then we have a curiously self-reflexive piece of writing. Marguerite as writer-narrator would be talking about herself ('Parlamente', the 'pearl' or 'marguerite') talking about herself ('Madame Marguerite') talking about writing a Decameron. The name Parlamente has in the past been associated with the old verb *parlementer*, and thus with talking, conversing, eloquence and urbanity. This suits the story-telling character, as well as the real Marguerite, who was often so described by her contemporaries. The name of Parlamente's fictional husband, Hircan, can be derived from *Henri* (alternatively spelt *Henric* or *Hanric*), the name of Marguerite's real-life second husband, Henri de Navarre. *Hircan* (*Hircain* in some versions) suggests the Latin for 'goatish' (*hirquinus*), but also Hircania, the rugged habitat of tigers and other wild beasts in Classical and Renaissance literature. Hircan is a warrior, jealous of his honour, and blunt in speech and manners. He is one of the main exponents of male dominance over women, and insists on the male right to intercourse with any female of his choice, while at the same time demanding the domestication and fidelity of wives.

These three, Oisille, Parlamente, Hircan, are at the apex of a miniature aristocratic society. They represent too a three-cornered antagonism that runs throughout the *Heptaméron* – an antagonism between female intelligence and love, masculine aggressiveness, and transcendent spirituality. The other characters and their names emerge in a similar fashion, and all contribute to a range of attitudes towards the topics of their stories and conversations, from the naturalistic cynicism of Saffredent to the Platonizing self-repression of Dagoucin. Above all they talk – some to flatter and flirt, some to dominate, some to resist, some to distort and deceive, some to preach and pray and some to extol the virtue of not speaking at all.

3. THE STORIES

The storytellers, then, have firm roots in their historical context, though their fictional context presents them in such a way as to focus on types of attitude towards the world. The stories also are interwoven with their historical context, not only in the sense that they actually refer to particular individuals – kings, princes, abbots, officers of the crown and so forth – but also in the sense that they present real contemporary social and spiritual problems. It is this dimension that makes the tales relevant also to our own historical context.

To summarize the complexities and conflicts of the first half of the sixteenth century in France would be impossible. But there are some major historical threads which it is useful to bear in mind while reading the *Heptaméron*. First, it is in this period that France begins to construct its identity as a nation-state controlled by a centralized monarchy, and to express itself in both political and cultural rivalry with Italy, Spain and England. Secondly, the traditional aristocracy (from which the *Heptaméron*'s storytellers are drawn) is confronted with changes such as the rise of the commercial, legal and bureaucratic classes. Thirdly, women may have been more self-assertive. Many noblewomen experienced increased independence and responsibility while their husbands were fighting in the Italian wars. There was certainly a flourishing literary debate on the status of women, which produced some remarkable declarations on both sides. Finally, the whole period is marked by the various ideological changes that go under the term Reformation, the most prominent of which are the emphasis on inner faith as opposed to external ritual, the emphasis on individual conscience as opposed to ecclesiastical authority and the challenge to the priesthood, monasticism and the doctrine of celibacy. In broad terms, it is a period of rapid cultural change, a period in which assumptions are being questioned and horizons broadened, both in the geographical sense (story 67 of the *Heptaméron*, for instance, concerns a voyage to Canada) and in the historical sense of the discovery of the values of the ancient non-Christian civilizations.

Academic introductions to the *Heptaméron* usually say that the main themes are various concepts of 'love' on the one hand offset on the other by 'religion', in particular the evangelism with the Platonic tinge that was characteristic of French attempts to reform the Church from within. Earlier generations who expurgated or excused the *Heptaméron* were possibly more aware that the principal themes of the stories and the conversations that accompany them are rape, seductions bordering on rape, incest and numerous infringements of the sex and marriage codes of aristocratic Europe. Sex is rarely fun in the *Heptaméron* (unlike Boccaccio's *Decameron*), and where characters do find enjoyment, it is accidental (as in story 8, or furtive and hypocritical (stories 43 and 49), or tragically revenged (story 32 and the clandestine marriage stories 21, 40 and 51) or guilt-ridden and roundly condemned (as in story 26). One has the impression that marriage and relationships between the sexes in general are deeply problematic for the world which the *Heptaméron* reflects. There are very few stories which do not directly concern such themes (story 17 about the prowess of François I; 28 and 52, which concern food and its debasement; 55 and 65, which are solely concerned with superstitious attitudes towards religion).

Rape in the *Heptaméron* sometimes takes place when the desires of a socially inferior male for a superior woman of conspicuous qualities are frustrated. This is so in the case of the mule-driver's wife and the servant who finally murders her (story 2), but it is also true in the long and tortuous tenth story, where the warrior Amador's attempts to transgress social barriers and possess the young Florida lead not only to violence against the woman, but to the woman's violence against herself. There is an element of pathological obsession in such stories. But the most pervasive motive has to do with the masculine ethos of honour and military glory. There are implicit structural parallels between military and sexual violence in the Amador story; in fact the whole story can be seen as a kind of exploration of the uglier implications of the concept and practice of chivalrous love.

Hircan openly *advocates* rape in order to avert the threat to a gentleman's honour posed by resistance to seduction. The borderline between the two is indeed frequently blurred, as in stories 14 and 16 (both told by men), where the valiant Admiral Bonnivet outdoes his Italian rivals and overcomes the resistance of two Italian women during the French occupation of Milan. Both the newer and the older senses of the term 'chauvinism' sum up these examples. To *fail* in an attempted rape constitutes the greatest humiliation for these men. Bonnivet again, in story 4, attempts to rape a high-born princess (rumoured by Brantôme to be Marguerite herself), only to be fought off by the lady's superior strength. Significantly, the storytellers agree that the woman was wise not to expose her attacker, since the prevailing view was (as also in story 62) that women only spoke of rape in order to mask their complicity, and that willing or not they were in any case dishonoured.

But the chief rapists and seducers are monks and friars. In fact almost all the many stories concerning monks and friars centre on this theme. They may rape or abduct in revenge for resistance (stories 5, 46), or because they take it to be some sort of right (stories 23, 31, 48 and 72, where the victim is a nun). They often associate it with punishment and penance (stories 46, 22, 41). In story 23 a rape-victim's suicide is actually attributed to the theology she learned from the Franciscans, with its stress on self-redemption by good works rather than on acceptance of human nature and grace freely given by a merciful God. But it is also stated that the woman feared for the purity of the family line. Even a story like story 11, which at first sight is purely scatological, is linked with monastic rape and fear of dishonour.

Coupled with the evangelical critique of Franciscan theology these tales are more than the traditional medieval farces about lecherous and gluttonous monks. Why are the religious orders depicted so consistently as sexually dangerous? It is not just criticism of the corruptness of monastic life, though it is that as well, or a portrayal of exploding frustrations. Clerical sexuality as such does not appear scandalous. There are two stories (56 and 61) in which women themselves initiate 'marriage' with clerics, creating situations which are treated humorously and somewhat ambivalently. It seems rather to be clerical aggression against, and degradation of, women that is presented in particularly horrific and horrified terms. Evangelical thinkers such as Erasmus and Rabelais had criticized the celibate life of monks and priests because it presupposed the inferiority of marriage. It also presupposed the biological, moral and intellectual inferiority of women (Rabelais's own views on this are not easy to determine). The reader of the *Heptaméron* may be able to link the work's evident dislike of friars to this background, that is, to the anti-feminist, anti-family and anti-marriage implications of the monastic outlook. Amongst other details it is worth noting that there is particular resentment in the *Heptaméron* of the intrusion of friars into family life, in part no doubt because of the threat to legitimacy and thus to a whole aristocratic society based on inheritance. Also, the victims of rape are frequently presented as women distinguished by being particularly active, clever or virtuous. Rape seeks to show that they are none of these. It has been claimed as a general principle that in periods when women show signs of assertiveness there is a corresponding preoccupation with violence against them. Be this as it may, in the *Heptaméron* the representation of rape is used in two main ways: as proof of the worth of women and as proof of the aggressive intentions of the men.

If one goes further and asks why the *Heptaméron* should be so concerned with the themes of celibacy and marriage, one possible answer is that an aristocratic society in a changing world was necessarily concerned with procreation and marriage rules in order to sustain itself. This concern is stated explicitly as well as implicitly, as we shall see. The ideology of marriage which emerges does so negatively, by way of examples of infractions, and is not without ambivalences and unresolved contradictions. Many stories deal with the infidelities of married people. The fate of the erring wife is usually different from that of the wenching husband. Thus the President of Grenoble poisons his wife for taking a lover (story 36). A German nobleman (story 32) imposes on his wife a macabre, ritualistic punishment, which eventually leads to expiation of her offence. A wife is beaten (story 35) for her 'spiritual' love for a visiting friar. Story 70 is an evocation of the claustrophobic atmosphere of a feudal court where private passion and public honour vie with one another; but at its core is the representation of the Duchess of Burgundy as a woman depraved by jealousy and lust whose verbal revenge leads to death and perpetual shame. The male fear of cuckoldry is everywhere, and in one case (story 47) becomes so obsessive as to actually provoke it.

Not all the *Heptaméron*'s women fare badly by any means. Some of the sexually enterprising ones reflect the *fabliau* tradition: wayward and wanton women of lowly station outwit old or stupid husbands. Their high-born counterparts in stories 43 and 49 have to go to extreme lengths for sexual gratification, and they have to resort to desperate measures in order to conceal their activities and conserve their reputation. Some of the more extended stories include tentative justification of the woman's action, even if the storyteller and his or her companions do not accept it in discussion. The woman in story 61, for example, escapes what is described as domestic 'slavery' to live happily (though not quite ever after) with a canon of the Church. The energetic lady in story 15 is eventually locked up for the tricks she perpetrates upon her husband, but not before she has hugely enjoyed herself and delivered a closely argued speech during the course of which she asserts that 'although the law of men attaches dishonour to women who fall in love with those who are not their husbands, the law of God does not exempt men who fall in love with women who are not their wives'. Here, as elsewhere in the *Heptaméron*, the prevailing ethos is being challenged in reforming evangelical terms.

When the husband is unfaithful in the stories the role of the wife is fairly clearly defined, although all the storytellers do not always agree with all the implications. The paradigmatic case is story 37, in which a husband has an affair with a chambermaid, who is made to symbolize disorder, dirt and decay of the family fortunes. He is 'converted' by several acts of ritual significance on the part of his devout and devoted wife, who simultaneously restores order, purity and prosperity. A similar role is assumed in stories 38, 54, 59, 68, 69 and 71, in all of which a man's unfaithfulness is arrested by a wife's patience and ingenuity. Fidelity and long-suffering virtually make a saint of the wife who is marooned with her husband on a desert island (story 67).

There are few stories of reciprocal infidelity. The Queen of Naples, however, does take as her lover the husband of her own husband's mistress, and does so out of revenge, though she never discloses what she has done (story 3). Ignorance is also important in the neat farce of story 8, where a husband is unknowingly faithful, and his wife unknowingly unfaithful: she substitutes herself for a chambermaid (compare also story 45), and he invites his drinking-companion to share the spoils. In both these stories it is the husband's own infidelity that brings about his cuckoldry. Thus alongside those tales advocating the wife's moral influence as the remedy for her partner's unfaithfulness, there is a small minority of stories claiming something approaching a symmetry of sexual rights in marriage. But only one form of extramarital relationship is overtly sanctioned – that of the *serviteur* and his lady. This too turns out to embody the same values as marriage itself. According to the *serviteur* practice as the *Heptaméron* presents it, a married aristocratic woman has the right to maintain several devoted knights in her service. Such men are clearly not on a par with chambermaids, as story 58 makes clear. 'Fidelity' is required of both partners: ladies who betray their admirers are denigrated in stories 20 and 53, and the rule for *serviteurs* themselves is made clear in 58 and 63. Indeed story 63 implies that fidelity to one's lady is a stronger influence than fidelity to one's wife – a position which Parlamente at least criticizes. Since it is supposed to be chaste, the *serviteur* relationship, this remnant of courtly and chivalric love, can coexist with faithful marriage; in fact it is virtually a simulacrum of marriage. Nevertheless, there is evidently considerable anxiety about the institution as such, as the Amador and Florida story strongly indicates.

The stories of wanton women were traditionally *exempla* of their inferior nature, and this is how some of the male storytellers use them. But in the context of the work as a whole they emerge more as a means of rejecting the asymmetrical marriage in which the male has greater sexual freedom. In practice, of course, lineal purity was so important to the aristocratic circle that female infidelity could not be condoned; so the symmetry is achieved by demanding male fidelity and seeking to achieve it by any means. If those means involve sacrifice and humiliation, the suffering takes on a sanctifying quality. The nature of the importance of marriage for the storytellers becomes clear when one looks at the numerous stories which are essentially concerned with the question: 'Who may marry whom upon whose authority?' This was a question much discussed by sixteenth-century jurists and others (Erasmus and Rabelais, for example) who rejected the purely sacramental view of marriage to concentrate on its social and political function.

Stories 21 and 40, which are concerned with clandestine marriages entered into without family consent, pinpoint the issues. In both tales the family in question is probably the ancient family of Rohan. Story 40 gives us a count (the father of the heroine of 21) who preserves the honour of his blood by slaughtering his sister's secret husband, a lesser nobleman, and by locking his sister up in a castle in a forest. After the story Saffredent demands to know *why* a lesser nobleman should not marry a lady of higher status. He is told by Dagoucin:

The reason is . . . that in order to maintain peace in the state, consideration is given only to the rank of families, the seniority of individuals and the provisions of the law, and not to men's love and virtue, in order that the monarchy should not be undermined.

Men or women in the *Heptaméron* who transgress or try to transgress this rule frequently come to a tragic or 'piteous' end. There is sympathy for individual affections, but the social imperative remains paramount, and the resulting conflict is presented as a natural inevitability. It is a conflict which is generally 'resolved' or sublimated in some sort of religious transcendence. Discussing story 40, Parlamente verbalizes such a 'solution' in the language of evangelism, expressing a hope that somehow personal, parental and social preference will merge in submission to divine will. Her own earlier story about Rolandine (Anne de Rohan) is structured to the same end. The thirty-year-old heroine's secret marriage to a bastard is disapproved of by the Queen (Anne of Brittany), and she is locked up in the forest castle mentioned in story 40. But the marriage falls *within* the letter of ecclesiastical law. There is thus a confrontation of church and state. Evangelical opinion was in general opposed to the ecclesiastical marriage laws, not least because it was mainly the friars who were called upon to exploit them. However, in the story Rolandine's feelings are treated with great respect by the storyteller, and there is no clear taking of sides on the issues involved. Rather, the story is so set up that the conflict is resolved by the course of events which are narrated. Rolandine's 'perfect' love for the bastard is preserved, but since he deserts her and dies, she is able to be reconciled with her family, make a suitable marriage (with Pierre de Rohan) and produce suitable heirs.

The problem in these two stories is how to dissolve misalliances once they have been contracted. Some stories deal with the prevention of misalliances. Men and women whose choices are disapproved of and effectively suppressed vent their emotions in expressions of mystical union. Thus the man in story 9 is not permitted to love the lady of his choice within marriage, and his love is too 'perfect' to love her outside of marriage, so the only possible union is a deathbed embrace which assimilates human love to mystical love of God. Story 19 works this solution out in more explicit detail. A misalliance between a rich lady and a poor nobleman is blocked, and the lovers enter the religious life, he the Observant Franciscans, she the sister order of St Clare. Paradoxically united in their separation they transform their desires for one another into parallel mystical marriages. It is in the ensuing dialogue that Parlamente expounds her famous Platonic doctrine of 'perfect' love, a doctrine that enables tragic contradictions to be transcendentally resolved – that is, not resolved at all but merely mystified. Adulterous affections may be 'resolved' in the same way. In story 24, the narcissistic knight Elisor, who loves above his station, converts his chivalrous love and becomes a hermit. There is a not dissimilar pattern in story 13. But almost the reverse seems to be the case in story 64, where we have family *approval* of a marriage apparently producing the lady's rejection of her suitor, who subsequently consoles himself with the cloister. Even here, however, it is hinted that the girl's self-frustration is the result of an excessive sense of family honour seeking to outdo her parents and relatives. All four of the tales of the transformation of frustrated love into spiritual love contain verse passages – passages in which linguistic resonances are fully (if somewhat cumbersomely) exploited in order to express the notion of transcendent passion.

With the tales of perfect lovers turning into mystical recluses we come full circle from the image of friars as wandering sexual predators. Just as in the Prologue the storytellers visit a 'good' and a 'bad' monastery, so the monastic institutions portrayed in the stories are double-edged. On the one hand there is sexual aggression and abasement; friars attack women, intrude into the family, disrupt the social order. On the other hand, there is sexual suppression and sublimation; frustrated lovers leave society in order not to transgress its rules, entering the inner mystical world in order to resolve their conflict with such rules. Thus the obverse of the image of the monk as rapist is the image of the secular person ravished by divine love. The religious outlook which condemns the worldliness of corrupt religious orders, but espouses the direct mystical approach to God, is typical of moderate reforming evangelism such as Marguerite's own. It is possible to consider its manifestation in the *Heptaméron* in isolation, but to do so is to fail to interpret its significance in relation to the work as a whole. In the world of the *Heptaméron* there is a thematic logic which relates the image of the religious life not only to the contemporary problem of the nature and status of women, but also to an intense preoccupation with preserving the fine nuances of the aristocratic hierarchy through the rules and rites of marriage. This by no means exhausts the fictional fabric of the *Heptaméron* and its implications; there are many more intricate patterns which the reader may wish to puzzle out for himself.

4. TRANSLATIONS

The first work of Marguerite of Navarre to attract the attention of an English translator was not the *Heptaméron* but a long religious poem called *Le Miroir de l'ame pécheresse* (*The Mirror of the Sinful Soul*), first published in 1531. It appeared in England in 1548 and again in 1570 with the title *A Godly Meditation of the Christian Soul*. There are two reasons why it is worth mentioning. One is that it had been condemned by the Sorbonne because it was alleged to contain heretical elements. The other is that the translator, according to the title page, was none other than the eleven-year-old daughter of Henry VIII, Elizabeth, the future queen and head of the English church.

It was during Elizabeth's reign that the *Heptaméron* itself was first translated, with the title *The Queen of Navarre's Tales Containing Verie pleasant Discourses of fortunate lovers*. Seventeen tales only were included: the first nine from the first day, stories 2, 4, 5 and 6 from the second day, stories 9 and 10 from the third day and two tales that do not appear to belong to the French corpus at all. The discussion passages linking the stories were omitted altogether. The title suggests that Boaistuau's edition was the basis of the translation, but unlike Boaistuau's version it clearly attributes the collection to Marguerite. Indeed the writer of the preface (who admits that he has not even read the book!) regards Marguerite's name on the title page as sufficient recommendation to English readers, and so feels confident in offering to them 'pleasure and recreation . . . contained within the limits both of wit and modesty'.

The first complete translation appeared during Cromwell's Commonwealth, and was by Robert Codrington, who also translated a number of theological and devotional works. He followed the Gruget text (although his title partly follows Boaistuau's), with the exception of the verse passages, which he left out. In his 'To the Reader', Codrington gives a glimpse of the way the *Heptaméron* was interpreted. Marguerite was still associated primarily with reformed religion and the *Heptaméron* is presented as above all an edifying text. Though slightly uncertain of Marguerite's exact theological orientation ('For the Divinity of this great Lady in many places here inferred, it is left to your Candor to interpret of it'), he thinks the moral and philosophical content indubitable:

> . . . for the Philosophy you shall undoubtedly find, that most wisely she hath sorted her discourse, in fit persons, to the four Complexions of the Natural Body. Besides, you shall everywhere read most excellent Precepts of Moral Philosophy . . .

Moreover, he regards the *Heptaméron* as aimed at ecclesiastical authority, Catholic theologians and the religious orders: the 'Canonists', the 'Casuists' and the 'Friers and Religious Men'. Indeed, according to Codrington it was the 'Friers and Religious Men' who had deliberately suppressed the last three days of tales, and Gruget's preface was essentially a complaint about such interference. As well as appealing to the religious content of the work, Codrington found it necessary to appease the puritanical spirit by apologizing for anything that might appear 'too light'. He begs the reader to balance it with 'that which shall be found more solid', and to attribute lapses of taste to the 'simplicity of those times, and to the condition of that Court, where Mars and Venus were for a long time the two culminating Planets'.

An attempt to produce a popular English version was made around 1750 in a collaborative translation: *Novels, Tales and Stories. Written Originally in French, by Marguerite de Valois, Queen of Navar.* There were only eight tales (the first six, the eighth and ninth), no Prologue, and none of the discussion passages. The anonymous translators gave no indication of the text they used. It could have been a stylistically updated edition which first appeared in France in 1698, and which became the standard eighteenth-century version.

Codrington's translation remained the only serious attempt until Victorian scholars got to work on Le Roux de Lincy's new French edition of 1853–4, apparently as much in search of the erotic as in a desire for scholarly accuracy. Walter Keating Kelly came to the *Heptaméron* after translating Boccaccio's *Decameron* (1864), and after editing and translating two volumes entitled *Erotica* (1848). His *Heptameron of Margaret, Queen of Navarre* proclaims the authenticity of Le Roux de Lincy's text, on which the translation is supposed to be based. It also includes the three alternative stories of dubious authenticity found only in Gruget's edition. But the verse passages (stories 13, 19, 26 and 64), which are an intrinsic part of the French versions, are either completely omitted or briefly summarized in prose. Kelly's translation proved fairly successful. There were re-issues incorporating the engraved illustrations of Leopold Flameng, which had been used in a French edition of 1870–72 by Paul Lacroix, and there were others using the engravings of S. Freudenberger and B. A. Dunker found in French editions of the eighteenth century. Like all the Victorian and early-twentieth-century translators of the *Heptaméron* Kelly is anxious about its content. Whereas Codrington had been able to emphasize uplifting philosophy, Kelly can only worry about 'the questionable morality' and the 'free language'. Inexplicably, he believes that the *Heptaméron*'s first editors ('those manifold offenders') were responsible for what he calls 'grossly obscene passages'. The attitude still persists in a selection from Kelly's version published in 1927, which suppresses what are described as 'such discussions as are . . . of a tiresomely waggish turn' and modifies 'an occasional phrase that seemed unnecessarily crude'. The Kelly translation itself is frequently inaccurate, and, with its literary archaisms embedded in nineteenth-century literary syntax, largely indigestible.

Arthur Machen, a translator of Casanova's *Mémoires* and a prolific editor and essayist, took up the cudgels against his predecessors in the preface to his own, new and (so he claimed) complete, accurate and stylistically appropriate translation, which was privately printed in 1885. Codrington's translation he thought 'careless and hasty', Kelly's marred by 'phenomenal ignorance and portentous blundering'. True, Kelly omits some passages, mistranslates others and misunderstands sixteenth-century customs. But Machen's own attempts to 'give the work a thoroughly English dress' are not altogether happy, either. He, too, misunderstands sixteenth-century social institutions. A significant example is marriage by '*paroles de présent*' ('words in the present'), which, stretching syntax and vocabulary beyond credibility, is translated as 'word and gift'. However, Machen's great pride is his style. He feels impelled, he declares, to choose an older form of English: 'The work is calculated to remind readers rather of Walton than Macaulay.' No attention was given apparently to the stylistic variation *within* the text, which distinguishes speakers and types of discourse. The result, when it is not some species of mistranslation, constitutes a serious stylistic obstacle for a twentieth-century reader. For example, the apothecary's servant in story 52, which is essentially a scatological farce, picks up some frozen excrement. 'Straightway,' goes the translation, 'he wrapped it in a brave white paper.' Archaisms like 'much folk' (Prologue), 'arrant knave' and 'fain to try to make a child' (story 41) can only be read ironically in current English. Machen's version has one merit, however, and that is its relative completeness: Le Roux's text with the alternative Gruget tales for 44 and 46 (the alternative for 11 is omitted without comment), and translations of the original verse passages into English verse.

The handsomest and most scholarly of the nineteenth-century translations was by John Smith Chartres, a lawyer, and a translator of Flaubert's *Salammbô*. Published in 1894 in five volumes for the Society of English Bibliophilists, it had an introduction by George Saintsbury, was extensively annotated on the Le Roux model and carried the Freudenberg and Dunker engravings. The text is complete and the verse passages rendered in verse. The translation is predominantly accurate, though a few problems ('*paroles de présent*', again) persist. The style does not suffer from imposed archaisms. The greatest disadvantage of this version is that like its source, the Le Roux edition, it does not make use of the de Thou manuscript.

The last in the line of Victorian translations is stamped *Unexpurgated*. It was claimed to be a totally new rendering by 'W' –

that is, W. M. Thomson, who was responsible for translations of an astonishingly wide variety: the *Song of Songs*, Boccaccio, Rabelais, Renan, Schopenhauer and Tolstoy. This 'unexpurgated' translation of the *Heptaméron* is actually the most coy of all. Without comment it suppresses the story of the lady in the latrines (story 11) and the story of the frozen faeces (story 52), and makes many verbal modifications. Without stating his source text W. M. Thomson appears to be using Le Roux selectively, with an admixture of an earlier edition by Lacroix. He follows Kelly in glossing over the verse passages.

It is worth repeating that there exists no definitive critical edition of the *Heptaméron*. What we have from Marguerite's day are the seventeen variant manuscripts and the two conflicting printed editions. Codrington's translation represents the most complete of these two early editions, that of Gruget. The Victorian translators represent an attempt to establish a translation on the basis of the manuscript sources. Since then there have been improvements (though not as many as one might wish) in our knowledge of these sources. It is on the most up-to-date accessible edition of the manuscript source – that of Michel François – that the present translation is based. In addition, however, and for the first time in an English translation, it utilizes the de Thou manuscript of 1553. Though clearly heavily edited by de Thou, this manuscript is linguistically the most coherent in the corpus, and offers a sixteenth-century reader's clarification of the difficulties found in the other manuscripts. But the present translation does not pretend to be a critical edition, so the de Thou variants are not quoted systematically, but incorporated in the text according to two criteria. They are used (a) if they make better sense contextually than the François version and (b) if they offer a bolder or more illuminating reading from a historical point of view. All readings from de Thou are indicated by [ ]. Variants from Gruget's edition have not been used, and this includes his three alternative tales, which at the present time are still difficult to attribute. The summaries of the tales are based on de Thou.

The most obvious of the problems any translator of the *Heptaméron* faces is the confused condition of numerous passages in his source. Fortunately, where the sense is contradictory or obscure, or where narrative sequence is awkward, it is possible to make plausible deductions from the surrounding context, as would any French reader of the original. The guiding principle has been to reproduce in English a meaningful *reading* of the original, not a mechanical transcription of words on a page. There are, however, more serious and more interesting problems, and they are of three kinds.

The problem of the first kind is that of 'accessing' a world that is at once familiar yet not familiar. Translation is only possible to the extent that the cultures (in the broadest sense) on which the two languages depend overlap. There is sufficient cultural difference in the case of the *Heptaméron* to make the task of translation interesting and revealing, but sufficient cultural overlap for translation to be relatively direct. Nonetheless this leaves a large area of meaning where the sets of words encoding social institutions, relationships, moral categories and the like do not coincide exactly with those of modern English (or those of modern French, for that matter). This kind of problem is closely linked to the second and third. The second kind of problem results from the unique peculiarities of the source language. Two or more different words or parts of words may be phonologically similar in the language of the original, but their available translation equivalents may be dissimilar. In other words, puns, ambiguities and verbal associations cannot always be transposed, which means that important aspects of the original mental world may be lost. The third kind of problem has to do with personal style of speech and with 'register', that is, with variation in style depending on who is speaking on which topic in which circumstances. This is a delicate matter in translation, since it has to do with highly variable and rapidly changing social expectations of one kind or another. With these three perennial translation problems in mind the most a translator can do is indicate his own practice and point out the areas where there appear to be inherent blockages in transmission.

Certain of the social institutions in the *Heptaméron* seem to be best dealt with by using *loan-words* – that is, by keeping French originals, many of which may already be familiar to English speakers. Thus terms like *gouvernante*, *maître des requêtes*, etc., seem to be culturally specific enough, yet intelligible enough, to warrant their retention in a number of instances. The same is true of terms of address like *Monsieur*, *Madame*, which are also used in circumstances (such as conversation between spouses) where their rough equivalents would sound distinctly odd to modern readers. Important words and concepts such as *gentilhomme* ('noble-man') and *serviteur* (a servant – who could be a lesser noble serving a superior, but also a nobleman chivalrously 'serving' a lady) are sufficiently remote as to require varying treatment to bring out relevant meanings in specific contexts. Such terms often cover a semantic space that is now subdivided and covered by several specialized words in modern English. This is particularly true of vocabulary denoting moral categories and emotional reactions. The word *honnête* is one of the most crucial in the whole *Heptaméron*. Its semantic space is covered by many different modern English words, from 'aristocratic' to 'chaste'. The conflation of categories of this kind is thematically important in a number of stories – for instance, the storytellers' surprise that a low-born working woman (story 5) or a *bourgeoise* (story 42) could have 'noble' principles, where 'noble' merges social with moral categories. While the English word 'noble' does in fact in this case cover something of the appropriate area of meaning, it is not always a feasible translation for a specific context. Faced with this situation, translators have various courses. They can opt for *loan translation*, that is, consistently use some such word as 'honest' or 'honourable', and extend the normal boundaries of its English meaning and use, at the cost of linguistic awkwardness. Or they can vary the translation depending on context, possibly disturbing the original conceptual world. In other words, although it might be consistent to use, say, 'honest' to translate *honnête*, 'honest' may not 'sound right' in all those instances where consistency would require it. For the sake of naturalness and fluency, I have generally chosen to vary the translations according to English context.

Amongst other things the *Heptaméron* is concerned with language itself, with the expression, disguise and distortion of meaning, and with the sensuous substance of speech. There is thus in the original a whole stratum of meaning which derives from the particular shapes and sounds of the French used, and which is manifested in numerous kinds of repetition, multiple meaning and word-play. When it is purely a matter of rhetorical repetition of words or phrases, this can usually be matched in English, and similar effects reproduced, though where it seems likely to appear so heavy-handed as to impede reading, I have taken the liberty of reducing it. But there are many instances where the structure of English simply does not permit one to suggest the same associations and categorizations as the original. The term *Cordelier* is a significant example. One possible translation is 'Cordelier', but this would not be widely understood, and I have preferred to use the more intelligible 'Franciscan' or simply 'friar'. In so doing I have lost some of the semantic possibilities of *Cordelier*, which incorporates the word 'cord', but many others would have been lost in any case. Only just beneath the surface of the *Heptaméron* there are some surprisingly relevant ramifications of the French word *Cordelier*. *Corde* ('cord') may be obvious; *lier* ('bind', 'tie') is less so; *délier* ('unbind', 'untie') even less so. But there is a constant harping on the theme of bonds, obligations, ties and relationships, and the various ways in which they can be made, maintained or undone. Moreover, this gives sense to an otherwise obscure exchange between Oisille and Nomerfide after story 5, where a pun on the word *nouer* ('to tie', but also 'to swim') carries both a sexual connotation (derived from the tying knots meaning) and an allusion to the Cordeliers (tiers of knots). In fact, one of the storytellers explicitly defines the Franciscans as those who both bind and unbind bonds – in this instance, the bonds of marriage. There are many other such examples. Here are a few. The contrast between *ordre* and *ordure* is one that can be carried into English, and one which is thematically important, since the *Heptaméron* is concerned with order, with purity in its various senses, and hence with disorder and impurity. The word *mystère* (in story 61, for instance) means both 'sacred mystery' and 'play-acting'. *Oraison* (story 58) means both 'speech' (in its two senses) and 'prayer'. The *laboureur* in story 29 cannot be translated 'labourer', since the term actually denotes a well-off peasant farmer, but the point of the story thereby becomes obscured, because the erotic connotation of 'labouring' or 'working', which recurs throughout the book, is excluded. Play on words is most prominent, as one would expect, in the verse passages, some of which in fact explicitly refer to their own use of language. A typical example is the pun on the word *diamant* ('diamond') in the verse epistle in story 13. From *diamant* is extracted the two words *dy* (a sixteenth-century form of the imperative 'say') and *amant* ('[male] lover'). It may be no coincidence that this tale is told by Parlamente, whose very name contains the words *parle amante* ('speak [female] lover'). The *Heptaméron* probably contains more such covert meanings than is generally realized; many of them are untranslatable, and the reader of any translation should bear this in mind.

Some critics have found the style of the *Heptaméron* flat, others have thought it marked by a lively variety of tone. In my view the second assessment is the correct one, and it is important to try to convey this in an English translation. It is a feature that the earlier translations tended to mask with their uniformly archaic style. Discrepancy or inconsistency of style needs to be sharply distinguished from stylistic variation related to subject matter, communicative intention, speaker's personality and so on. It is certainly true that there appear to be discrepancies and inconsistencies in parts of the original. These are probably due to the unfinished or unpolished state of the manuscripts, and they are found particularly in tales where distinct episodes amounting to sub-stories seem to have been cobbled together. The changing narrative style in story 15 is a case in point, and there are others too (stories 21, 22, 23, 26, 42). Even these examples, however, can, if one so decides, be regarded as part and parcel of the spontaneous story-telling in which the narrators are supposed to be engaged.

The type of stylistic variation resulting primarily from subject matter, intention and personality is considerably more complex. Of these factors the most obvious is personality. If one looks carefully at the speech of the ten storytellers, it becomes clear that there is not only variation between male and female speech (in itself an important concretization of a central theme), but also variation between the speech of soldiers, courtiers, priests, youth and age. And there are other roles adopted by the storytellers as they discourse with one another: they may temporarily take on the language of preachers, philosophers, poets, lovers, wives, husbands . . . This accounts for the highly variable style of the dialogues, which ranges from personal bickering to earnest evangelical sermonizing.

Since the stories themselves are presented as told by ten different individuals, the stories too display differences of tone and content. One would not expect the cynical Saffredent to talk like the devout Oisille, or the young and forthright Nomerfide to talk like the ageing soldier Geburon. Nor should one expect their stories to be uniform in manner. There is in fact a clear positive correlation between individual storytellers and the length, content and language of the stories they tell. To complicate matters further, the storytellers recount narratives which themselves contain different characters and therefore different styles. Many stories contain set-piece speeches which in their rhetorical formality, and in some cases in their pomposity, stand out starkly against the surrounding text. Yet even this is not the final complication. Irony and parody are extremely important features of the dialogue passages, though they may easily go unnoticed. It sometimes happens that a given story-telling character, with his or her own already distinctive style of speech, may seek to incorporate within that style the distinctive style of somebody else. Thus one of the defining features of Saffredent's style of speech is the way he frequently takes over the biblical style of evangelical speech or the idealizing vocabulary of Platonic love. Oisille actually complains about this in the discussion following story 36, and Parlamente after story 44 makes remarks about the difficulty of distinguishing true from specious language. This is another major theme of the *Heptaméron*, and since stylistic variations contribute to expressing it, it is important to try to maintain such variations in the translation.

In the last analysis it is of course vocabulary and the grammatical shape of sentences which expresses the oscillations between different styles. The present translation makes use of archaic wording and phrasing where it suits the character of the speaker and his or her purpose. The language of the Authorized Version of the Bible seems an effective (if strictly anachronistic) way of conveying the appropriate tone. And if plainer vocabulary appears alongside, this is not stylistic inconsistency, but an attempt to reflect the variety of the original. The *Heptaméron*'s syntax can be dauntingly contorted. There is one permanent stylistic *tic* which seems to be peculiar to the work, and that is the relatively high frequency of 'consecutive' ('so . . . that') clauses. So common are these that I have felt obliged to retain the construction; equally, however, the self-embedding of 'so . . . that' clauses can become so impossibly convoluted for modern English that I have felt obliged to reduce them in some passages. There are other kinds of syntactic complexity that remain because they seem to serve some stylistic end. The speech of Oisille, for instance, is marked by long but coherent sentences. Sometimes (though certainly not always) clumsy and difficult syntax may be parodistic in intent – as in the case of the English lord in story 57, who is the target of general ridicule.

Probably the strongest stylistic contrast in the *Heptaméron* is between prose and verse. In spite of the obvious pitfalls it seems to me to be essential to attempt to retain this distinction in translation, quite apart from the fact that the verse has, as has already been suggested, its own peculiar means of expressing obscure meanings. The renderings of the verse will doubtless appear trite, clumsy and pompous. Fortunately most of Marguerite's verse (and the *Heptaméron*'s verse closely resembles it) is generally described in those terms by literary critics and historians. It is probably not part of the translator's job to try to improve on the original, at least where taste rather than intelligibility is concerned. One can also take comfort in the fact that some of the verse passages are apparently regarded by some of the storytellers themselves as slightly ridiculous or even in some way suspect. After all, in the Prologue we are told that the storytellers had agreed to exclude men of letters. Moreover, the idea that poetry cannot really be translated at all is present in the book itself. Parlamente is using a conventional modest disclaimer in story 64 when she says that the hero's verse epistle is a translation, and a bad one at that, from the Spanish. It is intriguing to realize that translation is actually an intrinsic part, even a theme, of the original *Heptaméron* text. An association is established in the Prologue with the enterprise of translating. More importantly, the text itself incorporates translations, paraphrases and parodies of various sources – mainly Scripture, but also Plato, Old French, Latin, Italian and Spanish. Any translation of the work is thus, at least in part, a translation of translations. In a curious sense translating it may even implicitly add to its meaning, for one of its essential themes is precisely the communication (or non-communication) of meaning.

BIOGRAPHICAL AND HISTORICAL SUMMARY

Life of Marguerite de Navarre		*Politics and Culture*	
		1483	Birth of Luther
		1486	First printed edition of *Cent Nouvelles Nouvelles*
1492	Birth of Marguerite, to Charles d'Angoulême and Louise de Savoie	1492	Columbus discovers America
1494	Birth of her brother, François	1494	First French invasion of Italy
1498	François becomes heir apparent	1498	Death of King Charles VIII without heir; the Duke of Orleans becomes Louis XII, and re-starts Italian wars
1509	Marguerite marries Charles, duc d'Alençon		
		1514	Louis XII marries Henry VIII's sister Mary
		1515	Louis XII dies; François I accedes
		1516	Erasmus's edition of the New Testament
1517	Marguerite concerned with reform of convents. Has contacts with humanist reformer Lefèvre d'Étaples. Poet Marot enters her service	1517	Luther's theses against papal indulgences
		1519	Charles I of Spain, François I's main enemy, elected Holy Roman Emperor
1521	Marguerite starts correspondence with Briçonnet, Bishop of	1521	Luther condemned by Sorbonne and excommunicated. First

	Meaux, moderate reformer and mystical theologian.		war between François and Charles V
		1522	Lefèvre d'Étaples's *Commentaries* on the Gospels. Alliance of Charles V and Henry VIII against France
		1523	Lefèvre's French translation of the *New Testament*. Zwingli reforms Zurich
1524	Composes *Dialogue in the form of a Nocturnal Vision*, not published till 1533. Has Luther's treatise on monastic views translated	1524	François conquers Milan
1525	Marguerite's husband dies. She goes to Madrid to negotiate her brother's release	1525	Battle of Pavia. François captured. Louise de Savoie regent
		1526	Treaty of Madrid. François freed
1527	Marries Henri d'Albret, King of Navarre		
1528	Her daughter, Jeanne d'Albret, future mother of Henri IV, born	1528	Castiglione's *Book of the Courtier* translated into French. Bâle, Berne, Strasbourg join Reformation
1529	Participates in peace negotiations led by her mother and Margaret of Austria	1529	War in Italy, defeat of French. Peace of Cambrai
1530	Lefèvre residing at Marguerite's court at Nérac		
1531	Her mother dies. *Mirror of the Sinful Soul* published		
1532	Marguerite and François encourage reformist preaching	1532	Rabelais's *Pantagruel*
1533	Marguerite's *Mirror* condemned by the	1533	Sorbonne accuses Marguerite's chaplain,

	Sorbonne after re-edition including Marot's translation of psalm 6; François intervenes		Gérard Roussel, of heresy
1534	Marguerite bides her time in Navarre	1534	Anti-Catholic poster campaign triggers persecution of Protestants ('affaire des placards'). Rabelais's *Gargantua*. Henry VIII established head of English Church
1535	Marguerite returns to François's court		
1536	Takes Bonaventure des Périers into her service	1536	Calvin's *Institutes of the Christian Religion*. War with Charles V
1536–8	Active participation in brother's policies and in peace talks		
		1538	Geneva joins Reformation
1541	Marguerite's daughter, Jeanne, forced by François to marry William, Duke of Cleves. Marguerite's prestige waning	1541	French version of Calvin's *Institutes*
1524–4	Marguerite at Nérac, Mont-de-Marsan and Pau. Returns to Court	1542–4	Further war against Charles V. Ends with Peace of Crépy
1545	Jeanne's unconsummated marriage annulled	1545	Beginning of Council of Trent. Calvin criticizes 'spirituallibertine sect' patronized by Marguerite. French translation of *Decameron*, dedicated to Marguerite
1546	Marguerite and husband return to Navarre	1546	Luther dies. Rabelais's *Third Book*
1547	Marguerite mourns François. Retreat in convent at Tusson. Publication of her *Marguerites de la Marguerite des Princesses*	1547	François I dies. Henri II accedes

	and *Suyte des Marguerites* ...		
1548	Returns to Court. Strained relations with Henri II, who imposes marriage of Marguerite's daughter to the duc de Vendôme		
1549	Retires to Navarre and dies at castle of Odos on 21 December	1549	Rabelais's *Fourth Book*. England declares war on France

THE NAMES OF THE STORYTELLERS

Oisille Variously identified with Marguerite de Navarre, with Marguerite's mother, Louise de Savoie, and with Louise de Daillon (Brantôme's grandmother and *dame d'honneur* to Marguerite). The latter identification seems most plausible. *Loise* (a common spelling of *Louise*) could become the anagram *oisel* ('bird'), whence the feminine form *oiselle*, becoming *Oisille* in manuscripts. The name suggests spiritual flight.

Parlamente Usually identified with Marguerite de Navarre. The name may derive from *perle amante* ('loving pearl'). Marguerite and her contemporaries often punned on the word *marguerite*, which also means 'pearl'. If the name is read *parle amante*, it suggests the expression of love in speech; the word *parlementer* means 'to speak' or 'to discourse'. Married to Hircan, according to the text.

Longarine Widely accepted to be based on an anagram of Longrai. She would thus be Aymée Motier de La Fayette, baillive de Caen and dame de Longrai, who was one of Marguerite's ladies-in-waiting, accompanied her to Spain to negotiate François's release and was *gouvernante* to her daughter and grandchildren. The name suggests *langue orine* ('golden tongue'). Longarine's husband is killed during the Prologue. She has a *serviteur*, who may be either Dagoucin or Saffredent.

Ennasuite Can be resolved into *Anne* and *suite* ('retinue'), which has been taken to support Ennasuite's identification with Anne de Vivonne, daughter of Louise de Daillon (who could be Oisille) and mother of Brantôme. The latter actually states that his mother was one of the storytellers. The name does not seem to have any obvious associated meanings.

Nomerfide Has for a long time been linked with the name *Fiedmarcon*, an alternative spelling of *Fimarcon*. Nomerfide could thus be Françoise de Fimarcon, who was married to one Jean Carbon de Montpesat. This has been questioned on the grounds that the couple had only tenuous links with Marguerite. An alternative possibility is another prominent member of Marguerite's entourage, Françoise de Silly, daughter of the baillive de Caen. Nomerfide could thus be the daughter of Longarine, though this is not mentioned in the text. Françoise de Silly was married to the vicomte de Lavedan, who has been proposed as the original of Saffredent (see below). There is nothing in the text to suggest that Nomerfide either is or is not Saffredent's wife. Her name has evoked *nom* ('name') and the Latin *fides* ('faith') for some people, but can also be associated with *non perfide* ('not perfidious', hence 'honest', 'frank', 'loyal').

Hircan Generally agreed to represent Marguerite's second husband, Henri de Navarre. *Hircan* could be an anagram of *Hanric*, a possible spelling of *Henri*. The Prologue makes it clear that he is married to Parlamente. The name suggests *Hircania* and its proverbial wildness, and *hircin* ('goatish', 'goat-like' and associations with sexuality and Satan).

Dagoucin Can be linked with Nicolas Dangu, natural son of a Cardinal; Abbot of Juilly, Abbot of Saint-Savin of Tarbes and Bishop of Séez and Mende. The text does not state that he is a priest. He is the *serviteur* of either Parlamente or Longarine. The name is a fairly obvious pun: *de goûts saints* ('of saintly tastes').

Saffredent Has been identified with the Admiral Bonnivet, Jean de Montpesat and with Jean (or Gensanne) de Bourbon, vicomte de Lavedan. Anagrams do not seem to lead very far. The vicomte de Lavedan was close to Henri of Navarre and *gouverneur* to Marguerite's daughter. The name *Lavedan* could give rise to a pun: *lave* ('wash') *dent* ('tooth'). So can the name *Saffredent*: *saffre* ('lecherous', 'gluttonous'), *dent* ('tooth'). Lavedan's second wife was Françoise de Silly, who could be Nomerfide (see above). But the text does not say that Saffredent and Nomerfide are married, though we *are* told that Saffredent is *serviteur* to either Longarine or Parlamente. Note that Longarine could be his mother-in-law.

Geburon Most generally accepted to be Charles de Coucy, Seigneur de Burye, and a member of Marguerite's circle in the later part of her life. There is some support for this if one accepts a near anagram between *Gebur* and *Burye* (*Yebur* could become *Gebur*). The name suggests a paradoxical mixture of liveliness and austerity. The first syllable (*Ge* in some versions, *Gé* in others, and *Gue* in others) evokes 'jay', 'gay', 'lively', 'active', 'bright', in sixteenth-century French. The second syllable associates with *buron* ('hut'), *bure* ('homespun') and *bur* ('dark', 'sombrely clad').

Simontaut The accepted identification is with François de Bourdeille, the father of Brantôme, and husband of Anne de Vivonne. Simontaut could be married therefore to Ennasuite. The text does not state this, although it does tell us that he is a long-standing *serviteur* to Parlamente. The name could be an anagram of *Montauris*, a fief owned by Bourdeille's family. There were also connections with the family of *Montaut*. But there is a fairly direct pun in the name: *monte* ('mounts', 'rises'), *haut* ('high'), an allusion to the character's sexual prowess.

BIBLIOGRAPHY

I. MAIN EDITIONS OF THE HEPTAMÉRON

Histoires des Amans fortunez. Dédiées à trés illustre princesse, Madame Marguerite de Bourbon, Duchesse de Nivernois, edited by Pierre Boaistuau, Paris, Gilles Robinot, 1558.

Sixty-seven tales not divided into days, without linking discussions, and in an idiosyncratic order.

L'Heptaméron des Nouvelles de très illustre et très excellente Princesse Marguerite de Valois, Royne de Navarre, remis en son vray ordre, confus auparavant en sa première impression, et dédié à trés illustre et très vertueuse Princesse Jeanne de Foix, Royne de Navarre, edited by Pierre Gruget, Paris, J. Caveillier, 1559.

Seventy-two tales in standard order. Tales 11, 44 and 46 are Gruget's own substitutions.

L'Heptaméron des nouvelles de . . . Marguerite d'Angoulême, reine de Navarre. Nouvelle édition, publiée sur les manuscrits pour la société des bibliophiles français . . ., 3 vols., Paris, C. Lahure, 1853–4.

First edition to use manuscript sources. The editor was A.-J.-V. Leroux de Lincy. A re-edition in 1880 with the collaboration of A. de Montaiglon includes valuable essays and notes.

L'Heptaméron, texte établi sur les manuscrits avec une introduction, des notes et un index de noms propres par Michel François, Paris, Garnier Frères, 1943.

Reproduces Bibliothèque Nationale manuscript Fr. 1512 with some revisions. Some variants given from Boaistuau, Gruget and de Thou. Seventy-two tales. Appendix includes the Gruget substitutions for tales 11, 44 and 46 as well as an alternative version of 52 found in de Thou, a tale found only in the Bibliothèque Nationale's manuscripts Fr. 1513 and Dupuy 736 and the Pierpont Morgan Library's Ms. 242, plus a fragment of dialogue in Fr. 1513 and Dupuy 736.

Nouvelles, texte critique établi et présenté par Yves Le Hir, Paris, Presses Universitaires de France, 1967.

Reproduces Bibliothèque Nationale's Fr. 1524, which is an edition of the *Heptaméron* by Adrien de Thou. Seventy-two tales without the Gruget substitutions but with its own version of tale 52 and reworkings of the transitional dialogues.

Three Sixteenth-Century Conteurs, selected and edited with introductions and notes by A. J. Krailsheimer, MA, Oxford University Press, 1966.

As well as extracts from Des Périers and du Fail there are extracts from the *Heptaméron*: the Prologue, and tales 17, 31, 35, 49, 50, 60, 65, 67. François's text is reproduced. There is a useful introduction.

Tales from the Heptaméron, selected and edited by H. P. Clive, London, The Athlone Press, 1970.

Reproduces the de Thou manuscript with a small number of corrections. Selects Prologue and tales 4, 5, 8, 9, 12, 18, 19, 24, 26, 29, 31, 34, 35, 36, 37, 40, 44, 53, 55, 56, 57, 63, 67. Useful introduction, notes and glossary.

2. MAIN ENGLISH TRANSLATIONS

The Queene of Navarre's Tales. Containing Verie pleasant Discourses of fortunate lovers. Now newly translated out of French into English, London, printed by V. S. for John Oxenbridge, and are to be sold at his shop in Paule's churchyard at the sign of the Parot, 1597.

Heptameron or the History of the Fortunate Lovers; Written by the most Excellent and most Virtuous Princess Margaret de Valoys, Queen of Navarre; Published in French by the Privilege and immediate Approbation of the King; Now made English by Robert Codrington, Master of Arts, London, printed by F. L. for Nath. Ekins, and are to be sold at his Shop at the Gun, by the West-End of St Paul's, 1654.

Novels, Tales and Stories. Written Originally in French, by Marguerite de Valois, Queen of Navar. And Printed by Order of the French King. Translated into English by several Hands, London, printed for W. Chetwood, at Cato's Head, in Russel-Street, Covent Garden, and T. Edlin over-against Exeter Exchange in the Strand. (Price 6d.) (Published about 1750.)

The Heptameron of Margaret, Queen of Navarre. Translated from the French, with a Memoir of the Author, by W. H. Kelly, London, Henry G. Bohn, 1855. (In *Bohn's Extra Volume.*)

The Heptameron of Tales and Novels of Marguerite, Queen of Navarre, now first completely done into English prose and verse, from the original French, by A. Machen, privately printed, 1885.

The Heptameron of the Tales of Margaret, Queen of Navarre. Newly Translated [by John Smith Chartres] *from the Authentic Text of M. Le Roux de Lincy. With an Essay upon the Heptameron by George Saintsbury*, MA. *Also the Original Seventy-three Full-page Engravings Designed by S. Freudenberg and One Hundred and Fifty Head and Tail Pieces by Dunker*, 5 vols., London, printed for the Society of English Bibliophilists, 1894.

Unexpurgated Edition. The Heptameron. Tales of Marguerite, Queen of Navarre. New Translation from the French, London, The Temple Company, n.d. (The introduction is signed 'W'. Cataloguers attribute the translation to W. M. Thomson and give the date as 1896.)

3. SELECTED READING RELATING TO THE HEPTAMÉRON

Brantôme (Pierre de Bourdeille), *Oeuvres Complètes*, ed. L. Lalanne, vol. 8, *Des Dames*, Paris, 1875.

N. Cazauran, *L'Heptaméron de Marguerite de Navarre*, Paris, 1976.

B. J. Davies, *The Storytellers in Marguerite de Navarre's Heptameron*, Lexington, 1978.

C.-G. Dubois, 'Fonds mythique et jeu des sens dans le "Prologue" de l'*Heptaméron*', in *Etudes seizièmistes offertes à V.-L. Saulnier*, Geneva, 1980.

J. Gelernt, *World of Many Loves: The Heptameron of Marguerite de Navarre*, Chapel Hill, 1966.

P. Jourda, *Marguerite d'Angoulême, Duchesse d'Alençon, Reine de Navarre* (1492–1549), Paris, 1930.

A. J. Krailsheimer, 'The *Heptaméron* Reconsidered', in *The French Renaissance and its Heritage*, London, 1968.

D. Stone, Jr, 'Observations on the Text of the Histoires des amans fortunez', *Renaissance Quarterly*, vol. XXXIII, no. 2, 1980.

E. V. Telle, *L'Oeuvre de Marguerite d'Angoulême, reine de Navarre, et la Querelle des Femmes*, Toulouse, 1937.

M. Tetel, *Marguerite de Navarre's Heptaméron: Themes, Language, and Structure*, Durham, NC, 1973.

THE HEPTAMERON

NOTE Square brackets [ ] denote readings from de Thou – see Introduction, p. 26.

SUMMARIES OF THE STORIES

FIRST DAY: A COLLECTION OF LOW TRICKS PLAYED BY WOMEN ON MEN AND BY MEN ON WOMEN

SECOND DAY: ON WHICH IS DISCUSSED ALL MANNER OF THOUGHTS, AT THE PLEASURE OF THE STORYTELLERS

Story 72 While enacting the last rites and laying out a corpse, a monk turns to works of the flesh with a nun and gets her with child. 540

PROLOGUE

On the first day of September, when the springs of the Pyrenees are just beginning to be at their most potent, there were a number of people staying at the spa town of Cauterets. They had come from Spain [and other countries] as well as from France, some to drink the waters, some to bathe in them, and some to be treated with the mud. These are all very remarkable cures, so remarkable that patients long given up by their physicians go home completely restored to health. But it is not my purpose here to expatiate on the powers of these waters and their fine situation. I wish merely to relate those details which will serve the subject I have in hand.

The patients all remained at the spa for over three weeks, until their condition improved and they felt they could return home. But as they were preparing to leave, the rain came. It fell in such torrents and with such extraordinary force, you would have thought that God had quite forgotten that once He had promised to Noah never again to destroy the world by water. In Cauterets the huts and houses were all so badly flooded that it was impossible for anyone to stay there. Visitors who had come from the Spanish side went back over the mountains as best they could, with those among them who knew the tracks coming off the best. But the French lords and their ladies, thinking they could get back to Tarbes just as easily as they had come, discovered that the streams were so swollen they they could ford them only with difficulty. And when they came to the Gave de Pau, which on the way there had not been two feet deep, they found that it had turned into a raging torrent. So they turned back to look for the bridges, only to find that the flimsy wooden structures had been swept away by the force of the water. Some of the party thought they might be able to resist the current if they waded across in groups. But they were carried off so swiftly that those who had been about to follow them could not bring themselves to make the attempt. At this point, disagreeing on what they should do next, they split up to look for different routes. Some of them crossed the mountains, passed through Aragon into Roussillon, and from there went to Narbonne. Others went straight to Barcelona, from where they went by sea to Marseilles and Aigues-Mortes. But one of the travellers was an old lady named Oisille, a widow, with much experience of life. She resolved not to let the treacherous roads frighten her, and made her way to the abbey of Our Lady at Sarrance. Not that she was so superstitious as to believe that the glorious Virgin should leave her seat at her Son's right hand in order to come and take up residence in such a desolate spot. She simply had a desire to see this holy place about which she had heard such a lot, and was also fairly certain that if there was any way at all of finding refuge from danger, the monks were sure to have found it. Eventually, she reached her destination, but only after struggling through rugged and hostile terrain. Indeed, so arduous were the climbs with which she was confronted, that in spite of her age and weight, she was obliged for the most part to go on foot. But the most tragic thing was that most of her horses and servants died on the way, so that by the time she arrived at Sarrance she was accompanied only by one man and one woman. There the monks received them charitably.

Amongst the French travellers there were also two noblemen who had gone to the spa more because they were devoted to the service of two ladies who were there than because they had anything wrong with their health. When they saw the party was breaking up, and that the ladies were being led off by their husbands in another direction, these two gentlemen decided to follow at a distance, without saying anything to anyone. One evening during the journey the two married men and their wives arrived at the house of a man who was more of a bandit than a peasant. The two young gentlemen who were following behind stayed in a farm cottage nearby. Towards midnight they were woken up by a tremendous din. They jumped out of bed, roused their servants, and asked their host what was going on. The poor man was in a fair state of fright. It was a band of outlaws, he told them, and they had come to get their share in some loot that their comrade was keeping in his house next door. Immediately the two men grabbed their swords, and, taking their servants with them, dashed to the aid of their ladies, counting death for their sakes a far happier fate than a long life without them. When they got to the house, they found the outside door broken in, and the two other men and their servants putting up a valiant fight. But they were already badly wounded, and outnumbered by the bandits. Most of their servants were dead. They were beginning to give way. Through the window the two younger men could see the ladies wailing and weeping. So inflamed were their hearts by pity and by love, they fell upon the outlaws in a paroxysm of fury, like two enraged bears coming down from the mountains, and killed so many that the rest fled for safety to their hideout. The villains having been thus defeated, and the host himself being among those killed, it remained only for the two young noblemen to send his wife, who they had learned was even worse than he, the same way. A single thrust of the sword did the job. They then went into a downstairs room, where they found one of the married gentlemen breathing his last. The other was not hurt, although his clothes were torn to shreds and his sword had been broken. The poor man thanked the pair for coming to his aid in the way they had, embraced them, and asked them not to leave him and those of his party who had survived. The two young men were only too glad to agree. And so, after burying the dead man, and consoling his wife as best they could, they took to the road again, not knowing which way they should go, but trusting in God's guidance.

If you would like to know the names of the three gentlemen and the two ladies with them, they were Hircan, his wife Parlamente, and Longarine, the young widow. The two young men were Dagoucin and Saffredent. They rode all day, and towards evening they glimpsed a church tower in the distance. Eventually, after a hard struggle along the tracks, they arrived at the abbey of Saint-Savin, where the monks received them humanely. The abbot, who was himself of a good family, provided them with accommodation worthy of their station and asked them about their adventures, as he showed them to their quarters. When he had heard what had happened to them, he was able to inform them that there were others in the same boat. There were, in fact, in another room, two young ladies who had escaped from dangers just as great or even greater, inasmuch as they had had to deal, not with men, but with wild beasts. Half a league this side of Pierrefitte they had met a bear coming down the mountain. They had taken flight and galloped so fast that their horses had dropped dead beneath them as they rode through the abbey gates. Two of their women had arrived some time after them, and reported that the bear had killed all their male servants. So the three newly arrived gentlemen and the two ladies went in to see them, and recognized them at once as their companions Nomerfide and Ennasuite. They were both in tears, but once they had all embraced, told one another about their misfortunes, and heard a few [pious] exhortations from the good abbot, they began to take some consolation from their reunion. The next morning they heard mass with great devotion, praising God for delivering them from the perils of the mountains.

While they were at mass a man came rushing into the church in his shirt sleeves, shouting for help as if someone was chasing him. Hircan and the other two gentlemen got up at once to see what was the matter. Two men with drawn swords were in hot pursuit. When they saw so many people about they tried to get away, but Hircan and the others ran after them and made sure they did not get away with their lives. When Hircan came back he found that the man in the shirt sleeves was another of their companions, a man by the name of Geburon. He told them how he had been in a farm cottage near Pierrefitte, when three men had appeared. He had been in bed at the time, and dressed in nothing but his shirt. But he had jumped up, grabbed his sword, and had managed to wound one of the men and immobilize him. While the other two were busy picking up their companion, he had weighed up the odds, and decided that rather than face two armed men in his present state of undress, his best chance was to make a run for it. He thanked God now that he had been so lightly dressed, and he expressed his gratitude to Hircan and the other two for avenging him.

After they had heard mass and dined, they sent someone to find out if it was possible yet to cross the Gave de Pau. When they learned that the river was still impassable, they were extremely worried, in spite of the fact that the abbot repeatedly reassured them that they could have lodging in the abbey until the floods subsided. For that day they accepted this offer, and the same evening, as they were about to go to bed, an old monk turned up. He had come from Sarrance where he went every year for the Nativity of our Lady. On being asked about the journey, he told how, because of the floods, he had come over the mountains, and found the tracks more treacherous than he had ever seen them. On the way he had witnessed a very moving spectacle. He had come across a gentleman by the name of Simontaut, who, tired of waiting for the flood waters to go down, had decided to try to attempt a crossing. He had placed his trust in his excellent horse, and had grouped his servants round him to break the force of the current. But in the middle all the men on weaker mounts had been swept off down the stream. Neither men nor horses were ever seen again. The gentleman, finding himself completely alone, turned his horse back. But the animal could not make it, and collapsed under him. By God's will he was close enough to the edge to be able to drag himself on all fours out of the water and up the hard stony bank, though he had swallowed a good deal of water, and was so exhausted that he could hardly keep going. He lay amongst the rocks, soaked through and sick at heart at having seen his servants perish before his eyes. By a stroke of good fortune he was found in the evening by a shepherd bringing home the sheep. The mere sight of the gentleman, let alone the tale he had to tell, was enough to make the shepherd understand his plight. He had taken him by the hand and led him to his humble abode, where he had kindled a few sticks to dry him out as best he could. That same evening God had brought to the shepherd's house the old monk, who had told Simontaut the way to Sarrance, and assured him that he would find better accommodation there than anywhere else. He had also told him that he would meet there an old widow by the name of Oisille, who had suffered misfortunes similar to his own.

When they heard the old monk mention the name of the good Lady Oisille and the gentle knight Simontaut, they were overjoyed beyond description. They praised their Creator that He had been satisfied to take the servants and save their masters and mistresses. Parlamente in particular gave heartfelt thanks to God, for Simontaut had long served her as her devoted and loving servant. They pressed the monk to tell them the road to

Sarrance, and although he made it sound very difficult, they were not deterred from setting out that very day. The abbot provided them with everything they needed – [the best horses in Lavedan, good Béarnese cloaks,] wine and victuals, as well as guides to conduct them safely over the mountains. Most of the journey had to be done on foot rather than on horseback, but eventually they arrived, exhausted and bathed in sweat, at the abbey of Our Lady at Sarrance. The abbot was not a particularly nice character, but he did not dare to refuse them board and lodging, for fear of offending the Seigneur de Béarn, who, as he knew perfectly well, was on friendly terms with them. Hypocrite that he was, he put on as pleasant an air as he was able, and took them to see the good Lady Oisille and the noble Simontaut. They were overjoyed to be reunited so miraculously, and they spent the whole night in the church without finding it a moment too long, praising and thanking God for the great mercy He had bestowed upon them. In the morning they took a little rest, then heard mass. They all received the holy sacrament of union, in which all Christians are united in one, beseeching Him, who in His goodness had brought them together, that their journey might be finished to His glory.

After they had dined they sent someone to inquire whether the water had gone down, only to learn that the river was more swollen than before, and that it would be a long time before they could cross with safety. So they decided to build a bridge, using two rocks which were fairly close to one another. To this day there are planks at this point for the use of foot-travellers coming from Oléron who do not want to use the ford. The abbot was rather pleased that they were offering to put themselves to this expense, because it meant that he might get an increased number of pilgrims. So he provided the necessary workmen, but he was so mean that he contributed not a penny to the actual cost. The workmen said that they could not do the job in under ten or twelve days. This was rather a boring prospect for all of them, men and women alike. However, Parlamente, the wife of Hircan, was not one to let herself become idle or melancholy, and having asked her husband for permission, she spoke to the old Lady Oisille.

'Madame,' she said, 'you have had much experience of life,

and you now occupy the position of mother in regard to the rest of us women, and it surprises me that you do not consider some pastime to alleviate the boredom and distress that we shall have to bear during our long stay here. Unless we have some amusing and virtuous way of occupying ourselves, we run the risk of [falling] sick.'

Longarine, the young widow, added, 'What is worse, we'll all become miserable and disagreeable – and that's an incurable disease. There isn't a man or woman amongst us who hasn't every cause to sink into despair, if we consider all that we have lost.'

Ennasuite laughed and rejoined, 'Not everyone's lost a husband, like you, you know. And as for losing servants, no need to despair about that – there are plenty of men ready to do service! All the same, I do agree that we ought to have something to amuse us, so that we can pass the time as pleasantly as we can.'

Her companion Nomerfide said that this was a very good idea, and that if she had to spend a single day without some entertainment, she would be sure to die the next.

All the men supported this, and asked the Lady Oisille if she would kindly organize what they should do.

'My children,' replied Oisille, 'when you ask me to show you a pastime that is capable of delivering you from your boredom and your sorrow, you are asking me to do something that I find very difficult. All my life I have searched for a remedy, and I have found only one – the reading of holy Scripture, in which one may find true and perfect spiritual joy, from which proceed health and bodily repose. And if you ask what the prescription is that keeps me happy and healthy in my old age, I will tell you. As soon as I rise in the morning I take the Scriptures and read them. I see and contemplate the goodness of God, who for our sakes has sent His son to earth to declare the holy word and the good news by which He grants remission of all our sins, and payment of all our debts, through His gift to us of His love, His passion and His merits. And my contemplations give me such joy, that I take my psalter, and with the utmost humility, sing the beautiful psalms and hymns that the Holy Spirit has composed in the heart of David and the other authors. The contentment this affords me fills me with such well-being that whatever the evils of the day, they are to me so many blessings, for in my heart I have by faith Him who has borne these evils for me. Likewise, before supper, I withdraw to nourish my soul with readings and meditations. In the evening I ponder in my mind everything I have done during the day, so that I may ask God forgiveness of my sins, and give thanks to Him for His mercies. And so I lay myself to rest in His love, fear and peace, assured against all evils. And this, my children, is the pastime that long ago I adopted. All other ways have I tried, but none has given me spiritual contentment. I believe that if, each morning, you give one hour to reading, and then, during mass, say your prayers devoutly, you will find even in this wilderness all the beauty a city could afford. For, a person who knows God will find all things beautiful in Him, and without Him all things will seem ugly. So I say to you, if you would live in happiness, heed my advice.'

Then Hircan spoke: 'Madame, anyone who has read the holy Scriptures – as indeed I think we all have here – will readily agree that what you have said is true. However, you must bear in mind that we have not yet become so mortified in the flesh that we are not in need of some sort of amusement and physical exercise in order to pass the time. After all, when we're at home, we've got our hunting and hawking to distract us from the thousand and one foolish thoughts that pass through one's mind. The ladies have their housework and their needlework. They have their dances, too, which provide a respectable way for them to get some exercise. All this leads me to suggest, on behalf of the men here, that you, Madame, since you are the oldest among us, should read to us every morning about the life of our Lord Jesus Christ, and the great and wonderful things He has done for us. Between dinner and vespers I think we should choose some pastime, which, while not being prejudicial to the soul, will be agreeable to the body. In that way we shall spend a very pleasant day.'

Lady Oisille replied that she herself found it so difficult to put behind her the vanities of life, that she was afraid the pastime suggested by Hircan might not be a good choice. However, the question should, she thought, be judged after an open discussion, and she asked Hircan to put his point of view first.

'Well, my point of view wouldn't take long to give,' he began, 'if I thought that the pastime I would really like were as agreeable to a certain lady among us as it would be to me. So I'll keep quiet for now, and abide by what the others say.'

Thinking he was intending this for her, his wife. Parlamente, began to blush. 'It may be, Hircan,' she said, half angrily and half laughing, 'that the lady you think ought to be the most annoyed at what you say would have ways and means of getting her own back, if she so desired. But let's leave on one side all pastimes that require only two participants, and concentrate on those which everybody can join in.'

Hircan turned to the ladies. 'Since my wife has managed to put the right interpretation on my words,' he said, 'and since private pastimes don't appeal to her, I think she's in a better position than anyone to know which pastime all of us will be able to enjoy. Let me say right now that I accept her opinion as if it were my own.'

They all concurred in this, and Parlamente, seeing that it had fallen to her to make the choice, addressed them all as follows.

'If I felt myself to be as capable as the ancients, by whom the arts were discovered, then I would invent some pastime myself that would meet the requirements you have laid down for me. However, I know what lies within the scope of my own knowledge and ability – I can hardly even remember the clever things other people have invented, let alone invent new things myself. So I shall be quite content to follow closely in the footsteps of other people who have already provided for your needs. For example, I don't think there's one of us who hasn't read the hundred tales by Boccaccio, which have recently been translated from Italian into French, and which are so highly thought of by the [most Christian] King Francis I, by Monseigneur the Dauphin, Madame the Dauphine and Madame Marguerite. If Boccaccio could have heard how highly these illustrious people praised him, it would have been enough to raise him from the grave. As a matter of fact, the two ladies I've mentioned, along with other people at the court, made up their minds to do the same as Boccaccio. There was to be one difference – that they should not write any story that was not truthful. Together with Monseigneur the Dauphin the ladies promised to produce ten stories each, and to get together a party of ten people who were qualified to contribute something, excluding those who studied and were men of letters. Monseigneur the Dauphin didn't want their art brought in, and he was afraid that rhetorical ornament would in part falsify the truth of the account. A number of things led to the project being completely forgotten – the major affairs of state that subsequently overtook the King, the peace treaty between him and the King of England, the confinement of Madame the Dauphine and several other events of sufficient importance to keep the court otherwise occupied. However, it can now be completed in the ten days of leisure we have before us, while we wait for our bridge to be finished. If you so wished, we could go each afternoon between midday and four o'clock to the lovely meadow that borders the Gave de Pau, where the leaves on the trees are so thick that the hot sun cannot penetrate the shade and the cool beneath. There we can sit and rest, and each of us will tell a story which he has either witnessed himself, or which he has heard from somebody worthy of belief. At the end of our ten days we will have completed the whole hundred. And if, God willing, the lords and ladies I've mentioned find our endeavours worthy of their attention, we shall make them a present of them when we get back, instead of the usual statuettes and beads. I'm sure they would find that preferable. In spite of all this, if any of you is able to think of something more agreeable, I shall gladly bow to his or her opinion.'

But everyone of them replied that it would be impossible to think of anything better, and that they could hardly wait for the morrow. So the day came happily to a close with reminiscences of things they had all experienced in their time.

As soon as morning came they all went into Madame Oisille's room, where she was already at her prayers. When they had listened for a good hour to the lesson she had to read them, and then devoutly heard mass, they went, at ten o'clock, to dine, after which they retired to their separate rooms to attend to what they had to do. At midday they all went back as arranged to the meadow, which was looking so beautiful and fair that it would take a Boccaccio to describe it as it really was. Enough for us to say that a more beautiful meadow there never was seen. When they were all seated on the grass, so green and soft that there was no need for carpets or cushions, Simontaut said: 'Which of us shall be [the one in charge]?'

'Since you have spoken first,' replied Hircan, 'it should be you who give the orders. Where games are concerned everybody is equal.'

'Would to God,' sighed Simontaut, 'that the one thing in all the world I had were the power to order everyone in our party to comply with my wishes!'

Parlamente knew very well what he meant by this remark, and started to cough. Hircan did not notice the colour rising in her cheeks, and simply went on to invite Simontaut to start, which he did at once.

'Ladies, I have been so ill rewarded for my long and devoted service, that, in order to avenge myself on Love and on the woman who is so cruel to me, I shall do my utmost to collect together all the accounts of foul deeds perpetrated by women on us poor men. And every single one will be the unadulterated truth.'

FIRST DAY

STORY ONE

In the town of Alençon, during the lifetime of the last Duke Charles, there was a procurator by the name of Saint-Aignan. He had married a noblewoman of the region who was more beautiful than she was virtuous, and who, on account of her charms and well-known flightiness, was the object of the attentions of the Bishop of Sées. To achieve his ends the prelate took care to humour the husband. The result was that not only did the husband fail to notice the wicked behaviour of his wife and the Bishop, but he even came to forget the affection he had always had for his master and mistress. Indeed, things went so far, that although he had in the past been their most loyal servant, he turned so much against them that he even brought in a sorcerer to procure the Duchess's death. And so the Bishop continued his affair with the wretched woman, who for her part continued to do his bidding more out of greed than love. Besides, the husband had urged her to go on cultivating him. However, in the town of Alençon there also lived a certain young man. He was the son of the Lieutenant-General, and the procurator's wife became half demented with infatuation for him. She frequently made use of the Bishop in order to obtain commissions for her husband that would get him out of the way while she saw the son of the Lieutenant, who was called du Mesnil. This arrangement persisted for quite some time. She had the Bishop for profit, and young du Mesnil for pleasure. Of course she swore to du Mesnil that if she bestowed favours on the Bishop, it was only so that they themselves would have more freedom to indulge in their pleasures. In any case, she assured him, the Bishop got nothing from her but fair words, and nobody but he, du Mesnil, would get anything else.

One day, when Saint-Aignan had gone to visit the Bishop, his wife asked him if she might go into the country. The town did not agree with her, she said. No sooner had she arrived at her husband's farm in the country than she wrote a note to du Mesnil, telling him to come and see her there around ten o'clock the same evening. This the poor young man duly did. But as he was about to go through the door, the chambermaid, who usually let him in, came out to meet him.

'Go somewhere else, friend,' she said. 'Your place is already taken!'

Du Mesnil thought the husband must have turned up, and asked her how things stood. The good woman felt sorry for him. There he was, a good-looking, well-bred young man, so much in love, and so badly treated in return! So she told him all about his mistress's wild behaviour. That will teach him to fall in love like that, she thought to herself. She told him how the Bishop of Sées had only that moment arrived and was already in bed with Madame, who, as a matter of fact, had been rather taken aback, since she had not expected him till the following day. The Bishop had managed to keep the husband busy back in his residence, and had got away to see her secretly under cover of darkness. Well, you never saw anyone so flabbergasted as du Mesnil was at that moment. He could not believe his ears. What he did was to hide in a nearby house, where he kept watch till three o'clock in the morning, when he saw a figure emerge. And it was a figure that, in spite of the disguise, he recognized only too well as that of the Bishop.

Du Mesnil was in despair as he rode back to Alençon. It was not long before his obnoxious mistress followed on, and went to see him, assuming that she would be able to go on leading him by the nose as usual. However, he told her that as she had been in contact with sacred things she was too holy to speak to a sinner such as himself. He was very penitent, though, he said, and hoped that his sin would soon be forgiven. She realized that the game was up, and that it was no use making excuses, or promising and swearing never to do it again. So she went off and complained to her Bishop. Then, after due deliberation on the matter, she spoke to her husband, saying that she could not bear to stay in Alençon any longer. It was that Lieutenant's son, the man whom he, her husband, had regarded as a friend. He was for ever pestering her in a most dishonourable fashion, and in order to raise herself above any possible suspicion, she wanted her husband to take a house in Argentan. The husband, being in the habit of taking orders from his wife, agreed.

They had not been living at Argentan very long before the wretched woman sent word to du Mesnil that in her opinion he was the most despicable man alive, that she knew all about the way he had maligned the Bishop and herself in public, and that she would see to it that he came to regret it. The poor young man had actually never said anything to anybody except her, and was extremely worried lest he find himself in the Bishop's bad books. So he rode over to Argentan with a couple of servants, and eventually found the good lady attending vespers at one of the Dominicans'churches. He went up to her, knelt down at her side, and said:

'Madame, I'm here to swear before God that I've never spoken to anyone except yourself about matters that could affect your honour. You've behaved in an abominable way towards me, and what I've said to you is only half of what you really deserve. If any man or woman dares say to the contrary that I've maligned you in public, then here I am in person to deny the charge!'

There were a lot of people in the church, and du Mesnil had his two sturdy servants with him. So she forced herself to address him as agreeably as she could. She had no doubt, she assured him, that what he said was true. She knew he was far too decent a man to speak ill of anyone, let alone speak ill of her, the woman who was so fond of him. But her husband had heard rumours, and she would be glad if he would go and speak to him personally, in order to make it clear that he had not said the things he was accused of saying, and that he did not believe such tales either. Du Mesnil agreed to this. Thinking she wanted him to go back to her house with her, he took her by the arm. But she said that it would not be a good idea to go back together, because her husband would think that she had primed him on what to say. Grabbing hold of one of his servants by the sleeve, she said: 'Leave this man with me, and when the time's ripe, I'll send him to let you know. In the meantime go back to where you're staying and lie low.'

Off he went, never dreaming that she was planning to trap him, while she took his servant back to her house and gave him some supper. The man kept asking her when it would be time to go to fetch his master, to which she replied that he would be coming shortly. But when it got dark, she secretly sent one of her own serving-men to bring du Mesnil, who, not suspecting the danger ahead, went back to the house quite fearlessly, accompanied only by the one servant, the other having been detained by Saint-Aignan's wife. As he went in, his guide told him that the mistress would like to speak to him first, before he spoke to her husband, that she was waiting for him in a room with his other servant, and that he ought to send the one he had with him out by the front door. This he did, and went on alone up a dark staircase. But Saint-Aignan had prepared an ambush, and there were men hidden in a closet, waiting for du Mesnil. Hearing the noise on the stairs, Saint-Aignan asked what it was, and [was told] that it was a man trying to get in the house without being seen. At this point, out jumped an individual by the name of Thomas Guérin, who was a professional assassin, and had been hired for the occasion. Defend himself as he might, the poor young man could do nothing against the hail of blows from Guérin's sword, and he fell dead at his assailant's feet. The servant who had been with the lady of the house said: 'I can hear my master's voice on the stairs. I'm going to him.'

But she held him back, saying, 'Don't worry about him. He'll be coming up shortly.'

But then he heard his master shouting out: 'I'm dying! God have mercy on my soul!'

The servant wanted to run to his aid, but Saint-Aignan's wife still managed to hold him back.

'Don't worry about it,' she said. 'It's my husband teaching the young rascal a lesson. Let's go and see what's happening.'

Leaning over the top of the stairs she called out to her husband: 'Well then? Have you done?'

To which came the reply: 'Come and have a look. I have just avenged you on the man who has brought so much shame upon you!' So saying, he thrust his dagger a dozen or so times into the body of the man on whom he would never have dared lay a finger had he been alive.

Now that the murder had been committed, and the dead man's servants had got away to take the news to his poor father, Saint-Aignan realized that it could not be kept quiet. But he reckoned that du Mesnil's servants would not be regarded as credible witnesses, and that no one in his own household had seen the deed, apart from an elderly chambermaid and a girl of fifteen. The old woman he tried to seize without anyone knowing, but she managed to escape and get safely to the Dominican convent. She turned out to be the most reliable witness to the murder. The young girl stayed in the house for a few days and he managed with the help of one of the murderers to win her round. Then he took her off to Paris, and got her into a brothel, so that no one would take her seriously as a witness. To cover up all traces of the murder he burned the body of the deceased man, and put the bones which had not disappeared in the fire into the mortar he was using at that time to build an extension on his house. Finally, he sent an urgent message to court to ask for a pardon. He maintained that he had on several occasions forbidden entrance to a certain person whom he suspected of having dishonourable intentions with regard to his wife, that this person had, notwithstanding, come under suspicious circumstances to visit his wife and that, in consequence, having discovered the said person outside his wife's bedroom door, he had, being emotionally disturbed and not in a rational state of mind, killed him. However, before he could have the letter dispatched to the chancellory, the distressed father informed the Duke and Duchess of what had happened, and they in turn informed the chancellor, in order to prevent the pardon being granted. Realizing that his request was not going to succeed, Saint-Aignan fled to England, along with his wife, and a number of her relatives. Before he left he told the assassin who had committed the murder on his orders that he had [received] official instructions from the King to arrest him and have him put to death, but that in view of his services, he was prepared to save his life. So he give him ten écus to get out of the country. The man accepted, and was never seen again.

However, the murder was clearly authenticated by the two servants of the dead man, by the old chambermaid who had taken refuge with the Dominicans, and by the bones that were later discovered in the mortar. The case was brought and tried in the absence of Saint-Aignan and his wife. Judgement was pronounced on the two defaulters, the sentence being death. Their property was to be forfeited to the sovereign, and they were to pay fifteen hundred écus to the father to cover his legal expenses. Saint-Aignan, now safe in England, realized that he was a dead man if he went back to France. He ingratiated himself into the service of one or two eminent noblemen, and, partly through this and partly through the influence of his wife's family, he managed to get the King of England to forward a request to the King of France for a pardon and the restoration of his property and privileges. But the King had heard what an appalling case it was, and merely sent the details of the trial to the King of England, inviting him to see for himself whether a pardon was warranted, and informing him at the same time that the Duke of Alençon alone in the realm had the right to confer pardons within his own duchy. In spite of these protestations the King of England would not rest. Indeed, he was so persistent in the matter that in the end Saint-Aignan got what he had been asking for, and eventually returned to his house in France.

To crown his criminal career, he then fell in with a sorcerer called Gallery, in the hope that the occult arts would enable him to avoid paying the fifteen hundred écus to the deceased man's father. To this end he and his wife travelled, in disguise, to Paris, where he spent a great deal of time closeted in a locked room with his sorcerer friend. He had not told his wife what he was up to, and so one morning she spied on him, and saw Gallery showing him five wooden dolls. Three of the dolls had arms hanging by their sides, and two had their arms up in the air. Gallery was explaining:

'We've got to make dolls like these, but out of wax. The ones with their arms hanging down are the ones we're going to cause to die. The ones with their arms up are the ones whose favours and goodwill we're after.'

To which Saint-Aignan replied: 'This one here will be the King. He's the one whose good books I want to be in. And this one will be the chancellor of Alençon, Jean Brinon.'

'We have to put the dolls underneath the altar,' Gallery went on, 'so that they can hear mass being said, and when we put them there we have to say certain words, which I'll tell you later.'

When they came to the dolls with the arms hanging down, Saint-Aignan said that one of them was Gilles du Mesnil, the father of the dead man, because he knew that for as long as the

Lieutenant had breath in him he would never give up trying to track him down. The other two were women. One of them was the Duchess of Alençon, the King's sister, because she was so fond of her old servant du Mesnil, and because she knew so much about Saint-Aignan's other evil doings that if she too did not die, he, Saint-Aignan, could not hope to live. The other doll was his own wife. It was she who was at the bottom of all this trouble, and he was quite certain she would never renounce her wicked ways.

Seeing all this through the keyhole, and realizing that her husband had her marked as a dead woman, the wife decided to beat him to it. So, on the pretext that she had to go to borrow some money, she went off to an uncle of hers, called Néaufle, who was the Duke's *maître des requêtes*, and told him what she had overheard. Néaufle, loyal servant that he was, reported the story to the chancellor of Alençon. As it happened the Duke and Duchess were not at court at the time, so the chancellor took the whole extraordinary affair to Madame la Régente, the mother of the King and of the Duchess herself. She immediately called in the provost of Paris, La Barre, who got to work so efficiently that Saint-Aignan and the sorcerer were both arrested. They both confessed voluntarily, without torture or any other means of coercion having to be employed.

The case was duly brought to law, and laid before the King. There were some people who wanted the lives of the accused spared, and pleaded that the pair had merely sought by their magic practices to obtain the King's good graces. But the King held his sister's life as dear as his own, and ordered them to be sentenced as if they had made an attempt on his own person. His sister, the Duchess of Alençon, however, begged him to spare Saint-Aignan's life, and commute the death sentence into some other form of harsh punishment. Her request was granted, and Saint-Aignan and Gallery were sent to Baron de Saint-Blancard's galleys at Marseilles. In the galleys they ended their days, and with plenty of time to reflect on the seriousness of their crimes. As for the depraved wife, she led a more immoral life than ever, once her husband was out of the way, and died a most miserable death.

*

'Just consider now, Ladies, the amount of trouble that was caused by one woman. Just think of the whole train of disasters that this one woman's behaviour led to. I think you'll agree that ever since Eve made Adam sin, women have taken it upon themselves to torture men, kill them and damn them to Hell. I know. I've experienced feminine cruelty, and I know what will bring *me* to death and damnation – nothing other than the despair that I'm thrown into by a certain lady! And yet, I am mad enough to admit that though I suffer Hell, it's a Hell far more delightful to me than any Paradise that any other woman could offer.'

Parlamente, pretending she did not know that it was to herself that he was referring, replied: 'Since Hell is as agreeable as you say, you presumably have no fear of the devil who put you there.'

'If my devil,' retorted Simontaut with some irritation, 'were to turn black, as black as it has been cruel to me, then the fright it would give you all would be as great as the pleasure the mere sight of her gives me. But the fire of love makes me forget the fire of this Hell. So, I will say no more, and invite Oisille to tell the next story. I'm sure that if she'll tell us what she knows about women, she'll corroborate my own view.'

They all turned towards Oisille, and urged her to start. She accepted, and, with a laugh, began.

'It seems to me, Ladies, that the person who's just asked me to tell the next story has, by telling a true story about *one* wretched woman, succeeded in casting such a slur on *all* women, that I have to think back a very long way to find a story that will belie the low opinion he has of us. But there is one that comes to mind. It's a story that deserves not to be forgotten, so I shall tell it to you.'

STORY TWO

In the town of Amboise there was a certain mule-driver in the service of the Queen of Navarre, the sister of King Francis I, and it all happened while the Queen was staying at Blois, around the time when she gave birth to a son. The mule-driver had gone over to collect his quarterly pay, while his wife stayed behind in their house on the other side of the bridges in Amboise. Now the husband had a servant, and this man had been desperately in love with the wife for quite a while. One day, unable to stand it any longer, he had come out with his declaration. But being a very virtuous woman, she had given him a very sharp reply, and threatened to get her husband to give him a beating and throw him out of the house. After that the man had never dared open his mouth to her in this fashion again, or in any other way indicate his feelings. However, the flames of passion smouldered secretly away, until the fateful day when the husband went off to Blois. The lady of the house had gone to vespers in the church of Saint-Florentin, in the [castle, and a long way] from the house. Left to himself in the house, the servant got it into his head that he would take by force what he had failed to obtain by supplication and service. He broke an opening in the partition that separated the room where he slept from that of his mistress. The hole could not be seen, because it was covered by the curtain of his master's bed on one side, and by the curtain round the servant's bed on the other. So his foul intentions were not suspected, until the good lady had actually got into bed, accompanied by a little lass of eleven or twelve years of age. The poor woman had just fallen asleep, when the servant jumped through the hole and into bed with her, wearing nothing but his shirt, and clutching his bare sword in his hand. The moment she felt him by her side, she jumped up, and told him what she thought of him, like the virtuous woman she was. His love was no more than animal lust, and he would have understood the language his mules spoke better than he understood the virtuous appeals to reason that she now made. Indeed, what he did next proved him even more bestial than the animals with whom he had spent so much of his life. She ran too fast round the table for him to catch her, and was in any case so strong that she had already twice managed to struggle free from his clutches. He despaired of taking her alive, and stabbed her violently in the small of the back, thinking no doubt that the pain would make her surrender, where terror and manhandling had failed. However, the very opposite happened. Just as a good soldier will fight back all the more fiercely if he sees his own blood flowing, so the chaste heart of this lady was only strengthened in its resolve to run, and escape falling into the hands of this desperate man. As she struggled to get away, she reasoned with him as well as she was able, thinking she might somehow bring him to recognize the wrongness of his acts. But by now he was worked up into a frenzy, and was in no state to be moved by words of wisdom. He went on lunging at her with his sword, while she ran as fast as she could to get away. When at last she had lost so much blood that she felt death approaching, she raised her eyes to heaven and, joining her hands in prayer, gave thanks to her God.

'Thou art my strength, my virtue, my suffering and my chastity,' she prayed, humbly beseeching that He would receive the blood, which, according to His commandment, was shed in veneration of the blood of His son. For she truly believed that through Him were all her sins cleansed and washed from the memory of His wrath. And as she sank with her face to the floor, she sighed, 'Into thy hands I commend my spirit, my spirit that was redeemed by thy great goodness.'

Then the vicious brute stabbed her several times again, and, once she could no longer speak, and all her physical resistance was gone, he took the poor defenceless creature by force. When he had satisfied his lusts he made a speedy getaway, and in spite of all subsequent attempts to track him down, it has proved impossible to find him. The young girl who had been sleeping with the poor woman had been terrified, and had hidden under the bed. Once the man had disappeared she came out and went to her mistress. Finding that she was unable to speak and just lay there motionless, she ran to the window and called out for help from the neighbours. There were plenty of people in the town who were fond of her and thought highly of her, and they now rallied round immediately and fetched doctors to tend her. When they examined her they found twenty-five fatal wounds. They did what they could to help her, but to no avail. She lingered on for another hour, unable to speak, but indicating by movements of her eyes, and gestures of the hands, that her mind was still clear. A man of the church came and questioned her about the faith in which she died, and about her hope for salvation through Christ alone. Although she could only reply by signs, no words could have conveyed her meaning more clearly. And so, with joy on her face, and her eyes turned heavenwards, her soul left this chaste body to return to its Creator. No sooner had the corpse been lifted from where it lay, prepared for burial and placed before the door of the house to await the burial party, than the poor husband arrived. There, completely unforewarned, he was confronted with the spectacle of his wife lying dead in front of his own house. When he heard how she had died, his grief was doubled. Indeed, so deep was his sorrow that he too came near to death. His wife, this martyr of chastity, was then laid to rest in the church of Saint-Florentin. All the virtuous women of the town were present, as was their duty, to do all possible honour to her name. For them it was a great blessing to have lived in the same town as one so virtuous. For women of more wanton ways the sight of such respect being paid to her body made them resolve to amend their lives.

*

'Here we have, Ladies, a true story – a story that should strengthen our resolve to preserve this most glorious virtue, chastity. And we, who are all of good birth, ought to die of shame at the thought that our hearts may be tinged with worldly feelings, when in order to shun those very feelings, even a poor mule-driver's wife does not fear to face what was a most cruel death. Can any woman regard herself as virtuous unless she has, like this woman, resisted till the last? So let us humble ourselves, for God's graces are not given to men for their noble birth and for their riches, but according as it pleases Him in His goodness. He has no regard for persons, but elects whom He will, and those whom He has elected He honours with virtues and [crowns with His glory.] Often does He choose that which is low, that He might confound that which the world places high and considers worthy, even as He himself has said, "Let us not rejoice in our own virtues, but let us rejoice that we are inscribed in the Book of Life, from which nor Death, nor Hell, nor Sin can erase us." '*

There was not a lady in the company who did not have tears in her eyes, so moved were they all by the tragic and glorious death of the mule-driver's wife. Each and every one vowed that should the same happen to her, she would do all in her power to follow this martyr's example. Then, seeing that they were losing time in praising the dead woman, Madame Oisille turned to Saffredent and said: 'If *you* don't tell us something to make us laugh, I don't think there's anyone here who can make up for what I've done in making you all weep! So it's you I choose to tell us the next story.'

Saffredent replied that he would be only too happy if he could tell his companions, and a certain lady in particular, something to please them, but that this would be unfair, since there were others older and more experienced than he who ought to be allowed to speak first. However, he finally agreed that since it fell to his lot, he might as well speak now – after all, the longer he delayed, the more competition he would have, and the worse his story would be judged.

* Variant reading given in the de Thou MS: Let us not *place our trust in* our own virtues, but *in that* we are inscribed in the Book of Life, *from which for the multiplicity of our sins He may erase us.*

STORY THREE

I've often wished, Ladies, that I'd been able to share the good fortune of the man in the story I'm about to tell you. So here it is. In the town of Naples in the time of King Alfonso (whose well-known lasciviousness was, one might say, the very sceptre by which he ruled) there lived a nobleman – a handsome, upright and likeable man, a man indeed whose qualities were so excellent that a certain old gentleman granted him the hand of his daughter. In beauty and charm she was in every way her husband's equal, and they lived in deep mutual affection until a carnival, in the course of which the King disguised himself and went round all the houses in the town, where the people vied with one another to give him a good reception. When he came to the house of the gentleman I have referred to, he was entertained more lavishly than in any of the other houses. Preserves, minstrels, music – all were laid before him, but above all there was the presence of the most beautiful lady that the King had ever seen. At the end of the banquet, the lady sang for the King with her husband, and so sweetly did she sing that her beauty was more than ever enhanced. Seeing such physical perfection, the King took less delight in contemplating the gentle harmony that existed between the lady and her husband, than he did in speculating as to how he might go about spoiling it. The great obstacle to his desires was the evident deep mutual love between them, and so, for the time being, he kept his passion hidden and as secret as he could. But in order to obtain at least some relief for his feelings, he held a series of banquets for the lords and ladies of Naples, to which he did not, of course, omit to invite the gentleman and his fair wife.

As everyone knows, men see and believe just what they want to, and the King thought he caught something in the lady's eyes which augured well – if only the husband were not in the way. To find out if his surmise was correct, therefore, he sent the husband off for two or three weeks to attend to some business in Rome. Up till then the wife had never had him out of her sight, and she was heartbroken the moment he walked out of the door. The King took the opportunity to console her as often as possible, showering blandishments and gifts of all kinds upon her, with the result that in the end she felt not only consoled, but even content in her husband's absence. Before the three weeks were up she had fallen so much in love with the King that she was every bit as upset about her husband's imminent return as she had been about his departure. So, in order that she should not be deprived of the King after her husband's return, it was agreed that she would let her royal lover know whenever her husband was going to his estates in the country. He could then come to see her without running any risks, and in complete secrecy, so that her honour and reputation – which gave her more concern than her conscience – could not possibly be damaged in any way.

Dwelling on the prospect of the King's visits with considerable pleasure, the lady gave her husband such an affectionate reception that, although he had heard during his absence that the King had been paying her a lot of attention, he had not the slightest suspicion of how far things had gone. However, the fire of passion cannot be concealed for long, and as time went by its flames began to be somewhat obvious. He naturally began to guess at the truth, and kept a close watch on his wife until there was no longer any room for doubt. But he decided to keep quiet about it, because he was afraid that if he let on that he knew, he might suffer even worse things at the hands of the King than he had already. He considered, in short, that it was better to put up with the affront, than to risk his life for the sake of a woman who apparently no longer loved him. He was, all the same, angry and bitter, and determined to get his own back if at all possible.

Now he was well aware of the fact that bitterness and jealousy can drive women to do things that love alone will never make them do, and that this is particularly true of women with strong feelings and high principles of honour. So one day, while he was conversing with the Queen, he made so bold as to say that he felt very sorry for her when he saw how little the King really loved her. The Queen had heard all about the affair between the King and the gentleman's wife, and merely replied:

'I do not expect to be able to combine both honour and pleasure in my position. I am perfectly well aware that while I receive honour and respect, it is *she* who has all the pleasure. But then, I know too that while she may have the pleasure, she does not receive the honour and respect.'

He knew, of course, to whom she was referring, and this was his reply: 'Madame, you were born to honour and respect. You are after all of such high birth that, being queen or being empress could scarcely add to your nobility. But you are also beautiful, charming and refined, and you deserve to have your pleasures as well. The woman who is depriving you of those pleasures which are yours by right, is in fact doing herself more harm – because her moment of glory will eventually turn to shame and she will forfeit as much pleasure as she, you or any woman in the Kingdom of Naples could ever have. And if I may say so, Madame, if the King didn't have a crown on his head, he wouldn't have the slightest advantage over me as far as giving pleasure to ladies is concerned. What is more, I'm quite sure that in order to satisfy a refined person such as yourself, he really ought to be wishing he could exchange his constitution for one more like my own!'

The Queen laughed, and said: 'The King may have a more delicate constitution than your own. Even so, the love which he bears me gives me so much satisfaction that I prefer it to all else.'

'Madame, if that were the case, then I would not feel so sorry for you, because I know that you would derive great happiness from the pure love you feel within you, if it were matched by an equally pure love on the part of the King. But God has denied you this, in order that you should not find in this man the answer to all your wants and so make him your god on earth.'

'I admit,' said the Queen, 'that my love for him is so deep that you will never find its like, wherever you may look.'

'Forgive me,' said the gentleman, 'but there are hearts whose love you've never sounded. May I be so bold as to tell you that there is a certain person who loves you, and loves you so deeply and so desperately, that in comparison your love for the King is as nothing? And his love grows and goes on growing in proportion as he sees the King's love for you diminishing. So, if it were, Madame, to please you, and you were to receive his love, you would be more than compensated for all that you have lost.'

The Queen began to realize, both from what he was saying, and from the expression on his face, that he was speaking from the depths of his heart. She remembered that he had some time ago sought to do her service, and that he had felt so deeply about it that he had become quite melancholy. At the time she had assumed the cause of his mood lay with his wife, but she was now quite convinced that the real reason was his love for her. Love is a powerful force, and will make itself felt whenever it is more than mere pretence, and it was this powerful force that now made her certain of what remained hidden from the rest of the world. She looked at him again. He was certainly more attractive than her husband. He had been left by his wife, too, just as she had been left by the King. Tormented by jealousy and bitterness, allured by the gentleman's passion, she sighed, tears came to her eyes, and she began: 'Oh God! Must it take the desire for revenge to drive me to do what love alone would never have driven me to?'

Her words were not lost on the gentleman who replied: 'Madame, vengeance is sweet indeed, when instead of taking one's enemy's life, one gives life to a lover who is true. It is time, I think, that the truth freed you from this foolish love for a man who certainly has no love for you. It is time that a just and reasonable love banished from you these fears that so ill become one whose spirit is so strong and so virtuous. Why hesitate, Madame? Let us set aside rank and station. Let us look upon ourselves as a man and a woman, as the two most wronged people in the world, as two people who have been betrayed and mocked by those whom we loved with all our hearts. Let us, Madame, take our revenge, not in order to punish them as they deserve, but in order to do justice to our love. My love for you is unbearable. If it is not requited I shall die. Unless your heart is as hard as diamond or as stone, it is impossible that you should not feel some spark from this fire that burns the more fiercely within me the more I try to stifle it. I am dying for love of you! And if that cannot move you to take pity on me and grant me your love, then at least your own love for yourself must surely force you to do so. For you, who are so perfect that you merit the devotion of all the honourable and worthy men in all the world, have been despised and deserted by the very man for whose sake you have disdained all others!'

At this speech the Queen was quite beside herself. Lest her face betray the turmoil of her mind, she took his arm and led him into the garden adjoining her room. For a long time she walked up and down with him saying nothing. But he knew that the conquest was almost complete, and when they reached the end of the path, where no one could see them, he expressed in the clearest possible way the love that for so long he had kept concealed. At last they were of one mind. And so it was, one might say, that together they enacted a Vengeance, having found the Passion too much to bear.*

Before they parted they arranged that whenever the husband made his trips to his village, he would, if the King had gone off to the town, go straight to the castle to see the Queen. Thus they would fool the very people who were trying to fool them. Moreover, there would now be four people joining in the fun, instead of just two thinking they had it all to themselves. Once this was settled, the Queen retired to her room and the gentleman went home, both of them now sufficiently cheered up to forget all their previous troubles. No longer did the King's visits to the gentleman's lady distress either of them. Dread had now turned to desire, and the gentleman started to make trips to his village rather more often than he had in the past. It was, after all, only half a league [out of the town]. Whenever the King heard that the gentleman had gone to the country, he would make his way straight to his lady. Similarly, whenever the gentleman heard that the King had left his castle, he would wait till nightfall and then go straight to the Queen – to act, so to speak, as the King's viceroy. He managed to do this in such secrecy that no one had the slightest inkling of what was going on. They proceeded in this fashion for quite a while, but the King, being a public person, had much greater difficulty concealing his love-affair sufficiently to prevent anyone at all getting wind of it. In fact, there were a few unpleasant wags who started

* An allusion to medieval mystery plays: after the Passion and Resurrection, the mystery of the Vengeance depicted the punishment of Christ's slayers.

to make fun of the gentleman, saying he was a cuckold, and putting up their fingers like cuckold's horns whenever his back was turned. Anyone with any decency felt very sorry for the man. He knew what they were saying, of course, but derived a good deal of amusement from it, and reckoned his horns were surely as good as the King's crown.

One day when the King was visiting the gentleman and his wife at their home, he noticed a set of antlers mounted on the wall. He burst out laughing, and could not resist the temptation to remark that the horns went very well with the house. The gentleman was a match for the King, however. He had an inscription placed on the antlers which read as follows:

Io porto le corna, ciascun lo vede,
Ma tal le porta, che no lo crede.

Next time the king was in the house, he saw the inscription, and asked what it meant.

The gentleman simply said: 'If the King doesn't tell his secrets to his subjects, then there's no reason why his subjects should tell their secrets to the King. And so far as horns are concerned, you should bear in mind that they don't always stick up and push their wearers' hats off. Sometimes they're so soft that you can wear a hat on top of them, without being troubled by them, and even without knowing they're there at all!'

From these words the King realized that the gentleman knew about his affair with his wife. But he never suspected that the gentleman was having an affair with *his* wife. For her part, the Queen was careful to feign displeasure at her husband's behaviour, though secretly she was pleased, and the more she was pleased, the more displeasure she affected. This amicable arrangement permitted the continuation of their amours for many years to come, until at length old age brought them to order.

*

'Well, Ladies,' concluded Saffredent, 'let that story be a lesson to you. When your husbands give you little roe-deer horns, make sure that you give them great big stag's antlers!'

'Saffredent,' said Ennasuite, laughing, 'I'm quite sure that if you were still such an ardent lover as you used to be, you wouldn't mind putting up with horns as big as oaks, as long as you could give a pair back when the fancy took you. But you're starting to go grey, you know, and it really is time you began to give your appetites a rest!'

'Mademoiselle,' he replied, 'even if the lady I love gives me no hope, and even if age has dampened my ardour somewhat, my desires are as strong as ever. But seeing that you object to my harbouring such noble desires, let me invite you to tell the fourth story, and let's see if you can produce an example to refute what I say.'

During this exchange one of the ladies had started to laugh. She knew that the lady who had just taken Saffredent's words to be aimed at her was not in fact so much the object of his affections that he would put up with cuckoldry, disgrace or injury of any kind for her sake. When Saffredent saw that she was laughing and that she had understood him, he was [highly] pleased, and let Ennasuite go on. This is what she said:

'I have a story to tell, Ladies, which will show Saffredent and everyone else here that not *all* women are like the Queen he has told us about, and that not all men who are rash enough to try their tricks get what they want. It's a story that ought not to be kept back, and it tells of a lady in whose eyes failure in love was worse than death itself. I shan't mention the real names of the people involved, because it's not long since it all happened, and I should be afraid of giving offence to their close relatives.'

STORY FOUR

In Flanders there once lived a lady of high birth, of birth so high, indeed, that there was no one higher in the land. She had no children and had been twice widowed. After her second husband's death she had gone to live with her brother, who was very fond of her. He was himself a noble lord of high estate, married to the daughter of a King. This young Prince was much given to his pleasures, being fond of the ladies, of hunting and generally enjoying himself, just as one would expect of a young man. His wife, however, was rather difficult, and did not enjoy the same things as he did, so he always used to take his sister along as well, because she, while being a sensible and virtuous woman, was also the most cheerful and lively company one could imagine.

Now there was a certain gentleman attached to the household, an extremely tall man, whose charm and good looks made him stand out among his companions. Taking careful note of the fact that his master's sister was a very lively lady who liked to enjoy herself, it occurred to him that it might be worth seeing if an amorous overture from a well-bred gentleman might not be to her taste. So he approached her, only to find that her reply was not what he would have expected. Nevertheless, in spite of the fact that she had given him the sort of answer that becomes an honest woman and a princess, she had had no difficulty in forgiving this good-looking and well-bred man for having been so presumptuous. Indeed, she made it plain that she did not at all mind his talking to her, though she also frequently reminded him that he must be careful what he said. In order to continue to enjoy the honour and pleasure of her company, he was only too glad to promise not to return to his earlier overtures. But as time went by his passion grew stronger, until he forgot his promises altogether. Not that he dared risk opening the subject again verbally – he had already to his cost had a taste of her ability to answer him back with her words of wisdom. No, what he had in mind was this. If he could find the right time and place, then might she not relent and indulge him a little, and indulge herself at the same time? After all, she was a widow and young, healthy and vivacious. To this end he mentioned to his master that he had lands adjoining his home that offered excellent hunting, and assured him that if he came and hunted a stag or two in May he would have the time of his life. Partly because he liked the gentleman and partly because he was addicted to hunting, the Prince accepted this invitation, and went to stay at his house, which was, as one would expect of the richest man in the land, a very fine place and very well maintained. In one wing of the house the gentleman accommodated the Prince and his wife. In the other wing opposite he accommodated the lady whom by now he loved more than he loved life itself. Her room had been luxuriously decorated from top to bottom with tapestries, and the floor was thickly covered with matting – so that it was impossible to see the trap-door by the side of the bed which led down to the room beneath. The gentleman's mother, who normally slept in this room, was old, and her catarrh made her cough in the night, so, in order to avoid disturbing the Princess, she had exchanged rooms with her son. Every evening this old lady took preserves up to the Princess, accompanied by her son, who, being very close to the brother of the Princess, was naturally permitted to attend both her *coucher* and her *lever*. Needless to say, these occasions constantly served to inflame his passion.

So it was that one evening he kept her up very late, and only left her room when he saw she was falling asleep. Back in his own room, he put on the most magnificent and most highly perfumed nightshirt he possessed, and on his head he placed the most beautifully decorated nightcap you ever saw. As he admired himself in his mirror, he was absolutely convinced that there was not a woman in the world who could possibly resist such a handsome and elegant sight. He looked forward with satisfaction to the success of his little plan, and went off to his bed. Not that he expected to stay there long, burning with desire as he was, and quite confident that he was soon to win his place in a bed that was both more pleasurable and more honourable than his own. Once he had dismissed his attendants, he got up to lock the door, and listened carefully for noises in the Princess's room above. When he was sure all was quiet, he turned to the task. Bit by bit he gently lowered the trap-door. It had been well constructed and was so densely covered with cloth, that not a sound was made. He hoisted himself through the aperture and into the room above. The Princess was just falling asleep. Without more ado, without a thought for her rank and station, or for the duty and respect he owed her, without, indeed, so much as a by-your-leave, he jumped into bed with her. Before she knew where she was he was lying there between her arms. But she was a strong woman. Struggling out of his clutches, she demanded to know who he was, and proceeded to lash out, scratching and biting for all she was worth. He was terrified she would call for help, and felt obliged to stuff the bedclothes into her mouth in a vain attempt to prevent her doing so. She realized that he would use all his strength to dishonour her, and fought back with all *her* strength in order to stop him. She shouted at the top of her lungs for her lady-in-waiting, a respectable elderly lady, who was sleeping in the next room, and who, as soon as she heard the shout, rushed to her mistress's rescue, still wearing her night attire.

When the gentleman realized that he had been caught, terrified of being recognized by the Princess, he beat a hasty retreat down through his trap-door. He arrived back in his room in a very sorry state indeed. It was a shattering experience for a man who had set out burning with desire, fully confident that his lady was going to receive him with open arms. He picked up his mirror from the table and examined himself in the candlelight. His face was streaming with blood from the bites and scratches she had inflicted. His beautiful embroidered nightshirt had more streaks of blood in it than it had gold thread.

'So much for good looks!' he groaned. 'I suppose you've got what you deserve. I shouldn't have expected so much from my appearance. Now it's made me attempt something that I should have realized was impossible from the start. It might even make my situation worse, instead of making it better! If she realizes that it was I who did this senseless thing, breaking all the promises I had made, I know I shall lose even my privilege of visiting her chastely and openly. That's what my vanity's done for me! To make the most of my charm and good looks, and win her heart and her love, I ought not to have kept it so dark. I ought not to have tried to take her chaste body by force! I ought to have devoted myself to her service, in humility and with patience, accepting that I must wait till love should triumph. For without love, what good to a man are prowess and physical strength?'

And so he sat the whole night through, weeping, gnashing his teeth and wishing the incident had never happened. In the morning he looked at himself again in the mirror, and seeing that his face was lacerated all over, he took to his bed, pretending he was desperately ill and could not bear to go out into the light. There he remained until his visitors had gone home.

Meanwhile, the Princess was triumphant. She knew that the only person at her brother's court who would dare to do such an extraordinary thing was the man who had already once made so bold as to declare his love. In other words, she knew perfectly well that the culprit was her host. With the help of her lady-in-waiting she looked round all the possible hiding-places in the room, without, of course, finding anybody. She was beside herself with rage. 'I know very well who it is!' she fumed. 'It's the master of the house himself! That's the only person it can be. And mark my words, I shall speak to my brother in the morning, and I'll have the man's head as proof of my chastity!'

Seeing how angry she was, her lady-in-waiting just said: 'I am pleased to see that your honour means so much to you, Madame, and that in order to enhance it you have no intention of sparing this man's life – he has already taken too many risks with it because of his violent love for you. But it very often happens that when people try to enhance their honour, they only end up doing the opposite. I would therefore urge you, Madame, to tell me the plain truth about the whole affair.'

When she had heard the whole story, she asked: 'Do you assure me that all he got from you was blows and scratches?'

'I do assure you,' came the reply, 'that that was all he got, and unless he manages to find a very good doctor indeed, we'll see the marks on his face tomorrow.'

'Well, that being so,' the old lady went on, 'it seems to me that you should be thinking about giving thanks to the Lord, rather than talking about revenge. It must have taken some courage, you know, to make such a daring attempt, and at this moment he must be feeling so mortified by his failure, that death would be a good deal easier for him to bear! If what you want is revenge, then you should just leave him to his passion and his humiliation – he'll torture himself much more than you could. And if you're concerned about your honour, then be careful not to fall into the same trap as he did. He promised himself all kinds of pleasures and delights, and what he actually got was the worst disappointment that any gentleman could ever suffer. So take care, Madame – if you try to make your honour even more impressive, you may only end up doing the opposite. If you make an official complaint against him, you will have to bring the whole thing into the open, whereas at the moment nobody knows anything, and he certainly won't go and tell anybody. What is more, just suppose you did go ahead, and Monseigneur, your brother, did bring the case to justice, and the poor man was put to death – people will say that he *must* have had his way with you. Most people will argue that it's not very easy to accept that a man can carry out such an act, unless he has been given a certain amount of encouragement by the lady concerned. You're young and attractive, you're very lively and sociable in all kinds of company. There isn't a single person at this court who hasn't seen the encouraging way you treat the man you are now suspecting. That could only make people conclude that if he did indeed do what you say, then it couldn't have been without some blame being due to you as well. Your honour, which up till now has been such that you've been able to hold your head high wherever you went, would be put in doubt wherever this story was heard.'

As she listened to the wise reasonings of her lady-in-waiting, the Princess knew that what she was saying was true. She would indeed be criticized and blamed, in view of the encouraging and intimate way she had always treated the gentleman, so she asked her lady-in-waiting what she thought she ought to do.

'It is most gracious of you, Madame,' the old lady replied, 'to heed my advice. You know that I have great affection for you. Well, it seems to me that you should rejoice in your heart that this man – and he is the most handsome and best-bred gentleman I saw in my life – has been completely unable to turn you from the path of virtue, in spite of his love for you, and in spite of using physical violence against you. For this you should humble yourself before God, and acknowledge that it was not your virtue that saved you. For there have been many women, women who have led a far more austere life than you have, who have been humiliated by men far less worthy of affection than the man we are talking of. From now on you should be even more cautious when men make overtures to you, and bear in mind that there are plenty of women who have escaped from danger the first time, only to succumb the second. Never forget that Love is blind, Madame, and descends upon his victims at the very moment when they are treading a path which they think is safe, but which in reality is slippery and treacherous. I think also that you should never allude in any way to what has happened, either to him or anyone else, and even if *he* were to bring it up, I think you should pretend not to understand what he is talking about. In this way there are two dangers that you will be able to avoid. First of all, there's the danger of glorying in your triumph. And then there's the danger that you might enjoy being reminded of the pleasures of the flesh. Even the most chaste of women have a hard time preventing some spark of pleasure being aroused by such things, however much they strive to avoid them. Finally, Madame, so that he should not get it into his head that you in some way enjoyed what he tried to do, I would advise you to gradually stop seeing so much of him. In that way you will bring home to him what a low opinion you have of his foolish and wicked behaviour. At the same time he will be brought to see what a good person you are to have been satisfied with the triumph that God has already granted you, without seeking any further revenge. May God grant you the grace, Madame, to continue in the path of virtue wherein he has placed you, to continue to love and to serve Him even better than hitherto, in the knowledge that it is from Him alone that all goodness flows.'

The Princess made up her mind to follow the wise counsel of her lady-in-waiting, and slept peacefully for the rest of the night, while the wretched gentleman below spent a night of sleepless torment.

The next day the Princess's brother was ready to depart, and asked if he could take his leave of the master of the house. He was astonished to hear that he was ill, could not tolerate the light of day and refused to be seen by anyone. He would have gone to see him, but was told that he was sleeping, and decided not to disturb him. So together with his wife and his sister he left the house without being able to say goodbye. When his sister, the Princess, heard about their host's excuses for not seeing them before they left, she knew for certain that he was the one who had caused her so much distress. Obviously he did not dare to show his face because of the scratches he had received. Indeed, he refused all subsequent invitations to attend court until all his wounds – except, that is, for those he had suffered to his heart and to his pride – had healed. When eventually he did go back to court to face his triumphant enemy, he could not do so without blushing. He, who was the boldest man at court, would completely lose his self-assurance in her presence, and would frequently go quite to pieces. This only made the Princess the more sure that her suspicions had been well-founded. Gently, and little by little, she withdrew her attentions – but not so gently that he failed to appreciate what she was doing. Scared lest anything worse befell him, he dared not breathe a word. He simply had to nurse his passion in the depths of his heart, and put up with a rebuff that had been justly deserved.

*

'And that, Ladies, is a story that should strike fear into the hearts of any man who thinks he can help himself to what doesn't belong to him. The Princess's virtue and the good sense of her lady-in-waiting should inspire courage in the hearts of all women. So if anything like this should ever happen to any of you, you now know what the remedy is!'

'In my opinion,' said Hircan, 'the tall lord of your story lacked nerve, and didn't deserve to have his memory preserved. What an opportunity he had! He should never have been content to eat or sleep till he'd succeeded. And one really can't say that his love was very great, if there was still room in his heart for the fear of death and dishonour.'

'And what,' asked Nomerfide, 'could the poor man have done with two women against him?'

'He should have killed the old one, and when the young one

realized there was no one to help her, he'd have been half-way there!'

'Kill her!' Nomerfide cried. 'You wouldn't mind him being a murderer as well, then? If that's what you think, we'd better watch out we don't fall into *your* clutches!'

'If I'd gone that far,' he replied, 'I'd consider my honour ruined if I didn't go through with it!'

Then Geburon spoke up: 'So you find it str-nge that a princess of high birth who's been brought up in the strict school of honour should be too much for one man? In that case you'd find it even stranger that a woman of poor birth should manage to get away from *two* men!'

'I invite you to tell the fifth story, Geburon,' said Ennasuite, 'because it sounds as if you have one about some poor woman that will be far from dull.'

'Since you've chosen me [to speak],' he began, 'I shall tell a story that I know to be true because I conducted an inquiry into it at the very place where it happened. As you'll see, it isn't only princesses who've got good sense in their heads and virtue in their heart. And love and resourcefulness aren't always to be found where you'd expect them, either.'

STORY FIVE

At the port of Coulon near Niort, there was once a woman whose job it was to ferry people night and day across the river. One day she found herself alone in her boat with two Franciscan friars from Niort. Now this is one of the longest crossings on any river in France, and the two friars took it into their heads that she would find it less boring if they made amorous proposals to her. But, as was only right and proper, she refused to listen. However, the two were not to be deterred. They had not exactly had their strength sapped by rowing, nor their ardours chilled by the chilly water nor, indeed, their consciences pricked by the woman's refusals. So they decided to rape her, both of them, and if she resisted, to throw her into the river. But she was as sensible and shrewd as they were vicious and stupid.

'I'm not as ungracious as you might think,' she said to them, 'and if you'll just grant me two little things, you'll see I'm just as keen to do what you want as you are.'

The Cordeliers swore by the good Saint Francis that they'd let her have anything she asked for, if she'd just let them have what they wanted.

'First of all, you must promise on your oath that neither of you will tell a soul about it,' she said.

To this they readily agreed.

'Secondly, you must do what you want with me one at a time – I'd be too embarrassed to have both of you looking at me. So decide between you who's to have me first.'

They thought this too was a very reasonable request, and the younger of the two offered to let the older man go first. As they sailed past a small island in the river, the ferrywoman said to the younger one: 'Now my good father, jump ashore and say your prayers while I take your friend here to another island. If he's satisfied with me when he gets back, we'll drop him off here, and then you can come with me.'

So he jumped out of the boat to wait on the island till his companion came back. The ferrywoman then took the other one to another island in the river, and while she pretended to be making the boat fast to a tree, told him to go and find a convenient spot.

He jumped out, and went off to look for a good place. No sooner was he on dry land than the ferrywoman shoved off with a kick against the tree, and sailed off down the river, leaving the two good friars stranded.

'You can wait till God sends an angel to console you, Messieurs!' she bawled at them. 'You're not going to get anything out of me today!'

The poor friars saw they had been hoodwinked. They ran to the water's edge and pleaded on bended knees that she would take them to the port. They promised not to ask her for any more favours. But she went on rowing, and called back: 'I'd be even more stupid to let myself get caught again, now I've escaped!'

As soon as she landed on the other side, she went into the village, fetched her husband and called out the officers of the law to go and round up these two ravenous wolves, from whose jaws she had just by the grace of God been delivered. They had plenty of willing helpers. There was no one in the village, great or small, who was not anxious to join in the hunt and have his share of the fun. When the two good brothers, each on his own island, saw this huge band coming after them, they did their best to hide – even as Adam hid from the presence of the Lord God, when he saw that he was naked. They were half dead for shame at this exposure of their sins, and trembled in terror at the thought of the punishment that surely awaited them. But there was nothing they could do. They were seized and bound, and led through the village to the shouts and jeers of every man and woman in the place. Some people said: 'There they go, those good fathers who preach chastity to us yet want to take it from our wives!* Others said: 'They are whited sepulchres, outwardly beautiful, but within full of dead men's bones and all uncleanness!' And someone else called out, 'Every tree is known by his own fruit!' In fact, they hurled at the two captives every text in the Gospels that condemns hypocrites. In

* The 1559 edition adds: *The husband said: 'They dare not touch money with their bare hands, but they like to feel our wives' thighs, which are even more dangerous.'*

the end their Father Superior came to the rescue. He lost no time in requesting their custody, reassuring the officers of the law that he would punish them more severely than secular law could. By way of reparation, they would, he promised, be made to say as many prayers and masses as might be required! [The Father Superior was a worthy man, so the judge granted his request and sent the two prisoners back to their convent, where they were brought before the full Chapter and severely reprimanded.] Never again did they take a ferry across a river, without making the sign of the cross and commending their souls to God!

*

'Now consider this story carefully, Ladies. We have here a humble ferrywoman who had the sense to frustrate the evil intentions of two vicious men. What then ought we to expect from women who all their lives have seen nothing but good examples, read of nothing but good examples and, in short, had examples of feminine virtue constantly paraded before them? If well-fed women are virtuous, is it not just as much a matter of custom as of virtue? But it's quite another matter if your're talking about women who have no education, who probably don't hear two decent sermons in a year, who have time for nothing but thinking how to make a meagre living, and who, in spite of all this, diligently resist all pressures in order to preserve their chastity. It is in the heart of such women as these that one finds pure virtue, for in the hearts of those we regard as inferior in body and mind the spirit of God performs his greatest works. Woe to those women who do not guard their treasure with the utmost care, for it is a treasure that brings them great honour if it is well guarded and great dishonour if it is squandered!'

'If you ask me, Geburon,' observed Longarine, 'there's nothing very virtuous in rejecting the advances of a friar. I don't know how anyone could possibly feel any affection at all for them.'

'Longarine,' he replied, 'women who are not so used as you are to having refined gentlemen to serve them find friars far from unpleasant. They're often just as good-looking as we are, just as well-built and less worn out, because they've not been knocked about in battle. What is more, they talk like angels and are as persistent as devils. That's why I think that any woman who's seen nothing better than the coarse cloth of monks' habits should be considered extremely virtuous if she manages to escape their clutches.'

'Good Heavens!' exclaimed Nomerfide loudly. 'You may say what you like, but I'd rather be thrown in the river any day, than go to bed with a friar!'

*'So you're a strong swimmer, are you then!'** said Oisille, laughing.

Nomerfide took this in bad part, thinking that Oisille did not give her as much credit as she would have liked, and said heatedly: 'There *are* plenty of people who've refused better men than friars, without blowing their trumpets about it!'

'Yes, and they've been even more careful not to beat their drums about ones they've accepted and given in to!' retorted Oisille, amused to see that she was annoyed.

'I can see that Nomerfide would like to speak,' Geburon intervened, 'so I invite her to take over from me, in order that she may unburden herself by telling us a good story.'

'I couldn't care less about people's remarks,' she snapped, 'they neither please nor annoy me. But since you ask me to speak, will you listen carefully, because I want to tell a story to show you that women can exercise their [cleverness] for bad purposes as well as for good ones. As we've sworn to tell the truth, I have no desire to conceal it. After all, just as the ferry-woman's virtue does not redound to the honour of other women unless they actually follow in her footsteps, so the *vice* of one woman does not bring dishonour on all other women. So, if you will listen . . .'

* The original is: *vous scavez doncques bien nouer*. '*Nouer*' meant both 'to swim' and 'to tie'. In the second sense it had sexual connotations.

STORY SIX

Charles, the last Duke of Alençon, had a valet de chambre who was blind in one eye, and who was married to a woman a good few years younger than himself. Now, of all the men of that rank in the household this man was particularly well-liked by his master and mistress. This meant that he could not get home to see his wife as often as he would have liked, which in turn led to her neglecting her honour and conscience to the extent that she fell for a young man. There was so much malicious gossip about this affair that the husband eventually got wind of it, although he found it difficult to believe, as his wife always seemed to be very affectionate with him. One day he decided to check up on her and, if he could, get his own back on her for disgracing him. So he told her that he had to go away for two or three days to some place not far off. No sooner was he out of the door than the wife invited her young man round. But he had not been there above half an hour when back comes the husband and hammers loudly on the front door. She recognized the knock and told her lover, who was so terrified he wished he had never been born. He cursed his mistress and the whole wretched love-affair for placing him in such a tight corner. But she told him not to worry, she would find some way of getting him out of it without injury either to himself or his honour, and instructed him to get his clothes on as fast as he could. The husband was still banging at the door, and shouting for his wife at the top of his voice. But she pretended not to recognize him, and called out, as if to [the servants]: 'Why don't you get up, and tell whoever it is out there to be quiet? This is no time to be knocking at respectable people's doors! If my husband were here, he'd soon put a stop to it!'

Hearing his wife's voice, the husband called out as loud as he could: 'Open up, wife. Are you going to keep me standing here till morning?'

Seeing that her lover was ready to be off, she opened the door, and said to her husband: 'My dear husband, how glad I am to see you! I've just had a marvellous dream, and I've never felt so happy, because I dreamt that you'd got the sight back in your eye!'

She put her arms round him and kissed him, took his head in both hands, and covered up his good eye.

'Is it not true that you can see better than before?' she demanded. He could not see a thing, of course, and the wife gave her lover the sign to make his getaway.

Guessing what was going on, the husband said: 'By Heavens, woman, I'm not going to spy on *you* any more! I thought I was going to catch you out, but in return you play me the most cunning trick anyone's ever thought of. May God give you the punishment you deserve! Because there's not a man alive can make a bad woman behave herself, short of murdering her! Since treating you kindly as I've done up till now, hasn't made you mend your ways, perhaps you'll be brought to heel if from now on I treat you with the contempt you deserve!'

So saying, he stormed off, leaving her quite distressed, though in the end, by dint of tears, excuses and the mediation of her friends, she managed to get him to come back to her.

*

'So you can see, Ladies, that women can be very cunning when they're in a scrape. And if they're clever enough to cover up something bad, I think they'd be even more ingenious in avoiding bad deeds or in doing good ones. A shrewd wit is always stronger in the end, as everybody always says.'

'You can talk about your feminine cunning as much as you like,' said Hircan, 'but in my opinion, if anything like that happened to *you*, you would be incapable of covering it up!'

'I'd rather you thought I was the stupidest woman in the world!' replied Nomerfide.

'I don't say *that*,' he went on, 'but I do think you're the sort of woman who gets worked up over a rumour, instead of thinking of some clever way of putting an end to it.'

'You think that everyone's like you,' she replied, 'quite ready to cover up one rumour with another. But there's always the risk that a cover-up will end up destroying the very thing it was meant to conceal, like a building that collapses because the roof's too heavy for the foundations. However if you think that [male] cunning – and everyone knows you've got your fair share of *that* – is superior to female cunning, then I'll make way for you, so that you can tell us the seventh story. And if you'd like to tell us about yourself by way of example, I'm sure you'd teach us all a good deal about wickedness and trickery!'

'I'm not here to give myself a worse reputation than I've already got. There are already enough people willing to say worse things about me than I care for!' said Hircan, glancing at his wife, who quickly replied:

'Don't be afraid to tell the truth because of me. It will be easier for me to hear about your little games than to have had to watch you playing them under my nose – though nothing you may do could diminish the love I bear you.'

'Then I shan't complain about all the wrong opinions that you have held about me. So, since we know and understand one another, there is reason to feel more reassurance for the future. All the same I wouldn't be so foolish as to tell you a story about myself, when the facts might be hurtful to you – but I *will* tell one about a man who was a close friend of mine.'

STORY SEVEN

In the town of Paris there was once a merchant who was in love with a young girl who was a neighbour of his. To be more accurate, it was the girl who was in love with him, rather than the other way round. He merely pretended to be devoted to her in order to cover up a more exalted and honourable passion for someone else. But she let herself be deceived, and was so infatuated that she had completely forgotten that it is the custom for women to reject men's advances. For a long while the merchant had taken the trouble of going to seek her out, but eventually he was able to persuade her to come to meet him where it suited him. Her mother, who was a most respectable person, realized what was going on, and forbade the girl ever to speak to the merchant again, or she would be sent straight to a convent. But the girl was more in love with her merchant than she was in awe of her mother, and only did her best to see him more often than ever.

One day the merchant happened to find her alone in her dressing-room. It was a convenient place for his purposes, so he proceeded to make overtures to her in the most intimate fashion. But some chambermaid or other who had seen him going in ran off and told the mother, who flew into a rage and immediately came along to catch them. The girl heard her coming and burst into tears.

'Alas! Alas! My love,' she wailed to her merchant, 'my hour is come and I shall pay the price for the love I bear you! Here's my mother coming. This is what she's feared and suspected all along, and now she'll discover that it's true!'

The merchant was not the sort of man to be upset by a situation of this kind. He jumped up and went to meet the mother, put his arms around her and hugged and kissed her as hard as he could. Already in a passionate mood after flirting with her daughter, he flung the poor old woman on to a couch. She found this so extraordinary that all she could manage to say was: 'What do you want? Have you gone mad?'

But he was not deterred. Indeed, he went about it as if she had been the most attractive young girl he had ever seen. If her screams had not brought her servants and chambermaids running to her rescue, she would have gone the same way she feared her daughter was going! The servants extricated the poor old dear from the merchant's embraces without her having the vaguest idea why he had given her such a mauling. While all this was going on, the girl escaped to a neighbour's house, where there happened to be a wedding reception going on.

The merchant and the girl often had a good laugh together at the mother's expense, and the old woman never found them out.

*

'So, you can see, Ladies, how male cleverness succeeded in outwitting the old woman and in saving the young girl's honour. But anyone who knew the names of the people involved, or who saw the merchant's face or the old woman's astonishment, would have to be very afraid for his conscience if he refused to laugh. But I'll be quite satisfied if my story has proved to you that men are just as resourceful and quick-witted as women when they need to be. So, dear Ladies, you should have no fear of falling into their hands, because, should you be lost for a way out, they will always be able to cover up and save your honour!'

'Yes, Hircan, I agree that it's a very funny story,' said Longarine, 'and that the man was very clever. All the same, I don't think it's an example that young girls should follow. I suspect there are some you'd like to persuade to do so. But I don't think you're so stupid as to want your wife to play such games, or the lady whose honour is dearer to you than pleasure. I don't think there's anyone who would keep a closer watch on them than you, or anyone who would more promptly put a stop to such things.'

'On my oath,' replied Hircan, 'if [the ones] you refer to *had* done anything like that, I wouldn't think any the less of them for it – provided I knew nothing about it! For all I know, someone might have played just as good a trick on me, but if so, I know nothing about it, so it doesn't worry me.'

Parlamente could not resist commenting: 'It's impossible for men who do wrong themselves not to be suspicious of others.

But it's a happy man who gives no cause for others to be suspicious of him.'

'Well, I've never seen fire without smoke,' said Longarine, 'but I have seen smoke without fire! Malicious people are often just as good at smelling something bad when it doesn't exist, as they are when it does.'

'Since you speak so strongly in favour of women who get suspected wrongly, Longarine,' said Hircan, 'I choose you to tell us the eighth story, on condition that you don't make us all weep, like Madame Oisille did, with her excessive zeal for stories in praise of virtuous women.'

Longarine broke into a hearty laugh, and said: 'Since you want me to make you laugh, in my usual fashion, it won't be at the expense of women. Yet I *shall* tell you something to show how easy they are to deceive when they fill their heads with jealous thoughts, and pride themselves on their good sense for wanting to deceive their husbands.'

STORY EIGHT

In the county of Alès there was once a man by the name of Bornet, who had married a very decent and respectable woman. He held her honour and reputation very dear, as I am sure all husbands here hold the honour and reputation of *their* wives dear. He wanted her to be faithful to him, but was not so keen on having the rule applied to them both equally. He had become enamoured of his chambermaid, though the only benefit he got from transferring his affections in this way was the sort of pleasure one gets from varying one's diet. He had a neighbour called Sendras, who was of similar station and temperament to himself – he was a tailor and a drummer. These two were such close friends that, with the exception of the wife, there was nothing that they did not share between them. Naturally he told him that he had designs on the chambermaid.

Not only did his friend wholeheartedly approve of this, but did his best to help him, in the hope that he too might get a share in the spoils.

The chambermaid herself refused to have anything to do with him, although he was constantly pestering her, and in the end she went to tell her mistress about it. She told her that she could not stand being badgered by him any longer, and asked permission to go home to her parents. Now the good lady of the house, who was really very much in love with her husband, had often had occasion to suspect him, and was therefore rather pleased to be one up on him, and to be able to show him that she had found out what he was up to. So she said to her maid: 'Be nice to him, dear, encourage him a little bit, and then make a date to go to bed with him in my dressing-room. Don't forget to tell me which night he's supposed to be coming, and make sure you don't tell anyone else.'

The maid did exactly as her mistress had instructed. As for her master, he was so pleased with himself that he went off to tell his friend about his stroke of luck, whereupon the friend insisted on taking his share afterwards, since he had been in on the business from the beginning. When the appointed time came, off went the master, as had been agreed, to get into bed, as he thought, with his little chambermaid. But his wife, having abandoned her position of authority in order to serve in a more pleasurable one, had taken her maid's place in the bed. When he got in with her, she did not act like a wife, but like a bashful young girl, and he was not in the slightest suspicious. It would be impossible to say which of them enjoyed themselves more – the wife deceiving her husband, or the husband who thought he was deceiving his wife. He stayed in bed with her for some time, not as long as he might have wished (many years of marriage were beginning to tell on him), but as long as he could manage. Then he went out to rejoin his accomplice, and tell him what a good time he had had. The lustiest piece of goods he had ever come across, he declared. His friend, who was younger and more active than he was, said: 'Remember what you promised?'

'Hurry up, then,' replied the master, 'in case she gets up, or my wife wants her for something.'

Off he went and climbed into bed with the supposed chambermaid his friend had just failed to recognize as his wife. *She* thought it was her husband again, and did not refuse anything he asked for (I say 'asked', but 'took' would be nearer the mark, because he did not dare open his mouth). He made a much longer business of it than the husband, to the surprise of the wife, who was not used to these long nights of pleasure. However, she did not complain, and looked forward to what she was planning to say to him in the morning, and the fun she would have teasing him. When dawn came, the man got up, and fondling her as he got out of bed, pulled off a ring she wore on her finger, a ring that her husband had given her at their marriage. Now the women in this part of the world are very superstitious about such things. They have great respect for women who hang on to their wedding rings till the day they die, and if a woman loses her ring, she is dishonoured, and is looked upon as having given her faith to another man. But she did not mind him taking it, because she thought it would be sure evidence against her husband of the way she had hoodwinked him.

The husband was waiting outside for his friend, and asked him how he had got on. The man said he shared the husband's opinion, and added that he would have stayed longer, had he not been afraid of getting caught by the daylight. The pair of them then went off to get as much sleep as they could. When morning came, and they were getting dressed together, the husband noticed that his friend had on his finger a ring that was identical to the one he had given his wife on their wedding day. He asked him where he had got it, and when he was told it had come from the chambermaid the night before, he was aghast. He began banging his head against the wall, and shouted: 'Oh my God! Have I gone and made myself a cuckold without my wife even knowing about it?'

His friend tried to calm him down. 'Perhaps your wife had given the ring to the girl to look after before going to bed?' he suggested. The husband made no reply, but marched straight out and went back to his house.

There he found his wife looking unusually gay and attractive. Had she not saved her chambermaid from staining her conscience, and had she not put her husband to the ultimate test, without any more cost to herself than a night's sleep? Seeing her in such good spirits, the husband thought to himself: 'She wouldn't be greeting me so cheerfully if she knew what I'd been up to.'

As they chatted, he took hold of her hand and saw that the ring, which normally never left her finger, had disappeared. Horrified, he stammered: 'What have you done with your ring?'

She was pleased that he was giving her the opportunity to say what she had to say.

'Oh! You're the most dreadful man I ever met! Who do you think you got it from? You think you got it from the chambermaid, don't you? You think you got it from that girl you're so much in love with, the girl who gets more out of you than I've ever had! The first time you got into bed you were so passionate that I thought you must be about as madly in love with her as it was possible for any man to be! But when you came back the *second* time, after getting up, you were an absolute devil! Completely uncontrolled you were, didn't know when to stop! You miserable man! You must have been blinded by desire to pay such tribute to my body – after all you've had me long enough without showing much appreciation for my figure.

So it wasn't because that young girl is so pretty and so shapely that you were enjoying yourself so much. Oh no! You enjoyed it so much because you were seething with some depraved pent-up lust – in short the sin of concupiscence was raging within you, and your senses were dulled as a result. In fact you'd worked yourself up into such a state that I think any old nanny-goat would have done for you, pretty or otherwise! Well, my dear, it's time you mended your ways. It's high time you were content with me for what I am – your own wife and an honest woman, and it's high time that you found *that* just as satisfying as when you thought I was a poor little erring chambermaid. I did what I did in order to save you from your wicked ways, so that when you get old, we can live happily and peacefully together without anything on our consciences. Because if you go on in the way you have been, I'd rather leave you altogether than see you destroying your soul day by day, and at the same time destroying your physical health and squandering everything you have before my very eyes! But if you will acknowledge that you've been in the wrong, and make up your mind to live according to the ways of God and His commandments, then I'll overlook all your past misbehaviour, even as I hope God will forgive me *my* ingratitude to Him, and failure to love Him as I ought.'

If there was ever a man who was dumbfounded and despairing, it was this poor husband. There was his wife, looking so pretty, and yet so sensible and so chaste, and he had gone and left her for a girl who did not love him. What was worse, he had had the misfortune to have gone and made her do something wicked without her even realizing what was happening. He had gone and let another man share pleasures which, rightly, were his alone to enjoy. He had gone and given himself cuckold's horns and made himself look ridiculous for evermore. But he could see she was already angry enough about the chambermaid, and he did not dare tell her about the other dirty trick he had played. So he promised that he would leave his wicked ways behind him, asked her to forgive him and gave her the ring back. He told his friend not to breathe a word to anybody, but secrets of this sort nearly always end up being proclaimed from the [roof-tops,] and it was not long before the facts became public knowledge. The husband was branded as a cuckold without his wife having done a single thing to disgrace herself.

*

'Ladies, it strikes me that if all the men who offend their wives like that got a punishment like that, then Hircan and Saffredent ought to be feeling a bit nervous.'

'Come now, Longarine,' said Saffredent, 'Hircan and I aren't the only married men here, you know.'

'True,' she replied, 'but you're the only two who'd play a trick like that.'

'And just when have you heard of us chasing our wives' maids?' he retorted.

'If the ladies in question were to tell us the facts,' Longarine said, 'then you'd soon find plenty of maids who'd been dismissed before their pay-day!'

'Really,' intervened Geburon, 'a fine one you are! You promise to make us all laugh, and you end up making these two gentlemen annoyed.'

'It comes to the same thing,' said Longarine. 'As long as they don't get their swords out, their getting angry makes it all the more amusing.'

'But the fact remains,' said Hircan, 'that if our wives were to listen to what this lady here has to say, she'd make trouble for every married couple here!'

'I know what I'm saying, and who I'm saying it to,' Longarine replied. 'Your wives are so good, and they love you so much, that even if you gave them horns like a stag's, they'd still convince themselves, and everybody else, that they were garlands of roses!'

Everyone found this remark highly amusing, even the people it was aimed at, and the subject was brought to a close. Dagoucin, however, who had not yet said a word, could not resist saying: 'When a man already has everything he needs in order to be contented, it is very unreasonable of him to go off and seek satisfaction elsewhere. It has often struck me that when people are not satisfied with what they already have, and think they can find something better, then they only make themselves worse off. And they do not get any sympathy, because inconstancy is one thing that is universally condemned.'

'But what about people who have not yet found their "other half"?' asked Simontaut. 'Would you still say it was inconstancy if they seek her wherever she may be found?'

'No man can know,' replied Dagoucin, 'where his other half is to be found, this other half with whom he may find a union so equal that between [the parts] there is no difference; which being so, a man must hold fast where Love constrains him and, whatever may befall him, he must remain steadfast in heart and will. For if she whom you love is your true likeness, if she is of the same will, then it will be your own self that you love, and not her alone.'

'Dagoucin, I think you're adopting a position that is completely wrong,' said Hircan. 'You make it sound as if we ought to love women without being loved in return!'

'What I mean, Hircan, is this. If love is based on a woman's beauty, charm and favours, and if our aim is merely pleasure, ambition or profit, then such love can never last. For if the whole foundation on which our love is based should collapse, then love will fly from us and there will be no love left in us. But I am utterly convinced that if a man loves with no other aim, no other desire, than to love truly, he will abandon his soul in death rather than allow his love to abandon his heart.'

'Quite honestly, Dagoucin, I don't think you've ever really been in love,' said Simontaut, 'because if you had felt the fire of passion, as the rest of us have, you wouldn't have been doing what you've just been doing – describing Plato's republic, which sounds all very fine in writing, but is hardly true to experience.'

'If I have loved,' he replied, 'I love still, and shall love till the day I die. But my love is a perfect love, and I fear lest showing it openly should betray it. So greatly do I fear this, that I shrink to make it known to the lady whose love and friendship I cannot but desire to be equal to my own. I scarcely dare think my own thoughts, lest something should be revealed in my eyes, for the longer I conceal the fire of my love, the stronger grows the pleasure in knowing that it is indeed a perfect love.'

'Ah, but all the same,' said Geburon, 'I don't think you'd be sorry if she did return your love!'

'I do not deny it. But even if I were loved as deeply as I myself love, my love could not possibly increase, just as it could not possibly decrease if I were loved less deeply than I love.'

At this point, Parlamente, who was suspicious of these flights of fancy, said: 'Watch your step, Dagoucin. I've seen plenty of men who've died rather than speak what's in their minds.'

'Such men as those,' he replied, 'I would count happy indeed.'

'Indeed,' said Saffredent, 'and worthy to be placed among the ranks of the Innocents – of whom the Church chants "*Non loquendo, sed moriendo confessi sunt*"! I've heard a lot of talk about these languishing lovers, but I've never seen a single one actually die. I've suffered enough from such torture, but I got over it in the end, and that's why I've always assumed that nobody else ever really dies from it either.'*

'Ah! Saffredent, the trouble is that you desire your love to be returned,' Dagoucin replied, 'and men of your opinions never die for love. But I know of many who *have* died, and died for no other cause than that they have loved, and loved perfectly.'

'As you seem to know some stories on the subject,' said Longarine, 'I would like to ask you to take over from me and tell us one. That will be the ninth story of the day.'

'In order that signs and wonders may prove the truth of my words, and bring you to believe in them,' he began, 'I shall recount to you something that happened not three years ago.'

* Saffredent quotes from the *Oratio* for the Feast of the Holy Innocents: 'not by speaking, but by dying have they confessed'.

STORY NINE

There was once a nobleman who lived in the land between Dauphiné and Provence. Better endowed with virtue, good looks and good breeding than he was with material possessions, he loved a lady of high birth. I shall not tell her name, out of consideration for her family, all of whom are of exalted lineage, but you may rely upon it that the story is a true one. Because this gentleman was not of the lady's stock, he did not dare to reveal his feelings. Knowing that he was of such lowly station, he could never hope to marry her, yet his love for her was so deep and so perfect that he would have rather died than wish anything to her dishonour. So his love was founded on no other desire than to love her with a love as perfect as it was in his power to make it, and so long did he love her in this fashion that in the end the lady herself became aware of his devotion. It was, she knew, a noble love, full of goodness and virtuous intent, and she deemed it an honour to be adored by one so pure. The kindness she showed him exceeded anything he had dared to expect, and he was well contented.

But Envy and Malice, enemies of all repose, could not suffer them to live this life so sweet and yet so virtuous. For there were people only too ready to run to the girl's mother and say to her how surprised they were to see the gentleman at her house so often, how they suspected that he came because he was attracted by her daughter and how he had frequently been seen talking to her. But the mother entertained no doubts whatsoever concerning the gentleman's virtue; indeed she had no less confidence in him than she had in her own children. It was therefore with some distress that she learnt that his visits were being seen in a bad light. In the end, afraid lest, human nature being what it is, malicious gossip might lead to some sort of scandal, she decided to ask him not to come to the house for a while. This was very hard for him to bear, because he knew that his conversation with the daughter of the house had been entirely honourable and that he in no way deserved to be estranged from her in this fashion. But in order to put a stop to mischievous talk, he submitted, and remained away from the house until the rumours had died down.

When he resumed his visits, he was as steadfast as ever. Absence had not caused his love to diminish. But he heard during one of his visits that there was talk of the girl being married to a gentleman who was not, in his opinion, so much richer than himself that he had any superior claim to her. So he began to take courage, and persuaded his friends to speak up in his favour, for he was sure that if the lady were given the choice, it would be himself that she would choose. But the fact remained that the other man *was* somewhat richer, and it was consequently he who was the choice of the mother and the family. The poor gentleman, who knew that his lady's loss was no less than his own, was utterly downcast, and, though he was otherwise a healthy man, began little by little to waste away. His handsome features became obscured by the mask of death, as he sank hour by hour towards a welcome grave. Yet he could not resist the compulsion to visit the lady he loved so much, so that he might speak with her. But his strength was draining from him, and at length, unable to rise from his bed, and unwilling to force his suffering on his beloved, he abandoned himself to sorrow and despair. He lost all desire to eat or drink. He could neither sleep nor rest. His friends could no longer recognize his haggard face.

However, the girl's mother was a lady of great charity, and was, moreover, well-disposed towards the gentleman. Indeed, had hers been the prevailing view in the family, they would have preferred his good qualities to all the wealth of the other man, but the father's relatives in particular were opposed to him. This did not stop the mother, once she was informed of the poor man's state, taking her daughter to visit him in his distress. They found him more dead than alive. He had that very morning, feeling that his end was nigh, made his confession and received the sacrament. He had expected to die without seeing anyone again, but the sight of the lady who was his life and his resurrection brought him back from the brink of death. As she entered, his strength returned. He started up in his bed, and addressed her mother:

'What has moved you to come to see me, Madame? What has

brought you to see a man who already has one foot in the grave, and of whose death you yourself are the cause?'

'How is it possible,' she exclaimed, 'that the man we are so fond of should die because of us? Tell me, I beg you, why you say such things.'

'Madame,' he began, 'I have disguised to the utmost of my ability the love which I bear your daughter. But, alas, my relatives have spoken to you of marriage, and in so doing they have made known my love more freely than I desired, for now I must suffer the blow of seeing my hopes dashed to the ground. It is not my happiness alone that concerns me, because I know that with no one else could she ever be so deeply loved or so lovingly cared for. Now she is to lose a friend, the best and most loving friend she has, and that she should lose such a blessing is more painful to me than death itself. While I lived, I lived for her alone. But now my life can be of no more service to her, so I lay it down, and losing little, gain much.'

The gentleman's words moved the mother and daughter to do their best to comfort him.

'Take heart,' said the mother, 'I promise on my word that when God has restored your health, my daughter shall marry you, and no one else. Here she is, and I'll tell her to give you her word as well.'

The girl wept, and earnestly assured him she would do as her mother promised. But he knew that if he recovered he would not be granted his beloved. He knew that their earnest words were only meant to raise his spirit a little. Had they but spoken in that fashion three months ago, he sighed, then he would today have been the happiest and healthiest man in France. But it was now too late to help him. He could place no trust in the succour they offered, nor rest any hopes on it. When they protested and tried again to reassure him, he went on:

'Since you promise me a blessing that can never come to pass, even if it were your wish, and since I am sinking fast, I shall ask you a lesser favour, but a favour that I have never before had the boldness to ask.'

Together they swore that they would grant him his wish, however bold.

'Then I implore you,' he said to the mother, 'to place in my arms her whom you promised me as wife, and to tell her to embrace me and to kiss me.'

The daughter, unaccustomed to such intimacies, began to protest. But her mother ordered her to do as the gentleman requested, for it now seemed that all strength and all feeling had left him. So she leaned over the poor sick gentleman's bed, saying: 'Dear friend, do not be so downcast.'

The dying man stretched out his emaciated arms, and with all the strength remaining in his bones embraced her who was the sole cause of his death. He placed his cold pale lips on hers, and kissed and held her as long as he was able. Then he said:

'The love I have borne you has been deep and noble, so deep and so noble that never did I wish to be granted other than in marriage the blessing that now I have received. That was not to be, but with the blessing I now have, I gladly commend my spirit unto Him who is all perfect love and charity, and who knoweth how deep was my love, how noble my desire, beseeching Him, that having my desire in my arms, He may receive my spirit into His.'

So saying, he clasped her in his embrace again, and with such force, that his already weakened heart could not sustain the effort. All his vital spirits left him, dilated in the rapture. The seat of his soul was no more, and his soul itself took wing to its Creator. Long after the poor lifeless body had loosened its grip, the girl lay in its embrace. The love she had always felt but kept concealed broke forth now with such vehemence that her mother and the servants were able only with difficulty to separate their united bodies. Alive, but worse than dead, she was pulled from the corpse's embrace.

The gentleman was buried with due honour. But the highest tribute at his burial were the tears and lamentations of the girl. As she had hidden away her love during his life, so after his death she made it known to all. It was as if she desired to make up for the wrong she had done him, and I have heard that for all they gave her a husband to console her, she never in her life knew true happiness.

*

'Now, Gentlemen,' concluded Dagoucin, 'you who refused to believe what I said before, do you not find this case enough to force you to admit that perfect love can, through being too carefully concealed and too little known, lead lovers to their death? There isn't one among you who doesn't know the families concerned, so you can have no doubts as to the facts, though no one who has not had personal experience may actually believe them.'

There was not a lady present who did not have tears in her eyes. But Hircan said: 'I've never heard of such a fool in all my life! Does it make sense, I ask you, that we men should die for the sake of women, when women are made solely for our benefit? And does it make sense to hesitate to demand from them what God Himself has commanded that they should let us have? I'm not speaking for myself, of course, or for other married men. As far as women and so forth are concerned, I'm quite satisfied already – more than satisfied! But I mean those who aren't – they're very stupid to be afraid of women, when it's women who should be afraid of them! And as for the girl, don't you see how much she regretted having been so silly? She was happy enough to kiss the corpse, repugnant to nature though it is. So she wouldn't have refused physical contact if the man had had a little more nerve while he was alive, and been a little bit less pathetic on his deathbed!'

'Nevertheless,' said Oisille, 'the gentleman clearly showed that the love he bore her was noble and good, and for that he deserves high praise before all men. For chastity in a lover's heart is a thing more divine than human.'

'Madame, I support Hircan's point of view,' said Saffredent, 'and if you want confirmation of what Hircan says, bear in mind that Fortune favours the bold. There was never a man, you know, who didn't in the end get what he wanted from any lady who really loved him, so long as he went about wooing her ardently and astutely. But because of ignorance and some sort of stupid timidity there are men who miss many a good opportunity in love. Then they attribute their failures to their lady's virtue, even though they never get anywhere near testing it. To put it another way, you've only got to attack your fortress in the right way, and you can't fail to take it in the end!'

'I'm shocked that you two can talk like that!' exclaimed Parlamente. 'From what you've just said, the ladies you've been in love with can scarcely have been very faithful to you – or else you've only gone for immoral women anyway, and think that all the others are like them!'

'Mademoiselle, I do not have the good fortune to be able to boast of my conquests,' Saffredent replied, 'but I attribute my misfortune less to ladies' virtue than to my own failure to undertake my ventures with the right degree of care and astuteness. I don't want to quote the learned doctors to you. My sole authority is the old woman in the *Roman de la Rose*, who said:

> "Remember, sir, it's Nature's plan,
> It's every man for every maid,
> And every maid for every man!"

So I shall always believe that once a woman has love in her heart the outcome cannot fail to be happy for the man concerned, provided he does not persist in his own stupidity.'

'And just suppose,' said Parlamente, 'that I were able to name a lady who had been truly in love, who had been desired, pursued and wooed, and yet had remained an honest woman, victorious over the feelings of her heart, victorious over her body, victorious over her love and victorious over her would-be lover? Would you admit that such a thing were possible?'

'Certainly I should,' replied Saffredent.

'Then if Saffredent can accept a case like that,' she concluded, 'the rest of you would be hard to convince indeed, if you didn't accept it also.'

'Madame,' said Dagoucin, 'I have proved to you by means of an example that a man may continue in the way of virtuous love even unto death. If you know of a lady to whom similar honour is due, then I should like to ask you to finish our day of stories by telling us about her. We shall not mind if the story is a long one. We have time enough to listen to a good tale.'

'Since I am allotted what time is left,' she began, 'I shall not delay my story by giving you a wordy preamble. It's such a true, such a lovely story, that I'm anxious for you to hear it without more ado. I was not an eye-witness to the facts, but they were recounted to me by a very close friend of mine, a man who was devoted to the hero of the story and wished to sing his praises. He made me swear, however, that if I should ever tell the story to anyone else, I would alter the names of the people involved. So everything that I shall tell you is true to life, except the names of the people and the places.'

STORY TEN

In Aragon, in the province of Aranda, there once lived a lady. She was the widow of the Count of Aranda, who had died while she was still very young, and left her with a son and a daughter, who was called Florida. As was right and proper for the children of a noble lord, they were brought up by her according to the strictest codes of virtue and honour. So carefully did she school them that her house was known far and wide as the most honourable in the whole of Spain. She would often go to Toledo, which was then the seat of the King of Spain, and when she visited Saragossa, which was not far from the family home, she would spend her time at the Queen's court, where she was as highly esteemed as any lady could be.

One day, when the King was in residence at his castle in Saragossa, the Castillo de la Aljafcria, the Countess, on her way to pay her respects as was her wont, was passing through a little village that belonged to the Viceroy of Catalonia. Normally the Viceroy never moved from the border at Perpignan, where he was in command during the war between France and Spain, but peace had just been declared, and he returned with his officers in order to do homage to his King. He knew that the Countess would be passing through his lands, and went to meet her, not only to do her the honour that was her due as the King's kinswoman, but also because of the goodwill that he had long borne her. Now in the Viceroy's entourage there were not a few noblemen of outstanding valour, courageous men, who, after long service in the wars had earned such heroic reputations that there was no one in the land who was not anxious to meet them and be seen in their company. Amongst these men there was one by the name of Amador. Although he was only eighteen or nineteen years of age, he had such confidence, and such sound judgement, that you could not have failed to regard him as one of those rare men fit to govern any state. Not only was he a man of sound judgement, he was also endowed with an appearance so handsome, so open and natural, that he was a delight for all to behold. This was not all, for his handsome looks were equally matched by the fairness of his speech. Poise, good looks, eloquence – it was impossible to say with which gift he was more richly blessed. But what gained him even higher esteem was his fearlessness, which, despite his youth, was famed throughout all lands. For he had already in many different places given evidence of his great abilities. Not only throughout the kingdoms of Spain, but also in France and Italy people looked upon him with admiration. Not once during the recent wars had he shrunk from battle, and when his country had been at peace, he had gone to seek action in foreign parts, and there too had been loved and admired by friend and foe alike.

This young nobleman had devotedly followed his commander back home, to meet the Countess of Aranda. He could not fail to notice her daughter, Florida, who was then but twelve years of age. Never, he thought to himself, as he contemplated her grace and beauty, had he beheld so fair and noble a creature. If only she might look with favour upon him, that alone would give him more happiness than anything any other woman in the world could ever give him. For a long while he gazed at her. His mind was made up. He would love her. The promptings of reason were in vain. He would love her, even though she was of far higher birth than he. He would love her, even though she was not yet of an age to hear and understand the words of love. But his misgivings were as nothing against the firm hope that grew within him, as he promised himself that time and patient waiting would in the end bring his toils to a happy conclusion. Noble Love, through the power that is its own, and for no other cause, had entered Amador's breast and now held out to him the promise of a happy end, and the means of attaining it.

The greatest obstacle was the distance that separated his own homeland from that of Florida, and the lack of opportunity to see her. To [overcome] this problem he decided, contrary to his previous intentions, to marry some lady from Barcelona or Perpignan. His reputation stood so high there that there was little or nothing anyone would refuse him. Moreover, he had spent so long on the frontier during the wars, that although he came from the region of Toledo, he was more like a Catalan than a Castilian. His family was rich and distinguished, but he was the youngest son, and possessed little in the way of inheritance. But Love and Fortune, seeing him ill-provided for by his parents, and resolving to make him their paragon, bestowed upon him through the gift of virtue and valour that which the laws of the land denied him. He was experienced in matters of war, and much sought after by noble lords and princes. He did not have to go out of his way to ask for rewards. More often than not he had to refuse them.

The Countess meanwhile continued on her way, and arrived at Saragossa, where she was well received by the King and the whole court. The Viceroy of Catalonia visited her frequently, and Amador took the opportunity of accompanying him. In this way he might at least have the chance of looking at Florida, for there was no way in which he might be able to speak to her. In order to introduce himself into the society of the Countess, he approached the daughter of an old knight, who came from his home town. Her name was Avanturada, and she [had been brought up alongside] Florida, so that she knew the innermost secrets of her heart. Since she was a good, respectable girl, and expected to receive three thousand ducats a year by way of dowry, Amador made up his mind to address himself to her as a suitor, and seek her hand in marriage. She was only too willing to listen. But her father was a rich man, and she felt that he would never consent to her marriage with a man as poor as Amador unless she enlisted the aid of the Countess. So she first approached Florida.

'My lady, you have seen the Castilian gentleman, who often talks to me,' she said. 'I believe that it is his intention to ask my hand in marriage. But you know what my father is like. You know that he will never consent, unless the Countess and yourself persuade him.'

Florida, who loved the young lady dearly, assured her that she would do everything she could for her, just as if her own interests were at stake. Then Avanturada presented Amador to Florida. As he kissed her hand, he almost fainted in rapture. He, the most eloquent man in Spain, was speechless as he stood before her. This somewhat surprised Florida, for, although she was only twelve years of age, she knew well enough that there was not a man in Spain who could express his mind more eloquently than Amador. He stood there in silence, so she said to him:

'Señor Amador, your reputation has spread through all the kingdoms of Spain, and it would be surprising indeed if you were not known to us also. All of us who have heard about you are anxious to find some way in which we can be of service. So if there is anything I can do, I hope you will not be afraid to ask.'

Amador stood gazing at his lady's beauty. He was transported with joy, and was only just able to utter a few words of grateful thanks. Florida was astonished to see that he was still incapable of making any kind of reply, but she attributed it to some momentary whim, completely failing to see that the true cause of his behaviour lay in the violence of his love. She ignored his silence, and said no more.

Amador, for his part, had perceived what great virtue was beginning to appear in Florida, young as she was, and later he said to the lady he was planning to marry:

'Avanturada, do not be surprised that I couldn't speak a word in front of Lady Florida. She is so young, yet she speaks so well and so wisely, and behind her tender years there clearly lie hidden such virtues, that I was overcome with admiration and didn't know what to say to her. Tell me, Avanturada, since you are her friend and must know her closest secrets, how is it possible that she hasn't stolen the heart of every single man at court? Any man who has met her, and hasn't fallen in love with her, must be a dumb beast or made of stone!'

Avanturada, who by now was much in love with Amador, could keep nothing from him. She told him that the Lady Florida was indeed greatly loved by everyone, but that very few people actually spoke with her, that being the custom in that part of the land. There were only two men who seemed to show any inclination – Don Alfonso, son of Henry of Aragon, otherwise known as the Infante of Fortune, and the young Duke of Cardona.

'Tell me,' said Amador, 'which of the two do you think she likes the best?'

'She is so good and wise,' replied Avanturada, 'that she would never confess to anything that was not in accordance with the wishes of her mother. But, as far as we can judge, she prefers the son of the Infante of Fortune to the Duke of Cardona, although it is the Duke of Cardona her mother prefers, because with him she would stay closer to home. But you are a man of perception and sound judgement, so perhaps you would help us decide what the truth of the matter is. It's like this. The son of the Infante of Fortune was brought up at this court, and he is one of the most handsome and most accomplished young princes in Christendom. What I and the other girls think is that he is the one she should marry – they'd make the loveliest couple in the whole of Spain. And I ought to tell you as well that although they're both very young – she's only twelve and he's fifteen – they've been in love for three years already. If you want to get in her good books you ought to make a friend of him and enter into his service.'

Amador was relieved to hear that his lady was capable of love at all. One day, he hoped, he might win the right to become her true and devoted servant, even though he might never become her husband. Of her virtue he was not afraid. His sole anxiety had been that she might reject love completely. From this conversation onwards, Amador made friends with the son of the Infante of Fortune. He had little difficulty in gaining his goodwill, for he was versed in all the sports and diversions that the young prince enjoyed, being an excellent horseman, skilled in the use of arms and indeed good at everything that a young man ought to be able to do.

War broke out again in Languedoc, and Amador was obliged to return with the governor. His sorrow was great, the more so as he had no means of ensuring that he would return to a post where he would still be able to see his Florida. So before his departure, he spoke to a brother of his, who was major-domo in the household of the Queen. He told him what an excellent match he had found in the Lady Avanturada while in the Countess's household, and asked him to do everything in his power during his absence to bring the marriage about, by drawing on the influence of the Queen, the King and all his other friends. The brother, who was very fond of Amador, not only because of their common blood, but because he admired his prowess, promised to do as he was bidden. He was as good as his word. The Countess of Aranda, the young Count, who was growing to appreciate virtue and valour, and above all the the beautiful Florida, joined in singing the praises of Amador. The result was that Avanturada's miserly old father put aside his grasping habits for once and was brought to recognize Amador's excellent qualities. The marriage was duly agreed upon by the parents of the couple, and, during the truce that had been declared by the two warring kings, Amador was summoned home by his brother.

It was at that time that the King of Spain withdrew to Madrid, where he was safe from the unhealthy air that was affecting a number of places throughout the country. Acting on the advice of his Council, but also at the request of the Countess, he had arranged a marriage between her son, the little Count, and a rich heiress, the Duchess of Medinaceli, in order to bring the two families together in an advantageous union and to please the Countess herself, whose interests were very dear to his heart. In accordance with his wishes the marriage was celebrated in the King's palace at Madrid. Amador was present, and was able to pursue his own matrimonial plans so successfully that he too was married – to Avanturada, in whom he inspired a good deal more love than he returned. His marriage was no more than a cover, no more than a convenient excuse to enable him to visit her on whom his mind constantly dwelled.

After his marriage he made himself so familiar in the Countess's household that no one took any more notice of him than if he had been a woman. He was only twenty-two at this time, but had such good sense that the Countess used to keep him informed of all her business affairs. She even instructed her son and her daughter to listen carefully to his conversation, and heed any advice he might give. Having reached these heights in the Countess's esteem, he behaved in such a sensible, such a restrained manner, that even the lady whom he loved so dearly failed to perceive his feelings. In fact, being so fond of Amador's wife, she hid nothing from Amador himself, not even her most intimate thoughts, [and went so far as] to tell him about her love for the son of the Infante of Fortune. Amador's sole concern was to win her completely, and he talked to her constantly about the

Infante's son. Provided he was able to converse with her, he did not care what was the topic of their conversation. However, he had been there hardly a month after his marriage when he was obliged to go back to the wars. Not once, during the two years that followed, did he return to see his wife, who waited for him, living as she always had done in the household of the Countess. Throughout this time Amador would write to his wife, but his letters consisted principally of messages for Florida. She for her part would reply, and even insert something amusing in her own hand in Avanturada's letters – which alone was enough to make Amador very conscientious in writing to his wife. But throughout all this Florida was aware of nothing, except perhaps that she was as fond of Amador as if he had been her own brother.

Several times Amador came and went, but for five whole years he never saw Florida for two months together. Yet in spite of these long absences, and the long distances that separated them, his love grew. At last he was able to travel to see his wife. He found the Countess far from the court, for the King had gone into Andalusia, taking with him the young Count of Aranda, who had already started to bear arms. The Countess had moved to a country house she owned on the borders of Aragon and Navarre. She was delighted to see Amador, who had been away now for three years, and commanded that he was to be treated like a son. There was nobody who did not make him welcome. During his stay, the Countess told him all her domestic business, and asked his advice on almost every aspect of it. The family's regard for him was unbounded. Wherever he went, there was always an open door. He was looked upon as a man of such integrity that he was trusted in everything. Had he been a saint or an angel, he could hardly have been trusted more. Florida, fond as she was of Avanturada, went straight to Amador whenever she saw him. Having not the slightest suspicion as to his true intentions, she was quite unreserved in her behaviour towards him. There was not a trace of passion in her heart, unless it was a feeling of contentment at being by his side. Nothing else occurred to her. But there are people who can guess from the expression in a man's eyes whether that man is in love or not, and Amador was constantly anxious lest he be thus found out. When Florida came to speak to him alone, in complete innocence, the fire that burned in his breast would flare up so violently that, do what he might, the colour would mount to his cheeks and the flames of passion would gleam in his eyes.

In order that no one should guess from his intimacy with Florida that he was in love with her, he began to make approaches to an extremely attractive lady called Paulina, whose charms were highly celebrated in her day, and from whose snares few men managed to escape. She had heard how Amador had been successful with the ladies in Barcelona and Perpignan, and how he had won the hearts of the most beautiful and most noble ladies in the land; in particular she had heard how a certain Countess of Palamos, who was regarded as the most beautiful woman in Spain, had lost her heart to him. So she told him how deeply she pitied him for having married such an ugly wife, after all his past good fortunes in love. Amador realized from what she said that she was ready to provide him with any consolation he might require, and replied with as encouraging words as he was able, thinking that it would be possible to cover up the truth of his real feelings by making her believe a lie. But she was shrewd, experienced in the ways of love, and not a woman to make do with mere words. She sensed that his heart was not entirely taken up with love for her, and suspected that he wanted to use her as a cover. She watched him so closely that not a single glance escaped her. Amador's eyes were well-practised in the art of dissembling, however, and Paulina could get no further than her vague suspicions. But it was only with extreme difficulty that he was able to hide his feelings, especially when Florida, who had not the slightest idea of the game he was playing, talked to him with her customary intimacy in front of Paulina herself. It was only by making the most painful effort that on such occasions he was able to control the expression in his eyes, and prevent them reflecting the feelings in his heart. So to forestall any unfortunate consequences in the future, he said to her one day as he leaned against the window where they had been chatting: 'Tell me, [my Lady], is it better to speak or to die?'

'I would always advise my friends to speak,' she replied

quickly, 'because there are very few words that can't be remedied, but once you've lost your life, there's no way of getting it back.'

'So will you promise that you will not only not be angry at what I am going to say, but also, if you are shocked, that you will not say anything until I have finished?'

'Say whatever you please,' she said, 'because if *you* shock me, then there's no one in the world who could reassure me.'

So he began.

'My Lady, there are two reasons why I have not yet told you of the feelings I have for you. One reason is that I hoped to give you proof of my love through long and devoted service. The other is that I feared that you would consider it [overweening presumption] that I, an ordinary nobleman, should dare to aspire to the love of a lady of birth so high. Even if I were, like you, my Lady, of princely estate, a heart so true and loyal as your own would not suffer such talk of love from anyone but the son of the Infante of Fortune, who has taken possession of your heart. Yet, my Lady, just as in the hardships of war one may be compelled to destroy one's own land, to lay waste one's rising crops, in order to prevent the enemy taking advantage of them, even so do I now seek to anticipate the fruit that I had hoped to reap only in the fullness of time, in order to prevent our enemies from taking advantage of it to your loss. I must tell you, my Lady, that from the time I first saw you, when you were still so young, I have wholly consecrated myself to your service. I have never ceased to seek the means to obtain your good grace, and it was for this reason alone that I married the very lady who is your own dearest friend. Knowing, too, that you loved the son of the Infante, I did my utmost to serve him, to become his friend. In short, I have striven to do everything that I thought would give you pleasure. You have seen how the Countess, your mother, has looked favourably upon me, as has the Count your brother, and all those of whom you are fond, with the result that I am treated in this house, not as a man serving his superiors, but as a son. All the efforts that I made five years ago were for no other end than to live my whole life by you. But you must believe me, my Lady, when I tell you that I am not one of those men who would exploit this advantage. I desire no favour, nor pleasure, from you, except what is in accordance with the dictates of virtue. I know that I cannot marry you. And even if I could, I should not seek to do so, for your love is given to another, and it is he whom I long to see your husband. Nor is my love a base love. I am not one of those men who hope that if they serve their lady long enough they will be rewarded with her dishonour. Such intentions could not be further from my heart, for I would rather see you dead, than have to admit that my own gratification had sullied your virtue, had, in a word, made you less worthy to be loved. I ask but one thing in recompense of my devotion and my service. I ask only that you might be my true and faithful Lady, so true, so faithful, that you will never cast me from your good grace, that you will allow me to continue in my present estate, and that you will place your trust in me above all others. And if your honour, or any cause close to your heart, should demand that a noble gentleman lay down his life, then mine will I gladly lay down for your sake. On this you may depend. Know, too, that whatsoever deeds of mine may be counted noble, good or brave, these deeds will be performed for love of you alone. Yes, and if for ladies less exalted my deeds have met acclaim, then be you assured that for a lady such as you I shall perform such deeds of greatness, that acts which once I deemed impossible I shall now perform with ease. But if you will not accept me as wholly yours, my Lady, then I shall make up my mind to abandon my career at arms. I shall renounce the valour and the virtue that were mine, for they will have availed me nought. Wherefore, my Lady, I do humbly beseech that my just demand might be granted, since your honour and your conscience cannot refuse it.'

The young Lady Florida changed colour at this speech, the like of which she had never heard before. Then she lowered her gaze, like a mature woman, her modesty shocked. Then, with all the virtue and good sense that was hers, she said:

'If, as seems to be the case, Amador, you're only asking me for something that you already have, then why do you insist on making such a long, high-flown speech about it? I am rather afraid that there is some evil intent hidden away underneath all these fine words, and that you're trying to beguile me because

I'm young and innocent. It makes me very uncertain as to how I should reply to you. If I were to reject the noble love that you offer me, I would only be contradicting the way I've behaved towards you up till now, because in you I've placed more trust than in any other man in the world. Neither my honour nor my conscience stand in the way of your request. Nor does the love I bear the son of the Infante of Fortune, for my love for him is founded on marriage, to which you lay no claim. In fact I can think of no reason why I should not grant your wishes, except perhaps for one anxiety that troubles my mind. You have no reason to address me in the way you do. If you already have what you desire, what can it be that now makes you tell me about it in such an emotional manner?'

Amador was ready with his reply.

'My Lady, you speak most prudently,' he said, 'and do me great honour to place in me such trust as you declare. If I were not happy to receive this blessing from you, I should be unworthy indeed to receive any other. But let me explain, my Lady, that the man who desires to build an edifice that will endure throughout eternity should take the utmost care to lay a safe and sure foundation. So it is that I, who desire most earnestly to serve you through all eternity, should take the greatest care that I have the means to ensure not only that I shall remain always by you, but that I shall be able to prevent all others from knowing of the great love I bear you. For, though my love is pure and noble enough to be announced to the whole world, yet there are people who will never understand a lover's soul, and whose pronouncements will always belie the truth. The rumours that result are none the less unpleasant for being untrue. The reason why I have made so bold as to say all this to you, is that Paulina has become very suspicious. She senses in her heart that I am unable to give her my love, and she is constantly on the watch for me to give myself away. And when you come to talk to me alone in your affectionate way, I am so nervous lest she discern something in my expression to confirm her suspicions that I find myself in just the awkward situation that I am most anxious to avoid. So I made up my mind to beg you not to take me unawares when Paulina is present, or anyone else whom you know to have an equally malicious disposition.

For I would die rather than let any living creature know of my feelings. Were it not that your honour is so dear to me, I should never have entertained the idea of speaking to you in the way I have spoken. For I feel myself so content in the love that you have for me, that there is nothing further that I desire, unless it be that you should continue in the same for ever.'

At these words Florida was filled with delight beyond bounds. Deep within her heart she began to feel stirrings that she had never felt before. And as she could see that the arguments he brought forth were honourable and good, she was able to grant his request, saying that virtue and honour answered for her. Amador was transported with joy, as anyone who has ever truly loved will understand.

However, Florida took his advice too seriously. She became nervous, not only in the presence of Paulina, but in other circumstances too, until she began not to seek Amador's company at all in the way she had in the past. Moreover, she took it badly that he spent so much time with Paulina, who seemed so attractive that she felt it impossible for Amador not to be in love with her. To relieve her distress she would talk at great length with Avanturada, who was herself beginning to be jealous of her husband and Paulina, and often bemoaned her lot to her friend. Florida, suffering from the same affliction, would offer what consolation she was able. It was not long before Amador noticed Florida's strange behaviour, and concluded that she was keeping away from him, not just as a result of his advice, but because she was displeased with him. One day, as they were returning from vespers at a monastery, he said to her: 'My Lady, why do you treat me the way you do?'

'Because that is the way I thought you wanted it,' she replied.

Then, suspecting the truth of the matter. and wishing to know whether he was right, Amador said: 'My Lady, because of the time I have spent with her, Paulina no longer suspects you.'

'Then you couldn't have done better, either for yourself or for me,' she answered, 'for in giving yourself a little pleasure, you are acting in the interests of my honour.'

Amador understood from these words that she thought he derived pleasure from talking with Paulina. So hurt was he that he could not restrain his anger:

'Ah! My Lady, so you're starting already to torment your servant, by hurling abuse at him for [acting in your interests!] There's nothing more irksome and distressing than being obliged to spend one's time with a woman one isn't even in love with! Since you take exception to tasks I undertake solely in your service, I'll never speak to her again. And let the consequences take care of themselves! To cover up my anger, just as in the past I've hidden my joy, I shall go away to a place not far from here, and wait until your mood has passed. But I hope that when I get there I shall receive orders from my commanding officer to return to the wars, where I shall stay long enough to prove to you that nothing keeps me here but you, my Lady.'

So saying, he went, without even waiting for her reply. Florida was left utterly dejected and downcast. Love, having been thwarted, was aroused now, and began to demonstrate its power. She acknowledged that she had wronged Amador, and wrote to him over and over again, beseeching him to come back to her – as indeed he did several days later, once his anger had subsided. I could not begin to tell you in detail what they said to one another to resolve their jealousies. To cut a long story short, he won the day. She promised that she would never again suspect him of being in love with Paulina. More than that, she swore she was and would remain convinced that it was for Amador almost unbearable to have to speak with Paulina or any other woman, nay that it was a martyrdom suffered for no other reason than to render service to his lady.

No sooner had Love overcome these first suspicions and jealousies, no sooner had the two lovers begun to take more pleasure than ever from talking together, than word came that the King of Spain was sending the entire army to Salces. Amador, who was accustomed to be the first to join the royal standards, was as eager as ever to follow the path of honour and glory. Yet this time it was with particular regret, a regret deeper than that which he had experienced before, for not only was he relinquishing the one pleasure of his life, but he now feared that Florida might change during his absence. She had already reached the age of fifteen or sixteen, and was wooed by lords and princes from far and wide. He feared that she might be married while he was away, and that he might never see her again. He had one safeguard, however – that the Countess should make his wife the special companion to Florida. Accordingly, he employed his influence to obtain promises both from the Countess and from Florida herself that wherever she should go after her marriage Avanturada should go with her. And so, in spite of the fact that the talk at that time was of a marriage in Portugal, Amador was certain in his mind that she would never abandon him. With this assurance, yet none the less filled with sorrow beyond words, he departed for the wars, leaving his wife with the Countess.

After her faithful servant had left, Florida found herself quite alone. She set herself to perform all manner of good and virtuous deeds, hoping thereby to acquire the reputation of being the most perfect lady in the land, and worthy to have a man such as Amador devoted to her service. As for Amador himself, when he arrived at Barcelona, he was, as he had been in the past, greeted with delight by all the ladies. But they found him a changed man. They would never have thought that marriage had such a hold over a man, for he now seemed to have nothing but distaste for all the things that before he had pursued. Even the Countess of Palamos, of whom he had once been so enamoured, could no longer find a way of luring him even as far as the door of her residence. Anxious to be away to the scene of battle [where glory was to be won], Amador spent as little time as possible in Barcelona. No sooner had he arrived at Salces, than war did indeed break out between the two kings. It was a great and merciless war. I have no intention of relating the course of events in detail, or even of recounting the many heroic deeds accomplished by Amador, for to tell you all this I should need a whole day. Suffice it to say that Amador won renown above all his comrades in arms. The Duke of Nájera arrived at Perpignan in charge of two thousand men, and invited Amador to be his second-in-command. He answered the call of duty, and led his men with such success that in every skirmish the air rang with shouts of 'Nájera! Nájera!'

Now it came to the ears of the King of Tunis that the kings of Spain and France were waging war on the border between Perpignan and Narbonne. He had long been at war himself with the King of Spain, and he now saw that he could not wish for a better opportunity to harass him more. So he sent a large fleet of galleys and other vessels to pillage and lay waste every inch of unguarded territory that he could find along the Spanish coasts. When the inhabitants of Barcelona saw the vast number of sailing ships looming on the horizon, they immediately sent word to their Viceroy at Salces, who reacted by sending the Duke of Nájera to Palamos without delay. The Moors arrived to find the coasts well garrisoned and acted as if they were sailing on. But towards midnight they returned, and put large numbers of men ashore. The Duke was taken completely by surprise, and was in fact taken prisoner. Amador, vigilant as ever, had heard the noise, marshalled as many of his men as he could and defended himself so effectively that it was a long time before the stronger forces of the enemy were able to make any inroads. In the end, however, realizing that the Duke of Nájera had been captured, and that the Turks were determined to set fire to the whole of Palamos, and destroy the building which he had defended against them, he thought it better to surrender than to be the cause of the annihilation of his valiant comrades. It was also in his mind that if he were held to ransom, there would be some hope of seeing Florida again. Without more ado, he gave himself up to the Turkish chief-in-command, a man called Dorlin, who took Amador before the King of Tunis himself. He was received respectfully and treated well. He was guarded well, too, for the Turkish King was aware that the man he had in his hands was the veritable Achilles of Spain.

For two years Amador remained the prisoner of the King of Tunis. When the news reached Spain, the family of the Duke of Nájera was stricken with grief, but people who held the honour of their country dear judged the capture of Amador an even greater loss. It was broken to the Countess of Aranda and her household at a time when the poor Avanturada lay seriously ill. The Countess (who had guessed how Amador felt about her daughter, and had kept quiet, raising no objections, because she appreciated the young man's qualities) called Florida to one side to tell her the distressing news. But Florida knew how to hide her true feelings, and merely said that it was a great loss for all the family, and that she felt especially sorry for Amador's poor wife lying sick in bed. But seeing her mother weeping bitterly, she shed a few tears with her, lest her secret be discovered by being too well disguised. From this time on the Countess often spoke to Florida about Amador, but never once was she able to draw from her any reaction that would confirm her thoughts. I shall leave aside for now the pilgrimages, the prayers, the devotions, the fasts, which Florida began regularly to offer for Amador's salvation. As for Amador himself, as soon as he reached Tunis, he lost no time in sending messengers to his friends. To Florida he naturally sent the most trustworthy man he could find, to let her know that he was well and living in the hope of seeing her again. This was all she had to sustain her in her distress, but you may be sure that since she was allowed to write to him, she assiduously performed this task, and Amador did not go without the consolation of her letters.

The Countess of Aranda was summoned to Saragossa, where the King had taken up residence. There she found the young Duke of Cardona, who had been actively seeking the support of the King and Queen in his suit for the hand of Florida. Pressed by the King to agree to the marriage, the Countess, as a loyal subject, could not refuse his request. She was sure that her daughter, still so young in years, could have no other will than that of her mother, and, once the agreement was concluded, she took her on one side to explain how she had chosen for her the match which was most fitting. Florida knew that the matter was already settled and that further deliberation was useless. 'May the Lord be praised in everything,' was all she could bring herself to say, for her mother looked so stern, and she judged it preferable to obey rather than indulge in self-pity. To crown all her sorrows, she then heard that the son of the Infante of Fortune had fallen sick and was close to death. But never once in the presence of her mother, or of anyone else, did she show any sign of how she felt. So hard indeed did she repress her feelings that her tears, having been held back in her heart by force, caused violent bleeding from the nose which threatened her life. And all the cure she got was marriage to a man she would gladly have exchanged for death. After the marriage was over she went to the Duchy of Cardona. With her went Avanturada, to whom she was able to unburden herself, bemoaning the harsh treatment she had received from her mother and the sorrow she nursed in her heart at the loss of the son of the Infante. But never once did she mention the fact that she missed Amador, except by way of consoling Avanturada herself. In short, the young Lady Florida resolved to have God and honour constantly before her eyes, and she so carefully hid her troubles, that no one had the slightest suspicion that her husband gave her no pleasure.

For a long time Florida lived this life, a life that seemed to her little better than death. She wrote of her woe to her servant Amador, who, knowing how great and noble was his lady's heart, and how deep was her love for the son of the Infante, could only think her end was nigh. This new anguish heightened his affliction, and he grieved bitterly, for Florida's plight seemed already worse than death. Yet he knew what torment his beloved must be suffering, and his own paled into insignificance. Gladly would he have stayed a slave to the end of his days, if only that might have ensured Florida the husband of her desires. One day he learned from a friend he had made at the court of Tunis that the King, who would have liked to keep Amador in his service, provided he could make a good Turk of him, was planning to threaten him with impalement if he did not renounce his faith. To forestall this move, therefore, he prevailed upon the man who had captured him and had become his master to let him go on parole, without informing the King. The ransom was set so high that the Turk reckoned no one as poor as Amador could ever possibly find the money to pay it.

So, having been allowed to depart, he went to the court of the King of Spain, from where, as soon as he was able, he set off again to seek his ransom amongst his friends. He went straight to Barcelona, where the young Duke of Cardona, his mother and Florida were staying on account of some family business. As soon as Amador's wife, Avanturada, heard the news, she told Florida, who, as if for Avanturada's sake, expressed her joy. But she was afraid lest the joy she felt at seeing him again should show in her face, and lest people who did not know her well should put a bad interpretation on it. So instead of going to meet him, she stood at a window to watch his arrival from afar. Immediately he came into sight she went down by way of a staircase, which was dark enough to prevent anybody seeing whether her cheeks changed colour. She embraced Amador, took him to her room, and then to meet her husband's mother, who had not yet made his acquaintance. Needless to say, he had not been there two days before he had endeared himself to the whole household, exactly as he had in the house of the Countess of Aranda. I shall leave you to imagine the words that passed between him and Florida, and how Florida sorrowfully told of all that she had been through during his absence. She wept bitterly at having had to marry against her inclinations, and at having lost the man whom she loved so dearly, without hope of ever seeing him again. Then she made up her mind to take consolation in her love for Amador and the sense of security it afforded her, though she never once dared declare to him her intent. Amador guessed, however, and never lost an opportunity to make known to her how great was his love for her.

Florida was almost won. She was almost at the point where she was ready not merely to accept Amador as a devoted servant, but to admit him as a sure and perfect lover. But it was then that a most unhappy accident occurred. Amador had received word from the King to go to him immediately on urgent business. Avanturada was very upset at the news, and fainted. Unfortunately she happened to be standing at the top of a flight of stairs. She fell, and injured herself so badly that she never recovered. Florida was deeply affected by Avanturada's death. There could be no consolation for her now. It was as if she felt herself bereft of all relatives and friends. She went into deep mourning for her loss. To Amador the blow was even more overwhelming, for not only had he lost one of the most virtuous wives who ever lived, but he had also lost all hope now of continuing to be near Florida. He sank into a state of such dejection, that he thought he himself had not long to live. The old Duchess of Cardona visited him at frequent intervals, and quoted the sayings of the philosophers, in the hope of inducing him to bear the death of his wife with fortitude. But to no avail. The spectre of death tormented him from one side. From the other, his martyrdom was made more painful by the force of his love. His wife was dead and buried. His sovereign lord had called him. What further reason could he have for staying where he was? In his heart was such despair that he thought he would lose his reason. Florida sought to give consolation, but desolation was all she brought him. One whole afternoon she spent in an attempt to console him with gentle words, doing all she would to lessen the pain of his grief, and assuring him that she would find a way of seeing him far more often than he supposed. Since he was due to depart the following morning, and since he was so weak that he was unable to move from his bed, he begged her to come and visit him again that same evening, when everyone else had gone. This she promised to do, not realizing that such extremity of love as Amador's knew no rational bounds. He had served her long and well, without any reward other than what I have described in my story. Now he despaired of ever being able to return to see her again, and, racked by a love that had been hidden away within him, he made up his mind to make one last desperate gamble – to risk losing all, or to gain everything and treat himself to one short hour of the bliss that he considered he had earned. He had his bed hung with heavy curtains, so that it was impossible for anyone in the room to see in, and when his visitors came he moaned even more than before, so that people thought that he must surely die before another day passed.

In the evening, when all the visitors had gone, Florida came, with the full approval of her husband, who had encouraged her to tend the sick man. She hoped to give him consolation by declaring her feelings and her desire to love him within the limits permitted by honour. She sat down on a chair at the head of his bed, and began, as she thought, to comfort him, by joining her tears to his. Seeing her so overcome with sorrow and regret, Amador judged that it was now, while she was in this state of torment, that his intentions would most easily be accomplished. He rose from his bed. Florida, thinking he was too weak for such exertions, tried to stop him. But he fell on his knees in front of her, saying, 'Must I lose you for ever from my sight?' Whereupon he collapsed into her arms, as if all his strength had suddenly drained from him. The poor Florida put her arms around him and supported him for a while, doing her utmost to console him. He said not a word, and pretending still that he was at the brink of death, began to pursue the path that leads to the forbidden goal of a lady's honour. When Florida realized that his intentions were not pure, she found it beyond belief. Had not his conversation in the past always been pure and good? She asked him what he was trying to do. Amador still said nothing. He did not want to receive a reply that could not but be virtuous and chaste. He struggled with all the strength in his body to have his way. Florida, terrified, thought he must be out of his mind. Rather that, than have to admit he had desired to stain her honour. She called out to a gentleman who she knew would be in the room. Amador, now utterly despairing, threw himself back on the bed with such violence that the other man thought he had breathed his last. Florida, who had now got up from her chair, said: 'Quick, go and fetch some fresh vinegar!'

While the gentleman was doing as he had been bidden, she turned to Amador.

'What kind of madness is this, Amador? Are you beginning to lose your mind? What did you think you were trying to do?'

'What cruelty!' exclaimed Amador, now bereft of all reason through the violence of love. 'Is this the only reward I deserve after serving you so long?'

'And what,' she replied, 'has become of the honour you preached about so often?'

'Ah! my Lady,' he said, 'no one in the world could possibly hold your honour as dear as I do! Before you were married I was able to overcome the desires of my heart so successfully that you knew nothing at all of my feelings. But now you are a married woman. You have a cover and your honour is safe. So what wrong can I possibly be doing you in asking for what is truly mine? It is I who have really won you, through the power of my love. The man who first won your heart so irresolutely pursued your body that he well deserved to lose both. As for the man who now possesses your body – he's not worthy of the smallest corner in your heart. So you do not really belong to him, even in body. But consider, my Lady, what trials and tribulations I have gone through in the last five or six years for your sake. Surely you cannot fail to realize that it is to me alone that you belong, body and heart, for is it not for you that I have refused to give thought to my own body and my own heart? And if you are thinking that you can justify yourself on grounds of conscience, bear in mind that no sin may be imputed when the heart and the body are constrained by the power of love. When men kill themselves in a violent fit of madness, in no way do they commit a sin. For passion leaves no room for reason. And if it is the case that the passion of love is the most difficult to bear of all, if it is – as indeed it is – the passion that most completely blinds the senses, then what sin can you impute to a man who merely lets himself be swept along by an insuperable force? Now I must depart. All hope of seeing you again is gone. Had I but the guarantee that my great love deserves, I would have all the strength I need to endure in patience what will surely be a long and painful absence. If, however, you do not deign to grant me my request, then ere long you shall hear that your severity has brought me to a cruel and unhappy end!'

Florida was as distressed as she was taken aback to hear a speech like this from a man of whom she would never have expected anything of the kind, and her tears flowed.

'Alas! Amador,' she began, 'what has happened to all the virtuous things you used to say to me when I was young? Is this the honour, is this the conscience, for which you so often told me to die, rather than lose my soul? Have you forgotten all the lessons you taught me from examples of virtuous ladies who resisted senseless and wicked passion? Have you forgotten how you have always spoken with scorn of women who succumb to it? It is hard, Amador, to believe that you have left your former self so far behind that all regard for God, for your conscience, and for my honour is completely dead. But if it really is as you seem to say, then I thank God that in His goodness He has forewarned me of the disaster that was about to befall me. By the words you have uttered God has revealed to me what your heart is really like. How could I have remained ignorant for so long? I lost the son of the Infante of Fortune, not just because I was obliged to marry somebody else, but because I knew that he really loved another woman. Now I am married to a man whom I cannot love and cherish however hard I try. That is why I had made up my mind to give you all the love that is in me, to love you with my whole heart. And the foundation of this love was to have been virtue, that virtue which holds honour and conscience dearer than life itself, that virtue which I first found in you, and which, through you, I think I have now attained. Thus it was that I came to you, Amador, firmly resolved to build upon this rock of honour. But in this short space of time you have clearly demonstrated to me that I would have been building not upon the solid rock of purity, but upon the shifting sands, nay, upon a treacherous bog of vice. I had begun to build a dwelling in which I could live for evermore, but with a single blow you have razed it to the ground. So now you must abandon hope. You must be resolved never again, wherever it may be, to seek to speak to me or look into my eyes. Nor may you hope that one day I could change my mind, even should I so desire. My heart brims with sorrow for what might have been. But had it come to pass that I had sworn myself to you in the bond of perfect love, my poor heart would have been wounded unto death by what has transpired. To think that I have been so deceived! If it does not bring me to an early grave, I shall surely suffer for the rest of my days. This is my final word to you. Adieu. For ever more adieu!'

I shall not try to describe Amador's feelings as he listened to these words. It would be impossible to set such anguish down in writing. It is difficult even for anyone to imagine such anguish, unless they have experienced the same kind of suffering themselves. What a cruel end! Realizing that she was going to leave him on this note, and that he would lose her for ever if he did not clear his name, he seized her by the arm.

'My Lady,' he said, putting on the most convincing expression he could manage, 'for as long as I can remember I have longed to love a good and honourable woman. But I have found few who are truly virtuous, and that is why I wanted to test you out – to see if you were as worthy to be admired for your virtue, as you are to be loved for your other attributes. And now I know for certain that you are. For this I praise God, and give Him thanks that He has brought my heart to love such consummate perfection! So I beseech you, forgive this whim, pardon my rash behaviour. For as you can see, all has turned out for the best. Your honour is vindicated, and I am happy indeed that this should be so!'

But Florida was beginning to understand the evil ways of men. If she had before found it hard to believe that Amador's intentions were bad, she now found it even harder to believe him when he said that in reality they were good.

'Would to God that you were speaking the truth!' she said. 'But I am a married woman, and I am not so ignorant that I do not clearly realize that it was violent passion that drove you to do what you did. If God had not stood by me, and my hold on the reins had slackened, I am not at all convinced that you would have been the one to tighten the bridle. Those who truly seek virtue do not take the route that you took. But enough has been said. I was too ready to believe you were a good man. It is time that I recognized the truth, for it is by truth that now I am delivered from your clutches.'

With these words, Florida left the room. The whole night long she wept. This sudden change caused her such pain that her heart was hard pressed to withstand the assaults of bitter regret which love hurled against it. For, while in accordance with reason she was determined to love him no more, the heart, over which none of us has control, would never yield. Thus, unable to love him less than before, she resolved to propitiate love, since love it was that was the cause. She resolved, in short, to go on loving Amador with all her heart, but, in order to obey the dictates of honour, never to let it be known, either to him or to anyone.

The next morning Amador departed in a state of mind which I leave to your imagination. But no one in the world had a more valiant heart than he, and, instead of sinking into despair, he began to seek new ways of seeing Florida again, and winning her. So, being due to present himself to the King of Spain, who at that time was in residence at Toledo, he went by way of the County of Aranda. He arrived late one night at the castle of the Countess, and found her ailing, and pining for her daughter. When she saw Amador she put her arms around him and kissed him, as if he were her own son, for she loved him dearly, and had guessed that he was in love with Florida. She pressed him for news, and he told her as much as he could without telling the whole truth. Then he told her what her daughter had always concealed, and confessed their love, begging the Countess to help him have news of Florida, and to bring her soon to live with her.

The next morning he left, and continued on his journey. When his business with the King had been dispatched, he went off to join the army on active service. He was downcast and so changed in every respect that the ladies and officers whose company he had always kept no longer recognized him. He continually dressed himself in clothes of coarse black cloth, much more austere than was called for by the death of his wife. But the death of his wife served merely as a cover for a much deeper grief. Three or four years went by, and Amador never once returned to court. The Countess meanwhile had word that such a change had come over her daughter that she was piteous to behold. She summoned Florida to her, in the hope that she might want to come back and live with her permanently. But Florida would not hear of it. When she heard that Amador had told her mother about their love, and that her mother, good and wise as she was, had confided in Amador and told him she approved, her consternation was great indeed. On the one hand, she could see that her mother had considerable admiration for Amador, and that if she had the truth told to her, it might bring him harm. That was the last thing she wanted, and in any case, she felt quite well able to punish him for his outrageous behaviour without help from her family. On the other hand, she could see that if she concealed the bad things she knew about him, she would be obliged by her mother and all her friends to talk with him and receive him favourably. That, she feared, could only strengthen him in his base intentions. However, he was in distant parts, so she made little fuss, and wrote him letters whenever the Countess asked her to do so. But when she did write, she made sure that he would realize that they were written out of obedience, and not from any inclination of her own. There had once been a time when her letters had brought him transports of joy. Now he felt nothing but sorrow as he read them.

Three years went by, during which time Amador performed so many glorious deeds that no writer could ever hope to set them all down, even if he had all the paper in Spain. It was now that he devised his grand scheme – not a scheme to win back Florida's heart, for he deemed her lost for ever, but a scheme to score a victory over her as his mortal enemy, for that was how she now appeared. Throwing all reason to the winds, and setting aside all fear of death, he took the greatest risk of his life. His mind was made up. He was not to be deterred from his aim. Since his credit stood high with the governor, he was able to get himself appointed to a mission to the King for the purpose of discussing some secret campaign directed against the town of Leucate. He also managed to get himself issued with orders to inform the Countess of Aranda of the plan, and to take her advice before meeting the King. Knowing that Florida was there, he went post-haste into Aranda, and on his arrival sent a friend in secrecy to tell the Countess that he wished to see her, and that they must meet only at dead of night, without anyone else knowing about it. Overjoyed to hear that Amador was in the neighbourhood, the Countess told Florida, and sent her to undress in her husband's room, so that she should be ready to be called once everyone had retired. Florida made no objection. But she had not yet recovered from her earlier terrifying experience, and, instead of doing as she was bidden, went straight to an oratory to commend herself to our Lord, and to pray to Him that He might preserve her heart from all base affections. Remembering that Amador had often praised her beauty, which in spite of long sickness had in no way diminished, she could not bear the thought that this beauty of hers should kindle so base a fire in the heart of a man who was so worthy and so good. Rather than that she would disfigure herself, impair her beauty. She seized a stone that lay on the chapel floor, and struck herself in the face with great force, severely injuring her mouth, nose and eyes. Then, so that no one would suspect her when she was summoned, she deliberately threw herself against a [large piece of stone] as she left the chapel. She lay with her face to the ground, screaming, and was found in this appalling state by the Countess, who immediately had her wounds dressed and her face swathed in bandages.

Once she had been made comfortable, the Countess took her into her chamber and told her that she wanted her to go and talk to Amador in her private room till she had dismissed her attendants. Thinking that Amador would not be unaccompanied, Florida obeyed, but, once the door closed behind her, she was horrified to find herself completely alone with him. Amador, for his part, was not at all displeased, for now, he thought, he would by fair means or foul surely get what he had so long desired. A few words were sufficient to tell him that her attitude was the same as when he had last seen her, and that she would die rather than change her mind. In a state of utter desperation he said:

'Almighty God, Florida, I'm not going to have the just deserts of all my efforts frustrated by your scruples! Seeing that all my love, all my patient waiting, all my begging and praying are useless, I shall use every ounce of strength in my body to get the one thing that will make life worth living! Without it I shall die!'

His whole expression, his face, his eyes, had changed as he spoke. The fair complexion was flushed with fiery red. The kind, gentle face was contorted with a terrifying violence, as if there was some raging inferno belching fire in his heart and behind his eyes. One powerful fist roughly seized hold of her two weak and delicate hands. Her feet were held in a vice-like grip. There was nothing she could do to save herself. She could neither fight back, nor could she fight free. She had no other recourse than to see if there might not yet be some trace of his former love, for the sake of which he might relent and have mercy.

'Amador,' she gasped, 'even if you think I'm your enemy now, I beg you, in the name of that pure love which I used to think you felt for me in your heart, please listen to me, before you torture me!'

Seeing that he was prepared to hear her out, she continued: 'Alas, Amador! What is it that drives you to seek that which can give you no satisfaction, and to cause me the greatest sorrow anyone could ever cause me? You came to know my feelings so well in the days when I was young, when my beauty was at its most fresh, and when your passion might have had some excuse, that I marvel now that at the age I am, ugly as I am, ravaged by deepest sorrow as I am, you should seek that which you know you cannot find. I am certain that you can have no doubt but that my feelings remain as they have always been, and that [only by use of force therefore can you obtain that which you ask]. If you will look at the way my face is now adorned, you will lose all memory of the delights that once you found there, you will lose all your desire to approach it nearer! If there is the slightest trace in you of the love you used to bear me, you must surely have pity on me and overcome this violent madness. In the name of all the [pity and noble virtue] that I have known in you in the past, I plead with you, and beg you for mercy. Just let me live in peace! Let me live the life of honour and virtue to which, as you yourself once urged me, I have committed myself. And if your former love for me really has turned to hatred, and if, more out of a desire for revenge than some form of love, your intention is to make me the most wretched woman on earth, then I tell you plainly that you will not have your way. I shall be forced, against all my previous intentions, to make known your vicious designs to the very lady, who hitherto has held you in the highest esteem. You will realize that if I take this action, you will be in danger of your life . . .'

'If I am to die anyway,' Amador broke in, 'then the agony will be over all the sooner! Nor am I going to be deterred because you've disfigured your face! I'm quite sure you did it yourself, of your own volition. No! If all I could get were your bare bones, still I should want to hold them close!'

Florida could see that neither tears, nor entreaties, nor reasoning were to any avail. She could see that he was going to act out his evil desires, unmoved and merciless. Exhausted and unable to struggle any more, there was only one thing left she could do to save herself, the one thing that she had shrunk from as from death itself. With a heart-rending cry, she shouted out to her mother with all the strength that was in her. There was something in Florida's voice that made the Countess go cold with horror. Suspecting what had happened, she flew to the room with all possible haste. Amador, not quite so ready to die as he had just declared, had had enough time to gather himself together. When the Countess entered, there he was standing by the door, with Florida at a distance.

'Amador, what's the matter?' she demanded, 'Tell me the truth!'

Amador was never at loss when it came to finding his way out of a difficult situation. Looking shocked and pale, he gave his answer.

'Alas! Madame, what has come over Florida? I've never been

so astonished as I am at this moment. I used to think, as you know, that I had some share in her goodwill. But now I see that I have none at all. I do not think that she was any less modest, any less virtuous in the days when she was living in your household than she is now, but she used not to have such scruples about seeing men and talking to them. I only have to look at her now, and she can't bear it! I thought it was a dream or a trance, when I saw her acting like that, and I asked her if I could kiss her hand, which after all is quite normal in this part of the world, but she completely refused! I am prepared to admit that I was in the wrong over one thing, Madame, and for this I do ask your forgiveness: I'm afraid I did hold her hand as you might say by force, and kissed it. But that was the only thing I asked of her. But she seems to be so determined that I should die, that she called out to you, as you must have heard. I can't understand why she did it, unless she was afraid that I had other intentions. Anyway, whatever the reason, Madame, I take the blame for it. She really ought to show affection for all your loyal servants. But such is fate! I happen to be the one who's in love, and yet I'm the only one who loses favour! Of course, I'll always feel the same way about you, Madame, and about your daughter, as I have in the past, and I hope and pray that I shan't lose your good opinion, even if, through no fault of my own, I have lost hers.'

The Countess, who half believed, half doubted these words, turned to Florida. 'Why did you call out for me like that?' she asked.

Florida replied that she had been afraid, and, in spite of her mother's insistent and repeated questions, she refused ever to give more details. It was enough for her that she had been delivered from the hands of her enemy, and as far as she was concerned Amador had been quite sufficiently punished by being thwarted in his attempt. The Countess had a long talk with Amador, and then let him speak again to Florida, though she stayed in the room while he did so, in order to observe from a distance how he would comport himself. He had little to say, though he did thank Florida for not telling her mother the whole truth, and he did ask her that since he was banished from her heart for ever, she would at least not admit a successor.

'If I had had any other way of protecting myself,' came her reply, 'I would not have shouted out, and no one would have heard anything about what happened. Provided that you don't drive me to it, that is the worst you will have from me. And you need have no fear that I shall give my love to some other man. For since I have not found that which I desired in the heart which I regarded as the most virtuous in the world, I shall never believe it is to be found in any man. Thanks to what has happened I shall be free for ever more from the passions that can arise from love.'

So saying, she bade Amador farewell. The Countess had been watching closely, but she could come to no conclusion, except that her daughter plainly no longer felt any affection for Amador. She was convinced that Florida was just being perverse, and had taken it into her head to dislike anyone that her mother was fond of. From that time on, the Countess became so hostile towards her daughter, that for seven whole years she did not speak to her except in anger – and all this for the sake of Amador.

Up till this time Florida had had a horror of being with her husband, but during this period her attitude changed, and, in order to [escape] the harshness of her mother, she refused to move from his side. But this did not help her in her plight, so she conceived a plan which involved deceiving Amador. Dropping for a day or two her hostile air, she advised Amador to make amorous overtures to a certain woman, who, she said, had spoken of their love. The woman in question was a lady by the name of Loretta, who was attached to the household of the Queen. Amador believed Florida, and in the hope of eventually regaining her favour, he made advances to Loretta, who was only too pleased to have such an eminently desirable servant. Indeed she made it so obvious by her simperings, that the whole court soon got to hear of it. The Countess herself was at court at this time, and when she heard the rumours, she began to be less severe than she had been with her daughter. One day, however, it came to Florida's ears that Loretta's husband, who was a high-ranking officer in the army, and one of the King of Spain's highest governors, had become so jealous, that he had sworn to stop at nothing to kill Amador. Now Florida was incapable of wishing harm on Amador, however harsh a mask she might wear, and she informed him immediately of the danger he was in. Amador, anxious to return to her, replied that he would never again speak a word to Loretta, provided that Florida would agree to see him for three hours each day. To that she could not give her consent.

'Then why,' said Amador to her, 'if you do not wish to give me life, do you wish to save me from death? There can only be one reason – that you want to keep me alive in order to torture me, and hope thereby to cause me greater pain than a thousand deaths could ever do. Death may shun me, yet I shall seek it out, and I shall find it, for only in death shall I have repose!'

Even as they spoke, news arrived that the King of Granada had declared war on the King of Spain, and had attacked so fiercely that the King had had to send his son, the Prince, to the front, together with two old and experienced lords, the Constable of Castile and the Duke of Alba. The Duke of Cardona, too, and the Count of Aranda, were anxious to join the campaign, and petitioned the King for a commission. His majesty granted their requests, appointing each to the command appropriate to his birth. Amador was appointed to lead them. His exploits during that campaign were so extraordinary that they had more the appearance of acts of desperation than acts of bravery. Indeed, to bring my story to its conclusion, this bravery, going beyond all bounds, was demonstrated at the last in death.

The Moors had indicated that they were about to join battle. Then, seeing the size of the Christian forces, they had staged a sham retreat. The Spaniards had been about to follow in hot pursuit. But the old Constable and the Duke of Alba, realizing that it was a trap, had managed to restrain the Prince from crossing the river. The Count of Aranda and the Duke of Cardona, however, had defied orders. The Moors, seeing their pursuers were reduced in number, had wheeled round. Cardona had been killed, cut down by thrusts from Moorish scimitars. Aranda had been left gravely wounded, and as good as dead. In the midst of the carnage Amador arrived, riding furiously, and forcing his way like a madman through the thick of the battle. He had the two bodies transported back to the Prince's encampment. The Prince was as overcome as if they had been his own brothers.

When the wounds were examined, however, it was found that the Count of Aranda was still alive, so he was carried back in a litter to the family home, where he lay ill for a very long time. The Duke's corpse was sent back to Cardona. Amador, having rescued the two bodies, was so heedless of his own safety that he found himself surrounded by vast numbers of Moors. He made up his mind what he should do. His enemies would not enjoy the glory either of capturing him alive or of slaying him. Even as he had failed to take his lady, so now his enemies would be frustrated in taking him. His faith to her he had broken. His faith to God he would not break. He knew, too, that if he was taken before the King of Granada, he would have to abjure Christianity, or die a horrible death. Commending body and soul to God, he kissed the cross of his sword, and plunged it with such force into his body that he killed himself in one fell blow.

Thus died poor Amador, his loss bemoaned as his virtue and prowess deserved. The news of his death spread throughout Spain, and eventually reached Florida, who was at Barcelona, where her husband had expressed his wish to be buried. She conducted the obsequies with due honour. Then, saying not a word either to her own mother or to the mother of her dead husband, she entered the Convent of Jesus. Thus she took Him as lover and as spouse who had delivered her from the violent love of Amador and from the misery of her life with her earthly husband. All her affections henceforth were bent on the perfect love of God. As a nun she lived for many long years, until at last she commended her soul to God with the joy of the bride who goes to meet her bridegroom.

*

'I'm afraid, Ladies, that this story has been rather long, and that some of you might have found it somewhat tedious – but it would have been even longer if I'd done justice to the person who originally told it to me. I hope you will take Florida's example to heart, but at the same time I would beg you to be less harsh, and not to have so much faith in men that you end up being disappointed when you learn the truth, drive them to a horrible death and give yourselves a miserable life.'

Parlamente had had a patient and attentive audience. She now turned to Hircan, and said: 'Don't you think that this woman was tried to the limits of her endurance, and that she put up a virtuous resistance in the face of it all?'

'No,' replied Hircan, 'for screaming is the least resistance a woman can offer. If she'd been somewhere where nobody could have heard her, I don't know what she'd have done. And as for Amador, if he'd been more of a lover and less of a coward, he wouldn't have been quite so easily put off. The example of Florida is not going to make me change my opinion on this matter. I still maintain that no man who loved perfectly, or who was loved by a lady, could fail in his designs, provided he went about things in a proper manner. All the same, I must applaud Amador for at least partly fulfilling his duty.'

'What duty?' demanded Oisille. 'Do you call it duty when a man who devotes himself to a lady's service tries to take her by force, when what he owes to her is obedience and reverence?'

'Madame,' replied Saffredent, 'when our ladies are holding court and sit in state like judges, then we men bend our knees before them, we timidly invite them to dance, we serve them so devotedly that we anticipate their every wish. Indeed, we have the appearance of being so terrified of offending them, so anxious to serve their every whim, that anybody else observing us would think we must be either out of our minds, or struck dumb, so idiotic is our animal-like devotion. Then all the credit goes to the ladies, because they put on such haughty expressions and adopt such refined ways of speaking, that people who see nothing but their external appearance go in awe of them, and feel obliged to admire and love them. However, in private it is quite another matter. Then Love is the only judge of the way we behave, and we soon find out that they are just women, and we are just men. The title "lady" is soon exchanged for "mistress", and her "devoted servant" soon becomes her "lover".* Hence the well-known proverb: "loyal service makes the servant master."'

'They have honour, just as men, who can give it to them or take it away, have honour; and they see the things we patiently endure; but it is therefore only right that our long-suffering should be rewarded when honour cannot be injured.'

* *Maistresse*, *amye*, *serviteur*, *amy*, respectively, in the original.

'But you are not talking about true honour,' intervened Longarine, 'true honour which alone gives true contentment in this world. Suppose that everybody said I was a decent woman, while I knew that the opposite was true – then their praise would only increase my dishonour and make me feel inwardly ashamed. Equally, if everybody criticized me, while I knew that I was completely innocent, I would only derive contentment from their criticism. For no one is truly contented, unless he is contented within himself.'

'Well, whatever you all might say,' said Geburon, 'in my opinion Amador was the most noble and valiant knight that ever lived. I think I recognize him beneath his fictitious name, but since Parlamente has preferred not to disclose the identities of her characters, I shall not disclose them either. Suffice it to say that if it's the man I think it is, then he's a man who never experienced fear in his life, a man whose heart was never devoid of love or the desire for courageous action.'

Then Oisille turned to them all and said: 'I think it has been a delightful day, and if the remaining days are equally enjoyable, then we shall have seen how swiftly the time can be made to pass in refined conversation. See how low the sun is already. And listen to the Abbey bell calling us to vespers! It started ringing a while ago, but I didn't draw your attention to it because your desire to hear the end of the story was more devout than your desire to hear vespers!'

Upon these words they all got up and made their way to the Abbey, where they found the monks had been waiting for them for a good hour. After hearing vespers, they had their supper, and spent the evening discussing the stories they had heard that day and racking their brains for new stories to make the next day as enjoyable as the first. Then, after playing not a few games in the meadow, they retired to bed, thus bringing the first day to a happy and contented close.

END OF THE FIRST DAY

SECOND DAY

PROLOGUE

The next day they got up, eager to return to the spot where they had had so much pleasure the day before, for they had all prepared their stories, and could hardly wait to tell them. They listened to Madame Oisille's lesson and to mass, each of them offering their hearts and minds to God that He might inspire their words and grant His grace to continue their gathering. Then they dined, chatting one to another and recalling amusing stories from the past. After dinner they retired to their rooms to rest, and at the appointed hour reassembled in the meadow. The weather seemed to be smiling on their venture. The green grass provided a natural couch, and when they had all taken their seats upon it, Parlamente began:

'Since it was I who told the last story yesterday, it's up to me to choose who should start today. And since Madame Oisille, being the oldest and wisest, was the first woman to speak, today I shall choose the youngest (I do not say the most foolish), for I'm sure that if we all follow her example, we shan't hold up vespers as long as we did yesterday. Well then, Nomerfide, here is your opportunity to join the ranks of the eloquent – but please don't make us cry right at the beginning of our second day!'

'No need to make a special request,' replied Nomerfide, 'because one of the ladies told me a story last night which has stuck in my mind, and I couldn't tell another even if I tried. If this one makes you feel sad, you must have a very melancholy disposition indeed!'

STORY ELEVEN

In the household of Madame de La Trémoïlle there was a lady by the name of Roncex. One day she was visiting the Franciscan house at Thouars, and felt a sudden need to go where you can't send your servant for you. For company she asked a girl called La Mothe to go with her, but for the sake of privacy and modesty she left her in a room nearby, and went on her own into the privy, which was very dark. It was the place used by all the Franciscans, and all over the seat and everywhere else there was ample evidence that Franciscan bellies had been doing justice to the fruits of Bacchus and Ceres. Well, this poor lady, who was already in such a hurry that she scarcely had time to lift her skirts, went and sat down on the filthiest and dirtiest seat in the whole place. She stuck to it as if held on by glue! Her poor buttocks, her clothes, her feet, everything was in such a disgusting mess that she didn't dare take a step to one side or the other, for fear of even worse. So she started to scream for all she was worth.

'La Mothe! La Mothe!' she cried, 'I am undone, I am dishonoured!' The poor girl, who had heard plenty of stories about the vile behaviour of the Franciscans, thought that some of them must have been lying in wait, and that they must be trying to rape Madame de Roncex. So she ran to her aid as fast as her legs would carry her, shouting to everyone she met: 'Help! Help! The friars are trying to rape Madame de Roncex in the privy!'

Everyone dashed to the scene, only to find the wretched Madame de Roncex standing there, bottom bare lest her gown should be soiled, and shrieking for one of her women to come and clean her up. A splendid spectacle for the men who had come running to her rescue! And the only trace of a Franciscan was the filth stuck to the poor lady's behind! Needless to say it was all very amusing for the gentlemen, but somewhat humiliating for the lady, who after all had been expecting her women to run along to help her get clean. Instead there was a crowd of men to do her bidding, and there was she, exposed in the worst condition a woman could ever appear in! Immediately she saw them she let her skirts fall to cover herself up, thereby dirtying what little of her attire had remained clean. She quite forgot the filthy state she was in, so ashamed was she at the sight of the men. When she eventually managed to get out of the disgusting place, she had to be stripped naked and have all her clothes changed before she could leave the monastery. She felt very much inclined to be angry with La Mothe for bringing assistance in the way she had, but when she heard that the girl had thought there had been even worse things afoot, she forgot her anger, and laughed with the rest.

*

'Well, Ladies, I don't think that my story was either very long or very melancholy! So you've had what you expected!'

Thereupon her audience burst into peals of laughter, and Oisille said: 'It was a rather dirty story, but when one knows the people involved, one cannot really object to it. How I would have loved to see La Mothe's face – and the face of the lady she tried to rescue! Anyway, as you've finished so quickly, Nomerfide, will you choose us a new storyteller – someone perhaps who won't be quite so frivolous?'

'If you want me to make up for my naughtiness,' said Nomerfide, 'I think I shall choose Dagoucin, who's so wise and good that he would never for the life of him allow anything bad or foolish to pass his lips!'

Dagoucin thanked her for her high opinion of his good sense, and began.

'The story I have decided to tell you is to show you how love can blind even the greatest and most honourable of men, and how hard it is to overcome wickedness by means of kindness and generosity.'

STORY TWELVE

Ten years ago there was in Florence a Duke of the house of Medici who was married to Madame Marguerite, the natural daughter of the Emperor. Now, Madame Marguerite was still very young at that time, so young in fact that the Duke could not lawfully sleep with her until she was of a mature age. He treated her very gently, and to spare her, he pursued several love-affairs with women in the town, whom he visited at night while his wife was sleeping. Amongst these women there was one in particular with whom he was infatuated – a very beautiful woman, who was also virtuous and good. This lady happened to be the sister of a gentleman whom the Duke held almost as dear as he held himself. Indeed, this gentleman had been given such authority in the ducal household that his orders were obeyed and respected as if they came from the Duke in person. None of the Duke's secrets were hidden from him. He was told everything. He was in fact almost the Duke's second self.

The Duke realized that the gentleman's sister was a woman of virtue, and, after doing his utmost to find an opportunity, came to the conclusion that there was no way of declaring his love to her directly. So he addressed himself to her brother, the very same man who was his favourite.

'My good friend,' he said to him, 'there's nothing in the world that I wouldn't gladly do for you: if it were otherwise I should never dare to come to you and reveal what is in my mind, even less ask you to help me. But, as you know, I am extremely fond of you, and if I had a wife or a daughter who was in a position, as it were, to save your life, I would certainly let her serve you, rather than see you die in torment. I am sure that you feel the same way about me as I do about you. If I, as your master, bear you such affection, then, surely, to say the least, you can't feel less for me? So I am going to tell you a secret. I have kept it hidden for too long, and that is why you now see me in the state I am in. Death is the only hope for me, unless you agree to do me the service I am about to ask.'

The gentleman was moved to pity by the way his master pleaded, and by the unfeigned emotion on his tear-stained face.

'My lord, I am your creature. All that I have, all that I am in this world has come from you. You may speak to me as you would speak to your own soul, for you may be assured that whatever is in my power to perform shall be performed.'

So the Duke started to tell him how he was in love with his sister, and how his love was so deep and so strong that if his friend did not make it possible for him to enjoy her favours, then he could not see how he could go on living. He knew that gifts and entreaties would be of no avail, therefore he begged that if he cared for his master's life as he cared for his own, he would procure him the means of obtaining that which otherwise would be for ever beyond his grasp. But the brother had more concern for his sister's honour, and for that of his family name, than for the Duke's pleasures. He protested, and implored the Duke to use him for anything, but not to so callously take advantage of him as to force him to bring dishonour upon his own lineage. His honour, his heart, the very blood that flowed in his veins prevented him from lending himself to such a service. The Duke blazed with unbearable rage. He bit his nails in his wrath.

'So be it then!' he stormed. 'Since you are not my friend, I know what I have to do!'

Knowing what a ruthless man his master was, the gentleman, terrified, replied: 'My Lord, if it is your wish, then I will speak with her and bring you her reply.'

Whereupon the Duke walked out, saying: 'Take care for my life, and I will do the same for you.'

The gentleman understood well what this meant. For a day or two he saw nothing of the Duke, and wrestled alone with the dilemma before him. On the one hand he was aware of the strength of the obligations he owed to his master for all the honours and material benefits he had received from him. On the other hand, there was the honour of his family name, the chastity of his sister. He knew that she would never consent to sink to such vice, unless she were somehow tricked into it or taken by force – an eventuality so monstrous that it would bring down infamy on himself and his whole family for the rest of time.

Thus torn, he came to the conclusion that he would die rather than submit his sister, one of the most virtuous women in all Italy, to anything so vile, and that his duty was to rid his homeland of this tyrant who was bent on forcing disgrace upon his family name. He was convinced that if he did not remove the Duke, neither his own life nor the lives of those dear to him could be guaranteed. So, without breathing a word to his sister, or to anybody else, he made up his mind to save her life and avenge her honour at a single stroke.

When two days were up, he came back to the Duke, and told him that he had been successful in winning his sister round, that she had in the end agreed to do the Duke's bidding, provided that the affair was kept secret and that no one else but he, her brother, should know about it.

The Duke, only too anxious to believe this story, did not doubt it for one moment. He embraced the messenger who had brought him such good tidings, and promised him everything he could ask for. He begged him to bring his plan to fruition as speedily as possible, and together they arranged the time and the place. Needless to say the Duke was overjoyed.

On the day of the assignation, as the long-awaited night drew nigh when he would conquer her whom he had deemed unconquerable, the Duke retired early, accompanied only by the gentleman. He prepared himself with the utmost care, choosing his accoutrement for the occasion from amongst his most sweetly scented shirts and headgear. When everyone else had retired for the night, the Duke was taken to where the lady lived, and shown into an imposingly appointed bedchamber. There the gentleman helped him undress and get into bed, saying:

'My Lord, I shall now go to fetch a virtuous lady who will not enter this room without blushing, but before the morning I hope that she will be reassured.'

Leaving the Duke in the bedchamber, the gentleman went into his own room. There was still one servant who had not retired to bed, and to this one man the gentleman said: 'Are you bold enough to come with me? I am about to avenge myself of the greatest enemy I have in this world.'

'Certainly, Monsieur, even if it were the Duke himself!'

replied the man, who knew nothing of what was afoot. Without more ado the gentleman led him out of the room, giving him time to collect no weapon other than a dagger which he had.

The Duke heard their footsteps, and, thinking it was the lady he loved, he opened his eyes and drew back the bed-curtains, so that he might gaze upon his heart's desire and take her in his arms. What he saw was not his lady, but the gentleman's naked sword, not the preserver of his life, but the precipitator of his death. The gentleman struck him as he lay there in his night-shirt. Unarmed the Duke may have been, but his courage did not fail him. Raising himself up in bed, he seized his assailant about the body, saying: 'So this is the way you keep your promises?'

Fighting tooth and nail, for these were his only arms, the Duke sank his teeth into the gentleman's thumb, and struggled with all his might until they both fell to the ground at the side of the bed. The gentleman, uncertain now of his advantage, called out to his manservant, who ran in to find them so closely locked together that he could not make out who was who. He grabbed a pair of feet and dragged the two men, still grappling with one another, into the middle of the room. He then set to with his dagger, cutting the Duke's throat. The Duke fought back until loss of blood robbed him of his strength and he could struggle no more. The gentleman and the servant then lifted him back on to the bed, finished him off with their daggers, drew the curtains once again, locked the door behind them and left the corpse lying there.

Now that he was victorious over his mortal enemy, by whose death he hoped to set the state free, he began to think that his mission would be incomplete if he did not also dispatch the five or six men who had been close to the Duke. To this end, he gave orders to his manservant to fetch them all one by one, so that he might deal with them in the same way as he had dealt with their master. But the servant was a man of caution, neither foolhardy nor excessive in valour, and he replied:

'Monsieur, it seems to me that you've done enough for the time being, and that you'd do better to think about saving your own life than about taking still more. If we took as long to get rid of them as we did to get rid of the Duke, daylight would be upon us, and we'd be found out before we'd finished, even if we found our victims unarmed.'

The gentleman, with his crime fresh on his conscience, was nervous, and readily accepted this piece of advice. So, taking his servant with him, he made his way to the house of the Bishop, who had charge of the opening of the town gates and also had command over the post-horses.

'I have this evening received news that my brother is at the brink of death,' said the gentleman to the Bishop. 'I have just taken my leave of the Duke, and he has granted my request. I now ask you to give instructions to the posts to provide me with two good horses, and to instruct the gatekeeper to open the gates of the town.'

To the Bishop this request was as good as an order from his master the Duke himself, and he at once gave to the gentleman a pass which would guarantee two horses and unhindered passage through the town gates, just as he demanded. Once out of the town, instead of going to see his brother, he made his way to Venice, where he had the bites which he had received from the Duke treated, and thence to Turkey.

When the Duke failed to appear the next morning, his servants suspected that he had been to visit some lady. But later, when he still had not returned, they went out to search for him. The poor Duchess, who was beginning to love him dearly, was in great distress when she learned that he could not be found. As soon as it was realized that the gentleman who was the Duke's favourite had not been seen either, they went to look for him at his house. They found traces of blood at the chamber door, but no man or servant in the house could give any explanation. Following the blood stains, the Duke's miserable servants came to the door of the room where the murdered man was lying. The door was locked, but they broke it down. Seeing the whole place covered in blood, they drew back the bed-curtains and found the Duke's wretched body lying on the bed in the sleep of eternal rest. Picture to yourselves the grief of these servants as they carried the corpse back to the ducal palace, where the Bishop arrived to explain how the gentleman had made off post-haste during the night under pretext of visiting a sick brother. It was clear to everyone that it was the gentleman himself who was responsible for the murder. It was also evident that his sister had known nothing at all about it. She was horrified by what had happened, but loved her brother the more for having delivered her from a prince who was so cruel a foe. She continued her life of virtue, and grew in honour. Indeed, although the family house was confiscated and she was reduced to poverty, both she and her sister found husbands who were amongst the richest and most honourable men who ever lived in Italy. And ever after they enjoyed the highest esteem throughout the land.

*

'And so, Ladies, here we have a story that should make you truly fear that little god who delights in tormenting princes and poor alike, the mighty as much as the weak, and who blinds all men till they forget their God, their conscience and in the end their own lives. Princes, and all who have authority, should beware of offending those beneath them. For, when God desires to take vengeance on the sinner, there is no man [so humble] that he cannot inflict hurt, and no man so high that he has all power to harm those who are in God's charge.'

Everyone had listened attentively to Dagoucin's story. But it was a story that engendered diverse opinions. For some, the gentleman had clearly done his duty in saving his sister's life and honour, and in ridding his homeland of a tyrant by the same stroke. Others, however, did not agree. They said that it was the height of ingratitude for the gentleman to murder the very man from whom he had received such honour and advancement. The ladies said that he was a good brother and a virtuous citizen. The men, taking the contrary view, insisted that he was a traitor and a bad servant. It was most interesting to hear the arguments that each side advanced. But the ladies, as is their wont, spoke as much from passion as from reason, claiming that the Duke was so deserving of death that the man who had slain him was blessed indeed. Dagoucin, seeing that he had provoked such a heated debate, said:

'Do not, I beg you, Ladies, enter into dispute over something that is now long past, but take heed lest your beauty cause suffering a thousand times more cruel than the death that I have just described.'

'We learn from *La belle dame sans mercy*,' commented Parlamente, 'that "A malady so gracious, Ne'er put a man to death".'*

'I pray God, Madame,' replied Dagoucin, 'that all the ladies here realize how erroneous that view is! I truly believe that they do not desire to be referred to as "*sans mercy*", or to be likened to that fair lady of little faith who allowed her devoted servant to die for want of a kind and compassionate word.'

'So,' retorted Parlamente, 'in order to save the life of some man who claims to be in love with one of us, you want us women to put in peril both our honour and our conscience?'

'That is not what I said,' replied Dagoucin, 'for a man who loved perfectly would be even more afraid of wounding his lady's honour than would the lady herself. It seems to me, therefore, that a kind, compassionate and honourable response, such as perfect and noble love calls for, can only enhance one's honour and purify one's conscience. Any man who seeks the contrary is not a true servant of his lady.'

'But it's the contrary that's precisely the intention of all [their] fine speeches,' said Ennasuite. 'They start by preaching about honour, and end up with the opposite. And if all the men here would care to tell the truth about this, I'd gladly believe them on their oaths.'

So Hircan swore on his oath that he had never loved any woman but his wife, and that the last thing he wanted was to be the cause of her committing some grievous offence against the Almighty. Simontaut said the same, adding that he had often wished that all women, save his own wife, were wicked.

'Indeed!' retorted Geburon. 'Then you deserve to have a wife every bit as bad as you'd like to see the others! For my part, I can honestly swear to you that there is a certain lady whom I have loved so deeply that I would rather have died than that she should do for me anything that might have lowered her in my esteem. For my love was founded on her virtue, and I would not, for all the favours in the world, have desired to see her virtue stained.'

At this Saffredent burst out laughing.

'Geburon,' he said, 'I'd have thought your common sense and

* The quotation is from the famous poem by Alain Chartier.

your love for your wife would have saved you from the risk of playing the lover. However, I see it's not the case, since you're still employing the terms we generally use to get round the cleverest of women, and to get a hearing with the most modest. After all, what woman can turn a deaf ear when we start talking about honour and virtue? On the other hand, if we were to bare our souls, and show ourselves in our true light, there's many a man usually well-received by the ladies whom they would no longer deign to consider. So we devise the most angelic appearance we can, to cover up the devil inside, and thus disguised, we receive a good few favours before we're found out, and perhaps even manage to draw the ladies on so far, that, thinking they're set on the road to virtue, it's too late for them to beat a retreat when they find themselves in the midst of vice!'

'Indeed,' said Geburon, 'I didn't think that you were like that! I had thought that you found virtue more pleasing than pleasure.'

'What!' replied Saffredent. 'Can there be any greater virtue than loving according to God's commandment? It seems to me that it's far better to love one woman as a woman than to idolize several as if they were graven images! As far as I'm concerned, it's my firm belief that it's much better to use them than to abuse them!'

The ladies were all on Geburon's side, and told Saffredent to keep quiet.

'I'm quite happy to say no more on the subject,' he told them. 'In view of the bad reception I've had, I'd rather not return to it.'

'If you've been badly received,' said Longarine, 'you have only your own wickedness to blame for it. What honest woman would want you as her servant after the sort of things you've been saying?'

'Those women who have *not* taken exception to me wouldn't exchange their honesty for yours,' he replied. 'But let's say no more about it, lest I get angry, and upset myself and others too. Let's see who Dagoucin will choose to tell the next story.'

'I choose Parlamente,' said Dagoucin, 'because I think she is the one who above all others should know what noble and perfect love really is.'

'Since I have been chosen to tell the third story today,' she began, 'I shall tell you what happened to a lady who has always been a close friend of mine, and whose innermost thoughts were never hidden from me.'

STORY THIRTEEN

In the household of the Regent, the mother of King Francis I, there lived a certain lady, a very devout person married to a nobleman no less devout than herself. Although her husband was old, while she was young and attractive, she nevertheless loved and served him as if he were the handsomest young man in the world. To avoid causing him any distress she took pains to act as a woman of his own age would act, shunning all social gatherings, fine clothes, dances and all the diversions that young women normally enjoy. Her only recreation and delight was to render service to God. In consequence the husband bestowed such affection upon her and placed such trust in her that she was able to manage both him and the house as she pleased. One day he told her that ever since his youth he had had a longing to make a journey to Jerusalem, and asked her what she thought of the idea. She, whose sole wish was to please him, replied:

'My love, since God has deprived us of children but endowed us with riches, I should like us to use a part of our wealth to make this sacred journey. For, wherever you go, I am resolved never to leave you.'

The good husband was so happy that he could imagine himself already on Mount Calvary.

Now about the time they had decided on this pilgrimage a gentleman came to court who had seen much active service against the Turks. He was seeking support from the King for a campaign against one of the Turkish towns – a campaign which, it was hoped, would bring great advantage to the whole of Christendom. The old man asked him all about his expedition, and having heard what was being planned, asked him if, after his journey, he would care to make another to Jerusalem, which he and his wife were very anxious to visit. The captain, very gratified to hear of this devout desire to see the holy city, promised to take him there himself, and to keep the venture secret. The old man could hardly wait to tell his dear wife about the arrangements he had made. She, for her part, was scarcely less impatient for the day of their departure than her husband, and she talked about it continuously to the captain, who listened, but paid less attention to what the lady was saying than to the lady herself. In fact, he fell so violently in love with her, that while he was telling her about his adventures at sea, he would get completely confused, mixing up the port of Marseilles with the Archipelago, and talking about horses when he meant ships, like somebody who had quite lost his wits. But he found her so virtuous that he dared not make his feelings known, and his efforts to conceal them kindled such a fire in his heart that he began to suffer from frequent bouts of sickness. The lady took good care of him on these occasions, for he was, as it were, the cross that guided her on the road to Jerusalem. She would send so often for news of his progress, that in the knowledge that she was caring for him, he generally recovered without further treatment. But this was a man who had the reputation of being more a hearty comrade than a devout Christian, and there were not a few people who were somewhat surprised to see that the lady was giving him so much attention. When they saw that he appeared to be a completely changed man, that he was making a habit of going to church, listening to sermons and making his confession, they strongly suspected that he did it merely to win the lady's favour, and they could hardly resist pointing it out to her. The captain then became nervous lest she should hear something against him which would result in his being separated from her. So he told her and her husband that he was about to be dispatched by the King, and that he had many things to say to them before he left. But in order to keep the affair more secret, he preferred, he said, not to speak with them in front of other people, and therefore requested them to send for him privately when they had both retired for the night. The gentleman thought this was an excellent idea, and every evening without fail he went early to bed, and had his wife join him and take off her day-clothes. Then, when the household had retired, the couple would send for the captain, and would talk about their journey to Jerusalem. During these conversations the good old man would often fall devoutly asleep. Then the captain, sitting alone with the lady he esteemed the noblest and most beautiful in all the world, would often become lost for words, so torn was his heart between the desire to speak his love and the fear of doing so. In order that she would not notice his consternation, he would start to speak of the holy places of Jerusalem, of the places that bore the signs of that great love which Jesus Christ has borne us. And by talking about that love, he concealed his own as he sighed and gazed with tears in his eyes at his lady. She noticed nothing but his devout countenance, and took him for so holy a man that she asked him to tell her about his past life, and how he had come to such a fervent love of God. He recounted to her how he had been a poor nobleman, how he had neglected his conscience in order to acquire wealth and position, and how he had married a lady within the prohibited degrees because she was rich, although she was old and ugly and he had had no love for her. Once he had had all her money, he had gone to sea to seek his fortune, and by dint of hard work had eventually achieved an honourable position. But, he went on, from the moment he had met her, she, the wife of the old gentleman, had been the cause of a complete change in his life through her holy words and virtuous example. If he returned safely from his campaign he was now firmly resolved, he declared, to take her and her husband to Jerusalem. He hoped thereby to make amends for his grievous sins, which he believed he had now put behind him. His one outstanding obligation was to his wife, with whom he hoped to be reconciled in the near future. These words pleased the lady greatly, who was above all gratified to have drawn a man such as this to the love and fear of God. These long discussions continued night after night until it was time for the captain to leave the court, never once having dared to declare his true feelings. He made her a gift of a [crucifix and a pietà], beseeching her to remember him whenever she beheld them.

The day of the captain's departure came. He bade farewell to the old husband, who as usual was half asleep, and then turned to the lady. He could see tears in her eyes, drawn forth by the virtuous affection that she had come to feel for him. The sight made his love unbearable, so unbearable, that, still not daring to declare his passion, he almost fell in a faint as he said his adieu. He broke out all over in a sweat – it was as if not only his eyes but his whole body were shedding tears. Thus, without uttering a word, he departed, and the lady, who had never in her life seen sorrow shown in such a fashion, was left amazed and overcome. However, her good opinion of the captain did not change, and she sent her prayers and supplications with him. A month later, as she was on her way home, she met a gentleman, who gave her a letter from the captain, saying that she was requested to read it in private. The man told her how he had seen the captain embark, firm in his resolve that his expedition should be pleasurable to the King and advantageous to the cause of Christendom, and how he himself was returning to Marseilles to sort out the captain's affairs. Once home, the lady went discreetly to a window-recess where she could be alone, and opened the letter. It consisted of two sheets of paper on both sides of which were closely written the words that follow:

> My silent tongue has hid my love away
> So long in sorrow from the light of day,
> That if some final solace I would seek,
> My only way is death, or else to speak.
> Fair Speech, whom I forbade to show his face
> To you, fair Speech, has waited in this place,
> And waited long, to find me all alone
> And far from her who is my help, my own.
> Now in sore need he bids me set him free,
> To show himself, or else to stifle me.
> Yea, he is truly present even here,
> In this letter doth his very self appear,
> And says that since I may not look at all
> On her who holds my very life in thrall,
> On her from whom I nothing else would seek,
> Could I but see her face and hear her speak,
> He must into her gracious presence steal
> And there at once before your eyes reveal
> How in the depths of grievous woe I cry,
> So long concealed I fear I soon must die.
> Fain would I wipe him from this sorry screed,
> Lest you refuse his plaintive voice to heed,
> This voice of foolish, craven Speech, who now
> Does safe in absence boldly show his brow,

Where in your presence once he hung his head,
And sighs, 'T'were surely better I were dead
Than seek through words my sorry life to ease,
If I should then my lady sore displease
For whose dear sake I would most gladly die!'
Yet might my death bring sadness to the eye
Of her for whom alone I do desire
To save my health and save life's vital fire.
O Lady fair, how solemnly I swore
That when my journey happily was o'er
I would return to you with greatest speed,
Your husband and yourself straightway to lead
Unto the slopes of Sion's longed-for hill,
That you may kneel and pray and do God's will.
Yet if I die, there's none will take you there.
Too much my death would grieve my lady fair
To see the enterprise to nothing turned
For which her noble heart devoutly burned.
So will I live, will to my word be true,
And ere long time will I return to you.
It seems to me that death is good, I own,
And if I live, it is for you alone.
Therefore I needs must lighten my poor heart,
And now relieve him of that heavy part
Which pains us both all other pains above
By showing you my true and honest love,
Which is so great, which is so good and strong,
That no one ever loved so well so long.
What will you say, bold Speech, audacious friend?
Say, shall I let you go, and make an end?
Say, could you bring her heart to know at length
My love? Ah no! For yours is not the strength
E'en to convey of it one thousandth part!
Will you not tell her that my trembling heart
Was with such power captured by her eye
My body's but a husk all dead and dry,
If from her own I draw nor life nor light?
Alas, poor Speech, your weary strength is slight,
You cannot paint for her, with all your art,

How her pure eye can take a steadfast heart,
Nor can you praise the words that she can speak,
Your power is only faltering and weak.
If you could only venture to express
How all her virtue, grace and gentleness,
Rob me of words and even of my wit
So that from hour to hour I weeping sit,
As eyes that gazed on her shed forth their woe,
And words flow not as once they used to flow,
Yea, when I longed to tell her of my love,
I spoke of signs and times, the skies above,
And of the Arctic or Antarctic star!
O Speech, my friend, as skilful as you are,
You have no skill to tell my misery,
To tell how love brought me such agony,
To tell her all my sorrows and my pain,
You have no strength for that, and you remain
Too feeble to express my passion true.
This is a thing you have no power to do.
But if you cannot tell what's in my heart,
At least go to her now and make a start.
Say this: 'Although my will has served me well,
My fear lest I displease forbade me tell
This love so great, this love that should be told,
To you, to God, to all the Heav'ns unrolled.
For its foundation is your virtue fair,
Which makes my cruel torture sweet to bear.
Should not to all this treasure rich and rare
Be shown? To all one's very heart laid bare?
For who could blame a lover in this sort
For having dared admire, desire and court
A Lady in whom all virtue and all grace,
And honour too, do have their rightful place?
No! rather should you blame the man so wrought
That he could see all this, and love her nought.
But I have seen, and love her with such fire
That love with ease has won my heart entire.
Alas, this love is nothing feigned or slight,
Nor based on painted beauty's gaudy light.

This love so great which binds me is, far less,
A passion born of lust or wickedness.
It is not built upon the hope that's vain,
A bare enjoyment of your love to gain.
In this desire of mine there is no kind
Of which to bring displeasure to your mind.
I'd rather die in this strange land afar
Than know you less in virtue than you are,
Than know through me the honour any less
Which gives your soul, and body, goodly dress.
You, who in all the world most perfect art,
Have all my love: therefore my loving heart
Doth only wish Perfection to defend,
Of my affection only cause and end.
For you are good all other things above,
So do I think, and burn with perfect love.
I am not one who in the easy charms
Of Love finds solace, or some mistress' arms.
My Love is of a chaste and moderate mind,
Bestowed upon a Lady of such kind
That neither God nor Angel, seeing you,
Could do ought else but praise you as I do.
And if you cannot give your love to me,
I am content at least that I should be
Your servant true, and my devotion show,
For this you will believe of me, I know,
And length of time at last will prove to you,
That loving you I pay my homage due.
If I have nothing from my Lady fair,
Still am I glad to love, and glad to swear
That truly I ask nothing in return,
Save that you let my heart and body burn
Just for your sake, no matter what the price
Upon Love's altar as a sacrifice.
Believe me, if alive I come to you,
Your servant you will find me, pure and true,
And if I die, a servant dies in me
Such as my Lady never more will see.
So may the waves bear far from out your sight

A servant true, a perfect gentle knight.
My body might the ocean freely take,
But not my heart – there is no power can make
It leave your side, where always it shall stay,
And never seek me more nor steal away.
If I could change some of your heart for mine,
Your heart, so like an angel's, pure and fine,
I would not be afraid to win the fight,
Your heart alone would claim the victor's right.
Then let the future come, whatever will,
The die is cast, and my desire is still
Fixed in her place and never can depart.
Now so that you may better know my heart,
My loyalty, my faith so firm and sure,
This diamond take, a stone that will endure,
To wear on that white hand of yours, I pray,
And give me joy beyond what I can say.
Tell her, O stone: 'A lover sends me here,
Who takes a way that's fraught with doubt and fear,
Who hopes by worthy deeds to gain
Those regions where the perfect virtues reign,
May he one joyous day attain his certain place,
And take that longed for seat in your good grace!'

The lady read the letter through. She was the more astonished at this expression of the captain's feelings as she had never had cause to suspect their existence. She was greatly perplexed as she contemplated the surface of the beautiful big diamond set in its black-enamelled band. For what was she to do with it? All night long she pondered on the matter, and was glad that she had the opportunity to postpone her reply on the grounds that she did not have a messenger. She argued to herself that the messenger who had brought the letter had already suffered sufficiently in his master's service, and that there was no need to upset him by making him the recipient of her sharp reply – a sharp reply which she was fully intending to make, but which she now put off until the captain's eventual return. However, the diamond was an embarrassment. She was not in the habit of wearing jewelry obtained at the expense of anyone other than her husband. But being a lady of good sense, she decided to use the ring to the benefit of the captain's conscience. So she composed a letter, pretending that the writer was a nun from Tarascon, and sent it with one of her servants to the wife whom the captain had deserted. This is how it went:

'Dear Madame, your respected husband passed this way shortly before his embarkation, and, after making his confession and receiving communion like the good Christian he is, he revealed something to me that he had on his conscience. He told me of his sorrow that he had not loved you as much as he ought to have done, and before he left he asked me to send you this letter together with the enclosed diamond. I would ask you to look after this precious stone for his sake, and if God brings him safely home, I assure you that no woman in the world will ever have received such love and care as you will receive. May this stone be a pledge of the sureness of his word. Finally, I would ask you to remember him in your prayers, for I shall certainly remember him in mine for as long as I live.'

The letter was signed as from a nun, and duly sent to the captain's wife. As you may guess, when the old lady saw the letter and the accompanying diamond, she wept, her sorrow mingling with her joy at the thought that her husband, whom she had not seen for so long, loved and cared for her after all. She kissed the ring over and over again, letting her tears fall upon it. She praised God that at the end of her days He had brought back her husband's affection, though she had long accepted that it had gone for ever. To thank the nun for bringing her so much happiness, she wrote a most gracious reply, which she sent back post-haste by the same messenger. When the lady read the letter, and heard her servant's account, she laughed for joy. She had restored the bond of affection between man and wife, and so pleased was she at having disposed of the ring in this profitable fashion, that nothing, no, not the wealth of kings, could have pleased her more.

Shortly after, the news arrived that the captain had been killed. He had been abandoned by men whose duty it was to support him, and his plans had been disclosed by the Rhodians when they should have kept them secret. The result had been that the captain and the men who had made the landing with him had all been killed. Amongst these men there was a nobleman by the name of John, and also a converted Turk, at whose baptism the good lady had been godmother. Both of these men had in fact been appointed by her to assist in the captain's expedition. John had fallen at his captain's side and the Turk had managed to get away by swimming out to the French ships, in spite of the fifteen arrow wounds he had received to his body. It was by this man that the truth about the incident was revealed. There had been a certain nobleman, a man whom the poor captain had believed to be his friend and loyal companion, and for whom, moreover, he had obtained favour from the King and from the most elevated peers of France. No sooner had this man seen the captain set foot on dry land than he had ordered his ships out to sea. When the captain realized that his plans had been discovered and he found himself faced with four thousand Turks, he tried to beat a retreat, as was the correct thing to do. The gentleman in charge of the ships, however, on whom the captain was relying absolutely, could see perfectly well that if the captain was killed, he stood to take over the command of this not inconsiderable force, with all the benefits that such a command would bring. So he turned to his gentlemen officers, and put to them the view that the King's ships and the brave men who sailed in them ought not to be set at jeopardy for the sake of a landing party numbering a mere hundred. The officers were faint-hearted enough to express their agreement. Meanwhile, seeing that the more he called for assistance, the further his support drew off, the captain turned to face the Turks. Although he was up to his knees in the sand, he fought so valiantly that he looked almost as if he was going to beat them off single-handed. The captain's treacherous former companion watched anxiously, though not because he hoped for victory – on the contrary. The captain fought on, but in spite of his valour he now began to lose blood from the arrow wounds he had received from those Turks who had managed to get within bowshot of him. Seeing that these true Christians were weakening, the Turks then charged them with their scimitars. But for as long as God gave them strength the Christian band fought on. To the very end they fought, till at the last the captain called to his side the nobleman John, whom his lady had given him to serve under him, and the faithful Turk also he called to his side. Resting the point of his sword on the ground, he fell to his knees and embraced the cross, saying: 'Lord, into Thy hands I commend the spirit of one who has not feared to lay down his life to glorify thy name.'

Seeing that with these words his master's life was ebbing away, the nobleman John took him and the cross of his sword in his arms, in a desperate attempt to save him. At that moment a Turk came up from behind, and, with a blow of his scimitar, severed his legs at the thighs.

'Come, Captain,' he cried with his dying breath, 'let us fly to Paradise and gaze on the Lord for whose sake we give up our lives!'

Thus was he a faithful companion in death, even as he had been in life. The captain's Turk, realizing that there was nothing now that he could do, managed to drag himself, in spite of his fifteen arrow wounds, towards the ships that were standing off shore. There he was, the sole survivor of the eighty or so who had gone ashore, and his pleas to be taken aboard were rebuffed by the traitor who was now in command. However, being a good swimmer, he plunged into the waves and was eventually picked up by a small boat. He was cared for by his rescuers, and after some time recovered from his wounds. It was through this man, this poor foreigner, that the truth, to the great honour of the captain, and the equally great shame of his former companion at arms, became generally known. The King, and indeed all decent people who heard about what had happened, considered it an outrage towards God and humanity, an outrage so heinous that its perpetrator deserved to suffer the most painful death that could be devised. However, once the man got back, he succeeded, by dint of false assertions and presents offered in the right quarters, in escaping any punishment at all. What is more, he succeeded to the post that had been formerly held by the very man he did not deserve even to serve as lackey.

When this tragic tale reached the court, Madame la Régente, who had held the captain in high esteem, was profoundly affected by his loss, as was the King, and all worthy people who had known him. As for the good lady who had loved him most, when she heard what a moving and Christian end he had endured, the harsh words she had intended were turned to tears and lamentations. In this she was joined by her husband, who was bitterly disappointed at the frustration of his plans to journey to the Holy Land. I must not forget to mention also a certain young woman in the lady's retinue. She had been deeply in love with the nobleman called John, and, on the very day that the two men had been killed, she had come to her mistress to tell her about a dream she had had, in which her beloved John, all dressed in white, had come to bid her adieu before ascending to Paradise in the company of his master, the captain. When she had learned that the dream had come true, her grief was indescribable and her mistress was scarcely able to console her.

Some time later, the court moved to Normandy, which was where the captain came from, and his wife did not neglect to come and pay her respects to Madame la Régente. In order to obtain an audience, she first approached the woman whom her late husband had loved so much. While she was in a church waiting to be presented, the good widow began to talk about her husband, saying how much she missed him and what a good man he had been.

'Alas! Madame,' she said, 'I am the most miserable of women! God took him from me at the very time when he loved me more than he had ever done in his life!'

And as she said this she showed her companion the ring that she wore on her finger as a sign of the perfect love that her husband had borne her, and her tears flowed freely. The lady, in spite of her own sorrow, felt a strong desire to burst out laughing when she saw that her little deception had borne such good fruit. Indeed, so strong was her desire to laugh that she could not bring herself to go through with the presentation, and she handed the captain's widow over to another lady, while she herself went into a side-chapel until she had recovered!

*

'In my opinion, when ladies receive presents like the one which the lady in this story received, it ought to be their fervent wish to turn them to equally good account. They would find that in return they would be filled with the joy that all those who do good receive. And we mustn't accuse this lady of deception. On the contrary, we ought to admire her good sense for putting to good use something that in itself was of no value.'

'Do you mean,' said Nomerfide, 'that a beautiful diamond like that, worth at least two hundred écus, has no value! I can tell you, if that diamond had come into my hands, his wife wouldn't so much have set eyes on it, nor any of his relatives either! If something's given to you, then you have every right to keep it. The man was dead, nobody else knew anything about it, and if she had left well alone, she needn't have made the poor old lady cry!'

'By Heavens! I'm absolutely sure you're right, Nomerfide!' said Hircan. 'Because there are women who'll put on a show of doing good deeds – but it's always against their natural inclinations, and they only do it so as to look superior to other women. We all know that women are greedy and grasping. Even so, their pride often gets the better of their greed, and they end up doing things that in their hearts they don't really want to do. I think that the woman who let that diamond go like that didn't deserve to wear it anyway!'

'Not so fast, not so fast!' interrupted Oisille. 'I have a good idea who this lady really is, and I don't think you should condemn her without hearing her case.'

'Madame,' replied Hircan, 'I'm not condemning her, but if the gentleman in question was as valiant as you say, then it was to her honour that she should have a man like that devoted to her service and wear his ring. But it may have been that there was some other man less worthy of being loved who was hanging so tightly on to her finger that the ring couldn't be put on it anyway!'

'I really think,' said Ennasuite, 'that she could have kept it, seeing that nobody knew anything about it.'

'What's that?' said Geburon. 'Is it permissible for people in love to do anything at all, provided that nobody gets to know about it?'

'To tell you the truth,' intervened Saffredent, 'the only misdemeanour I've ever seen punished is stupidity. The law never caught up with anyone, be he adulterer, thief or murderer, nor did anybody in the slightest blame him, provided his cleverness matched his crime. However, it very often happens that people are so steeped in vice that they are totally blind, and become utterly stupid. As I've already said, it's only stupid people who get punished, not those who do wrong.'

'You may say what you like,' said Oisille. 'God may judge this lady's heart. As far as I'm concerned, I find that what she did was most honourable and virtuous. Let us not pursue the matter any further. Parlamente, I call upon you to choose who shall tell the next tale.'

'I should like to choose Simontaut,' she replied, 'because we've had two sad tales, and I'm sure that he's not one to make us all weep.'

'Thank you very much!' replied Simontaut. 'If that's why I'm chosen to speak, it's almost as good as calling me a clown – and that's not a title I particularly want! However, to get my own back I shall demonstrate to you that there are women who only *pretend* to be chaste, that is, they pretend to be chaste for certain people, or for a certain length of time, but in the end they show what they are really like – as you will see from my story, which is a very true one.'

STORY FOURTEEN

In the Duchy of Milan, during the period when the Grand Maître de Chaumont was governor, there lived a certain gentleman called the Seigneur de Bonnivet, who later earned for himself the rank of Admiral of France. Being a man of exceptional qualities, and consequently much in favour with the Grand Maître and everyone else in Milan, he not infrequently found himself a guest at banquets in the city. He was much sought after by the ladies, who invariably all appeared on these occasions. Indeed, his good looks, his charm, his nimble tongue and his reputation for being the ablest and bravest warrior of his age made him more sought after by them than any other Frenchman before him.

On one occasion when he was going about in a mask at a carnival, he danced with one of the proudest and most beautiful ladies of Milan. Every time the hautboys stopped playing, he would whisper words of love in her ear in his inimitable fashion. She felt no obligation to respond in any way to these advances, and decided to put a stop to them before they went any further by telling him that her husband was the only man she loved, the only man she would ever love, and that he, Bonnivet, was wasting his time if he expected the slightest favour from her. But he was not in the least daunted by this reply and continued to pursue the lady energetically until mid Lent, only to find that her resolve was firm, and that she still insisted that she would not fall in love with him or with anyone else. This he found somewhat difficult to believe, when be compared her considerable beauty with the unattractiveness of her husband. So he made up his mind that if she was going to dissemble, he would employ a little trickery himself, and he promptly ceased making his advances to her. Instead he made discreet inquiries about her private life, and managed to discover that she was actually in love with a very honourable and worthy Italian gentleman.

Little by little Bonnivet insinuated himself into this Italian gentleman's confidence. So subtle was his approach that the man had not the faintest idea what he was up to, and in fact became so fond of Bonnivet that, after his beloved lady, there was no one in the world of whom he could have been fonder. In order to extract the man's secret, Bonnivet pretended to reveal a secret of his own. He told him that he was in love with some lady or other – a lady he had never in fact once given a thought to, and begged him to keep it secret, adding that he hoped that in their friendship their hearts and minds might be one. To show that the friendship was indeed returned, the poor Italian then went and told Bonnivet the whole story about his love for the very lady upon whom Bonnivet was seeking love's revenge. The two men met every day in a quiet spot, so that they could tell one another what had befallen them in the preceding twenty-four hours and whether they had had any good fortune. Bonnivet made it up as he went along, of course, while the Italian told him the truth. In fact the Italian admitted that he had been in love with the lady for three years without receiving from her any concessions at all apart from fair words and assurances that she loved him. So Bonnivet advised him on the means whereby he might achieve his objective, and the advice was so effective that not many days after, the lady consented to grant the Italian everything he desired. It remained only to find some way of meeting, but this, with the expert advice of Bonnivet, was quickly arranged. One day, just before supper, Bonnivet's friend said to him:

'Monsieur, I'm more indebted to you than to any other man alive. Tonight is the night I expect to receive what I have longed for all these years – and all through your excellent advice.'

'Well, my friend,' replied Bonnivet, 'you had better tell me what plans you've made, just to see if there are any risks or traps of any kind, so that I can give you a helping hand if need be, as a true friend should!'

The Italian proceeded to explain how the lady had the opportunity of leaving the front door of her house open, on the pretext that it was necessary to keep sending servants to the town to fetch [drugs and others requisites] for one of her brothers, who was ill. She had told him that it was quite safe to go into the courtyard, though he should not go straight up the main steps, but round by a little staircase on the right. He should then go along the first gallery he came to, on to which the bedrooms of her father-in-law and brothers-in-law opened, take the third door from the stairs and try it gently. If it was closed, he should go away again, since that would mean that her husband had come back, although she did not in fact expect him for another two days. If, however, the door opened, he could go in quietly and bolt it firmly behind him, since there would be no one there but herself. She had also insisted that he must get some felt shoes made, so that he would not make any noise, and that he must not come before two hours after midnight, because her brothers-in-law, who were given to gambling, never retired till after one o'clock in the morning.

'I wish you God speed, my friend,' said Bonnivet. 'I'll pray to Him that you don't run into any trouble. If it would be of any help for me to come with you, I would gladly do so. There's nothing in my power that I wouldn't do for you!'

The Italian thanked him heartily, but told him that in a matter like this one could not be too much alone, and so saying he went off to get himself ready.

The Seigneur de Bonnivet did not go to bed that night. The time had come to take his revenge on the lady who had treated him so cruelly. He went back early to his residence, where he had his beard trimmed so that it was the same length and shape as the Italian's. He had his hair cut, too, so that to the touch at least it was indistinguishable from that of his rival. Nor did he forget the felt slippers, and other details of clothing that were like the Italian's. He had no qualms about going to the lady's house early, since he was on good terms with her father-in-law, and he considered that if he was seen, he could simply go straight to the good fellow's room to discuss a piece of business they had to settle. So, as midnight struck, Bonnivet went into the lady's house. There were still quite a few people coming and going, but he passed unrecognized through their midst, and made his way to the gallery. He tried the first two doors. They were locked. But the third door was not, and he gently pushed it open. Once inside he bolted it behind him. He found the whole room draped in pure white, flooring and ceiling as well as the walls. There was a bed, too, with a canopy of fine linen, also pure white, and decorated with the most beautiful embroidery. In the bed lay the lady, alone, her dainty cap and nightdress adorned with pearls and precious stones. A huge white wax candle was burning and the room was as light as day. He took in the whole scene through a chink in the curtain. So far he had not been seen, but lest he be recognized, he quickly snuffed the candle. Then he took off his clothes and got into bed with his lady. She, thinking it was the man who had loved her so long, welcomed him with open arms. He, however, knowing perfectly well that all this was for the sake of another man, took care not to utter a word. He was bent only on revenge – [to take her honour and her chastity, without obligation or gratitude on his part, and without will, forethought or intention on hers.] But the revenge was sweet to the lady, and she was happy to let it continue till one o'clock, when she deemed that her lover was sufficiently rewarded for his labours. Then it was time to say adieu, and Bonnivet, in as low a voice as he could manage, asked if she was as content with him as he was with her. She, thinking it was her Italian paramour, replied that not only was she very happy, but also that she was amazed to find he loved her so much that he had not spoken a word for a whole hour. Bonnivet burst out laughing at this, and said: 'Well now, Madame, are you going to turn me down yet again, as you've been doing up to now?'

She recognized him at once from his voice and the way he laughed, and was overcome with shock and shame. 'Traitor! Impostor! Villain!' she yelled at him over and over again, as she struggled to get out of the bed. It was in her mind to get a knife and stab herself to death, to release herself from the miserable fate of having lost her honour to a man whom she did not even love, a man who, moreover, for the sake of revenge would be quite capable of divulging the episode to the whole world. But he held her tight in his arms, and spoke to her gently, vowing that he loved her far more than the other man, that he would conceal everything that concerned her honour and that he would be so careful that not the slightest blame would attach to her name. The poor silly woman believed all this, and when she further heard from Bonnivet how ingenious and painstaking he had been in his plan to win her, she swore that she would love him more than the other man! After all, *he* had not even been able to keep the secret. Moreover, she now knew that what people said about the French was not true. Frenchmen were evidently not only cleverer, and more persistent than the Italians, but also more discreet. So she would have nothing more to do with what her fellow-Italians thought. She would stick to Bonnivet. She did, however, insist that for a while at least he should not appear at banquets or on any other occasion where she might be present, unless he was in disguise, for she knew that otherwise she would be so embarrassed that everybody would see her disgrace written all over her face. He gave her his word, and for his part insisted that when his friend came to her at two o'clock she should accord him the same favours as he had received. Later on she could gradually release herself from the attachment. She was very reluctant to agree to this, and would have refused outright, had it not been for the love she had now conceived for Bonnivet. At this point he took his leave, and the way he did it made her so satisfied that she would gladly have kept him there still longer!

He got out of the lady's bed, dressed himself and left the room, leaving the door ajar as he had found it. It was already nearly two o'clock, and, worried in case he met his Italian friend on the way to his tryst, he waited at the top of the staircase, until, not many minutes later, he saw him go into his lady's bedroom. He then went straight back to his house to recover from his exertions, and slept so soundly that he was still asleep in bed at nine o'clock the next day. While he was getting up, the Italian arrived to tell him all about the night's adventures. It had not, he told him, been so successful a night as he had hoped. When he had gone into the lady's room he had found her out of bed wearing her dressing-gown. She had a high fever, her pulse was racing, her face was flushed and she was starting to break out in a sweat. Her condition had been so bad that she had asked him to go away again at once, saying that she had not dared call her women, for fear of being found out, [though she felt] so ill that her thoughts were more on God and Death than on Love and Cupid. She was very sorry, she had said, that he had taken the risks he had for her sake, for she had no power in this world to surrender to him that which she feared she was soon to surrender to the next. He had been so surprised and upset at this that all his joy and all his fire had turned to ice and to sorrow, and he had left his lady's bedroom without more ado. At daybreak he had sent for further news of her condition, and he had received word that she was indeed very ill.

As he told his sorry tale, the Italian wept bitterly, so bitterly you would have thought his soul was about to flow out with the tears. Bonnivet, as much disposed to burst out laughing as his friend was to weep, consoled him as best he could. He told him that it is always rather difficult at the beginning when one has been in love for so long, and that the God of Love had only brought about this setback in order that his enjoyment should be increased later on. And on this note they parted.

The lady kept to her bed for a few days longer. When she recovered her health she dismissed her Italian, who had so long devoted himself to her service, her excuse being the fright she had had in the face of death, and the pangs of conscience that she was now experiencing. She gave herself entirely to Bonnivet, whose love, as usual, endured even as flowers of the field in their beauty endure!

*

'If you ask me, Ladies, the man's ingenuity was a match for the lady's hypocrisy, and hypocrisy it was, since she played hard at being an honest women, only to show that underneath she was a wanton.'

'Say what you like about women,' said Ennasuite, 'but the man played a mean trick. If a woman is in love with one man, does that make it alright for some other man to take her by trickery?'

'Take my word for it,' observed Geburon, 'you can't put goods like that up for sale without their being carried off by the highest bidder! Please don't think that men pursue ladies and take so much trouble just for *their* sakes – actually, they only do it for their own, and for the pleasure they get out of it!'

'Quite!' said Longarine. 'I'm sure that what you say is true. The fact is that every man who's ever wanted to be *my* devoted servant has always started by declaring that my life, my welfare and my honour were all he truly desired. But in the end it's always their own interests that count, only their own pleasure and their own glory that they really desire. Consequently, the best thing to do is to get rid of them before they've finished the first part of their speech. If one waits till they get into the second part, there is less honour in refusing them, for vice should be rejected as soon as it's recognized.'

'So,' said Ennasuite, 'as soon as a man starts to open his mouth, you ought to turn him down without even knowing what he's going to say?'

'That's not what my companion means,' said Parlamente. 'It's well known that when a man begins to speak, a lady should not let it appear that she understands what he is driving at; nor should she admit to believing him when he comes to the point. When he starts to swear on his oath, however, I think it's more becoming for a lady to leave him to continue that particular route alone, rather than accompany him down to the valley, so to speak.'

'But must we then take it that they only love us for bad reasons?' asked Nomerfide. 'Is it not a sin to judge one's neighbour?'

'You may believe what you please on this point,' said Oisille, 'but it is to be feared that what has been said is very much the case, so much so, indeed, that as soon as you see a spark you should flee from the fire immediately. It is a fire that has burnt more than one heart before it has even been noticed.'

'Really,' said Hircan, 'these laws you lay down are far too harsh! If women *were* as harsh as you want them to be, when it becomes them so well to be soft and gentle, we men would just have to give up submitting meek requests and turn to trickery and violence.'

'The best thing in my view,' said Simontaut, 'would be for everyone to follow his natural disposition. Whether you're in love or whether you're not in love, show it without dissimulation!'

'Would to God,' added Saffredent, 'that that law brought as much honour as it would pleasure!'

At this Dagoucin could not keep silent, and said: 'But those who would rather die than have their feelings known could not submit to this ordinance of yours.'

'Die!' exclaimed Hircan. 'A knight who'd consent to die for a cause like that has yet to see the light of day! Let's stop talking about impossibilities, and see who Simontaut will choose to tell the next story.'

'I choose Longarine,' replied Simontaut. 'I noticed a moment ago that she seemed to be talking to herself. I think she was rehearsing a piece for us. She's not in the habit of concealing the truth from anyone, man or woman, so it is she I choose to speak next.'

'Since you regard me as such a truthful person,' said Longarine, 'I'll tell you a story, which, although it doesn't praise women as much as I'd like, does, as you will see, show that there are women who are just as courageous, just as intelligent and just as shrewd as men. If it is a little long, I ask you to bear with me.'

STORY FIFTEEN

At the court of Francis I there lived a certain gentleman, a gentleman whom I know well, but whose name I prefer not to tell you. He was poor. He did not have five hundred livres a year to live on. But the King was very fond of him on account of his many excellent qualities, and he ended up marrying a woman rich enough to do justice to the highest lord of the land. As his wife was still only a young girl, the gentleman asked one of the greatest ladies of the court to take her into her household, which the lady in question gladly did. The gentleman himself was endowed with such good looks, such nobility, such charm and grace, that he was held in high esteem by the ladies at court, and in particular by one who happened at that time to be the object of the King's own affections. With this lady our handsome gentleman was passionately in love, though she was neither as beautiful nor as young as his own wife, of whom he took so little notice, that scarcely one night in a whole year did he sleep with her. What was even more insufferable to the girl was the fact that he never spoke to her or showed the least sign of affection. Moreover, although he drew on her wealth for his own pleasures, he gave her such a small share in it that she was not able to dress as she wished, or even as her station required. The lady in whose household she resided often complained to the husband about this state of affairs.

'Your wife is rich, beautiful and of good birth,' she would say, 'yet you treat her just as if she were the very opposite. So far she has put up with all this, being little more than a child, but I am afraid that when she grows up, and her mirror tells her how beautiful she really is, someone with little love for you will come along who will tell her the same thing. You have thought but little of her beauty, and I fear that in her resentment she will do things that she would never dare even to think about if she had been well treated by you.'

But the gentleman's heart was set on other things, and remonstrate as she might, he merely laughed at her and carried on as before.

Two or three years passed by, and the young wife began to turn into one of the most beautiful women in all France. It was said that no other woman at court could match her. The more she realized that she deserved to be loved, the more she became upset at her husband's lack of consideration for her. So distressed did she become, in fact, that had it not been for the efforts her mistress made to console her, she would almost have despaired. She tried everything in her power to win him round. How could it be possible, she asked herself, that he [did not] love her, when *she* loved *him* so dearly? In the end there seemed to her to be only one explanation – that his head had been turned by some fancy for another woman. She investigated this possibility with great shrewdness, until she eventually learned the truth. Every night he was occupied elsewhere. He had quite forgotten both his conscience and his duty to his wife.

Now that she knew for certain the kind of life her husband was leading, she sank into such a deep melancholy that she refused to wear anything but clothes of black and shunned all kinds of merrymaking. When her mistress noticed this, she did everything she could to draw her out of this gloomy frame of mind. But to no avail. The husband, although the situation was made abundantly clear to him, was more inclined to laugh at it than to do anything to remedy it.

Well now, as you know, Ladies, just as the heights of happiness may give way to tears, so the depths of misery may end in transports of joy. Thus it was that a certain noble lord of high estate, who was a close relative of the lady's mistress, and a frequent visitor, came to hear of the outlandish way the husband behaved towards her. He felt so sorry for her that he made an attempt to console her, and as he talked with her he was so struck by her goodness, her beauty and her modest demeanour, that he became rather more concerned to win her favour than to talk about her husband, except to show her what little cause she had to have any affection for the man. As for the lady herself, there she was, on the one hand abandoned by the very man who ought to have loved her, and on the other hand sought after and loved by a handsome prince, so it was hardly surprising that she felt overjoyed at having won his favour. Although she was concerned always to preserve her honour, nevertheless, starved as she was of love and consideration, she took the greatest delight in talking to him, and basking in his love and admiration. This tender friendship lasted for some time, but was eventually noticed by the King, who, being extremely fond of the lady's husband, was not prepared to let anybody cause him the least distress or disgrace. So he urged the prince to rid himself of his infatuation, and told him that if he did not, he was likely to incur royal displeasure. The prince was far more anxious to win the King's favour than he was to win all the favours of all the ladies in the world, so he promised that for the King's sake he would abandon his designs, and that he would go that very evening and take his leave of the lady.

True to his word, he went to the lady's house as soon as he was sure she had returned. As usual in the evening the husband was sitting at his window, so he saw the prince go into his wife's room, which was just beneath his own. But the prince, though he knew he had been seen, was not deterred. Once in her room, he told the fair lady, whose love was only beginning to blossom, that he was saying goodbye. The sole reason, he told her, was that he had been ordered to do so by the King himself. Till an hour after midnight the lady wailed and wept. Then by way of a parting speech she turned to him and said:

'Monseigneur, I give thanks to God that you no longer have the feelings you had before, for they must be weak indeed if you can pick them up and put them down again upon the orders of mere mortals! *I* asked permission neither from my mistress, nor from my husband, nor from myself, when I fell in love with you. It was Love alone, with the help of your handsome appearance and your charm, that had such authority over me that I recognized no other God and no other King. But since *your* heart is not so overflowing with love that all fear is banished from it, you cannot be a perfect lover, and I have no desire to take one who is imperfect, and make him, as once I was resolved to do, a lover loved with perfect love. So, Monseigneur, since you are too craven to deserve my true affection, I say farewell!'

And the noble lord went off in tears. [On his way out he noticed the husband watching again at the window,] so the next day he went to explain to him why he had been to see his wife, and what the King had ordered him to do. The gentleman was very gratified to hear all this, and thanked the King. However, seeing his wife growing daily more beautiful, while he was getting older and losing his good looks, he began to change his role. It was his turn now to play the part he had imposed on his wife for so long, for he spent more time with her than he had hitherto, and kept a constant watch on her actions. But the more he followed her about, the more she kept out of his way, since she had conceived a desire to pay him back for the sorrows that his lack of love had brought her in the past. What is more, she was beginning to learn the pleasures of love, and had no desire to be deprived of them so soon. So she made advances to a young nobleman. He was a very good-looking young man, very elegant, very nimble with his tongue, and consequently much adored by all the ladies at court. She bemoaned her lot to him, telling him how badly she was treated, and he was so moved by her tale that he left no stone unturned in an attempt to comfort her. In order to make up for the loss of her prince, she set about falling in love with this young man with such passion that she eventually got over her earlier disappointment. She no longer had any other concern than to carry on her new intrigue with as much finesse as possible. So careful was she, that her mistress, in whose presence she scrupulously avoided addressing the young man, suspected nothing at all. But when she did want to talk to him, she would go off to see some of the other ladies who resided at court, amongst whom there happened to be one with whom her husband was affecting to be in love.

One evening after supper, she slipped off in the dark on her own, and went straight to the ladies' chamber, where she met the man she loved more than life itself. She sat by his side, and, leaning over the table as if they were reading a book together, they chatted intimately. The husband, however, had set someone to watch her, and her whereabouts were soon reported back to him. Being a cautious man he said nothing, but made his way to the scene as fast as he could. He saw his wife sitting there reading as soon as he went into the room, but pretending not to have noticed her, he went straight over to the ladies on the other side. The poor wife, realizing that her husband had discovered her with a man to whom she had never spoken in his presence, was so unnerved that she completely lost her head. Unable to move along the bench, she jumped over the top of the table, as if her husband was after her with a naked sword, and went to find her mistress, who was just retiring for the night. Then she too undressed and retired, but one of her women arrived with a message to say that her husband was demanding her. She replied outright that she had no intention of going to him; he was so hard and cruel that she was afraid he might actually do her some harm. In the end, however, she did decide to go to him, for fear that worse might happen if she did not. The husband spoke not a word when she came in. [But she, not so good at dissembling as he was, started to cry as soon as they were in bed.] When he asked what was the matter with her, she replied that she was afraid he might be angry with her because he had found her reading a book with a gentleman. To this he answered that he had never forbidden her to speak to any man, and that he found nothing wrong with her talking to that one. What he did find suspicious was the way she had run off when she had seen her husband, as if she really was doing something reprehensible. And it was this alone, he said, which led him to think that she was in love with this particular gentleman. Consequently he was going to forbid her ever to speak to him again, either in private or in public. The first time he should catch her doing so, he warned her, he would kill her without pity or compassion. This she was ready to accept, resolving not to be so foolish a second time. But to forbid something is the surest way to make it even more ardently desired, and it was not very long before the poor young wife had forgotten her husband's threats, as well as the promises she herself had made. Indeed, that very evening, having gone back to sleep in another room with the other young ladies and their attendants, she sent word to her young gentleman that he was to come and see her during the night! But the husband, so racked by jealousy that he cannot sleep, gets up, dresses himself in a cloak, and calls a valet de chambre to accompany him. This, so he had heard, was how his rival equipped himself for his nocturnal visits. Then off he goes to his wife's quarters, and knocks at the door. She gets up, puts on the furry shoes and wrap lying by her side, and, seeing that the three or four women she had with her were asleep, goes alone out of the room straight to the main door. Her husband was the last person she expected to find there.

'Who is it?' she called out.

A voice replied, giving the name of the young man she was in love with. But to make certain, she opened a grating in the door, saying:

'If you're who you say you are, let me feel your hand, and I shall recognize it.'

As soon as she touched the hand, she knew it was her husband's. She slammed the grille shut, shouting, 'Ah! Monsieur, it's *your* hand!'

He was beside himself with rage.

'Yes, it is indeed my hand!' he shouted. 'And by this hand I shall keep my promise! Therefore do not fail to come when I command you!'

With these words he went back, and she, more dead than alive, returned to her room.

'Get up! Get up!' she shouted to her attendants. 'You have slept too long! I thought I was going to outwit you, but instead it is I who have been outwitted!'

As she spoke she fell in a faint in the middle of the room. The poor women scrambled out of bed, astonished to hear their mistress talking like that, and then to see her collapse on the floor as if she were dead. There was nothing to do but to run and find some means of reviving her. When she came round and could speak again, she said: 'My dear friends, the woman you see before you is the most miserable creature in all the world!'

Then she told them what had befallen her, and begged them to give her their help, for she thought that she was already as good as dead. As they were trying to console her, one of her husband's valets de chambre came in with the order that she was to appear before him at once. She threw her arms round two of her women, screaming and crying, and beseeching them not to let her go, for she was sure she would be going to her death. But the valet de chambre assured her that she would be alright, and that he would answer for her safety with his own life. She saw there was no way out, and threw herself into the poor servant's arms, saying, 'Since it must be so, bear this, my wretched body, unto death!'

In her despair she almost fainted, and the valet de chambre had to carry her bodily to his master. The poor lady fell at his feet, saying: 'Monsieur, I beg you to have pity on me. I swear to you, by the faith I owe to almighty God, that I will tell you the whole truth.'

'By God!' he replied, beside himself with rage, 'tell me you certainly shall!'

He then ordered all his servants out of the room. Knowing that his wife had always been devout, he felt that she would not dare to perjure herself if she was made to swear by the true cross. So he had a cross sent for, a particularly fine specimen which he happened to have in his possession, and when they were alone again, he made her swear on it that she would tell the truth in reply to his questions. But having overcome her initial fears of death, she took courage, and while resolving not to conceal the truth before she died, she also resolved to say nothing which might cause the young gentleman she loved to suffer. So, having listened to her husband's questions, she replied thus.

'It is not my intention, Monsieur, to justify my love for the young gentleman who has roused your suspicions, or to make light of it. After the evidence you have had of it today you would not be able to believe me, nor is there any reason why you should. But I do wish to explain to you how this friendship came about in the first place. You know, Monsieur, that no wife ever loved her husband as dearly as I did. From the day I married you until my present age, my heart knew no love but my love for you. You know, too, that when I was still only a child, my parents were anxious for me to marry a man who was much richer than you, and of higher birth. But from the moment I met you, I could not agree to their plans for me. In opposition to their wishes, in spite of your lack of means and in spite of the way everyone criticized me for what I was doing, I insisted on having you and you alone. Nor can you be exactly ignorant of the way you have treated me since we were married, of the way you've failed to show me any love and respect! I've been so wretched, so miserable, that if it hadn't been for the lady who has looked after me, I would have sunk into the depths of despair. But then I grew up. Everybody – except you – considered me beautiful. I began to be so acutely aware of the wrong you had done me that instead of loving you as I did before, I began to hate you. Before I had longed to do your bidding, now my longing turned into a desire for revenge. This was the desperate state I was in when I was found by a certain prince. And then, just as this honourable love was beginning to give me some relief from all my sufferings, he left me too, because he preferred to obey the dictates of the King rather than the dictates of Love. After he had left me, I met this other man. There was no need for him to approach me. He was handsome, refined, charming. He had manly qualities that made him sought after by every woman with any discernment. It was because I sought his love, not because he sought mine, that he came to love me with a love that was pure and virtuous. Never once did he demand of me anything that honour could not have granted. Although I had little enough reason to give you my love and had every excuse to break my loyal vows, the love which I have for God and for my honour have prevented me till now from doing anything that I need to confess or be in any way ashamed of. I don't deny that I went to talk to him as often as I could in a private room. I used to pretend I was going there alone to say my prayers, because I trusted no one, neither man nor woman, to assist me in this matter. I don't want to deny, either, that when I was alone with him in that intimate room where nobody could suspect us I often kissed him, and kissed him more gladly than I do you. But may I answer to God, if anything more than that ever passed between us, or if he ever demanded more, or if I ever had the slightest desire that he should do so. It gave me joy just to see him. I could have imagined nothing in the world more pleasurable. Now, Monsieur, do you intend, after being the sole cause of all my misery, to take revenge on me for the very kind of thing of which you yourself have been guilty for years – with the difference that the example *you* set was completely devoid of any scruple of honour or conscience? You know, and I know, that the woman you love doesn't content herself with what lies within the commands of God and reason. However, although the law of men attaches dishonour to women who fall in love with those who aren't their husbands, the law of God does not exempt men who fall in love with women who aren't their wives. Suppose that what each of us has done is weighed in the balance. There are you, a mature man with experience of the ways of the world, who ought to be able to tell right from wrong. There am I, young and with no experience of the violence and the power of love. You have a wife who wants to be with you, who admires you and loves you more than life itself. And what have I got? A husband who keeps out of my way as much as possible, who hates me and despises me more than if I were a humble chambermaid. You are in love with a woman who's already getting on in years, a shapeless creature far less beautiful than I, while my love is for a gentleman who's younger than you, more handsome than you and more worthy to be loved than you! Furthermore, this woman you're in love with is the wife of one of the closest friends you have and at the same time the mistress of your monarch, so that you violate the duty that you owe to both of them, betraying not only the bond of friendship, but also the obligation of respect and esteem; whereas the young man whom I love is under no bond, except the bond of love, the love that he bears for me. Well then, judge without bias. Which of the two of us most deserves to be punished, and which of us most deserves to be excused? Is it you, or is it I? Is it you, the man considered experienced and wise, who not only shamefully wrongs his wife, although she never gave him the least provocation, but also wrongs his King, to whom he owes his loyalty? Or is it I, the young and innocent girl, rejected and despised by you, who loves the finest and most honourable man in all France, and who loves him only because she despaired of ever being loved by you?'

The husband was overcome by these words, words so obviously full of truth, spoken from the lips of this beautiful woman, and spoken with such confident grace and bold assurance that it was evident she neither feared punishment nor considered she deserved it. So overcome was he that he did not know what to say, except that men's honour and women's honour were not the same thing. However, since she had sworn that there had been nothing [sinful] between her and the young man, it was not his intention to punish her further, provided that she did not see him again, and provided that both of them forgot all about the past. This she promised, and thus reconciled the two of them went to bed together.

The next day an elderly lady who attended the wife, and who had been extremely anxious for her mistress's life, came to her as she was rising, and asked: 'And how are you, Madame?'

'My dear,' replied the wife, laughing, 'I have the best husband in all the world. He believed everything that I swore to him!'

For the next five or six days the husband kept her under such close observation that she was spied on night and day. But guard her as he might, he could not stop her meeting her young man in some dark and [secret] corner. In fact she kept the affair so well concealed that there was not a man or woman in the place who could have guessed the truth. However, some servant or other spread a rumour that he had found a young lady and gentleman in the stable underneath the room occupied by the wife's mistress, and the husband became so suspicious at this report that he finally made up his mind to have the young man murdered. He called together a large number of relatives and friends with the intention of having him killed, if they could catch him in some [out-of-the-way] place. But the foremost of the relatives happened to be a great friend of the young man himself, with the result that instead of helping to take the intended victim by surprise, he actually warned him of all [the moves that were being made] against him. In any case the young man was so well liked at court and always surrounded by so many people that he was not at all afraid of his enemy's superior forces, and was in fact never [caught]. Moreover, he managed to go to a church to meet the Princess, who was the mistress of the lady he loved, and who had learned nothing of what had passed between the couple, since neither had so much as spoken to the other in her presence. The young gentleman told her that the husband was suspicious of him and full of ill-will, and declared that although he himself was innocent he intended to go to distant parts to escape the rumours that were starting to spread. The noble Princess who had his lady in her charge was astonished to hear this. She swore that the husband was completely in the wrong to suspect his wife, whom she had always known to be a model of virtue and honour. However, because of the husband's high position, and in order to put an end to the malicious gossip, she advised the young man to absent himself for a good while, assuring him at the same time that she personally placed no credence in any of these wild suspicions. Both the young man and his lady were overjoyed that they were still well regarded and still favoured by the Princess, who gave a final piece of advice – that the young man should speak to the husband before leaving, which he duly did.

It was in the gallery, near the King's own chamber, that he came across the husband. He approached him confidently, but with due respect for the man's rank, and said: 'Monsieur, all my life it has been my wish to render you service, yet I learn that for my sole reward you sent people yesterday evening to seize and kill me. I would beg you to bear in mind, Monsieur, that although you may have more power and influence than I have, I am, like yourself, a gentleman, and I should be very disinclined to give up my life for nothing. I would also beg you to bear in mind that you have a virtuous wife, and that if any man dares to assert the contrary, then I shall tell him that he has uttered a wicked lie! As far as I myself am concerned, I do not think I have done anything that ought to give you cause to wish me harm. Therefore, I shall remain your servant, if it so please you, and if it does not, then I remain the servant of the King, and that is sufficient for me!'

In reply to these words the husband said that he had indeed been suspicious of him in the past, but that he considered him an honourable man whose friendship he preferred to his enmity. So saying, he embraced him like a bosom friend, and, hat in hand, bade him adieu. You can imagine what the people who only the night before had been commissioned to murder him said, when they saw him being given such tokens of friendship and respect! They all had something to say about it.

And so the young man set off. Since he was not so well endowed with riches as he was with good looks, his lady presented him with a ring which her husband had given her. It was worth three thousand écus, and he pawned it for one thousand five hundred. Some time after he had left, the husband approached his wife's mistress, the Princess, and asked leave for his wife to go and stay for a while with one of his sisters [in the country.] The Princess thought this request rather curious, and insisted so strongly on being given a reason, that he was obliged to give her a partial, though not a complete, explanation. The young wife took leave of her mistress and the court without shedding a tear or showing any sign of regret. She then went off to the destination desired by her husband under the escort of a young gentleman who had been expressly instructed to keep a careful watch on her. In particular, he was to take care that she had no communication *en route* with the man who was the object of her husband's suspicions. She knew perfectly well what orders her escorts had been given, and every day took great delight in setting them on their guard and then teasing them for not being vigilant.

One day, as they were leaving the inn where they had spent the night, they came across a Franciscan friar on horseback. The lady rode along on her palfrey at his side, and chatted with him from midday till supper-time. When they were within a quarter of a league of their next lodging place, she said to him:

'Father, here are two écus for having been so kind to me this afternoon. I've wrapped them in a piece of paper, because I know you wouldn't dare to touch them with your bare hands! When you leave me will you please make off across the fields, taking care that the men don't see you. It's for your own good, and because of the debt I owe you.'

The Franciscan, pleased with his two écus, galloped off at top speed across the fields. When he was quite a long way off, the lady started to shout out to her attendants.

'A fine lot of servants you are! You are conscientious guards, aren't you! That man you were supposed to watch out for, he's been talking to me all day, and you've not done a thing about it! To think that your master trusted you! Really, it's a good beating you deserve from him, not your wages!'

When the gentleman in charge of her heard this, he was so angry that he could think of nothing to say in reply. He dug in his spurs, called to two of his men, and riding for all he was worth, managed to catch up with the good friar, who saw them coming and did his best to get away. However, being better mounted than he was, they eventually caught the poor man. He had not the faintest idea what it was all about, and begged for mercy. To make his pleas more effective, he pulled his hood off and bared his head. They realized at once that it was not the man they were after, and that their mistress had made fools of them. When they got back, she teased them even more than before.

'So,' she said, 'this is the sort of people they entrust ladies to! They let them talk all day long, without finding out to whom, and then, believing anything they're told, they go and insult the servants of God!'

After teasing them all in this fashion, she went to the place to which her husband had ordered her to be taken, and there her two sisters-in-law and the husband of one of them held her in strict subjection. During this time her husband found out that his ring had been pawned for fifteen hundred écus and was extremely angry about it. In order to save his wife's honour and get his ring back, he told her through his sisters that she was to redeem it, and that he would pay the fifteen hundred écus himself. The wife could not have cared less about the ring itself, since the money was now in the hands of the young man, to whom she promptly wrote a letter explaining that it was her husband who had ordered her to redeem the ring. [And] in order that he should not think that she had done so because of any lessening of her goodwill, she sent him a diamond, which her mistress had given her, and which she prized above any of her rings. The young gentleman willingly sent her the pawnbroker's bond, content to have had the fifteen hundred écus as well as the diamond, the assurance of his lady's favour – although, so long as the husband was alive, he was unable to address a single word to her except in writing. After the husband's death, assuming that she would be true to her word, he lost no time in seeking her hand in marriage, but he found that during his long absence, she had acquired another companion whom she now preferred. His sorrow was so great that he thenceforth shunned all female company, preferring to court danger and risk his life in battle. Thus he ended his days, having won as much esteem as ever a young man could.

*

'Without being in any way lenient to our own sex, Ladies, the point of this [example] is to show all husbands [that women of high spirit are more often] dominated by anger and the desire for revenge than by the [pleasures] of love. The lady in the story was able to resist these emotions for a long time, but in the end was overcome by despair. No good woman should let this happen, because, whatever the circumstances, she should not look for an excuse to act badly. In fact the more excuses she is offered for doing wrong, the more she should prove her virtue by resisting and overcoming evil with good, rather than rendering evil for evil – especially as the wrong one intends to inflict on another person often rebounds on to oneself. Happy are they in whom God manifests the virtues of chastity, gentleness, patience and long-suffering!'

'It seems to me, Longarine,' said Hircan, 'that this lady you've told us about was moved more by resentment than by love, because if she'd loved the young gentleman as much as she pretended, she wouldn't have left him for another man. It follows that she could reasonably be said to be resentful, bitter, vindictive, stubborn and fickle!'

'It's easy for you to talk,' said Ennasuite, 'but you don't know how heart-rending it is to love without having your love returned.'

'True,' he replied, 'because the moment a lady starts to be in the slightest way cold towards me, I forget all about love and all about her as well!'

'That may well be so,' said Parlamente, 'for you. All you care about is your own pleasure. But an honest woman shouldn't leave her husband in that fashion.'

'However,' said Simontaut, 'the woman in the story completely forgot she was a woman for a while, for even a man could not have taken his revenge so well!'

'Because one woman is not virtuous,' said Oisille, 'one should not think that all others are like her.'

'All the same,' said Saffredent, 'you *are* all women. You can cover yourselves up becomingly with all the finery you like, but the fact remains that anyone who looks carefully underneath all those skirts will find that you *are* all women!'

'If we listened to *you* all day,' said Nomerfide, 'we'd never stop arguing. But I'm waiting to hear another story, so I'll ask Longarine if she'll pick the next person to speak.'

Longarine looked at Geburon. 'If you know anything about a virtuous woman,' she said, 'then will you tell us, please?'

'Since I'm called upon to speak on this subject,' he said, 'I'll tell you a story about something that happened in Milan.'

STORY SIXTEEN

During the time when the Grand Maître de Chaumont was governor of Milan, there lived in that city a certain lady who was considered by all to be one of the most virtuous women of her age. She had married an Italian count, but after his death had gone to live as a widow with the brothers of her late husband. She would never hear of remarrying, and her conduct was so proper, indeed so saintly, that there was not a single Frenchman or Italian in the whole of the Duchy of Milan who did not look upon her with considerable esteem. One day, however, her brothers-in-law and her sisters-in-law were holding a banquet in honour of the Grand Maître, and this lady, though a widow and not accustomed to appearing in public, was obliged to be present. When the French visitors saw her they all formed a very high opinion of her elegance and beauty. One man in particular was impressed by her. I shall not tell you his name. Suffice it to say that there was not a Frenchman in all Italy who more deserved a lady's love, for he was as richly endowed with manly graces as ever a gentleman could be. Although he saw that the lady was dressed in black crêpe and remained seated in a corner with the old women, apart from the young people, he was not the man to be daunted by this, or by anything else. So, taking off his mask and leaving the dancers, he went to her side and set about engaging her in conversation. The whole evening he talked with her and the old women, and derived more pleasure from it than if he had been with the youngest and liveliest ladies at the court. Indeed, when the time came for everyone to retire, he found he had enjoyed himself so much that he could hardly believe he had had the time to sit down. As for the lady, although she had heard from him nothing but the light conversation that such occasions call for, she nevertheless knew full well that he was anxious to see more of her. In consequence she resolved that she would be on her guard. Never again would he see her at a banquet or any other public occasion.

The gentleman made inquiries about her habits, and discovered that she often visited churches and monasteries; he would keep such a careful watch on these places that however secret she kept her visits, he would always be there before her, and would linger as long as possible just for the pleasure of gazing upon her. From the rapt way he looked at her on these occasions she could be in no doubt that he was in love with her. Bent on avoiding such attentions, she decided to feign sickness for a while and have mass said at her home. The poor gentleman could scarcely have been more upset at this. There was no way now that he could see his lady. However, after a while, when she thought she must finally have thwarted him, she resumed her customary visits to the local churches. The god of love lost no time in communicating this fact to the French gentleman, and he too resumed his devotions.

He was worried lest she should invent some other means of avoiding him, and that as a result he would not have another opportunity to declare his feelings. So, one morning, in a chapel where the lady had gone to hear mass, thinking she would be hidden from view, he positioned himself at the end of the altar where she was kneeling. She had few attendants with her, and just as the priest was raising the *corpus Domini* above his head, the gentleman turned to his lady, and said softly in a voice quivering with emotion:

'Madame, in the name of Him whom the priest holds even now in his hands, may I be condemned to everlasting damnation, if I lie when I declare that it is you who are the cause of my death. For, though you take from me all means by which I might speak but a word to you, yet you cannot be ignorant of my feelings. For Truth declares to you that it is so by the languor in my eyes and by the deathly pallor of my countenance!'

The lady pretended she could not understand a word of all this.

'The name of God should not be taken in vain,' she said. 'Furthermore the poets say that the gods only laugh at the lying oaths which lovers swear. Therefore women who have any concern for their honour ought not to let themselves be taken in by them or be made to feel sorry for them.'

So saying she got up, and returned to her house.

Anyone who has had similar experiences will readily appreciate how grieved the gentleman was by her words. But his heart was not faint. Better, he felt, to have had a response like that, than not to have declared his feelings at all. His love endured for the next three years, during which time he continued at every available opportunity to woo his lady by writing her letters and sending messengers. But no other reply would she give him. [On the contrary], she fled from him as the wolf flees the wolf-hound! It was not that she hated him; it was more her honour and her reputation that she was afraid for. Aware that this was the real reason, the gentleman only conducted the chase more energetically than ever. In the end, after many a rebuff, much suffering, much torment and much desperation, the lady was moved by his persistence and the evident sincerity of his love to have pity on him. In short she granted him what he had so long desired and so patiently awaited. The time and place were agreed upon, and the gallant Frenchman ventured forth to the lady's house, despite the fact that he thereby put his life in great danger, for she lived there not alone, but with all her family and relatives.

But he was more than a fine figure of a man. He was also cunning, and managed the situation so skilfully that he succeeded in gaining access to the lady's bedroom at the appointed hour. He found her alone, recumbent upon a magnificent bed, and undressed hurriedly so that he could join her. As he did so he heard voices whispering outside the door, and the sound of swords grating against the walls. The widowed lady turned to him, her face deathly pale.

'This is an hour of great peril,' she declared, 'both for your life and for my honour, for I can hear my brothers who have come to kill you! Therefore, I beg you, hide yourself beneath my bed. When they come in and fail to find you, I shall rebuke them severely for alarming me without cause!'

But the gentleman, who had never known fear in his life, replied: 'And who are these brothers, then, that a man of honour such as I should be afraid of them? Were they and their whole breed assembled there, they would not, I am assured, wait for the fourth blow from my sword. So be at ease, lie in your bed, and let me guard the door!'

Winding his cloak round one arm, and brandishing his naked sword, he strode to the door to face the blades whose fearsome rattle dinned his ears. When the door opened there stood a couple of chambermaids with a sword in each hand. So they were the ones who had brought him leaping into action!

'We're very sorry, Monsieur,' they stammered, 'but Madame told us to do it. We won't disturb you any more.'

Seeing that his assailants were mere women, he contented himself with cursing them to Hell and slamming the door in their faces. Thereupon he went back to his lady and lost no time in getting into bed with her. It was hardly a question of fear dampening his ardour, and, completely forgetting to ask her what this rumpus had been all about, he thought only of satisfying his desire. But towards daylight he asked her not only about this latest episode, but also why she had in the past treated him so badly, and made him wait so long.

'My original intention was that I should never fall in love again,' she said, laughing, 'and for a long time after I became a widow I kept my resolution. But from the moment you spoke to me at the banquet, I thought you were such a fine man that I had to change my tune and return your love. All the same, it is true that I have always been guided by honour, and I was quite unable to do anything that would tarnish my reputation. Then, as the stricken deer runs from place to place to relieve its pain but only carries its wounds with it, so I wandered in and out of churches, thinking that I could escape from the man whom I carried with me in my heart. He had proved that he loved me perfectly, reconciling love and honour. But I wanted to be certain that I was giving my heart and my love to a man of honour who was perfect in every way. So I wanted to put you to one last test, and I enlisted the help of my maids. I assure you that if I'd found you so cowardly as to creep under the bed because you were afraid for your life, or for any other reason, I was fully intending to leave you there, get up, go into another room, and have nothing more to do with you! But in the event I've found that you're even more handsome, even more charming and even more valiant than people had told me. Fear had no hold over you, nor did it in the least cool your love for me. So my mind is made up. I shall stay by you for the rest of my days in the full certainty that neither my life nor my honour could be in better hands than in the hands of the bravest and best man in the world, the like of whom I think I have never seen!'

Thereupon, they solemnly swore, as if the will of man were immutable, an oath that they could never keep. Perpetual love was what they promised one another, perpetual love that can neither have birth in the hearts of men, nor have its abode therein. Those women alone know the truth of this who have learned from experience how short is the duration of such promises as these!

*

'And so, Ladies, if you are wise, you will beware us men, even as the deer would beware the hunter if it had understanding. For our one pride and joy, our one true delight, is to see you caught, and to take from you that which you prize more than life itself!'

'What's all this about, Geburon?' said Hircan. 'Since when have you turned preacher? I remember a time when you weren't in the habit of saying that sort of thing.'

'Quite true,' Geburon replied. 'What I've just said goes against everything I've said all my life. But my teeth aren't so strong as they used to be, and I can't chew venison any more, so I want to warn the little does to watch out for the huntsmen! In that way I can in my old age make up for all the wrong things I desired in my youth.'

'Thank you very much, Geburon, for informing us of our interests,' said Nomerfide, 'though I don't think we need be too grateful, because that isn't the way you've talked in the past to [girls] when you were in love with them. It just goes to show that you don't really love us, and don't want anyone else to love us either! I'm sure we're just as virtuous and wise as the girls you used to spend so much time chasing when you were younger. But then, old people are always so self-satisfied, and always think that they were more sensible than anyone born after them.'

'Well, Nomerfide,' he replied, 'when one of your devoted servants deceives you and teaches you all about the wicked ways of men, perhaps you'll believe that what I say is true.'

Then Oisille turned to Geburon and said: 'You have praised highly the valour of this gentleman, but in my opinion he ought rather to have been singled out as an instance of a man who was carried away by the madness of love, which is a force so powerful that it is capable of making the biggest cowards in the world do things that the bravest would think twice about.'

'Madame,' said Saffredent, 'if it weren't for the fact that he considered the Italians were better talkers than doers, I think he would have had good reason to be scared.'

'Yes,' said Oisille, 'if he hadn't had in his heart that fire which consumes fear itself!'

'Since you don't seem to think this man's bravery really deserves our admiration,' said Hircan, 'it sounds to me as if you know of somebody who deserves it more.'

'I admit that the gentleman deserved some praise,' said Oisille, 'but I do know of a man who deserves it more.'

'If that is so, Madame,' said Geburon, 'I beg you take my place and tell us about him.'

'If you regard the gentleman in the last story as a man of valour because he faced the Milanese in order to save his own life and preserve the honour of his lady, what will you think of a man who, not from necessity, but from true and genuine valour, performed the deed I shall now relate to you?'

STORY SEVENTEEN

In the town of Dijon in the Duchy of Burgundy a certain German count entered the service of King Francis I. His name was Wilhelm, and he was of the house of Saxony, a family so closely allied to that of Savoy that in times past the two were as one. This Count was widely regarded as the finest and bravest man in Germany, and was so well received by the King that not only was he accepted in the royal service, but was actually appointed to attend the King personally in his chamber. Now the governor of Burgundy at this time was the Seigneur de La Trémouïlle, who was an old knight and a faithful servant of the King. He was naturally anxious lest any harm should befall his master and was always on the watch for danger. His administration was hedged about by spies who kept him informed of his enemies' activities, and he was so efficient that there was very little he did not know about. Amongst other pieces of information he received a letter one day from one of his friends, revealing that Count Wilhelm had accepted a sum of money and had received promises of more to come, on condition that in some convenient fashion he had the King assassinated. The Seigneur de La trémouïlle duly went and warned the King. He made no secret of it either to the King's mother, Madame Louise of Savoy, who immediately repudiated the family alliance with the German and asked the King to dismiss the man at once. The King, however, asked her not to raise the subject again, maintaining that a man as gallant, noble and honourable as Count Wilhelm could not possibly embark on such a crime. Some time later a further piece of intelligence was provided which confirmed the earlier reports. The governor, burning with zeal for the King's cause as he was, asked royal permission either to get rid of the Count or to take other precautionary measures. But the King expressly commanded him to keep quiet, thinking that he would find some other way of discovering the truth of the matter.

One day the King took the Count on one of his hunting

expeditions, giving him instructions to stay close behind him, and arming himself with a sword, a very fine sword, to be sure, but with no other weapon than that. They followed the deer for a while, and then, when the King could see that his men were some distance off, he turned on to a side track. He was now alone with the Count in the thick of the forest. He turned to him, drew the sword, and said: 'What do think of this? Is it not a beautiful, well-made weapon?' The Count examined the blade from the tip, and replied that he thought he had never seen a better.

'You are quite right to say so,' said the King. 'Now let us suppose that there is some gentleman or other who has decided to try to kill me. Let us also suppose that he knows perfectly well that I possess a strong arm and a stout heart. If he knew as well that I had this sword at my side, I think he'd think twice before proceeding! On the other hand, I'd regard him as wicked indeed if he happened to find himself alone with me, without witnesses, and didn't attempt to carry out his plan!'

With a look of astonishment on his face, the Count replied: 'Sire, the wickedness of such an attempt would indeed be great, but no less great would be the madness of desiring to make it.'

Thereupon the King laughed out loud, sheathed his sword and, hearing the huntsmen approaching, dug in his spurs and galloped off to join them. Having rejoined the party he said nothing to anybody about what had happened. He was certain that Count Wilhelm, valiant and strong though he may have been, was not the man to make such a daring attempt. The Count thought that he had been found out, or at least that he was under serious suspicion, and the next day he went straight to Robertet, the King's secretary of finance, and told him that he had been considering the pay and other benefits he received from the King for his services. They were inadequate, he claimed, to live on for even half the year, and if the King did not double his income, he would be obliged to leave. He concluded by asking Robertet to ascertain the King's intention as soon as possible. Robertet answered that he would see the King about it at once, and that he could hardly do better for him than that. He was in fact only too anxious to take the matter to the King, because he had seen the reports obtained by the governor, La Trémouïlle.

As soon as the King was awake, Robertet laid the matter before him in the presence of Monsieur de La Trémouïlle and Admiral Bonnivet, neither of whom of course knew anything of the King's confrontation with Count Wilhelm in the forest.

'So you want to dismiss Count Wilhelm?' said the King, laughing. 'Well, as you can see, he's dismissing himself! So tell him that if he's not happy with the terms he accepted when he entered my service, terms which many a man of good family has readily accepted in the past, then he should go and see if he can do better elsewhere. I certainly shan't stop him, and shall be only too happy if he finds a position that enables him to lead the life he deserves.'

Robertet was as prompt in reporting back to the Count as he had been in taking his request to the King. The Count replied that he would, with his kind permission, leave forthwith. Having been forced by fear into resigning, he was unable to bear it for another twenty-four hours, and he presented himself as soon as the King was at table, in order to take his leave. He affected extreme regret that circumstances obliged him to leave the King's service and renounce the honour of being in his majesty's presence. He also went to take his leave of the King's mother, who was as glad to bid him farewell as she had once been to welcome him as kinsman and friend. Thus he went back to his own country. The King, seeing how surprised his mother and his courtiers were at this sudden departure, told them how he had given the man a fright in the forest, and how even though he was still innocent of the charge against him, he had been sufficiently afraid to want to leave a royal master whose ways he had not yet come to comprehend.

*

'In my view, Ladies, there can be only one reason why the King was moved to risk his life, alone against a man who was renowned for his prowess. He wanted to get away from the court entourage where no inferior would ever challenge a king to single combat, and he wanted to confront his suspected enemy as an equal, so that he could satisfy himself personally by proving that his heart was true and his courage unswerving.'

'Without a shadow of doubt, [what you say is correct],' said Parlamente. 'For the praises of all the men in the world cannot satisfy a true heart as much as the knowledge that it alone has of the virtues which God has placed in it.'

'Long ago,' said Geburon, 'the Ancients would have said that one cannot enter the Temple of Fame unless one has first passed through the Temple of Virtue. I know both of the people in your story, and I know that the King [justly deserves his reputation.] He is one of the most valiant men in his kingdom.'

'Yes, upon my honour!' said Hircan. 'At the time when Count Wilhelm came to France, I'd have been more afraid of the King's one sword than of *four* Italian blades, even if they were the boldest at the court!'

'We are all agreed,' said Ennasuite, 'that the King's renown is so great that any praise we might offer now could barely do justice to his merits, and the day would soon be gone if we were all to speak on this subject. Therefore, I beg you, Madame, to choose someone to tell us more about the good deeds of men – *if* such a thing is possible!'

'I think,' said Oisille, turning to Hircan, 'that you are so fond of speaking ill of women, that you wouldn't have great difficulty in finding something good to say about men. So will you tell us the next story?'

'That's easy,' he replied. 'Not long ago I was told a tale that was very much to the credit of a certain gentleman. This was a man whose love, long-suffering and loyalty were so praiseworthy that I believe it my duty to prevent them sinking into oblivion.'

STORY EIGHTEEN

My story is about a noble lord of excellent family. He was living in one of the important towns in the kingdom of France, and was studying at the schools there. His desire was to attain that knowledge which is the key to honour and virtue among men of worth. At the age of seventeen or eighteen he was so knowledgeable that one would have thought him a shining example, fit to instruct his fellow-students. However, he was also to become a pupil in the School of Love. Now Love is a subtle teacher, and to ensure that his lessons would be heard and taken to heart, he concealed himself behind the fair eyes and face of a certain lady. She was the most beautiful lady in all the land, and as chance would have it, was in the town at that time for some lawsuit. But before setting about the conquest of the heart of the noble young lord, Love first vanquished the heart of the lady herself, by bringing all his manly perfections before her eyes. For he was indeed so fair of face, so fair of speech, so fair in all his ways that there was not a man in all the land, whatever his station, who could surpass him. Those of you who know how quickly the fire of love spreads when it starts to smoulder in the heart and in the imagination will understand that once Love enters two such perfect subjects, he never stops until he has rendered them obedient to his commands, until indeed he has filled them both so full of his clear light that all their thoughts, all their desires and all their speech are nothing but the blazing forth of his flame. With the timidity of youth, the young lord pursued his desires with the utmost caution. But already the lady was conquered. There was no need of force. Yet Modesty, that persistent companion of ladies, prevented her for a while from showing her feelings. But in the end, the fortress of the heart where Honour dwells was destroyed, and the poor lady gave herself up to that which she had never wished to resist.

In order to test the long-suffering, constancy and love of her servant, she acceded to his demands on one exceedingly difficult condition. If he was able to keep this condition, then she would love him perfectly for evermore. If, however, he were to fail, then he would not possess her for as long as he should live. The condition was this. She would be happy to go to bed with him and to talk with him there. But they were both to keep their nightshirts on, and he was to demand nothing more than her discourse and chaste kisses! The young man, who felt that there was no joy in the world to be compared with that which she was promising him, agreed. Evening came, and the promise was kept. However much she encouraged him, however much he was tempted, he refused to break his word. Purgatory itself could not, he felt, be worse than what he went through that night. Yet so great was his love, so firm was his hope, that he was happy to wait in patience, for he was sure that the eternal love which it had cost him so much to win would in the end be his. So he left her bed without once [asking of her anything that would have gone against his promise.] But the lady was, I think, more astonished than pleased by his upright behaviour, and began to think that either he did not love her as much as he had said, or that he had found her less attractive than he had expected. [Completely disregarding his demonstration of honour, chastity, patience and fidelity,] she decided to put the young man's love to another test before keeping her own promise. To this end, she asked him to approach one of the girls in her entourage, a girl who was extremely attractive and somewhat younger than herself. The idea was that he should make amorous overtures to this young girl, so that people would think it was because of her that he came to the house so often. The young lord, quite certain that his lady loved him as much as he loved her, carried out to the letter everything she ordered him to do. He forced himself for her sake to pursue her young companion, who, seeing what a handsome, gently spoken young man he was, believed his lies rather than the truth, and promptly fell in love with him, thinking he loved her. When the lady realized things had gone as far as this, she decided at last to permit the young man, who was still pressing her to fulfil her promise, to come to her room at one hour after midnight. She had, she told him, tried out his love and tested his obedience so thoroughly that it was only right that she should reward his long and patient wait. There can be no doubt about the joy which her loving and devoted servant experienced.

At the appointed hour he went to his lady's room. But she still wanted to test the strength of his love. So before he arrived, she took the young girl on one side, and said to her: 'I know that there's a certain young gentleman who's in love with you, and I think you are no less passionately in love with him. Well, I feel so sorry for you both, that 'I've decided to give you the opportunity to talk on your own together for as long as you like.'

The girl was so transported, that she could scarcely conceal the love she felt, and said that she could never refuse such a proposal. Following her mistress's advice, indeed her orders, she went to the appointed bedroom, undressed and lay down on the magnificent bed. The door was left half open, and all the candles lit, so that the girl and all her charms could be clearly seen. Then, pretending to go away, the lady herself hid near the bed in a spot where she could not be seen. It was not long before her poor devoted servant arrived, prompt at the appointed hour and fully expecting to find his beloved waiting for him as promised. In he crept, closed the door behind him, took off his gown and his fur-lined shoes, and went over to the bed, thinking to find there his heart's desire. No sooner did he stretch out his arms to embrace the recumbent figure he took to be his lady, than the poor girl, thinking he was all hers, flung her arms around his neck. The expression in her eyes and the passionate words she murmured would have been enough to put the holiest hermit off his paternosters! But prompted by his great love for his lady, the young man recognized both the voice and the face, and jumped out of the bed even faster than he had jumped in, when he realized that this was not the woman for whom he had suffered so long and so deeply!

Angry not only with the girl herself, but also with her mistress, he said: 'I shall not be made other than I am either by your wild desires or by the wicked one who put you here! Seek to be an honest woman, for by no act of mine shall your good name be lost!'

Beside himself with rage, he marched out, and for a long time he did not come back to see his lady. However, Love, who never abandons hope, assured the young gentleman that the longer his constancy was tried and tested, the longer and pleasanter would be the enjoyment in the end. For her part, the lady, who had seen and heard everything, was surprised at the depth and constancy of his love, but it pleased her too, and she was anxious to see him again to ask his forgiveness for the pain she had inflicted in testing him. So at the earliest opportunity she addressed him in tones of such gracious tenderness that he not only forgot all his past torments, but even began to think of them with pleasure. For after all, it was through them that his constancy was honoured at last, and through them that his lady was convinced of his love. From that hour on there were no more obstacles and no more trials, and from his lady he received all that his heart could desire.

*

'Now, Ladies, can you tell me of a woman as constant, as patient and as faithful in love as the man in this story? Anyone who's been through such temptations will find the temptations we are shown in pictures of St Anthony as nothing by comparison. Anyone who can remain patient and chaste when beautiful women offer not only their beauty and their love, but also time, place and opportunity, will surely be virtuous enough to resist every single devil in Hell!'

'It is a great shame,' said Oisille, 'that he did not address himself to a woman who had the same resources of virtue as he. We should then have had the most perfect example of pure and perfect love that has ever been heard of.'

'Tell me,' said Geburon, 'which of the two trials do you think was the most difficult for the young man to bear?'

'I think the second,' Parlamente said, 'because disappointment and resentment are the strongest temptations of all.'

Longarine, however, felt that the first trial was the hardest, 'since he had to overcome Love as well as overcome himself, in order to keep his promise.'

'It is easy for you to talk,' said Simontaut, 'but those of us who know the truth in such matters ought to say what they think. As far as I'm concerned, he acted like an idiot the first time, and like a madman the second. You see, I think that by keeping his promise he only made his lady suffer as much as, or more than, he himself suffered. The only reason she made him make such a promise in the first place was so that she could make herself look more virtuous than she really was. She knew perfectly well that desperate love can't be held back by orders or oaths or by anything else in the whole world. But she wanted to make her vice look virtuous, and to make it appear that she could be won only by acts of virtue nothing less than heroic. The second time, he showed that he was mad to let the girl go, when she was so obviously in love with him and was certainly worth more than the woman he'd made his promise to. What is more, he had a good excuse, given the bitter disappointment he had just experienced.'

Dagoucin objected to this, saying that his opinion was exactly the opposite, and that on the first occasion the young man had shown himself patient, constant and true to his word, while the second occasion showed that in his love he was perfect, true and faithful.

'And how do we know,' said Saffredent, 'that he wasn't one of those referred to in a certain chapter headed *De frigidis et maleficiatis*?* If Hircan had really wanted to sing this man's praises, he should have gone on to tell us how he acquitted himself once he got what he wanted. Then we could judge whether it was his virtue or his impotence that made him so well-behaved!'

'You may be quite sure,' said Hircan, 'that if he'd told me, I wouldn't have kept it back, any more than I have the rest of the story. But knowing him as well as I do, and knowing what his temperament is like, I shall always take the view that he acted the way he did because of the power of his love rather than because of frigidity or impotence.'

'Well,' Simontaut replied, 'if he was the kind of man you say, then he ought to have broken his oath. After all, even if she had got annoyed at a little thing like that, it wouldn't have been too difficult to calm her down again!'

'But perhaps she didn't want him to do it just then?' said Ennasuite.

* Reference to the Decretals of Gregory IX, Liber iv, Titulus xv: *De frigidis et maleficiatis, et impotentia coeundi* ('On men who are impotent and under magic charms, and on the inability to copulate').

'So what? Wasn't he strong enough to force her,' Saffredent said, 'seeing that she led him on?'

'Holy Mary!' exclaimed Nomerfide. 'That's a fine way to talk! Do you think that's the way to win the favour of a lady you believe to be chaste and virtuous?'

'In my opinion,' said Saffredent, 'when a man desires that sort of thing from a woman, the greatest honour he can do her is to take her by force. Because, however humble a girl may be, she will want you to beg and beseech over and over again. There are others who have to be given a lot of presents before you can win them round. [Others are so stupid that they let themselves go at the slightest trick or guile, and with them it's merely a matter of finding the right method.] But when you're faced with one that's too sensible and good to be tricked, and too well-behaved to be won round by presents and talk, is one not justified in trying every possible means of conquering her? Whenever you hear that a man's taken a woman by force, you can take it from me that the woman in question must have deprived him of all hope of success by other means. You shouldn't think the worse of a man who risks his life like that in order to give vent to his love.'

Geburon started to laugh. 'I've often seen places besieged and taken by storm,' he said, 'because neither threats nor offers of money could persuade the defending forces to parley, for they say that once you engage in talks, you're already half defeated!'

'It would seem that all the love-affairs in the world are based on the kind of wicked passion [that Simontaut and Saffredent have just been talking about]!' said Ennasuite. 'But there *are* people who have been in love, and loved long and constantly, without having those motives.'

'If you know a story about somebody like that,' said Hircan, 'then I hand over to you for the next one.'

'I do know such a story,' she replied, 'and shall be only too happy to tell it to you.'

STORY NINETEEN

In the time of the Marquis of Mantua, who had married the sister of the Duke of Ferrara, there was in the Duchess's household a lady-in-waiting by the name of Paulina. She was deeply beloved of a certain gentleman in the service of the Marquis. People marvelled at his attachment to Paulina, for, though poor, he was a man of valour, and one would have expected him, in view of his master's great liking for him, to have sought a match with a lady of means. But in his eyes Paulina was worth all the treasure in the world, and it was she alone whom he desired to marry and make his own. The Marchioness wanted to use her influence to bring about a better marriage for Paulina and did her best to deter her from marrying the gentleman who loved her so much, and often stopped them talking together. They would, she warned them, be the poorest and most miserable wretches in the whole of Italy if their marriage took place. But the gentleman could not be convinced by such arguments as these. For her part Paulina disguised her love as best she could – but dreamt about it none the less. Thus they continued in their love, living in the hope that one day their fortunes would improve.

During this time war broke out, and the gentleman was taken prisoner along with a Frenchman, who had left his love at home in France, just as he had left his in Italy. Finding that they were companions in the same misfortune, the two men began to tell one another their secrets. The Frenchman confessed that his heart too was captive, though he did not name its captor. He knew already that his comrade was in love with Paulina, for he too was in the service of the Marquis, and he urged him, as a friend concerned for his interests and well-being, to abandon this infatuation. The Italian gentleman of course swore that it was not within his power to do so. He said that if the Marchioness did not let him marry his beloved in recompense for his sufferings in captivity and all his other services, then he would become a Franciscan friar and serve no other master than

God. His comrade could not believe this, for, apart from his devotion to Paulina, the Italian gentleman did not seem to him to show the slightest sign of monastic piety. Nine months later the Frenchman was set free, and succeeded in obtaining the subsequent release of his comrade, who then immediately approached the Marquis and Marchioness and pursued the matter of his marriage to Paulina for all he was worth. But he had no success. They constantly reminded him that if he and Paulina were to marry they would have to live in poverty. Moreover, neither his family nor hers were in favour of the match, and they forbade him to speak to her in the hope that his infatuation would vanish if he was deprived of all means of meeting her. He realized that he had no alternative but to obey. So he asked the Marchioness if he might say farewell to Paulina, promising that he would never thereafter speak to her again. Permission was granted, and he immediately went to Paulina and began [the following speech]:

['I can see,] Paulina, that both Heaven and earth are against us and desire not only that we should not marry, but that we should not even see one another and talk together. The orders of our master and our mistress are harsh indeed. Well might they boast that by uttering one word they have wounded two hearts, two hearts in two bodies that cannot now but languish unto death, and thus do our cruel master and our cruel mistress show that neither Love nor Pity ever entered their breasts. Their wish, I know, is that we should make rich marriages elsewhere, for they do not know that true riches are to be found in happiness alone. So badly have they treated me, so much grief have they caused me, it is impossible that I should any more do them service with a cheerful heart. If I had not mentioned marriage, I believe they are not so scrupulous that they would have prevented me meeting and talking with you. [But] I would sooner die than demean my love and, after having loved you with a love that is noble and good, [seek] to have that which I would defend against all others. Therefore, since to continue to be able to see you would be a penance too hard to bear, and since not to see you would fill my heart, which can never stay empty, with a despair that would bring me to a miserable end, I have resolved, and my resolve has long been firm, that I shall enter the religious life. It is not that I do not know well enough that all men can be saved, whatever their condition, but my wish is to have leisure to contemplate the divine Goodness, who will I hope take pity on my youthful faults and change my heart, that I may come to love spiritual things as I have loved those which are temporal. If God grants me [this grace], it shall be my continual occupation to pray for you. And I beg you, in the name of this true and faithful love that is ours, to remember me in your devotions and to pray to Our Lord that He will give me as much constancy when I cease to see you as He gave me contentment when I was able to look upon you. My whole life I have lived in the hope that one day I would through marriage to you have that which honour and conscience allow, but now that I give up that hope, now that I can never expect that you will treat me as a wife treats a husband, I beseech you that you treat me as a brother, and permit me to kiss you.'

Perceiving how deeply he was suffering, and yet how honourably even in the midst of such despair he contented himself with such a modest request, poor Paulina, who had always been severe, answered nothing, but threw her arms about his neck, weeping bitterly. So violent were her tears, that her voice, her faculty of speech and all her strength left her, and she fell into a faint in his arms. He, filled as he was with love and sorrow, was so overcome that he too fell in a faint. One of Paulina's companions, seeing them both collapse on the ground, called for help, and they were given medicaments which revived them.

When Paulina realized that she had revealed the strength of her feelings, she was overcome with shame, for she had always sought to disguise her love. But she was able to excuse herself on the grounds that she had been overwhelmed by compassion for the gentleman's plight. He, unable to bear the pain of uttering his final adieu, hastily left the scene, his face set, as he fought back the emotion that welled in his heart. No sooner had he returned home than he collapsed on his bed, a lifeless corpse. Throughout that night he lamented aloud, and his cries were so heart-rending that his servants thought he must have lost parents, friends and everything he had. The next day he commended himself to Our Lord, and shared out among his servants what little he possessed, taking only a small sum of money for himself. Then, forbidding anyone to follow him, he wended his way alone to the convent of the Observant Friars, where, in the firm resolve never again to leave those walls, he requested the friar's habit. The Superior, who had seen him in the past, thought at first that he must be dreaming or that it must be some sort of a joke. Indeed there could hardly have been a man in the whole land who was less endowed with the qualities and gifts required of a friar, for his gifts were the solid virtues of a gentleman of honour. But once the good father had heard the words he had to speak, once he had seen the tears pouring in torrents down his face, though he did not know their cause, he had compassion on him and took him in. It was not long afterwards that he acknowledged the gentleman's perseverance and granted him the habit, which the gentleman received with due devotion.

When the Marquis and Marchioness heard of this, they found it so strange that they could scarcely believe it. Paulina, desiring to show that she was not in any way subject to the dictates of love, covered up as best as she was able the sorrow she felt at the gentleman's departure. So complete was her dissimulation that all those around her said that she had at last forgotten the feelings she had once had for her faithful and devoted servant. Five or six months passed by, and still she revealed nothing. One day during this time a monk visited her and showed her a song that had been composed by her faithful servant shortly after he had taken the habit. The tune was Italian and is quite well-known, but I have translated the words as closely as possible. They go like this:

> What will she say,
> My Lady, pray,
> What will she do, when her fair eyes
> See me thus dressed in monkish guise?
>
> Dear one, my own,
> Sweet one alone,
> Long speechless, wond'ring will she be,
> Troubled and torn
> Lady forlorn.
> Strange will it seem, then presently

Her thoughts they will begin to dwell
On convent close and holy cell,
There to reside, eternally.
What will she say, etc.

What will they do,
Who from us two
Our love and joy did cause to go,
Seeing that love
Howe'er they strove
They yet more perfect caused to grow?
When they do look into our heart
They surely will repent their part
And bitter tears will surely flow.
What will she say, etc.

And if they say,
Oh come away!
And seek our souls so to divert,
Then you and I
Shall say, we'll die!
Far rather that than ever part,
For since we must their harshness bear,
We two do now the long robe wear
That we shall wear perpetually.
What will she say, etc.

And if again
With marriage then
They seek our souls to taunt and tempt,
While they relate
That pleasant state
And how we should be thus content,
Our soul, we'll say, is at God's side,
His holy spouse, His heavenly bride,
So shall it be, eternally.
What will she say, etc.

O love so great,
That through this gate
I have perforce for sorrow passed,

Ah! in this place
Grant me the grace
Without regret to pray and fast,
For this our love, our mutual love,
Shall rise so high, and dwell above
That God will be well pleased at last.
What will she say, etc.

Then put behind
The joys that bind
In iron-bonds so dire and fell!
Quit worldly fame
That leads in shame
Black souls through pride to depths of Hell!
Let us shun lust and vanity,
And take that love which in mercy
Lord Jesus gives, with Him to dwell.
What will she say, etc.

Come then away,
Make no delay,
And with your best beloved go,
Fear not, I pray,
The habit grey,
Nor yet to flee this world below.
For with that love that's live and strong
From ashes must arise ere long
The phoenix true, enduringly.
What will she say, etc.

Just as on earth
Our love had birth,
Pure and perfect, noble, rare,
It may appear,
Hidden here
In cloistered cell, beyond compare.
For loyal love that's true and sure
And endlessly shall e'er endure
Must lead to heav'n, eventually.
What will she say, etc.

She was sitting in a chapel as she read the song through, and when she had finished she wept bitterly, sprinkling the paper with the tears as they fell. Had it not been for her anxiety to avoid showing herself more moved than was becoming, she would even at that very moment have transported herself to some hermitage and shut herself away from all living creatures for evermore. But imbued as she was with the virtue of prudence, she was constrained to disguise her feelings for some little time longer. In her heart she was resolved to leave the world for ever, but in her outward appearance it was the very opposite she showed, for when in company she wore an expression that revealed nothing of her true self. For five or six months more she kept her intentions secret, appearing to the world gayer and happier even than she had used to be.

Then, one day, she went with her mistress to the Observant convent to hear high mass. As the priest, deacon and subdeacon came out of the sacristy and made their way to the high altar, she beheld her poor suitor, who had still not completed his one year of novitiate. He was serving as acolyte and walked with eyes bent to the ground, bearing in his hands the altar-cruets covered in their white silk cloth. When she saw him attired thus in his vestments, his looks enhanced rather than diminished, she was so overcome with emotion that she made herself cough in order to cover up the colour that had risen to her cheeks. Her poor servant could not fail to recognize the sound of her voice, a sound better known to him by far than the cloister bell. He dared not turn his head, yet as he passed by her, he could not prevent his eyes from turning in the direction that they had so long been accustomed to take. As he gazed sorrowfully upon her, he was so overwhelmed by the fire he believed almost extinct that in his desire to conceal it more than was [in his power] he fell to the ground at her feet. Fear lest the true cause be known led him to say that he had fallen over a broken paving-stone. But when Paulina realized that his change of habit could not change his heart, and that it was so long since he had entered the monastery that everyone would think she had forgotten him, she decided to carry out her long resolve. It was her desire that at the last their love should bring them together, that they should be alike in habit, condition and manner of life, just as at the beginning [they had] lived under the same roof, under the same master and under the same mistress. She had already more than four months previously made all the arrangements necessary for her entry into a convent, and one morning she asked the Marchioness for permission to go and hear mass at the convent of Saint Clare. Permission was granted, although the Marchioness was ignorant of the true reason for the request. As Paulina went past the Franciscan house, she stopped and asked the Father Superior to send her devoted servant, who, she said, was a relative, to speak to her. They met in a quiet chapel, and she addressed him thus:

'If my honour had allowed me to dare to enter the cloister as soon as you did, I should not have waited till now. But I have waited patiently, and now that my waiting has thwarted those who prefer to think ill of others than to think well, I am resolved to adopt the same condition of life and the same robes as you have adopted. I do not ask what people will say. For if your chosen way has brought you joy, I shall have my part therein. If it has brought you suffering, I have no wish to be spared. Whatever path you tread to Paradise, I wish to follow in your steps. For I believe that He who alone is worthy to be called true and perfect Love has drawn us to His service through a love that is reasonable and good, a love that through His Holy Spirit He will turn wholly unto Himself. And I beg you that we may put away the flesh of the old Adam that perisheth, and accept and put on that of Jesus Christ our Spouse.'

Paulina's devoted servant, now a servant of God, was so filled with joy when he heard her express this sacred wish that, weeping tears of happiness, he strove to strengthen her resolve. Since he could have nothing of her but the enjoyment of the words she spoke, he held his lot happy indeed, for henceforth he would always be able to hear her, and her words would be such that both he and she would profit by them, living as they would in one love, one heart and one spirit, drawn and guided by the goodness of God. And he prayed that God would hold them in His hand, for in His hands no man can perish. As he spoke, he shed tears of love and joy. Then he bent to kiss her hand, but Paulina lowered her face to his, and in true charity they exchanged the holy kiss of love. Her soul thus filled with happiness, Paulina departed and went to the sister convent of Saint Clare, where after being received she took the veil.

Later she had the news conveyed to the Marchioness, who was so surprised she could not believe it, and went the very next day to try to make her change her mind. But Paulina's reply was firm. The Marchioness might have the power to remove her fleshly husband, the one in the world whom she had loved above all others, but that being so, she should now be satisfied and not seek to separate her from Him who was immortal and invisible, for neither the Marchioness nor any creature on earth had such power. Seeing that Paulina was resolute, the Marchioness kissed her, and filled with sorrow and regret, went on her way. From that time on Paulina and her servant lived devout and holy lives in their Observant houses. So devout and so holy were they, one cannot doubt that He whose law has its end in charity would tell them at their lives' end, even as He told Mary Magdalen, that their sins were forgiven, for they had loved much, and that He would transport them in peace [to the] place whose recompenses surpass all human merits.

*

'Now you can't deny, Ladies, that the man's love was clearly the stronger. But it was so well repaid, that I only wish that everybody who fell in love had the same recompense.'

'If that were the case,' said Hircan, 'there'd be more self-declared fools around than ever!'

'Do you call it folly if one loves with an honourable love in one's youth, and then converts this love entirely unto God?' asked Oisille.

'If melancholy and despair deserve praise,' he replied laughing, 'then Paulina and her devoted servant certainly deserve praise!'

'Yet God has many ways of drawing us to Him,' said Geburon, 'ways whose beginnings may seem bad, but whose end is good.'

'Furthermore,' said Parlamente, 'I hold the view that no man will ever perfectly love God, unless he has perfectly loved some creature in this world.'

'What do you mean by perfectly loved?' said Saffredent. 'Is a perfect lover for you one of those paralytic individuals who adore their ladies from afar and never dare to bring their desires out into the open?'

'Those whom I call perfect lovers,' replied Parlamente, 'are those who seek in what they love some perfection, whether it be beauty, goodness or grace, those whose constant goal is virtue and whose hearts are so lofty and so pure that they would die rather than make their goal that which is low and condemned by honour and conscience. For the soul, which was created solely that it might return to its Sovereign Good, ceaselessly desires to achieve this end while it is still within the body. But the senses, by means of which the soul is able to have intelligence of its Sovereign Good, are dim and carnal because of the sins of our forefather Adam and consequently can reveal to the soul only those things which are visible and have some nearer approximation to perfection. The soul runs after these things, vainly thinking that in some external beauty, in some visible grace and in the moral virtues it will find the sovereign beauty, the sovereign grace and the sovereign virtue. But once the soul has searched out these things and tried and tested them, once it has failed to find in them Him whom it loves, it passes beyond. In the same way children, when they are small, like dolls and all manner of little things that are attractive to the eye and think that the pebbles they collect will make them rich; but then, as they grow up, the dolls they love are living people and the things they collect are the necessities of human life. [Then,] when they learn through experience that in earthly and [transitory] things there is neither perfection nor felicity, they desire to seek the source and maker of these things. Yet, if God does not open the eyes of faith, they will be in danger of leaving ignorance behind only to become infidel philosophers. For only faith can reveal and make the soul receive that Good which carnal and animal man cannot understand.'

'Do you not see,' said Longarine, 'that uncultivated ground is desirable, although it bears nothing but useless trees and grasses, because it offers the hope that one day, when it is sown, it will bring forth good fruit? In the same way, if the heart of man feels no love for visible things, it will never attain the love of God when His word is sown therein. For the earth of his heart is sterile, cold and damned.'

'So that's why most of your doctors of theology aren't spiritual doctors!' said Saffredent. 'It's because all they'll ever like is good wine and ugly, sluttish chambermaids. They never try out what it's like to love ladies who are more refined!'

'If I could speak Latin properly,' said Simontaut, 'I'd quote St John to you. He says "he who loves not his brother whom he has seen, how can he love God whom he cannot see?" For it is through things visible that one is drawn to the love of things invisible.'

'But who is the man who is so perfect?' asked Ennasuite. '*Quis est ille, et laudabimus eum*?'

To this Dagoucin replied: 'There *are* men,' he said, 'who love so deeply and so perfectly that they would rather die than feel any desire that was contrary to the honour and conscience of their ladies, and yet they would not wish their ladies or anyone else to be aware of their feelings.'

'Men like that,' said Saffredent, 'are chameleons – they live on nothing but air! The fact is that there's no such thing as a man who doesn't want to declare his love and know it's returned. What is more, if it *isn't* returned, I don't think there was ever a love fever that wasn't cured instantaneously. I've seen miracles enough to prove it!'

'Then, will you take my place,' said Ennasuite, 'and tell us about somebody who was raised from death to life when he found that his lady's feelings were not favourable to his desires?'

'I am so much afraid of offending the ladies,' he replied, 'whose most devoted servant I have been and always shall be, that without their express command, I should not have dared to tell a story about their imperfections. However, since I now have that command, I must obey, and I shall not hide the truth.'

STORY TWENTY

There once lived in the Dauphiné a gentleman named the Seigneur de Riant. He belonged to the household of King Francis I, and was as handsome and honourable a man as you could possibly wish to see. For a long time he had devoted himself to the service of a certain lady, a widow. So much did he love and revere her that, for fear of losing her good graces altogether, he did not dare demand from her that which above all things he desired. Feeling that he was a fine figure of a man and not unworthy of a lady's love, he firmly believed her whenever she solemnly swore, as she often did, that she loved him more than any other man in all the world. If ever she were obliged to do anything for a gentleman, she would declare, she would do it for him alone, for he was the most perfect gentleman she had ever known. Then she would beg and beseech that he would content himself with this, and not go beyond the bounds of respectable friendship. If she ever found him dissatisfied with what was reasonable and good, if she ever found him laying claim to other favours, then, she assured him, he would lose her for ever. Well, not only was the poor man satisfied with his lot, he deemed himself fortunate indeed to have won the heart of a lady who seemed so full of honour and virtue!

It would take me a long time to give you the whole account of his love for this lady, to tell you of all the time he spent with her, and how he made many a long journey to see her. To cut a long story short, suffice it to say that this wretched martyr to the sweet fire of love constantly went in search of ways of making his martyrdom worse – for the more you burn in such a fire, the more you want to burn. One day he was suddenly taken by a desire to see the one whom he loved more dearly than life itself, this fair one whom he adored above all other women in the world. So he went with all possible speed by post-horse to her house. On asking where she was, he was told that she had only just come in from vespers, and that she had gone into the game park to finish off her devotions. So he got down from his horse, and went straight to the park, where he found her women attendants, who said that she had gone for a walk on her own down a broad tree-lined path that ran through the grounds. This made him all the more hopeful that he was going to be in luck. So off he went to seek out his fair lady, treading ever so carefully so as not to make the slightest noise, and hoping above hope that he was going to find her alone. Then he came to a leafy bower, in the most delightful spot you ever did see, and, unable to contain himself any longer, he went bursting straight in. What does he find but his beloved stretched out on the grass in the arms of one of her stable-boys! A stable-boy as dirty, common and ugly as de Riant was handsome, gallant and refined! I shan't attempt to describe his feelings – enough to say that his indignation was sufficient to extinguish instantaneously the fire of a passion that had endured time and circumstance.

'Do as you please, Madame, and much good may it do you!' he cried, as impassioned with rage as he had been with love. 'This day I am cured by your wickedness and delivered from the perpetual suffering which was occasioned by what once I took to be your noble virtue!'

Without waiting to say goodbye, he turned, and went somewhat more quickly than he had come. The poor woman did not know what to reply. As she could not hide her shame, she covered up her eyes, so as not to see the man who in spite of her long dissimulation, could now see *her* all too clearly!

*

'And so, Ladies, if you don't intend to love perfectly, kindly do not try to deceive men of honour, or try to cross them for the sake of your pride and glory. Hypocrites get their just deserts, and God is good to those who love openly!'

'Well, indeed!' exclaimed Oisille. 'You certainly did keep a fine story to finish off the day! If it were not for the fact that we have all sworn to tell the truth, I could not believe that a woman of such station could be so corrupt – corrupt in her soul, corrupt in the sight of God and corrupt in her body. To leave an upright gentleman for a vulgar stable-boy!'

'Ah! Madame, if you only knew,' said Hircan, 'what a great difference there is between a gentleman who spends his whole life in armour on active service and a well-fed servant who never budges from home, you'd excuse the poor widow in this story!'

'You may say what you like, Hircan,' replied Oisille, 'but I do not think *you* would be capable of accepting excuses from her!'

'I've heard it said,' began Simontaut, 'that there are some women who like to have their "evangelists" to preach abroad their virtue and chastity! They treat them in the most encouraging and intimate way possible and assure them that if only they were not held back by honour and conscience they would grant them their heart's desire. Then when the poor fools get together with their friends, they start talking about their ladies, and swear that to uphold their beloved's virtue they'd stick their fingers in the fire and not feel a thing, because they believe they've personally tried and tested their love to the farthest extreme! That's the way women manage to get honourable men to spread their good name. But they show themselves in their true colours to those of their own kind. They pick men who would never be so bold as to talk about what they knew, and who, if they did happen to talk, wouldn't be believed in any case, because they're so base and common.'

'That,' said Longarine, 'is a point of view I've heard expressed before by men who are particularly jealous and suspicious. But it's all sheer fantasy. Just because something like that happens to some miserable wretch of a woman, there's no reason to go round suspecting all women of the same thing.'

'The more we pursue this subject,' said Parlamente, 'the more these fine gentlemen here will embroider on what Simontaut has already said, at the expense of us ladies. We had better go to vespers, so that we don't keep the monks waiting as long as we did yesterday.'

They were all in agreement, and, as they got up to go, Oisille said: ['May each and every one of us give thanks to God that we have today told the truth in the stories we have told. As for you, Saffredent, you ought to pray for forgiveness for having told one so insulting to women.']

'Upon my oath, Ladies,' replied Saffredent, 'although my story is a [curious] one, I heard it [from reliable people, and it is true.] If I were to tell you one about women that I know from first-hand experience, I'd have you making more signs of the cross than they do to consecrate churches!'

To this Geburon replied: 'You're a long way from repentance when your confession only makes your sin the worse!'

And Parlamente said: 'If that's your opinion of women, then they ought to deprive you of their refined conversation and cease to have anything to do with you.'

But Saffredent retorted: 'There are some women who have followed your recommendation and have banished me from all that is decent, good and refined, and have been so thorough about it that if I could say anything worse, or *do* anything worse to [each and every one of them, and to one in particular who does me considerable wrong,] then I wouldn't hesitate to do so and take my revenge!'

On hearing these words Parlamente raised her mask to her face, and went into the church. They found that although the bell had been ringing heartily for vespers, not a single monk had yet appeared. The fact was that they had heard that the ladies and gentlemen were meeting together in the meadow to recount all manner of amusing tales and, preferring their pleasures to their prayers, they had been hiding in a ditch behind a thick hedge, flat on their bellies, so that they could overhear. So attentively had they been listening, they had not even heard their own monastery bell ringing. The consequence was that they came scurrying to their places in such a hurry that they hardly had enough breath left to start singing the service! When vespers were over and they were asked why they had been so late and their chanting so out of tune, they confessed, and admitted that it was because they had been listening to the stories. When it was realized that they were so favourably disposed towards the proceedings, they were given permission to go along every day and listen from behind the hedge for as long as they wished. At supper everyone enjoyed themselves. The conversations that had remained unfinished in the meadow were continued and went on the whole evening, until Oisille urged them all to retire for the night. If they had a good long rest, their minds would be all the fresher the next day, for, as she said, an hour before midnight is worth three after. And so, taking their leave of one another, they went each to their respective rooms, and brought the second day to its close.

END OF THE SECOND DAY

THIRD DAY

PROLOGUE

In the morning everybody rose early and went into the hall, but early as it was, they found Oisille already there, having spent more than half an hour studying the lesson that she was to read to them. And on this the third day they were no less delighted by her reading than they had been on the first and second days. Indeed, if it had not been for one of the monks coming to call them to mass, they would never have gone at all, for they were so deep in contemplation that they had not heard the bell. Once mass had been devoutly heard, they had their meal, eating in moderation so that their memories would not be clouded and so that they would be able to perform to the best of their ability when their turn came. Then they all retired to their rooms to consult their notes until it was time to go out to the meadow.

At the appointed time they eagerly sallied forth. Those amongst them who had made up their minds to tell a funny story had such merriment written on their faces that the rest were already looking forward to a hearty laugh. Once they had arrived, they sat down and asked Saffredent whom he would choose to speak first for their third day of stories.

'It seems to me,' he replied, 'that since the fault I committed yesterday is as grave as you say it is, and since I don't know a story that could make up for it, I ought to call upon Parlamente, who, being a woman with plenty of good sense, will be able to praise ladies in such a way as to make everyone forget the truth I have told you.'

'I'm not undertaking to make up for your faults,' said Parlamente, 'but I do intend to take care not to commit similar ones myself. So, appealing to that very truth which we have all pledged to speak, it is my intention to demonstrate to you that there *are* women who in their love have had in view nothing other than honour and virtue. And because the lady I want to tell you about is from a good family, I shall change the heroine's name, but nothing more. I hope, Ladies, that you will believe that love does not have the power to change a heart that is chaste, virtuous and honourable. For such indeed is the case, as you will now see from my story.'

STORY TWENTY-ONE

There was once a Queen of France who had living in her household several of the daughters of important noble families. Amongst them she had one called Rolandine, who was a close relative. However, since she bore some grudge against Rolandine's father, the Queen did not treat her at all kindly. The young lady herself, although neither particularly beautiful nor particularly ugly, was so virtuous and chaste that several men of rank asked for her hand in marriage – only to receive a cold reply. The reason was that Rolandine's father was so fond of his money that he neglected the interests of his daughter. Also, her mistress, as I've already said, was so ill-disposed towards her that no one who wanted to win the Queen's favour would ever ask for Rolandine's hand in marriage. Consequently, through her father's negligence and her mistress's dislike the poor girl remained unmarried. As time went by this state of affairs came to distress her greatly, not because she actually wished to marry, but more because she was ashamed. And so she turned herself entirely to God, abandoning the elegant and worldly ways of the court. Her sole occupation was to pray to God and do a little sewing. Thus she spent her youth, withdrawn from the world and leading the most virtuous and saintly life imaginable.

When she was approaching thirty years of age, there appeared a certain gentleman, the bastard son of a good and noble family. He was as gallant and worthy as any man of his day, but bereft of means, and so ill-endowed with good looks that no lady, whoever she might have been, would have chosen him for her pleasure. This poor gentleman had also never found his match, and as two unhappy people often will, the one sought out the other. He introduced himself to Rolandine, knowing that in their temperaments, in their misfortunes and in their station in life, they had much in common. They poured out their sorrows to one another and soon formed a deep attachment. Companions as they were in misfortune, they would seek one another out wherever they might for their mutual consolation.

Thus it was that, as a result of seeing so much of one another, a deep and lasting affection came into being. Everyone who had known Rolandine as a quiet and withdrawn young woman who spoke to no one, was scandalized when they saw her constantly in the company of [the bastard,] and told her gouvernante that she ought not to tolerate the long conversations which the pair were in the habit of having together. So the gouvernante spoke to Rolandine about it, telling her that everybody was scandalized at the way she spent so much time talking with a man who was neither rich enough to marry her nor handsome enough to be her lover. Rolandine, who had always been reproached for her austerity rather than for worldliness, replied to her gouvernante thus:

'Alas, Mother, you know that I cannot find a husband to match my family and lineage, and that I have always shunned men who are young and good-looking, for fear of the troubles I have seen suffered by others. I [have found] this gentleman here, who is virtuous and good, as you know well, and who never speaks to me of anything that is other than virtuous and good. What harm, then, can I be doing either to you or to the others who are complaining, in seeking consolation with him for my sorrows?'

The old lady, who loved her mistress Rolandine more than she loved herself, said: 'Mademoiselle, I can see that you are telling the truth, and I know that you are not treated as you deserve either by your father or by your mistress. Even so, since people are talking about you in a way that concerns your honour, you must give up speaking to him. Even if it were your own brother, you ought to do so!'

'Since such is your advice, Mother, I will do as you say,' answered Rolandine, weeping as she spoke. 'But what a harsh thing it is not to have just one consolation in this world!'

The bastard wanted to come and talk with her as usual, but she told him everything that her gouvernante had said, begging him with tears in her eyes that he should not speak to her for a while, until all the rumours had died down. He complied with her request. Both of them had now lost their consolation, and during their separation from one another each began to feel a kind of torment neither had ever before experienced. She spent her time in constant prayer, on pilgrimages, in fasting and in acts of abstinence. For her love, of which she was as yet unaware, caused her an anxiety that gave her not even an hour's repose. The bastard of high birth was no less afflicted by the assaults of Love, but he had already resolved in his heart to love Rolandine and to endeavour to marry her. He considered too the honour that would redound to him if he could but win her, and concluded that he must find a way of declaring his desire to her, and above all of winning over the gouvernante. So he took the old lady to task, pointing out the misery that her mistress was being subjected to by those who wanted to deprive her of all consolation. The good woman wept, and thanked him for the worthy feelings he bore her mistress. And together they worked out a way for him to talk to her. Rolandine was to pretend to be suffering from a migraine that made her terrified of any noise; and when her companions went into the Queen's chamber, she and the bastard would remain alone together; in this way he would be able to talk with her. The bastard was extremely pleased at this prospect, and was happy to let himself be ruled entirely by the advice of Rolandine's gouvernante. Thus it was that he was able to talk to his beloved whenever he wished. But he did not enjoy this happy arrangement for very long, for the Queen, who had no affection for Rolandine, inquired of her why she spent so much time in her room. And although somebody told her that it was because of her illness, there was somebody else, with an over-ready memory for missing faces, who said pointedly that relaxing in conversation with the well-born bastard would be sure to cure Rolandine's migraine. The Queen, who regarded the venial sins of others as mortal in Rolandine, sent for her and forbade her ever to speak to the bastard again, unless it was in the Queen's own chamber or in the great hall. Rolandine did not demur, but simply said: 'If I had thought, Madame, that [he] or anyone else was displeasing to you, then I would never have spoken to him.'

However, she thought to herself that she would look for some other way, some way of which the Queen should know nothing. And so she did, for every Wednesday, Friday and Saturday, the days when she kept a fast, she would stay in her chamber with her gouvernante, and while the other girls were at supper, she would talk at leisure with the man whom she was now coming to love so deeply. And the less time they had to talk, the more ardent were the words they spoke. For time was precious, and they stole their comments as a thief steals a precious object. However, they were unable to keep the affair completely secret, and some servant or other who saw the bastard going in on Rolandine's fast days passed on what he had seen until it reached quarters where it was not concealed from the Queen. So angry was the Queen that the bastard no longer dared go near the ladies' chamber. But, in order not to lose completely the joy of talking with Rolandine, he would often pretend to go away on some journey, coming back in the evening dressed as a Franciscan or Dominican friar, or disguised in some other way so that no one would recognize him. He would then go to the church or to the castle chapel, where Rolandine would come to talk to him accompanied by her gouvernante. And seeing that Rolandine was now greatly in love with him, he did not shrink from saying to her:

'Mademoiselle, you see how I set myself at risk in order to serve you. You know, too, how the Queen has repeatedly forbidden you to speak with me. What is more, you know what your father is like, and that nothing could be further from his thoughts than arranging for you to marry. He has turned down so many good matches that I can think of no one, however far and wide he looked, whom he would accept as your husband. I know only too well that I am poor and that you could not marry any gentleman unless he were richer than myself. But if love and an honest heart were considered treasure, then I should regard myself the richest man in the world. God has endowed you with great wealth and you are likely to receive yet more. If I were so fortunate as to be chosen by you for your husband, then I would be your husband, your lover and your servant for the rest of my days. If you take a man who is your equal, and such a man will be difficult to find, he will want to be your master and will pay more attention to your wealth than to yourself, more attention to your beauty than to your virtue. He will have full right to enjoy your wealth, yet will treat your body other than it deserves. My desire to enjoy such happiness, and my fear that you will have none with anyone else, brings me to humbly beg of you that you will make me happy and at the same time make yourself the most satisfied and best treated wife there ever was.'

Rolandine listened. What she had heard were the very words that she herself had intended to speak, and she said with steadfast face: 'It gives me happiness to hear you say to me the very things which long ago I had resolved to say to you. During the two years I have known you I have turned over and over in my mind all the arguments I could invent both for you and against you. But, now at last, knowing that I sincerely wish to enter into the state of matrimony, it is time that [I should choose the man] with whom I believe I could best live in tranquillity of conscience. However handsome, however rich, of however high estate my suitors, I have not found one amongst them, save you alone, with whom my heart and mind could accord. I know that in marrying you, I would be doing no offence to God but would be carrying out His commands. As for my father, so little has he sought to further my well-being and so much has he denied me, the law permits me to marry without his being able to disinherit me. Even if I have nothing but what belongs to me personally, I would regard myself as the richest woman in the world to marry a man who is towards me as you are. And as for my mistress the Queen, my conscience need not be troubled if I displease her in order to obey God, since hers was not in the least troubled when she prevented me having the happiness I could have had when I was young. However, in order that you may know that the love I bear you is founded on virtue and on honour, you will promise me that if I agree to this marriage, you will not seek to consummate it until my father is dead or until I have found some way to obtain his consent.'

The bastard gladly gave her his word, and having exchanged promises, each gave the other a ring in token of the marriage. Then they kissed, in the church and in the sight of God, taking Him as witness of their vows. And never afterwards was there anything between them more intimate than kisses. This grain of happiness left the two perfect lovers with great contentment in their hearts and, secure in these feelings, they lived for some time without seeing one another. Wherever in the world honour was to be won the high-born bastard went with joy in his heart, in the knowledge that with the precious wife whom God had bestowed upon him he could never be poor. Rolandine kept intact her perfect love during his absence, paying no heed to any other man in the world. Although several asked for her hand, the only reply she would give them was that since she had already remained so long unmarried, she now had no wish ever to be otherwise. It soon became known that she was in the habit of giving this reply, and when the Queen heard about it, she asked Rolandine what was the reason for such language. To this Rolandine replied that it was in order to obey her majesty, and that her majesty knew well enough that she had never wished her to marry at a time when she might have been honourably and comfortably provided for. Moreover, age and long-suffering had taught her to content herself with her lot. And whenever anybody spoke to Rolandine about marriage, that was how she would answer.

When the wars were over and the bastard had returned to court, she never spoke to him in company, but always went to talk with him in a church under the pretence of going to confession. For the Queen had forbidden them on pain of death ever to speak to one another, unless they were in the company of other people. But noble love, which knows no prohibitions, was more prompt in finding a means whereby they could talk to one another than were their enemies in catching them out. Thus, under the cover of all the monastic habits they could think of they continued in their noble love until the King moved to a country seat near Tours. It was not, however, close enough to Tours for the ladies to walk to church there, and they had to use the chapel in the château, which was so inconveniently constructed that there was nowhere to go for confession without the confessor being clearly on view. But if one expedient had failed them, Love soon found them another, easier way. For there arrived at the court a lady to whom the bastard was closely related. This lady and her son were accommodated in the part of the building occupied by the King, and it so happened that the young prince was given a room which projected from the rest of the wing in such a way that it was quite possible for him to see and speak to Rolandine herself, since their windows were situated in the angle formed by the two parts of the building.

The room facing that of the young prince was in fact over the King's hall and was the chamber where all the young noblewomen, including Rolandine, had their quarters. Having noticed the young prince at his window several times, Rolandine sent word to the bastard through the gouvernante. The bastard then spied out the land and pretended to be seized with a sudden passion for reading a book about the Knights of the Round Table which the young prince had in his room. When everyone went to dinner he would ask a valet de chambre to let him in, lock the door and keep a careful watch while he finished his reading. As the servant knew that he was related to his master, and that he was a reliable man, he let him stay in the room to read for as long as he wished. On her side of the building Rolandine would come to the window, having made a pretence of suffering from a pain in the leg so that she could stay longer in her room, and having taken her dinner and supper so early that she did not need to join the other ladies at table. Also she had set about making an open-work bed cover in crimson silk, and this she would hang up in the window where she wanted to be left alone. Thus when the others had gone, she would talk with her husband, keeping her voice low so that no one could possibly hear. If anyone came near, she would cough and give a sign, so that the bastard had time to withdraw. All the people who had been keeping an eye on Rolandine were quite convinced that her attachment had worn off, for Rolandine never moved from this one room, where, so people thought, the bastard could not possibly be seeing her, since he had been expressly forbidden to enter.

One day the young prince's mother was in her son's room, and happened to go over to the window where the big book was. She had not been there many seconds when one of Rolandine's companions appeared at the window opposite, waved to the lady and started a conversation. The lady asked how Rolandine was, and was told that she could see her, if she so desired. Whereupon Rolandine was brought to the window in her nightcap. They talked a little about her illness, and then went inside again. As the lady who was the young prince's mother turned back into the room, she glanced at the big book about the Round Table, remarking to the valet de chambre: 'It amazes me that young people waste so much time reading such nonsense!' To which the valet de chambre replied that it amazed him even more that persons who were supposed to be older and wiser were even more given to it, and went on to tell her how astonished he had been to find her kinsman, the bastard, spending four or five hours every day with her son's book – a fine thing for him to be reading! Instantly, the explanation bore itself into the lady's mind. She instructed the valet de chambre to hide in the room and observe what the bastard did. The man did as he was asked and found that what the bastard was really doing was not reading the book, but standing in front of the window where Rolandine came to speak to him, and he also overheard them express to one another the love which they had believed to be secure. The next day he told his mistress, who sent for the bastard and, after severely reprimanding him, forbade him ever to come to the room again. In the evening she spoke to Rolandine, warning her that if she persisted in this foolish and wicked attachment, she would inform the Queen of her deceitfulness. Rolandine, giving not the slightest sign of dismay, swore that since her mistress's prohibition she had never once spoken to the bastard, whatever people might say, and that if she wanted to know the truth she could ask her companions [and her servants.] As for the window, she denied that she had used it in order to converse with the bastard. The bastard himself, afraid lest the affair be exposed, decided to avoid further risks and left court.

It was a long time before he returned, but he continued to write to Rolandine, sending letters to her by various means. So ingenious was he in this respect that, however careful a watch the Queen kept on Rolandine, never a week went by without her hearing from him twice. He enlisted the aid of monks, but when that method failed, he took to sending a little page, who would sometimes wear one set of colours, sometimes another. This young boy would wait by a door which all the ladies used, and, unnoticed in the crowd, would hand over the letters to Rolandine. One day, when the Queen had gone into the country, somebody recognized this page-boy, and chased him. But the cunning little fellow darted into a house, where an old woman was cooking her stew, and threw the letters straight on to the fire. When the gentleman who had been chasing him eventually caught him, he stripped him naked and searched through all his clothes, but, finding nothing, let him go. When he had disappeared, the old woman asked the man why he had searched the child in the way he had. He replied: 'To find some letters I thought he was carrying.'

'You didn't have much chance of finding them,' the old woman said. 'He'd hidden them too well!'

'Will you kindly tell me where?' asked the gentleman, hoping that he was about to retrieve them. But when he learnt that they were in the fire, he realized that the page had been cleverer than he, and went straight to tell the Queen about it. From that time on the bastard stopped using page-boys and other young children to carry his letters, and sent an old servant he had instead. Although the old man knew that anyone involved in the affair was under threat of death on the Queen's authority, he banished all fear from his mind and undertook to convey letters to Rolandine. Once inside the château where she was, he took up his watch by a door at the foot of a flight of steps which all the ladies used. But a servant who had seen him before recognized him and immediately went to tell the Queen's maître d'hôtel, who came at once with the intention of seizing him. The wise old servant, having noticed that he was being watched, turned to the wall as if to pass water, tore up the letters into the smallest pieces he could and threw them behind a door. Thereupon he was seized and searched all over, and when they found nothing he was interrogated on oath. They demanded to know whether he had any letters on him, using all possible means of persuasion and physical force to make him confess. But for all their threats and promises they were unable to extract anything. A report was duly sent to the Queen, and somebody had the idea of looking behind the door where the bastard's servant had been when he had been taken. Sure enough they found what they were looking for – the letter. They sent for the King's confessor, who assembled the pieces on a table and read the letter in its entirety. The truth about the marriage, so long kept secret, stood revealed, for throughout the letter the bastard had addressed Rolandine as 'my wife'. The Queen, not being minded to conceal a close relative's misdemeanour, as she should have done, made a great commotion about it. She gave orders that all possible means be used to make the wretched man confess the truth about the letter. He could scarcely deny having seen it, she insisted, if he had it presented to him. But whatever they said to him, and however much they thrust the letter in front of his eyes, the man never wavered from the story he had told at the beginning. Then the people in charge of him dragged him off to the river, put him in a sack, and told him that he had lied before God and before the Queen. But he would rather have lost his life than accuse his own master, and he requested a confessor to be sent to him. Having satisfied his conscience as best he could in the circumstances, he addressed his captors thus:

'Messieurs, I beg you, tell my master, my lord the bastard, that I commend to him my wife and my children, for my own life I cheerfully lay down in his service. Now do what you like with me, because you'll never get a word out of me against my master!'

After that, to give him an even bigger fright, they flung him into the river still tied up in the sack. 'If you'll tell the truth, your life is saved!' they shouted. However, seeing that he was not going to reply, they hauled him out again and reported his loyal behaviour to the Queen, who remarked that neither she nor the King had ever been so lucky with servants as the bastard, who did not even have the means to remunerate them. In fact she did her very best to persuade the man to enter her own service, but he refused ever to desert his master. Eventually, however, the bastard gave his consent, and the man entered the service of the Queen, to lead a happy and contented life.

Once the Queen had learnt the truth about the marriage from the bastard's letter, she sent for Rolandine and, far from addressing her as 'cousin', she told her repeatedly, her face contorted with rage, that she was a 'miserable wretch', and accused her of bringing dishonour upon her father's house, upon her relatives and upon her mistress, the Queen. Rolandine, who had long been aware that her mistress had little affection for her, gave as good as she received. As there was little love between them, there was also little room for fear. It seemed to her that this reprimand in the presence of several other people sprang not from loving concern, but from the desire to humiliate, and that the woman who was administering it was moved not by displeasure at the offence, but by pleasure in the punishment. Consequently, when she replied, she was as calm and composed as the Queen was violent and vehement.

'Madame, if you were not already fully aware of your own feelings,' she began, 'I would spell out to you the hostile attitude you have shown for a long time now towards Monsieur my father and towards myself. However, you know perfectly well what your own feelings are, and you will not be surprised that everybody else has a fair inkling of them too. For my part, Madame, I certainly know the way you feel, and know to my cost. If you had favoured me in the same way as you favoured the other girls, who were not even as closely related as I am, I would by now have been married in a manner that would have brought honour to yourself as well as to me. However, as far as your favour is concerned I have been totally ignored, so that every single good match that I might have made slipped away before my very eyes, thanks to my father's negligence and to your lack of regard for me. Consequently I fell into such a state of despair, that had it not been for my poor health I would certainly have entered the religious life to avoid the continual suffering that your harsh treatment caused me. While I was in this state of despair I was sought out by a man whose birth would have been the equal of mine, if only love between two persons carried as much esteem as a ring on the finger, for, as you well know, his father was more elevated than mine. He has for a long time loved and cherished me. You, Madame, have never forgiven me even the slightest fault, nor have you ever praised me for any good thing I may have done. Yet you know from your own experience that I was not one to be always talking about love and worldly vanities, and that I was fully resolved to lead a life more religious than otherwise. And now, Madame, you are surprised that I converse with a gentleman who is as unhappy in life as I am, a man in whose company I saw nothing other than spiritual solace, and sought nothing other than that. When I realized that this was taken from me, I again fell into such a state of despair that eventually I made up my mind to pursue my own happiness, however much you may desire to take it from me. It was then that we talked of marriage, and the words that we spoke were consummated in promises and the exchange of rings. It therefore seems to me, Madame, that you do me a grievous wrong, when you say that I am wicked, for throughout this deep and perfect love of mine, in spite of the opportunities that have presented themselves, never once has there been between this man and myself anything more intimate than a kiss. For it was my hope that God in His mercy would enable me to win my father's heart and obtain his consent before the consummation of the marriage. I have offended neither God nor my conscience, for I have waited till the age of thirty to see what you and my father would do for me. Throughout my youth I have kept myself in such virtue and chastity that no man alive could possibly reproach me in any way. Finally, in the light of my own reason with which I am endowed by God, realizing that I am old, and have no hope of finding a match worthy of my station, I have resolved to take a husband according to my own inclinations, not in order to satisfy the concupiscence of the eye, for as you know he is not handsome, nor to satisfy the lusts of the flesh, for there has been no carnal consummation, nor yet to satisfy pride and worldly ambition, for he is poor and has no prospects. No, my sole considerations were the virtue with which he is imbued, for which no one can deny him praise, and the deep love which he has borne me, a love which gives me hope that with him I will find kindness and contentment. I considered carefully the good and the evil that might befall me, and finally decided upon the course that seemed to me the best. For two long years I pondered this in my heart. My decision was to use up the rest of my days in his company, and I am determined to hold firm to this resolve, so firm indeed that no torment that I might endure, not even death itself, would make me swerve from what was in my mind. So, Madame, you will be pleased to excuse me for an eminently excusable offence, and permit me to enjoy the peace I hope to find with him.'

Seeing that Rolandine was resolute and that she meant every word she said, the Queen was quite incapable of making a reasonable reply. She burst into tears and went on raging at Rolandine, making accusations and hurling insults at her.

'Miserable wretch that you are! Instead of being humble and sorry for the serious offence you have committed, you dare to speak in this outrageous fashion with never a tear in your eye! That shows how obstinate you are and how hard your heart is! But if the King and your father heed my words, they'll put you where you'll be obliged to sing another tune!'

'Madame, since you accuse me of speaking outrageously,' replied Rolandine, 'I shall remain silent, unless it pleases you to give me leave to answer you.'

Having been given the order to speak, she then went on: 'It does not behove me, Madame, to address you in any way that is outrageous or lacking in the respect that I owe you, for you are my mistress and the greatest princess in Christendom. Nor has it ever been my desire or intention to do so. However, I have no advocate to speak in my defence. My only advocate is the truth, the truth which is known to me alone, and I am bound to declare it to you fearlessly, in the hope that once it is known to you, you will think better of me than to call me by the names you have so far been pleased to use. I am not afraid that any mortal creature should hear how I have conducted myself in the affair with which I am charged, since I know that there has been no offence either to God or to my honour. It is this that makes me speak fearlessly, for I am sure that He who sees my heart is with me, and if such a judge [is] in my favour, then indeed I would be wrong to fear those who are subject to His judgement. Why then should I weep? My heart and my conscience are clear in this matter. Far from being sorry for anything I have done, I would act exactly as I have acted, if I had to choose again. But you, Madame, you have very good reason to be weeping now. Not only did you do me grave injustices when I was young, but you have just committed another grave injustice against me in publicly accusing me of an offence that ought more properly to be imputed to yourself. If it were the case that I had sinned against God, the King, yourself, my parents and my own conscience, then indeed I should be obdurate not to weep tears of repentance. But there is no reason at all why I should weep for something that is holy, just and good, and which would never have been known to anyone except as something entirely honourable, were it not for the fact that you prematurely made it common knowledge [and turned it into a scandal] – an act which demonstrates that you are more interested in bringing about my dishonour than in protecting the honour of your own house and kindred. However, since such is your desire, I shall not contradict you. For whatever punishment you may choose to order, I shall derive as much pleasure from my undeserved suffering as you will derive in inflicting it. So, Madame, give orders to Monsieur my father to impose whatever tortures you think fit! I am sure that he will not fail to carry them out. At least I [shall] have the satisfaction of seeing him carry out your wishes to the sole end of bringing me unhappiness, the satisfaction of seeing him obediently applying himself to do me harm, exactly as in the past he has neglected my well-being to do your bidding. But I have a Father in Heaven, who, I know, will grant me patience enough to endure the evils which I see you preparing for me, and in Him alone do I place my trust.'

The Queen, beside herself with rage, ordered Rolandine to be taken out of her sight and shut up alone in a room where it would be impossible for her to speak to anyone. However, they did not deprive her of her gouvernante, and through her she was able to inform the bastard of what had befallen her and ask his advice on what she should do. The bastard, thinking that the services he had rendered the King in the past might stand in his favour, made his way post-haste to the court. He found the King out in the country and told him the truth about what had happened, requesting that his majesty would look kindly on a nobleman of slender means and appease the Queen, so that the marriage might be consummated. The King made no other reply than to say: 'Do you assure me that you have married her?'

'Yes, Sire,' answered the bastard, 'but only with "words in the present", and if it please you, proper conclusion shall be made.'*

The King looked down, and saying no more, went back to his château. No sooner was he there than he instructed his captain of the guards to take the bastard prisoner. However, a friend of the bastard, who knew the King well enough to guess his intention, warned him to go away and take refuge in a house that he had nearby. If the King ordered a search for him, as he suspected he would, then he would have him warned immediately

* A legal formula. Under ecclesiastical law exchange of promises followed by sexual intercourse sufficed to establish marriage.

so that he could flee the kingdom; equally, if things quietened down, he would have him informed, so that he could return. The bastard took his friend's advice and acted on it with such alacrity that the captain of the guards was quite unable to find him.

Meanwhile the King and Queen came together to discuss what they would do about the poor young woman who had the honour to be related to them. At the Queen's suggestion it was decided that she should be sent back to her father, who was duly apprised of the facts of the case. However, before they sent her, they arranged for several men of the Church and some members of the King's Council to speak with her. These men made it plain to her that since her marriage was established by nothing more than exchange of words, it could quite easily be dissolved, provided that they gave one another up entirely. It was, they informed her, the King's wish that she should do so, in order that the honour of her house should be upheld. Her reply was that she was ready to obey the King in all things, provided there was no conflict with her conscience. But that which God had joined together no man could put asunder, so let them not seek to induce her to do anything so unreasonable. For if love and honest intent founded on the fear of God were the true and sure bonds of marriage, then she was, she declared, so firmly bound that nothing, neither fire, nor steel nor water, could loose her bonds. Death alone could do so, and to Death alone and to no other would she give up her ring and her vows. She begged them, therefore, to speak to her no more of the contrary course of action. So resolute was she, that she would die to preserve her faith, rather than break it and live. The King's spokesmen reported how Rolandine had replied with firm determination. Once it was realized that there would be no other way of making her renounce her husband, it was decided to send her back to her father. She was dispatched in such a pathetic condition, that everyone who saw her as she passed by was moved to tears. Although she [had done] wrong, the punishment was so harsh and her constancy so great, that it made her offence seem a virtue. Her father, when he heard the pitiful news, refused to see her, and sent her to a castle in a forest – a castle which he had built in previous years for a purpose which is worthy of being recounted [in a later story.] There, in this castle in the forest, he kept her imprisoned for a long time and had it constantly impressed upon her that if she renounced her husband, he would acknowledge her once again as his daughter and set her free. But she held firm. To preserve the bond of marriage she preferred to endure the bonds of prison. Far rather that, than all the freedom in the world without her husband. It seemed, to see her face, that all her pains were a pleasant pastime, so gladly did she endure them for the one she loved.

And then – ah, what words can express the wickedness of men? – the bastard, despite his obligation to her, fled to Germany, where he had many friends. It was quite plain from his lack of constancy that it was not true and perfect love that had led him to attach himself to Rolandine but rather greed and ambition. In fact, he soon became so enamoured of a German woman that he totally neglected to write letters to the one who for his sake was enduring so much tribulation. Fortune had treated them harshly yet had never deprived them of the means of writing to one another. No, the cause was the base and senseless love to which the bastard had succumbed. Rolandine's heart was filled with such foreboding of the truth that she could take no more repose. When finally she heard from him, the way he wrote was so cool, so different in style from the way he had written in the past, that she began to suspect that it was some new love that was taking her husband away from her [and making him so distant.] Nothing, no, not all the pain and suffering that had been inflicted on her, had been able to accomplish such a thing. Yet her love was perfect and true, and she could not sit in judgement on the evidence of mere suspicion. So she found a way of sending a trusted servant in secret, not to bear letters or messages to the bastard, but to spy on him and discover the truth. And when the servant returned, he reported that he had found the bastard deeply enamoured of a German lady, and that he had heard a rumour that it was his intention to marry her, for she was a very wealthy woman. Poor Rolandine's heart was so utterly overcome with sorrow at these tidings that she fell gravely ill. People who knew the cause of her condition told her on her father's behalf that, since she could now appreciate the extent of the bastard's wickedness, she had every right to abandon him. And to this end they did everything in their power to persuade her. Yet, even though she was tormented to the utmost degree, there was nothing that could make her change her mind. In this her final temptation she showed how great was the power of her love and the extent of her virtue. For as the bastard's love diminished, so hers grew. In spite of all, her love remained perfect and whole, for as it drained from the bastard's heart, so it flowed into the heart of Rolandine. When she knew at last that in her heart alone was all the love that once had dwelt in two, she resolved to nourish it there till one of them should die.

Thus it was that the divine Goodness, who is perfect charity and true love, had pity on her sorrow and looked upon her long-suffering, for not many days later the bastard in full pursuit of another woman met his end. Rolandine, informed of his death by the very people who had been present at his burial, sent to her father a request that she might speak to him. He went to her at once, though since she had been locked away he had never once spoken a word to her. He heard her out while she delivered her just defence, and then instead of condemning her and killing her as he had often threatened, he took her in his arms and wept bitterly.

'There is more right on your side than on mine,' he said, 'for if any offence has been committed in what you have done, it is I who am to blame. But since God has ordained that it should be so, I will make amends for the past.'

So he took her back to his home and treated her as his eldest daughter. She was wooed by a gentleman who bore the same name and arms as her father and who was a sober and virtuous man. He spent a lot of time in Rolandine's company and held her in such high esteem, that he would praise her where others would have blamed her, for he knew that virtue had been her only goal. Both Rolandine and her father were favourable towards the marriage, and so it was concluded without delay. It is true that one of her brothers, who was the sole heir to the estate, refused to agree that she should have any share in it whatsoever, on the grounds that she had been disobedient to her father. Indeed, after the father's death he treated her so harshly that she and her husband, who was a younger son, were hard put to keep themselves alive. But God provided for them. For one day this brother who wanted to keep everything for himself died unexpectedly, leaving behind him both his own inheritance and the inheritance that rightly belonged to his sister. Thus she became heir to a fine large house, and there she lived a devout and respectable life in the company of her husband, whom she loved dearly, and by whom she too was much beloved. And at last, after having raised the two sons whom it had pleased God to grant them, she gave up her soul to Him in whom she had always had perfect trust.

*

'Well, Ladies, let the men, who are so fond of representing us women as lacking in constancy, produce an example of a husband who was as good, as faithful and as constant as the woman in this story. I'm quite certain that they would have a great deal of difficulty in doing so – so much, in fact, that I'd rather let them off than put them to such a lot of trouble! And as far as the ladies are concerned, [I would ask] that you will all either not love at all or else love as perfectly as Rolandine, so that our honour and reputation be upheld. And don't let anyone say to you that she sullied her honour, for through her steadfastness she has greatly magnified the honour of us all.'

'In all truth, Parlamente,' said Oisille, 'you have told us the story of a woman who possessed a noble and virtuous heart. But what enhances her constancy is her husband's disloyalty and the fact that he deliberately left her for someone else.'

'I think that was the hardest thing for her to bear,' said Longarine, 'for when a couple are completely united in love, no burden is so heavy that it cannot be carried with a cheerful heart; but when one of them fails to meet the demands of duty and leaves the full burden to be borne by the other, the weight is beyond endurance.'

'Well then,' said Geburon, 'you ought to take pity on us, seeing that we bear the whole burden of love and you never lift a finger to ease the load!'

'Ah, Geburon!' said Parlamente. 'The burdens borne by men and by women are often very different. A woman's love is rooted in God and founded on honour, and is so just and reasonable that any man who is untrue to such love must be considered base and wicked in the sight of God and in the eyes of all [good] men. But most [men's] love is based on pleasure, so much so that women, not being aware of men's evil intentions, sometimes allow themselves to be drawn too far. But when God makes them see the wickedness in the heart of the man of whom they had previously thought nothing but good, they can still break it off with their honour and reputation intact. Those wanton loves are best which are the shortest!'

'If what you're maintaining,' said Hircan, 'is that an honest woman can honourably abandon her love for a man, but that a man can't do the same, then it's just an argument made up to suit your own fancies. As if the hearts of men and women were any different! Although their clothes and faces may be, their dispositions are the same – except in so far as the more concealed wickedness is worse!'

'I'm well aware,' said Parlamente somewhat angrily, 'that you think more highly of women whose wickedness is *not* concealed!'

'Let's not pursue that particular topic,' intervened Simontaut. 'To put an end once and for all to this question of the difference between the hearts of men and women, I say that the best of them is good for nothing, be they men or women! So let's hear another good story instead, and see who Parlamente is going to choose to tell it.'

'I'll choose Geburon,' she said.

'Well, since I began by talking about the Franciscan friars,' he said, 'I don't want to overlook the monks of Saint Benedict. I must tell you about something that happened to one of them not so long ago. Of course, I don't mean to undermine your good opinion of decent people, just because I tell you a story of one bad monk. However, as the Psalmist has said: "All men are liars", and again, "There is none that doeth good, no not one." So it seems to me that one cannot go wrong in esteeming man for what he is. If there is good in him, one should attribute it to Him who is its source, not to those whom He has created. For in giving too much honour and glory to God's creatures, or in esteeming themselves too highly, most people are greatly deceived. And so that you won't think that extreme austerity makes extreme concupiscence impossible, I will tell you about something that happened during the reign of Francis I.'

STORY TWENTY-TWO

My story is about a Prior of Saint Martin-des-Champs in Paris. I shall not reveal his name, because of the friendship I have borne him. Up to the age of fifty he led such an austere life that his saintly reputation spread far and wide throughout the realm, and there was not a prince or princess who did not receive him with great honour when he paid them a visit. There was not a single piece of monastic reform for which he did not have some responsibility, and he was known as 'the father of true monasticism'. He was elected visitor to the celebrated order of the ladies of Fontevrault. The nuns were so much in awe of him that whenever he visited one of their convents, they would tremble in terror, and in an attempt to soften his severity they would treat him like royalty. At first he resisted this, but eventually, as he approached his fifty-fifth year, he began to rather enjoy this treatment in spite of having originally scorned it. He began, in fact, to regard himself as representing the general good of the monastic community at large, and so became very much more concerned to preserve his health than he had been in the past. Although the rule of his order forbade him ever to touch meat, he gave himself a dispensation – something that he never did for anybody else, saying that upon his shoulders rested the entire burden of the religious life. Accordingly he indulged himself to such an extent, that after having been once a very lean monk, he now turned into a very fat one. Now this transformation in his style of life was accompanied by a transformation in matters of the heart. He started to look more attentively at the faces around him, although previously the mere sight of them had been a matter of conscience for him. Then, as he gazed upon these fair countenances, which were all the more desirable for being veiled, he began to lust after them. And in order to satisfy his desire he invented all manner of ingenious methods, so that the good shepherd soon turned into a wolf. There were not a few respectable convents where he managed to find some slow-witted girl whom he could trick. However, after he had carried on in this wicked fashion for some considerable time, the divine Goodness had pity on his poor lost sheep, and unable to endure it any longer brought the reign of this overweening villain to an end in a manner which I shall now recount to you.

One day he was visiting a convent at Gif near Paris, and while he was hearing the nuns' confessions, he came across one by the name of Marie Héroet. Her voice was gentle and her words sweet, and gave promise that her face and her heart would be no less so. In fact, the mere sound of her voice fired the Prior with a passion far stronger than any he had felt for any of his other nuns. As he spoke to her he bent down low so as to see her. And what he saw was an adorable little mouth with lips so red that he could not restrain himself from lifting her veil to see if the eyes matched the rest. They did indeed, and his heart was overwhelmed with such a violent ardour that he lost all desire to eat and drink. His composure quite left him, however hard he tried to hide his feelings, and when he got back to his priory he simply could not settle down. For whole days and nights he fretted, searching desperately for some way of satisfying his desire and having from this nun what he had had from not a few before her. He feared it would be no easy task, for the girl had been very modest in her speech, and at the same time she was obviously too clever to be taken in. So his hopes were not high. Moreover, he knew he was old and ugly. He therefore decided that rather than try to talk her round, he would frighten her into doing his bidding. Before many days had elapsed, he was back at the convent of Gif, this time putting on a more austere manner than he had ever done before. He scolded every single nun in the convent. He told one she was not wearing her veil low enough, another that she carried her head too high, another that she did not curtsey the way a nun should, and so on. He was so severe about all these trivial things that they were terrified of him. He might have been God Almighty in some picture of the Last Judgement! Gout-ridden as he was, he wore himself out so much doing his rounds, that as the time for vespers approached, he found himself, as he had carefully planned, in the dormitory.

'It's time to say vespers, reverend Father,' the Abbess said to him.

'You run along and get someone else to say vespers, Mother,' he replied. 'I'm so tired, I think I'll stay here. It's not that I want to rest – I have something to say to Sister Marie. I've heard very bad reports about her. I'm told that she chatters in the most worldly fashion.'

The Abbess, who was the aunt of the girl's mother, asked him to give her a severe reprimand and then left her alone with him, the only other person there being a young monk who had accompanied the Prior. Once he was on his own with Sister Marie, he lifted her veil and told her to look at him. She replied that her rule forbade her to look at men.

'You speak well, my daughter,' came the reply, 'but you must not think of [us monks] as men.'

Afraid lest she be committing an act of disobedience, Sister Marie looked him in the face. She found him so ugly, that she felt that merely to look at him was more in the way of penance than sin anyway. Then our fine father said a few words about his great love for her, and tried to put his hand on her breasts. Quite rightly and properly she pushed it away. He was furious, and said: 'What business has a nun to know that she has breasts?'

'I know perfectly well that I have, and I also know that neither you nor anyone else is going to touch them. I'm not so young and so ignorant, you know, that I don't understand what is a sin and what isn't!'

Seeing that she was not going to be won over by this approach, he went on to try another.

'Alas, my daughter! I shall have to tell you what a desperate condition I am in. The fact is that I am suffering from an illness, and the doctors say that it is incurable unless I indulge myself and take my pleasure with a woman whom I love passionately. I would not for the life of me commit a mortal sin, but in such desperate straits I know that mere fornication is nothing compared with the sin of homicide. So if you have any concern for my life, you can save me and at the same time save your own conscience from the burden of an act of cruelty!'

She asked him what kind of a game he thought he was playing. He replied that her conscience might be guided by his, and that he would do nothing that would weigh on the conscience of either of them. To give her a preliminary idea of the sort of pastime he required, he flung his arms round her and tried to throw her on to a bed. Knowing full well what his intentions were, she cried out and struggled so hard that he only managed to get hold of her habit. His carefully laid plans frustrated, he turned on her like a madman. Not only had he apparently no longer any conscience, he was also completely deprived of his natural reason, for he thrust his hand under her robe and scratched wildly at whatever came in contact with his nails. The poor girl screamed at the top of her lungs and fell in a faint on the floor. Having heard the scream, the Abbess rushed into the dormitory. While she had been at vespers she had remembered leaving the nun, who was her own niece's daughter, with our fine father. She had suddenly felt a twinge of conscience and had felt impelled to leave the service and listen at the dormitory door. Hearing her niece's daughter cry out, she pushed open the door, which was being held by the young monk. When the Prior saw the Abbess standing there, he just pointed to the unconscious nun and said:

'Really, it was wrong of you, Mother, not to tell me about Sister Marie's state of health. Not knowing she had a weak constitution, I had her standing in front of me while I issued my reprimand, and she just fainted, as you can see.'

They brought her round with vinegar and other suitable medicaments, but found that she had also injured her head in the fall. Once she was conscious, the Prior, who was afraid lest she should tell her aunt what the true cause of her injury was, somehow managed to whisper in her ear:

'My daughter, I command you on pain of eternal damnation for disobedience never to say a word about what I have done. It was the extreme nature of my love that drove me to act as I did. And since I can see that you have no intention of returning my love, I will never mention it to you again. But let me assure you that if you did change your mind, I would have you elected as abbess of one of the three best abbeys in the kingdom!'

But she replied that she would rather languish in perpetual imprisonment than admit any other lover than Him who had died for her on the cross. With Him she would rather endure all the suffering in the world than enjoy all the pleasures in the world against His will. And she warned the Prior that if he ever spoke to her in this fashion again, she would tell the mother Abbess. Thereupon this bad shepherd made to leave his flock, but in order to appear in a favourable light and also to take one more look at the object of his passions, he lingered on to speak to the Abbess.

'Mother,' he said, 'would you have your daughters sing a *Salve Regina* in honour of the Virgin, in whom is my hope and trust?'

The Abbess did as he requested and as the nuns sang, the old fox did nothing but weep – not out of devotion, but because he was so disappointed at not having succeeded! The nuns imagined it was because of his love for the Virgin Mary, and thought what a holy man he was. But Sister Marie knew how bad he really was, and prayed inwardly to [Our Lord] that He would confound this man who had so little respect for virginity.

So it was that the hypocrite returned to Saint Martin's, where the sinful fire continued day and night to burn in his heart, as he turned over in his mind all possible ways of satisfying his desires. His greatest fear was the Abbess, who was a virtuous woman. So he set about devising a way of removing her from her convent. He went to see Madame de Vendôme, who at that time was living at La Fère, where she had founded and built a Benedictine house named Mont d'Olivet. In his self-appointed role of reformer-in-chief he informed her that the current Abbess of Mont d'Olivet was not competent to run a community of that kind. The good lady asked him to provide somebody else who would be worthy of the office. This was just what he was waiting for, and he recommended that she appoint the Abbess of Gif, who was, he told her, the most competent abbess in the whole of France. So Madame de Vendôme immediately sent for her and put her in charge of Mont d'Olivet, while the Prior, who held control of all the votes in the order, had elected as Abbess of Gif a nun who would bow to his wishes.

Once the new Abbess had been elected, the Prior went back to the convent of Gif to try once again to win Sister Marie Héroët round, this time by persuasion and kind words. But finding that he still could not prevail, he went home to his priory in a state of desperation. He was fearful now lest his doings should become known, and, partly in order to accomplish his original design, partly to take revenge for the way he had been so cruelly rejected, he arranged for somebody to go into the [Abbey] of Gif by night and make off with their relics. Then he accused their confessor, an aged and worthy man, of having committed the theft. He had him imprisoned in the priory of Saint Martin and in the meantime set up two false witnesses, who, on his instructions, signed a document according to which they had seen the confessor committing an improper and sordid act with Sister Marie in a garden. The aim was to force the old man to admit such an offence. However, the confessor knew all about the Prior's misdeeds, and requested to be sent before the Chapter, where he would tell the whole truth to the assembled monks. The Prior refused to grant the request for fear the confessor's defence should turn into a condemnation of himself. But the old man held firm, and as a result was treated so badly in prison that some say he actually died there. According to other stories he was forced to renounce his habit and was chased out of the kingdom. Be that as it may, the poor man was never seen again.

Thinking he now had a hold over Sister Marie, the Prior went off to her convent, where his Abbess, who bowed to his every whim, never contradicted a word he spoke. He started by exercising his authority as official visitor and had every single nun brought before him, one by one, in a room where he could interview them as part of his visitation. When it came to the turn of Sister Marie, he said to her:

'Sister Marie, you are aware of the crime that is laid against you and that your pretence of chastity has availed you nothing, for it is known now that you are the very opposite of chaste.'

Sister Marie, who no longer had her good aunt to guard her, replied firmly:

'Bring my accuser before me and we shall see whether he will maintain his evil opinion in my presence.'

'We need no further proof, since the confessor already stands convicted.'

'But I know that he is a good man and that he would never make a false confession. However, supposing he *has* made such a confession, if you bring him here, I shall prove the contrary of his statements.'

The Prior began to realize that she was not going to be shaken.

'I am your father, and my sole desire is to safeguard your honour. Therefore, I shall permit the matter to rest on your conscience and shall accept your word. I enjoin you to tell me the truth on pain of mortal sin and ask you to answer me this: when you were placed in this house, were you or were you not a virgin?'

'Father, I was five years of age when I came here. That should be sufficient evidence of my virginity.'

'Well then, my daughter, have you since the time of your entry lost that precious flower?'

She swore that she had not and that the only danger to its preservation had come from him. To which he replied that he was not able to believe her and that further proof was required.

'What proof do you require?' she asked.

'The same proof as I require from all the others,' he answered. 'In my capacity as visitor I not only examine the soul, but also the body. All your Abbesses and Prioresses have submitted themselves to inspection at my hands. You need have no fear, if my visitation extends to an inspection of your virginity. Kindly lie down on the bed and raise the front part of your habit over your face.'

'You've already talked enough about your base passion,' she replied in high indignation, 'to give me every reason to think that your intention as far as my virginity is concerned is to deprive me of it rather than to examine it in your capacity as visitor. So understand that I have no intention of consenting.'

Then he told her she was excommunicate for breaking her vow of obedience and that if she did not consent, he would dishonour her before the whole Chapter by making a statement about the offence she had committed with the confessor. Without a trace of fear Sister Marie replied:

'He who knows the heart of His servants will reward me with honour in His sight for the disgrace you threaten to bring upon me in the eyes of men. Therefore, since your viciousness has already reached such depths, I would far rather it carry through its cruelty towards me to the bitter end than that it carry through its evil designs and desires. For I know that God is a righteous judge.'

Thereupon the Prior called the whole Chapter together, forced Sister Marie to kneel before him, and in a state of extraordinary rage addressed her thus:

'Sister Marie, it is with extreme displeasure that I find the just admonitions which I have administered to you have been of no effect, and that you have lapsed to such a dangerous degree that I am constrained to impose on you a penance contrary to my custom. Having examined your confessor with regard to certain offences with which he has been charged, he has confessed to me that he has made abuse of your person [in] a place where he was seen by two people who have duly given testimony. Therefore, as you have been raised to the status of Sister in charge of novices, so now I command not only that you should be reduced to the lowest rank but that you should henceforth eat bread and water on the ground in front of all the Sisters, until such time as your contrition shall have been seen to be such as to merit mercy.'

Sister Marie had been warned by one of her companions who knew what had been going on that if she answered in any way that displeased the Prior again, he would surely place her *in pace* – in other words, have her locked away for life. So she heard her sentence in silence, her eyes raised Heavenward, as she prayed to Him who had been her stay against sin that He would now give her patience to endure her sufferings. The Prior further prohibited her from speaking to her mother and other relatives when they visited the convent for a period of three years, and she was not to write any letters other than those written in community.

After this the wretched man left the convent never to return again. As for the poor girl, she continued to suffer for some considerable time because of the punishment the Prior had imposed on her. However, her mother, who loved Marie the best of all her children, was extremely surprised when she stopped receiving news from her daughter. She spoke to one of her sons, a man of wisdom and honour, of how she believed that her daughter was dead, and that the nuns were concealing the truth for the sake of the annual payment. She begged him to find some way, no matter what, of finding out whether his sister was alive. So he went to the convent without delay, only to be told the usual tale – that his sister had been sick in bed for the past three years and was quite unable to move. He refused to be satisfied with this and swore that if he was not allowed to see his sister he would climb over the walls and force his way into the convent. The nuns were so alarmed that they brought his sister to the grille, but the Abbess kept so close to her that she could hear every word she spoke to her brother. However, Sister Marie, full of good sense as she was, had put in writing all that has been recounted above, together with a thousand other acts of deception committed by the Prior in his attempts to seduce her. It would take too long to tell you everything, but there is *one* thing I mustn't forget to tell. During the time when Sister Marie's aunt was still Abbess it had occurred to the Prior that he might have been rejected because he was ugly. So he arranged for temptation to be put in her way in the shape of another monk who was both young and handsome, hoping that if she yielded to the younger man for love, she might, if intimidated, yield to him also. But in the event, when the young monk accosted the poor girl in the garden with certain proposals and certain indecent gestures that I'd be too embarrassed to describe, she immediately ran off to the Abbess, who happened at the time to be in conversation with the Prior himself.

'Mother, Mother,' she cried, 'these monks that come to visit us, they're demons in disguise!'

The Prior, terrified in case he was found out, turned to the Abbess and said with a laugh: 'Without a shadow of doubt, Mother, she is right!'

Then he caught hold of Sister Marie's hand, and said for the Abbess's benefit: 'I had heard that Sister Marie spoke very well indeed that she had such a nimble tongue that she was generally thought to be rather worldly in her ways. So, much against my natural disposition I forced myself to say to her all the things that men of the world are accustomed to say to women – just as I have read in books, for I have never had any personal experience of such matters and am as ignorant about them as the day I was born. When she answered back in such a virtuous manner I thought it must be because I am so old and ugly. So I instructed my young brother to say the same sort of things to her, and as you see, she has virtuously resisted him also. I deem her exceedingly virtuous and good, and in view of her qualities I would like her from now on to have a position in this convent second only to your own and be in charge of the novices, so that her good intentions may flourish and continue to grow in virtue!'

This deed and several others were perpetrated by our fine monk during the three years he was enamoured of this nun – who, as I said, wrote the whole unhappy story down on paper and handed it to her brother through the grille. The brother sent the story to his mother, who in desperation came to Paris, where she found the Queen of Navarre, the King's only sister, and showed her the piteous account her daughter had written, saying, 'Never trust these hypocrites of yours again, Madame! I thought I had set my daughter on her way in the environs of Paradise, and I find I have placed her on the road to Hell, in the hands of the worst devils who could dwell there, for devils do not tempt us unless we so desire, but these men are willing to take us by force if desire is deficient!'

The Queen of Navarre was greatly distressed to hear this, for she had complete faith in the Prior of Saint Martin's – indeed she had placed him in authority over her own sisters-in-law, the Abbess of Montivilliers and the Abbess of Caen. But the crime so horrified her that she was anxious to avenge the innocence of the poor girl at once and promptly informed the King's chancellor, who at that time was the papal legate in France. The Prior of Saint Martin's was duly sent for. All that he could offer by way of excuse was that he was a poor old man of seventy. He made an appeal to the Queen, begging her [in the name of all the favours she might ever wish him], and in recompense for all his past services, that she would have the proceedings stopped. He would then publicly declare that Sister Marie Héroët was the very pearl of honour and virginity. The Queen was so amazed when she heard this that she did not know what to reply, and simply left him standing there. The poor man, covered in shame, went back to his monastery. He refused to be seen again by anyone and lived for only another year. Sister

Marie Heroët received the recognition she [deserved] for the virtues implanted in her by God. She was removed from the Abbey of Gif, where she had witnessed so much wickedness, and on the order of the King himself was appointed Abbess of the Abbey of Gy near Montargis. She reformed the Abbey, and there she continued to live, full of the spirit of God, and constantly praising Him for having restored her honour and her tranquillity.

*

'That, Ladies, is a story which demonstrates what we read in the Gospel [and in Saint Paul's Epistle to the Corinthians] – that God chooses the weak things of the world to confound the things which are mighty, and the things which are despised in the eyes of men to confound the glory of those who think they are something, yet are nothing. And note well, Ladies, that without the grace of God there is no man in whom we may believe goodness to dwell. Equally, there is no temptation which with Him one cannot victoriously overcome, as you can see from the discomfiture of this man who believed himself to be among the righteous, and from the exaltation of this girl whom he wished to appear sinful and wicked. And in this is proven the truth of the saying of Our Lord: "Everyone that exalteth himself shall be abased; and he that humbleth himself shall be exalted."'

'Ah! What a disgraceful thing!' exclaimed Oisille. 'To think that the Prior deceived so many good and decent people! For I can see that they placed more trust in him than in God.'

'Well, I wouldn't have been one of them,' said Normerfide. 'The mere sight of a monk fills me with horror – I couldn't even bring myself to make my confession to one. In my view they're the worst possible type of men and never attach themselves to a household without leaving a trail of dissension and disgrace behind them.'

'There are some good ones,' Oisille said, 'and one must not judge them all adversely merely because of the bad ones. But the best ones are the ones who are least given to frequenting the houses of the laity and keeping company with women.'

'What you say is true,' said Ennasuite, 'because the less you see of them, the less you know about them, and the less you know about them, the higher your opinion of them is. You soon find out what they're like if you have much to do with them.'

'Well,' said Nomerfide, 'let's leave it at that – *laissons le moustier où il est*,* as you might say, and see who Geburon is going to pick to speak next.'

Geburon was anxious to make amends for the offence, if offence it was, of having exposed the appalling and disgraceful life of a corrupt monk in order to give warning against those who were equally hypocritical. He held Oisille in high esteem – as indeed she deserved to be held, for she was a lady of great wisdom and as slow to speak ill of people as she was quick to praise and proclaim the good she knew to be in them – so it was she whom he asked to tell the next story.

'I ask Madame Oisille to speak next, in order that she may tell us something in favour of the religious life.'

'We have all so firmly sworn to speak the truth,' replied Oisille, 'that I could not undertake to plead that case. Moreover, your story has reminded me of a tale so tragic that I am compelled to tell it to you, for it happened in my time and near my part of the country. Therefore, Ladies, in order that your minds should not be so beguiled by the hypocrisy of men who consider themselves more religious than others that your faith, diverted from the straight and narrow path, seeks salvation in some other creature rather than in Him alone who desired no companion in our creation and redemption, in Him alone who is almighty to save us unto eternal life and in this temporal life to console us and deliver us from all our tribulations, knowing that often Satan transforms himself into an Angel of Light – in order, I say, that your eye should not alight on external things, blinded by the outward appearance of sanctity and devotion, and linger on those things that it ought to shun, it seems good to me that I should tell you this story, for it is a story that is of [our] time.'

* Proverb used by Villon in a famous passage (*Testament*, I. 265: 'Let's leave the monastery where it is?)

STORY TWENTY-THREE

There lived in the Périgord a certain gentleman who was so devoted to the cult of Saint Francis that he was under the impression that anyone who wore the Franciscan habit must be as holy as the good Saint himself. It was in the Saint's honour that he had had bedrooms and dressing-rooms built in his house to accommodate the Franciscan brothers, and he followed their advice in everything, even the smallest domestic matters. In that way, he thought, he must surely be on the right road. Now it happened that the gentleman's wife, who was very beautiful and no less wise and virtuous, produced a fine male child. Her husband's affection for her was doubled, and in order to provide a celebration for his dear wife, he sent for one of his brothers-in-law. As supper-time approached, along came a certain friar, whose name for the sake of his order I shall not reveal. The husband was delighted when he saw him, for the man was his spiritual father from whom he had no secrets. After the gentleman, his wife, his brother-in-law and the friar had talked for a while, they all sat down to supper. As they ate, the gentleman looked at his wife, who had all the grace and beauty required in a woman to arouse a husband's desire, and for all to hear he asked of the friar: 'Is it true, father, that it is a mortal sin for a man to sleep with his wife during the period after her confinement?'

The friar replied sternly, although the way he spoke and the expression on his face were the opposite of what he felt in his heart.

'There is no question, Monsieur. I believe it to be one of the most grievous sins that can be committed in matrimony. You have only to consider the example of the Blessed Virgin Mary, who would not enter the Temple until after her Purification, although of purification she had no need. It is plain, therefore, that you most certainly should abstain from this small pleasure, just as the Virgin Mary, in order to obey the Law, abstained from going into the Temple where alone she could find her consolation. What is more, Monsieur, the doctors of medicine say that there is considerable danger for any offspring that might be conceived under such circumstances.'

The gentleman was somewhat disappointed to hear this, because he had hoped that the good father would give him permission. But he did not pursue the matter any further. As for the good father himself, he had drunk somewhat more than he ought, and as he spoke he too was taking a look at the lady of the house, and thinking to himself that if he had been the husband, he would not have asked for advice before lying with her. Thus, even as a fire is kindled and spreads little by little until the whole house is alight, so [this poor] *frater* began to burn with such concupiscence that he resolved then and there to quench his desires once and for all – desires which he had for three whole years now kept hidden in his heart.

Once the tables had been cleared away, he took the gentleman by the hand, led him to his wife's bedside, and as she listened said to him: 'Monsieur, since I know well what great love is between yourself and Madame here present, and since such love combined with such youth can cause such torment, I am moved to compassion for you, and am minded to tell you a secret of our holy theology. For the law, which is so strict with regard to abuses on the part of indiscreet husbands, has no desire to permit men of good conscience such as yourself to be deprived of true understanding. Consequently, Monsieur, although when in the presence of other people I stated the rigour of the law's provisons, I must not conceal from you, who are wise, its provisions of mercy. Know therefore, my son, that there are women and women, even as there are men and men. In the first instance we must know from Madame here present, since it is now three weeks since the time of the birth, whether she is yet free of the flux of blood?'

To this she replied that she was completely clean.

The friar said, 'I can grant you permission to sleep with her, and you need have nothing on your conscience, provided that you promise me two things.'

The gentleman of course consented willingly.

'The first thing is that you speak of this to no one and go to your bed in secret. The second thing is that you do not go to your bed until after two o'clock in the morning, so that you do not disturb Madame's digestion with your pleasures.'

The husband promised solemnly on his oath to do these things. The good father knew the man was more a fool than a liar, and was quite sure he would be as good as his word. So after they had talked a little while longer he retired to his room, wishing them both a good night and piously pronouncing his benediction. As he went out, he took the gentleman by the hand, and said: 'Monsieur, you must be sure to go now, for you must not keep the dear lady awake any longer.' The gentleman gave his wife a kiss, saying, 'Leave your door open for me, my dear!' This the fine father heard and duly noted. The two men then went to their respective rooms. But the friar had no intention of sleeping or resting. As soon as the house had gone quiet, at about the time he was accustomed to go to matins, he rose and crept stealthily to the lady's bedroom. The door had been left open for the master of the house, so in he went, cunningly snuffed out the candle, and jumped straight into bed with his host's wife without uttering a word. Thinking it was her husband, the lady said: 'Now, now, my dear! You're not keeping that promise you made to our confessor! You said you wouldn't come till two!' Our Franciscan, by this time more intent on the active than the contemplative life, was afraid of being recognized, so concentrated more on satisfying the lusts that had so long infected his soul than on offering a reply, and this surprised the lady considerably. When the Franciscan saw that it was near the time when the husband was to come, he got out of bed and returned to his own room as quickly as he could.

Before it had been raging lust that had prevented him sleeping, now it was the terror that always follows vice [and sin] that robbed him of all repose. He went down to the porter, and said: 'My friend, I have been asked by Monsieur to go to our monastery at once to say some prayers which he devoutly desires. I beg you, fetch my horse for me, and open the door without making any noise, for it is a very secret and urgent matter that is in hand.' The porter, who thought that he would be doing his master a great service in obeying the Franciscan's instructions, quietly opened the door and let him out. It was then that the husband woke up and saw that it was nearly the time when the friar had said he could go to his wife. So he clambered out of bed and hurried along in his nightshirt to her bedroom – where by God's ordinance he had a perfect right to go without seeking permission from mortal men. His wife, who did not realize what had happened, was extremely surprised to hear his voice in the dark at her bedside and said:

'What is this? So this is how you keep your promises to the good father! You said you would be careful with your health and with mine, and now not only do you come earlier than you should do, but you come back again! What are you thinking of!'

The gentleman was so disconcerted to hear this that he could not hide his annoyance, and said: 'These are fine words! I know in all truth that I've not been to bed with you for the past three weeks, and you're complaining now because I come to your bed too often. If you continue in this way, you'll make me think that my company displeases you and force me against all my habits and inclinations to look elsewhere for the pleasures which according to God's law I should take with you!'

The wife, thinking he was joking, replied:

'Come now, Monsieur! Do not deceive yourself in thinking you're deceiving me! For though you did not speak to me last time you came, I knew full well that you were there!'

Then he realized that someone had deceived both of them, and he swore solemnly to his wife that he had not yet been to her bed. Overcome with despair at this she pleaded amidst tears and lamentations that her husband make all speed to discover who it could have been, for the only other people sleeping in the house were her brother and the friar. Strongly suspecting the friar, the gentleman went straight to the bedroom [where he had been staying] and found it empty. To be more sure that the friar had left the house, he called for his gatekeeper and asked if he knew what had become of the good father. The gatekeeper told him the truth, and the gentleman, now certain of the evil deed that had been done, went back to his wife's room and said: 'My love, it is certain that it was our fine father confessor who came to your bed and performed his good works!'

All her life this lady had been careful for her honour. She fell into such a state of desperation that all human compassion and all feminine gentleness deserted her, and on her knees she implored her husband to take vengeance for this outrage. The husband lost not a moment, but jumped on his horse in hot pursuit of the Franciscan. Meanwhile the lady lay alone in her bed, with no counsel or consolation apart from her little newborn son. She dwelt upon the terrible thing that had happened and with no excuse for her ignorance judged herself guilty, the most miserable woman in the world. She had learnt from the Franciscans nothing but confidence in good works, satisfaction for sins through austerity of life, fasting and chastisement. She had remained ignorant of the grace given by our good God through the merit of His Son, ignorant of the remission of sins by His blood, ignorant of the reconciliation of the Father with us by His death and ignorant of the life given to sinners through His goodness and mercy. So deeply was she disturbed, so sorely beset by despair which sprang from the gravity and enormity of the sin, from her love for her husband and from her concern for the honour of her lineage, that it seemed better by far to die than to live such a life. Overwhelmed by her grief, she sank into such despair that not only was she diverted from the hope in God that every Christian ought to have, but became alienated too from all rationality and all remembrance of her own nature. Overwhelmed by sorrow, driven on by despair, no longer in the knowledge of God, no longer knowing herself, and in a state of violent frenzy, she seized one of the cords hanging from her bed and strangled herself with her own hands. But worse still, in the agony of this horrible death, her body, still struggling against extinction, writhed in such a manner that her foot came down upon her little child's face. His innocence was no guarantee that he should not follow his sorrowing, suffering mother into death. As he died, he let out such a cry that a woman who slept in the room got up immediately and lit a candle. There was her mistress hanging strangled from the bed-cord, the child lying dead, suffocated beneath her foot. In horror the woman ran into the brother's room and brought him to behold this tragic spectacle.

He was as stricken with grief as ever a brother who loves his sister with all his heart could be or should be. He asked the chambermaid who had committed such a hideous crime. She replied that she did not know, that no one had come into the room except her master and that he had gone away not a moment ago. The brother went into the gentleman's room and, failing to find him there, concluded at once that it must have been he who had perpetrated the deed. Without further inquiry he jumped on his horse, rode after him, and met him coming back after chasing the friar, whom to his great chagrin he had been unable to catch.

'Defend yourself!' cried the brother as soon as he caught sight of his brother-in-law. 'Base coward and villain! I trust in God that with the sword I bear I shall take revenge on you this day!'

The husband attempted to explain, but the other man was bearing down on him with his sword, and he was forced to defend himself before he could find out what the cause of the challenge was. They dealt one another so many blows in the course of the ensuing struggle that they were eventually obliged through loss of blood and fatigue to separate and rest. Once they had regained their breath, the husband turned to the other and said:

'Brother, what has happened to turn our friendship, which in the past has always been so close, into this cruel battle?'

'And what can have caused you to put to death my sister, the best woman who ever lived? And in a way so foul that under pretext of wishing to sleep with her you enter her room only to strangle her and hang her with the cord from your own bed?'

Hearing these words, the husband, more dead than alive, went towards his brother-in-law, placed his arms around him, and said: 'Is it possible? Is it possible that you've found your sister in this state?'

When he was assured that such was indeed the case, he went on: 'Listen, my brother, I beg you. Listen to the reason why I left the house.'

He told the whole story, and the part the Franciscan friar had played in it. The brother was overcome with dismay, and, bitterly regretting the way he had attacked him, begged for forgiveness.

'I have wronged you. Forgive me,' he said.

And the husband replied: 'If I have wronged you, then I am punished for it. For I am badly wounded and I do not think I shall live.'

The brother-in-law set the wounded man on to his horse again as best he could, and led him back to the house, where the very next day he died. He then confessed before the dead man's relatives that he had been the cause of his death and was advised, in order that justice might be satisfied, to go and seek pardon from King Francis, first of that name. Once husband, wife and child had been laid honourably to rest, he left on Good Friday to seek remission from the royal court. His quest was successful, and he obtained his pardon through the good offices of François Olivier, who was the Chancellor of Alençon at that time, and who, because of his excellent qualities, was later chosen by the King to be Chancellor of France.

*

'Ladies, the story I've told you is very true, and now you've heard it, I don't think there'll be one amongst you who won't think twice before giving that sort of pilgrim shelter under your roof. Remember, too, that the most venomous poison is the poison that has been kept concealed.'

'But what a great fool the husband was,' said Hircan, 'to invite a gallant like that to supper with a wife as beautiful and good as his was!'

'I remember a time,' said Geburon, 'when there wasn't a house in the country that didn't have a room dedicated to the use of the good fathers. Nowadays though, everyone knows what they're like, and people are more frightened of them than they are of outlaws and bandits.'

'In my opinion,' said Parlamente, 'if a woman is in bed, she should never let a priest in her room unless it's to administer the sacraments of the Church. If I ever have one in my room, you can take it as a sure sign that I'm about to breathe my last!'

'If the whole world were as severe as you,' observed Ennasuite, 'the poor priests would be worse than excommunicated, being separated from women in that fashion.'

'No need to worry about that!' Saffredent said. 'They'll never want for women!'

'It's extraordinary!' said Simontaut. 'They're the ones who tie us to our wives in the bonds of matrimony, and then they're low enough to try to undo those bonds and make us break the very vows *they* made us take in the first place!'

'It is a great shame,' said Oisille, 'that men who are in charge of the administration of the sacraments should play about with them in this frivolous way. They ought to be burned alive!'

'You'd do better to show them respect than to [burn them,]' Saffredent said. 'Flattering them would be more advantageous than insulting them. After all, they're the ones with the real power to do the dishonouring and the burning. So, *sinite eos*,* and let's see who's going to take over from Oisille.'

'I call upon Dagoucin,' said Oisille. 'I can see that he's falling into deep contemplation – he must have something interesting to tell us.'

'Since I cannot and dare not say what is in my mind,' he answered, 'I will tell you instead about a certain man who suffered because of a certain lady's cruelty, but later on benefited greatly from it. Love, when he is powerful and strong, holds himself in such high regard that he wishes to walk around completely naked and finds it irksome, even unbearable to be covered up. Yet, Ladies, often it happens that those who follow his counsel and venture to uncover their love too soon, receive little return on their pains. And that is exactly what happened to a gentleman of Castile, whose story you shall hear forthwith.'

* Matthew 15:14: 'Let them alone.' The verse continues: '. . . they be blind leaders of the blind . . .'.

STORY TWENTY-FOUR

At the [court] of Castile in the time of a king and queen whose names I shall not reveal there was a gentleman so perfect in appearance and character that there was not his like in the whole of Spain. Everyone marvelled at his fine qualities, but even more at the strangeness of his character, for to no one's knowledge had he ever loved or served any lady. At that court there were many ladies who were fit to turn ice to fire, yet not one of them had had the power to capture the heart of Elisor, for such was the gentleman's name.

The Queen, a lady of great virtue, but by no means exempt from that fire which burns the more the less it is made known, had observed that this gentleman had entered the service of none of her ladies, and she wondered at it. Then one day she asked him whether it could be possible that he really was as much without love as he pretended. He replied that if she could but see his heart as clearly as she could see his face, she would not have asked that question. Eager to know what he meant, she pressed him so closely that he confessed, saying that he was in love with a lady whom he esteemed the most virtuous lady in the whole of Christendom. Whereupon she did everything she possibly could to find out who the lady was, begging, beseeching, even commanding him to tell her. But to no avail. Then she pretended to be exceedingly angry with him, and swore that she would never speak to him again, unless he named the lady with whom he was so much in love. His distress was so great that he was forced to say that it would be as death to him to be obliged to confess to her. But seeing that he was in danger of being cast from her sight and from her favour simply for not revealing a truth in itself so honourable that no one could ever have taken it amiss, he said in fear and trembling:

'Madame, I have neither the strength nor the courage to tell you. But the next time that you go out hunting, I shall show her to you, and I am sure that you will find her the most beautiful and the most perfect lady in all the world.'

This reply led the Queen to go hunting somewhat sooner than she would otherwise have done. When Elisor heard of this, he prepared to attend her majesty as usual. He had a huge steel mirror fashioned into a cuirass. This he strapped across his chest and concealed it beneath a voluminous cloak of heavy black cloth richly [embroidered] with thread of gold. He was mounted on a black horse, richly caparisoned, and decked with all the trappings a horse could require. The harness was gold, and enamelled in black in the Moorish style. On his head was a hat of black silk to which was attached an emblem, bearing as its device a figure of Love concealed by Force, the whole richly adorned with precious stones. His sword and dagger also were finely wrought and likewise decorated with fine devices. In short, he was well accoutred. Even more imposing was his horsemanship. So skilfully did Elisor handle his mount that those who saw him deserted the pleasures of the hunt in order to watch him race and jump. After he had escorted the Queen to the place where the nets were spread to trap the quarry, he dismounted from his noble steed and came to help the Queen climb down from her palfrey. As she held out her arms, he opened the cloak that had been gathered across his chest, and held her, revealing the mirror of his breastplate and saying: 'Madame, behold, I beseech you!' Without waiting for a reply, he set her gently on the ground.

When the hunt was over, the Queen went back to the castle without saying a word to Elisor. But after supper, she summoned him to her, and told him that he was the greatest liar she had ever seen, for he had promised that during the hunt he would show her the lady who was his love, and this he had not done. She was resolved, therefore, no longer to hold him in esteem. Elisor, fearing lest the Queen had misunderstood his words, replied that he had not failed to obey her command, for he had shown her not only the woman he loved most in all the world, but also the thing in all the world that he most loved. Then the Queen, feigning not to understand, said that she was not aware that he had shown her any of her ladies.

'That is true, Madame,' said Elisor, 'but [what] did I show you as you got down from your horse?'

'Nothing at all,' replied the Queen, 'except a mirror across your chest.'

'In this mirror, Madame,' said Elisor, 'what did you see?'

'I saw nothing but myself!' answered the Queen.

Then Elisor said:

'Therefore, Madame, I have kept my promise and obeyed your command, for there is no image within my heart, nor shall there ever be, save that image which you saw reflected on my breast without. That image alone will I love, revere and adore not as a woman, but as my God on earth in whose hands I place my life, humbly beseeching you that my deep and perfect love, which has been life itself to me while it remained concealed, should not be my death now that it is revealed. And if I am not worthy to look upon you or to be accepted as your servant, then at the least suffer me to live as hitherto I have, in the contentment I derive from the knowledge that my heart has dared to build its love in such a perfect and worthy place. I cannot hope for any satisfaction save that of knowing that my love is so deep and so perfect that I must content myself with loving, though I can never be loved. And if, in the knowledge of my great love for you, you should be no more pleased than before to look graciously upon me, then I beg that at the least you will not take my life, which consists for me in the joy of gazing upon you as I always have. That which you grant me is no more than that which I needs must have to sustain me in my extremity. Had I less than this, then you would be the less adored, for thus would you lose the best and the most devoted servant that you ever had or could ever have again.'

Now it may have been that the Queen wished to appear other than she really was; it may have been that she wished to put Elisor's love to the test of time; it may have been that she loved another man whom she did not wish to abandon for Elisor; or it may have been that she wished to hold him in reserve in case the other man should offend. Whatever the reason, she now replied, in a tone that expressed neither anger nor pleasure:

'Elisor, I shall not ask you, as if I were entirely ignorant of the power that love exerts over the hearts of men, what madness has driven you to undertake a love so arduous and so exalted as the love you profess for me. For I know that the heart of man is so little at his command, that it is not within his power to choose whom to love and whom to hate. But since you have concealed your feelings so well, I wish to ask you how long ago you first began to feel them?'

Elisor looked at her beautiful face, and seeing that she was asking about the sickness with which he was afflicted, hoped that she would bring him some relief. But he saw too that his questioner's countenance was chaste and grave and he began to be afraid, for it was as if he was standing before a judge, awaiting a sentence which he knew would be given against him. Yet in spite of this he swore that his love had taken root in his heart when he had still been very young, although it had only been for the past seven years that he had begun to feel a pain, which in truth was not real pain but rather a sickness which had brought such happiness that to be cured now would be his death.

'As you have given such long proof of your steadfastness,' said the Queen, 'it is not fitting that I should be [more] precipitate in believing you than you have been in declaring your love to me. Therefore, if it is as you have told me, I wish to test the truth so thoroughly that I shall never be able to doubt it. Once you have proved yourself, I shall believe that your feelings really are as you have sworn they are. And when I know for certain that you are what you declare, then you shall find me to be even as you desire.'

Elisor implored her to put him to whatever test she might wish. For there was nothing in the world, no matter how arduous, that he would not gladly undertake in order to have the [joy] of knowing that she acknowledged his love for her. He implored her, then, to command of him whatever she might wish.

'Elisor,' she began, 'if you love me as deeply as you say, then I am sure that in your desire to win my favour no task will seem too hard. Therefore I command you, on pain of forfeiting for ever that which you most desire to have and most fear to lose, that when tomorrow morning breaks you shall, without seeing me again, depart from this court, and that you shall go to a place where for seven whole years you shall not hear word of me, nor I of you. You, who have loved now for seven years, you know that you love me; but only when I too have had seven years in which to put your love to the test, only then shall I too know for certain that your love is true; only then shall I believe that which mere words are unable to make me believe or comprehend.'

On hearing this cruel command, Elisor began to think that it was her intention to remove him from her presence, but in the hope that the test would speak more eloquently on his behalf than words themselves, he accepted the command, saying:

'If I have lived for seven years without any hope, keeping the fire of my love concealed, how much more easily, how much more hopefully, shall I bear the next seven, now that my love is known! But, Madame, since in obeying your command I am deprived of the only joy the world affords me, what hope do you give me that at the end of these seven years you will recognize me as your most loyal and faithful servant?'

The Queen drew a ring from her finger, and said: 'I give you this ring. Cut it into two equal halves. I shall keep one, and you the other, so that if time erases the memory of your face, I shall nevertheless be able to recognize you, since your half of the ring will match mine.'

Elisor took the ring, and broke it in two, giving one piece to the Queen, and keeping the other for himself. Then, more dead than the dead themselves, he took his leave and retired to his quarters to make preparations for his departure. All his attendants and servants he sent back home, while he, accompanied only by one valet, went away to a place so remote that neither his family nor his friends could receive any news of him for the whole seven years. Of his manner of life during this time, of the sorrows he endured through his separation, nothing may be known. But no one who has ever loved can fail to imagine what they must have been. On the very day the seven years elapsed the Queen was approached on her way to mass by a hermit with a long beard who kissed her hand and presented her with a petition. She did not read it immediately – [contrary to her usual custom, which was to receive all such petitions and read them personally,] however poor the people who had presented them. However, half-way through mass, she opened it and found the half of the ring which she had given to Elisor. Her surprise was great, but not unmingled with pleasure, and before she had read the contents, she instructed her chaplain to bring to her the venerable hermit who had presented the petition. The chaplain looked everywhere for him, but failed to discover his whereabouts. The only thing anyone could tell him was that he had been seen on a horse. But nobody knew which way he was going. Meanwhile the Queen read the petition that had been handed to her. It turned out to be a letter composed in the most elegant manner. If it were not for my desire that you should know the contents of this letter, I should never have dared to translate it. For, Ladies, you must understand, the Castilian language is beyond compare as a means of expressing the passion [of love]. The substance of it is as follows:

Time, mighty Time all other things above,
Did bring me perfect knowledge of true Love.
Then Time itself I had, Time enough and more,
And in that Time such cruel pains I bore
That she who had no faith came finally
To see what Love could never make her see.
Time, which made Love to come and rule me so
Within my heart, has taught me Love to know
E'en as it is: so now I have perceived
And seen it other than I once believed.
Time has revealed to me on what a ground
My heart desired its steadfast Love to found.
That ground it was your own true Beauty bright
'Neath which was Cruelty concealed from sight.
Time has shown me Beauty's worthlessness,
While Cruelty has brought me happiness.
For thus from Beauty's face I did depart
On whom to gaze I'd striv'n with all my heart.
Seeing no more the Beauty of your brow,
Your cold hard heart I felt more keenly now,
Yet your commands I truly did obey,
Wherefore yet happy and content I stay,
For I see that Time, who caused my Love so strong,
Has shown me pity by his tarrying long,
Has served me well and served me with such grace,

I have no wish to come unto this place,
Except it be to say and say full well,
Not 'I greet you' but a last 'Farewell'.
Time has shown me Love's poor naked frame
E'en as it is and shown me whence it came,
And Time it is who makes me now to rue
That Time that once I loved for Love of you,
A Love that blinded all my senses so
That now no feeling save regret I know.
But as deceitful Love I came to see,
Time did the One True Love reveal to me,
Here in this solitary place where I
For seven silent plaintive years do lie.
Love from on high through Time I came to know,
And other Love seemed poorer then to grow.
Through Time I bowed to Love's supremacy,
And Time from lesser Love defended me.
My soul and flesh in sacrifice I give
To serve not you but true Love while I live.
When you I served, you valued me at naught,
But he this naught, though it offend, hath sought.
For all my service Death alone you give,
But he, though him I shunned, doth bid me live.
Through Time true Love with goodness from above
Hath vanquished and laid low that other Love,
And it hath melted back into the air,
Air once so sweet to me and falsely fair.
To you this Love I now entire restore,
For nor of him nor you have I need more,
Since perfect Love, the which shall never die,
Joins me to him with never-ending tie.
To him I fly, to him myself enslave,
No more to you nor to your god the slave.
I take my leave of Cruelty and pain,
Of torment, hatred, and of proud disdain;
Of burning fires, which fill your lovely breast
E'en as with perfect Beauty you are dressed.
My best adieu to all these miseries,
To all these woes and dire adversities,

To all the flames of love, that very Hell,
Is this one word to say, Madame: *Farewell*!
Without a hope, whatever is in store,
That e'er again we see each other more.

The Queen was overcome as she read these lines, and wept tears of regret beyond belief. For such a loss, the loss of a servant imbued with such perfect love, must be esteemed a loss so great that no treasure in the realm, no, not even the realm itself, could make her other than the poorest and most desolate lady in the whole world. For she had lost that which no riches on earth could replace. After she had heard mass, she retired to her room and there gave herself up to such sorrow as her cruelty had deserved. There was not a mountain, not a rock, not a forest that the Queen did not have searched for the hermit. But He who had taken him from her hands took care that he did not fall into them again, and transported him to Paradise before she was able to discover his whereabouts on earth.

*

'This example shows that a gentleman who serves a lady should not confess what can only harm and do no good. Even less, Ladies, should *you* be so distrustful as to demand such difficult proofs of love that though you obtain the proof, you lose your servant.'

'Well, Dagoucin,' said Geburon, 'I've always admired the lady in your story as the most virtuous woman in the world. But now I think she's the most wicked [and the most cruel] women that ever lived!'

'All the same, it seems to me that it was not wrong of her,' said Parlamente, 'to put him on trial for seven years to find out if he really loved her as much as he claimed. Men are in the habit of lying in such circumstances, as well you know, and one cannot put them on trial for too long before placing such trust in them – if indeed one should ever place one's trust in them!'

'Ladies are a good deal more sensible now, though, than they used to be,' observed Hircan, 'since they convince themselves of their servant's devotion after only seven *days'* trial, whereas they used to take seven *years*!'

'Yet there are women in this very gathering,' said Longarine, 'whose devoted servants have loved them through thick and thin for more than seven years and have still failed to win their hearts.'

'By God, how right you are!' said Simontaut. 'But you should put them with the ladies of a bygone age, because they wouldn't be accepted nowadays.'

'But the gentleman was indebted to his lady,' said Oisille, 'because it was through her that he turned his heart entirely to God.'

'Lucky for him it was God!' said Saffredent. 'Considering his plight, I'm surprised he didn't sell his soul to the Devil!'

'So when you've been treated badly in the past by *your* lady,' said Ennasuite, 'that's what *you*'ve done, is it?'

'Thousands of times!' retorted Saffredent. 'But the Devil would never take me, because he could see that all the torments in Hell could not possibly cause me any more pain than the pain *she* was making me suffer. He knew perfectly well that the most diabolical torture of all is when you love a woman who won't love you in return!'

'If I were you,' said Parlamente, 'and felt that way about women, I would not bother to do them service at all.'

'Ah, but such has always been the force of my feelings,' replied Saffredent, 'so swollen my [heart] with emotion, that I have been only too happy to serve, if I have been unable to give the orders. Whatever their malice, they shall never overcome the love I bear them! But tell me, do you, in all conscience, approve of this lady's extraordinary severity?'

'Yes, I do,' said Oisille, 'because I think she neither wanted to love him nor to be loved by him.'

'If that was her attitude,' said Simontaut, 'then why did she hold out some hope to him for after the seven years?'

'I agree with you,' said Longarine, 'because people who don't want love don't create situations which enable their admirers to persist.'

'Maybe she loved somebody else,' said Nomerfide, 'somebody who wasn't as good as the noble Elisor, and maybe she preferred him even though he was the worse of the two.'

'If you ask me,' said Saffredent, 'she was keeping him on one side so that she could have him when she eventually left the one she was temporarily attached to.'

Although what the Queen of Castile had done was certainly not something to be praised either in her or anybody else, Oisille could see that on the pretext of criticizing her behaviour the men would go so far in speaking ill of women in general [that] they would no more spare women who were modest and chaste than they would those who were wanton and lewd. She could not bear the men to proceed further, so she said: 'I can see that the more we pursue this subject, the more those men who complain of being harshly treated will try to speak ill of us. So, Dagoucin, I request you to choose the next storyteller.'

'I choose Longarine,' he said, 'because I'm sure that she'll tell us something far from melancholy, and that at the same time she'll tell us nothing but the truth, without concessions either to men or to women.'

'Since you consider me such a truthful person,' she began, 'I'll make so bold as to tell you about something that happened to a certain prince of high estate, a man whose qualities set him apart from all other men of his time. I'll tell you, too, how there is one vice that should be avoided above all others – lying and deceit. This is the most ugly and the most squalid of all vices, particularly for princes and high-born lords, for it is fitting that they of all people should have truth on their lips and in their eyes. However, there's no prince in the world, even if he had all the riches and honours one could ever desire, who isn't subject to the tyrannous sway of Love. It would seem, indeed, that the more valiant and noble the prince, the more Love strives to subjugate him and hold him in his grip. For this vainglorious god disdains the ordinary things in life that never change. His majesty Love delights in constantly working miracles – strengthening the weak, weakening the strong, making the ignorant wise, depriving the most learned of their wisdom, encouraging the passions and destroying reason. Turning things upside down is what the god of Love enjoys. Now, since princes are not exempt from this, they are not exempt either from [necessity, that necessity which desire and the servitude of love impose.] And by such necessity not only are they permitted, but are actually obliged, to employ fabrications, lies and hypocrisy, which, according to the teaching of Jean de Meung, are the weapons one needs in order to vanquish the enemy. Well, since one finds such behaviour praiseworthy in princes, though it is to be disapproved of in other mortals, I shall tell you about a trick played by a certain young prince, a trick which tricked the very people who usually do the trickery themselves!'

STORY TWENTY-FIVE

In Paris there was once an advocate, the most highly thought of man in his profession. Because of his ability everyone came to him, and he had become the richest amongst his learned colleagues. However, his first wife had not given him any children, and he thought to himself that he might manage to have some after all if he married again. Old in body though he was, he was ever hopeful, and his spirit was by no means dead. So he decided on one of the most attractive girls in town. She was about eighteen or nineteen years of age, with a lovely face, a lovely complexion and even lovelier figure. He loved her and did his best for her, but he no more succeeded in having children by her than he had by his first wife. As time went by she took this rather to heart. But youth does not suffer such setbacks for long, and she soon started to look for amusement outside the home. She went to dances and banquets, but conducted herself so properly the whole time, that her husband could not take offence. In any case, she was always accompanied by other women in whom he had complete confidence.

One day she was at a wedding, and there was a prince there of very high estate. He himself told me this story, but instructed me not to reveal his name. What I *can* say is that he was the most handsome and most elegant man there ever was in this realm, or ever will be. Well, this Prince saw the young girl. Her eyes and her whole expression simply invited love. So he went to talk to her, and uttered such sweet beguiling words that she did not in the least mind him holding forth. She made no attempt to disguise the fact that her heart had long harboured the love that he was begging her for, and told him that he must not put himself to such pains to persuade her, for love had made her consent at the mere sight of him. This was a prize that the young Prince would have gladly toiled long and hard to win, but when he realized that it was already his, thanks to the natural spontaneity of Love, he thanked the god with all his heart for bestowing such favour upon him. And from that moment on he handled things so well that it was not long before a way was agreed upon whereby they could meet alone and out of sight. The time and place were decided on, and the young Prince duly appeared. In order to safeguard his lady's honour he disguised himself in someone else's clothes. But with him he brought some trusted men, because of the violent characters who roamed the town at night and to whom he did not care to have his identity revealed. He left his men at the end of the street where the girl lived, saying,

'If you don't hear any noise within a quarter of an hour, go back home, and come to meet me here in three or four hours' time.'

So they waited, and hearing no noise, went back. Meanwhile the young Prince went straight to the lawyer's house, where he found the door open as promised. But on his way up the stairs he met the husband, candle in hand. The old man had seen him first. Fortunately the god of Love sharpens his victims' wits and fortifies their courage to meet the needs which he himself gives rise to. The young Prince marched straight up to the husband and said:

'Monsieur, you know that I, and my family too, have always had a great deal of confidence in you. I regard you as one of my best and most faithful servants. I've come to pay you a private visit, partly because I want to discuss my affairs and partly to ask if you'll give me something to quench a terrible thirst I have. And I'd be glad if you wouldn't tell anyone that I've been here, because I have to go on to another place where I don't want anyone to recognize me.'

The poor old advocate was so delighted to have the honour of a private visit from the Prince, that he took him straight up to his room and ordered his wife to prepare and serve the choicest fruit and preserves she had. Only too happy to obey, she presented the fairest collation she could devise. The young Prince pretended he did not even know her and managed not to look at her too obviously, in spite of the fact that her night attire revealed her as even more beautiful than she was accustomed to appear. He spoke the whole time about his business affairs to her husband, for it was he who had long been in charge of them. However, while the good lady of the house was kneeling before the Prince offering him the preserves, and while the husband was at the sideboard pouring him a drink, she whispered to him that he should slip into a dressing-room to his right and that she would join him there presently. When he had finished his drink, he thanked his lawyer friend, and said that he ought to go. The old man insisted on accompanying him back home, but the Prince assured him that where he was going he [had no need] of company! Then he turned to the wife, and said:

'Well, it would not be fair of me to deprive you of this husband of yours. He's one of my oldest servants, after all, and you're very lucky to have him. You should thank God that you have a man like him. So make sure you serve him properly and do what he tells you – it would be too bad of you, if you didn't!'

And with these noble sentiments, off he went, closing the door behind him, so that the old man would not follow him down the stairs. Then he went straight into the dressing-room, where, once the husband had fallen asleep, his lovely lady came to join him. She led him into a room furnished with the most wonderful paintings and statues. But the finest figures, however clad, were the figures of the pair themselves. And I've not the slightest doubt that she kept all the promises she had made him.

At the agreed time, he left her, and went to find his companions who were waiting for him at the appointed spot. He continued to see his lady in this fashion for some time, and eventually decided to use a short cut by way of a nearby monastery. He ingratiated himself with the Prior and had things so organized that every night the porter would open the monastery door for him around midnight and let him out again on his way back. As the lawyer's house was quite close, he was able to go without taking anyone with him. In spite of carrying on in the way he was, he remained a prince, a prince who feared and loved the Lord, and although he never stopped in the church on his way to his assignations, he never failed to stop on his way back and to spend a long time in prayer. The monks, who used to see him there on his knees as they went in and out to matins, came to regard him as the holiest man on the face of the earth.

Now the Prince had a sister who was in the habit of visiting this monastery quite frequently. She loved her brother above all other creatures in the world and liked to ask all the devout people she knew to remember him in their prayers. One day she earnestly asked the Prior if he would pray for the young man.

'Alas, Madame,' he replied, '[what] is this you ask of me? If there is any man in the world in whose prayers I myself should like to be remembered, it is the Prince, your brother. For if *he* is not a holy and righteous man, then I cannot hope to be found holy and righteous! Blessed is the man who can do evil and doeth it not, as the Scriptures say!'

The Prince's sister, eager to discover how the Prior knew her brother was possessed of such piety, questioned him so closely that eventually he told her what he knew, on condition that it was treated as a secret of the confessional.

'Is it not a remarkable thing that a young and handsome prince like your brother should give up his pleasure, give up his bed, in order to come so often to hear matins with us, and come not as a prince, not so as to win the respect of the world, but like an ordinary monk, all alone in the obscurity of a side chapel? His piety so confounds my brethren and myself that in comparison with him we are not worthy to be called men of religion!'

The Prince's sister was not sure what to make of these words. In spite of the fact that her brother was a man of the world, he was, she knew, also a man of conscience and a man who devoutly loved and trusted in God. But to make a practice of going to superstitious ceremonies other than those which a good Christian should attend – that was something of which she would never have suspected him. So when she saw him, she told him what a high opinion the monks had of him. He could not help bursting out laughing at this, and she could tell at once – for she knew him as well as she knew herself – that there was something else behind his apparent piety. She did not leave him alone until he had told her the truth – [the truth even as I have written it down, and even as she herself so graciously told it me.

*

'You see from this, Ladies, that however cunning your lawyers, however crafty your monks – and all of them are in the habit of tricking everybody and anybody – the god of Love can in cases of need outwit them all, and make fools of them at the hands of those whose only experience is to have been in love.

So if Love can trick the tricksters, then the rest of us ordinary ignorant folk ought indeed to fear it!']

'I think I can guess well enough who the hero of that story is,' said Geburon, 'but I must still say that one can have nothing but praise for the way he acted. One sees only too few men of such elevated rank who care either about women's honour or about public scandal, provided they enjoy themselves; and very often they don't even care if people suspect them of being worse than they really are.'

'I do wish that all young lords would follow his example,' said Oisille, 'because often the scandal is worse than the sin itself.'

'Don't forget,' exclaimed Nomerfide, 'that he had every good reason to be saying his prayers!'

'But you should not seek to judge,' replied Parlamente, 'because it's possible that afterwards his repentance was such that his sin was forgiven.'

'It's very difficult to repent something as enjoyable as that!' said Hircan. 'I've often made my confession about that sort of thing, but I've scarcely ever repented!'

'It would be far better,' said Oisille, 'not to confess at all if one does not feel true repentance.'

'But, Madame,' he replied, 'I don't approve of sin, and I'm always very sorry if I offend God – but I still enjoy it!'

'So you and your ilk would rather there wasn't any God at all,' Parlamente replied, 'and that there was no law either, unless it was laid down according to your own inclinations?'

'I admit that I'd be very glad,' said he, 'if God enjoyed what I enjoy as much as I do – I'd be able to give Him plenty of opportunity to have a good time!'

'Well, you're not going to be able to make a new god,' commented Geburon, 'so you'd better obey the one we've got. Let's leave this dispute to the theologians, and ask Longarine to choose the next person to speak.'

'I choose Saffredent,' she said, 'but I would request him to tell us the best story he can think of and not to concentrate so much on speaking ill of women that in cases where there is something good to say he does not tell the whole truth.'

'Willingly,' began Saffredent. 'I'll do just as you ask, because the story I have in mind is in fact about a woman who was wanton and a woman who was wise. You may please yourselves which example you follow! You will see that love makes bad people do bad things, and virtuous people do things we should respect. For in itself love is good, but if the individual is bad, then you might choose to call it something else – foolish, fickle, cruel, or depraved. What you will see, then, from the story I am about to tell you, is that love doesn't change the heart but shows the heart as it really is – wanton in women who are wanton, wise in women who are wise.'

STORY TWENTY-SIX

In the time of Louis XII there was a young lord by the name of d'Avannes. He was the son of the Seigneur d'Albret, the brother of Jean de Navarre, and it was with the latter that d'Avannes resided. Now, already at the age of fifteen this young lord was so good-looking and so charming that it seemed his only role in life was to be loved and gazed upon in admiration. Indeed, everyone who saw him did love and did admire him, in particular a certain lady who lived in Pamplona, in Navarre. She was married to a very rich man and she led a quiet and respectable life. In fact, although she was only twenty-three, she dressed so modestly in order to conform with her husband, who was nearer fifty, that she looked more like a widow than a married woman. She was never seen at weddings or any other celebrations without her husband, whose good qualities she held in such high regard that she preferred him to all other men, no matter how young or good-looking they might be. For his part, the husband had found her so good and so wise, and had such confidence in her, that he placed her in charge of all his domestic affairs.

One day this rich man and his wife were invited to the wedding of a relative, and it so happened that d'Avannes himself was there to honour the bridal pair. He was naturally fond of dancing, for there was no one in his day could match him. After dinner, when the music started, the rich man asked d'Avannes if he would dance for them. D'Avannes replied by asking who was to be his partner, to which the rich man answered:

'Monseigneur, if there were any woman here more beautiful than my wife, and more ready to do my bidding, I would present her, humbly beseeching you to do me the honour of taking her as your partner.'

The Prince accepted readily, but young as he was, he took more pleasure in skipping and dancing than in eyeing the charms of the ladies. His partner, on the other hand, was rather more interested in d'Avannes's looks than in the dance – though of course, being a prudent lady, she was careful not to let her interest become obvious. When supper was served, d'Avannes took his leave of the guests and went back to the château. The rich man accompanied him on his mule, and said to him as they went along:

'Monseigneur, you have done me and my family a great honour in being with us today, and I should be very ungrateful if I did not offer to perform for you some service that lies within my power. I know, Monseigneur, that noble lords like yourself often have fathers who are harsh and parsimonious and that you are often more in need of money than are the likes of us who live very quietly and frugally and only think about saving. Now God has given me a wife who is everything that I could desire, but it has not been His will that I should enjoy complete Paradise in this life, for He has deprived me of the joy of being a father. I know, Monseigneur, that it is not for me to adopt you as my son, but if you would deign to accept me as a servant and confide your little affairs in me you may depend on me to help you out in your needs to the extent of a hundred thousand écus.'

D'Avannes was extremely pleased to receive this offer, because he had exactly the kind of father the rich man had described. So he thanked him warmly, and called him his father by alliance.

From that moment on the rich man was so devoted to d'Avannes that he never ceased inquiring from morning till night whether the young man was in need of anything. He made no secret to his wife of his attachment to the young lord, or of his desire to serve him, and she loved him all the more. As for d'Avannes himself, he never from that time on went in want of anything. He would often go and visit the rich man, and eat and drink with him. If the rich man was not at home, his wife would supply everything he asked for, and not only that, but she would talk to him very wisely, and exhort him to live a wise and virtuous life, with the result that he came to love and respect her more than any other woman in the world. She for her part kept God and honour firmly in mind and satisfied herself with seeing him and hearing him speak, for in the faculties of sight and hearing lies the whole satisfaction of love that is noble and good.

She never once gave any sign that might suggest she had any feelings other than Christian, sisterly affection.

During this secret friendship d'Avannes was able, thanks to the rich man's help, to cut an elegant figure, and as he approached his seventeenth birthday, he began to pay more attention to the ladies than he had been accustomed to do. He would far rather have given his love to the wise lady than to any other, but he was afraid that if she heard him speak of it he would lose her friendship altogether. So he kept quiet, and pursued his pleasures elsewhere. Thus it was that he went and paid his attentions to a lady from near Pamplona who had a house in town. This lady was married to a young man whose ruling passion was horses, hounds and hawks. In order to please her, he took to putting on all manner of entertainments – tournaments, races, wrestling-matches, masked balls, banquets and other diversions. The lady would always be present, but her husband was a jealous man, and her mother and father, who knew that she was not only very attractive, but also somewhat flighty, were very cautious about her honour and reputation. Consequently, she was so closely guarded that d'Avannes never managed to get anything more out of her than a brief exchange of words during one of the balls. All the same, he could tell even from this brief encounter that the time and place to meet were all that would be required for the attachment to flourish. So he approached his good 'father', the rich man, and told him he had conceived a devout desire to visit the monastery of Our Lady of Montserrat and that he would like him to give lodging to his entire retinue, because he wanted to make the pilgrimage alone. To this the rich man readily agreed. But his wife, in whose heart was lodged that great prophet Love, who sees all, suspected at once what the true reason for the journey was, and could not resist saying: 'Monsieur, the lady that you adore does not live beyond these city walls. Therefore I beg you, take care above all for your health!' D'Avannes, who loved and respected her, blushed so deeply at these words that, without uttering a word, he confessed the truth. And thereupon he left.

What he did then was to buy himself a pair of fine Spanish horses, dress himself up as a stable-lad and disguise his face so well that he was quite unrecognizable. The husband of the foolish lady from Pamplona, devoted to horses as he was, spotted the pair that d'Avannes had with him and lost no time in offering to buy them from him. When the deal was done he watched the disguised d'Avannes handle the horses, and was so impressed that he asked him if he wanted a job. D'Avannes replied yes, he was just a poor stable-lad, and looking after horses was the only work he knew, but he would do it very well, and the gentleman would be well pleased with him. So the gentleman, delighted by these words, placed him in charge of all his horses. When he arrived back at his house he told his wife that he was just going to the château and that she was to look after his horses and the new groom. While he was gone she went out to inspect the stables, partly to humour her husband and partly to amuse herself. She looked the new groom up and down. He seemed highly presentable, but she did not recognize him. Realizing that she did not know who he was, d'Avannes bowed to her in the Spanish style, taking hold of her hand and kissing it. As he did so, he squeezed so hard, that she realized who he was, because he had played exactly the same trick when she had danced with him at the ball. From that moment on she thought of nothing but how to get to talk to him on his own. That very evening she found the answer. She and her husband had been invited to a banquet, so she pretended to be ill. Her husband was anxious not to disappoint his friends, so he said: 'As you don't feel like coming, my dear, will you look after the dogs and the horses for me, in case they need anything?'

This was a task highly to her taste, though she was careful not to show it. She replied that since he could not give her anything better to do, she would just have to show how much she desired to please him by doing something menial. The husband had scarcely gone through the door before she was downstairs in the stable. It had not taken her long to find something that needed to be done – and to make sure that it was done, she sent the servants off on errands all over the place! Now she was alone with her groom, but she was still afraid lest anyone came and found them, so she said:

'Go into the garden. There's a leafy bower at the end of the path. Wait for me there.'

Without stopping to express his gratitude, he dashed off to

the appointed spot. As for the lady, once she had finished her jobs in the stables, she went to take a look at the dogs. She took as much trouble over them as she had over the horses, busily instructing the servants to make sure that the animals had everything they needed. She worked so hard, anyone would have thought she was a chambermaid rather than the mistress of the house. When she had finished she went to her room, feeling so tired that she got straight into bed, saying that she needed to rest. All her serving women went out, except for one, in whom she confided.

'Go into the garden,' she told her, 'and fetch me that man who's waiting at the bottom of the path!'

Off went the chambermaid, found the groom, brought him straight back to his lady, and then went to keep a look-out for the husband coming back. Now that he had his lady alone, d'Avannes stripped off his stable-boy's gear, removed his false nose and his false beard, and, without so much as a by your leave, hopped boldly into bed with her. Gone was the cringing stable-lad. In his place was a bold young lord, the finest youth of his age, and as such he was received by the loveliest and most lascivious lady in the land. He stayed with her till the husband got back. Then, as soon as he heard him coming, he put on his disguise again and vacated the place which with such low cunning he had usurped. As he walked into the courtyard, the husband was told with what diligence and dispatch his wife had carried out his instructions, and he went to thank her.

'I only did my duty, my dear,' she said. 'You were quite right, if one didn't keep one's eye on these wretched men of yours, all your dogs would be mangy and all your horses reduced to skin and bones. But since I know how lazy they are and how you like things, you'll be better served than ever before!'

The husband then asked her what she thought of the new groom, being himself convinced that he had made the best choice in the world.

'Well, I admit he does his job as well as any servant you could have chosen, but he does need to be pressed hard, because he's the sleepiest individual I ever came across!'

As a result of this she and her husband actually lived for a long time on better terms than they had before. The husband ceased to be jealous and suspicious, because now she devoted as much attention to running the house as previously she had devoted to balls and banquets. Not only that, but whereas before she had been in the habit of spending four hours every day dressing herself up, she was now content to wear a simple tunic over her shift, and her husband and everybody else were very pleased with her, little knowing that it was a case of a worse devil taking the place of a lesser. Thus in the hypocritical guise of a virtuous wife, the lady lived a life of such sensual pleasure that reason, conscience, order and moderation no longer had any place in her. But the delicate constitution of d'Avannes, who after all was still very young, could not tolerate this state of affairs for long. He became so pale and thin that even without his disguise you would not have recognized him. But his wanton passion for this woman so dulled his senses that he made demands on his strength that would have exhausted Hercules himself. As a result he eventually fell sick, and on the advice of his lady, who was less fond of him in that condition than when he was well, he asked his master for leave to go and visit his parents. The husband granted him his request reluctantly, and made him promise that he would return to his service once he had recovered. So d'Avannes set off – on foot, of course, because he only had to go down the street to reach the house of his good father, the rich old man. When he got there he found no one at home but the wife, whose virtuous love for him had not in the least diminished while he had been away. But when she saw how thin and wan he was, she could not help saying to him:

'Monsieur, I cannot guess what state your conscience is in, but you do not look as if your body has benefited from your pilgrimage. If I am not mistaken, it has been even harder going for you at night than during the day. Why, if you'd walked all the way to Jerusalem, you might have been more sunburnt, but you could scarcely have been thinner and weaker. But it's all over now, so stop doing service to such idols, which instead of bringing the dead to life put the living to death. I could say a good deal more, but if your body has sinned, then it has been punished enough, and I feel too sorry for you to add to your sufferings!'

When d'Avannes heard these words he was as much ashamed as he was aggrieved, and said: 'Madame, I have always been told that repentance follows sin. To my cost I have now found out how true that is and I beg you to excuse my youthfulness, for youth will learn its lesson only by experiencing the bad things it refused to believe in.'

Thereupon the lady dropped the matter, and put him in a comfortable bed, where he remained for the next fortnight, taking nothing but light, nourishing food. Both she and her husband were so attentive that he was never without one or the other of them at his bedside. And in spite of the fact that he had against all her wishes and all her advice behaved in the wanton manner I have described, the wise lady continued to love him as virtuously as before. For it was still her hope that after sowing his wild oats he would quieten down, bring himself back to the way of virtuous love and so be wholly hers. During the fortnight he spent in her house, she talked so inspiringly about love and virtue, that he began to abhor the wild and wanton life he had been leading. And as he gazed upon the lady, who in beauty far surpassed the wanton woman, he came more and more to recognize the virtue and the graces that were hers. Then, one day when the light was dim, he banished all fear, and could no longer hold back from saying:

'Madame, I can see no better way to be as virtuous and good as you have exhorted me to be than to give my heart and my whole being to the love of virtue. So tell me, Madame, I beg you, will you not be so good as to give me all the help and favour that you can?'

The lady was overjoyed to hear him talking like this, and replied: 'I promise, Monseigneur, that if as behoves a noble lord of your station you make virtue the object of your love, then I shall use all the strength that God has given me to serve you, and help you achieve your goal.'

'Then may you heed your promise, Madame,' replied d'Avannes, 'and know that God, whom no man may know but by faith alone, did deign to take on flesh, even the same flesh as the sinful flesh of man, so that in drawing our flesh to the love of His humanity, he would draw our spirit to the love of His divinity. And by means of things visible did it please Him to make us love through faith the things that are invisible. Thus is that virtue, which my whole life through I desire to love, a thing that is invisible unless it show external effects. It must therefore take on a bodily form, so that it may make itself known unto men. Indeed, it has done so, for it has clothed itself in your body, Madame, the most perfect it could find. Therefore, I acknowledge and confess that you are not merely virtuous, but Virtue itself. And I, who see that Virtue shining through the veil of the most perfect body that ever existed do desire to serve and honour it for the rest of my days, for its sake renouncing all vain and vicious love!'

The lady was as pleased as she was surprised to hear these words coming from him, but she concealed her feelings, and said: 'Monseigneur, I shall not attempt to reply to your theology; but as I am inclined rather to fear evil than to believe goodness, I would beseech you to desist from addressing such words to me, for I know how little you respect those women who have believed them. I know well that I am a woman, not only a woman like any other, but a woman [so full of imperfections that] Virtue would be performing a greater act in transforming me into herself than in taking on my form, unless she wished perchance to remain unknown to the world. For, hidden beneath such a garb as mine, Virtue could never be known as she truly is. Yet for all my imperfection, Monseigneur, I do not cease to bear you such love as a woman who fears God and has care for her honour [can] and ought. However, this love shall not be declared until the day when your heart shall be capable of the long-suffering that virtuous love demands. When that time comes, I know what language I must speak, but for the present, Monseigneur, be you assured that you yourself cannot hold any dearer than I your life, your honour and your whole welfare.'

Trembling, and with tears in his eyes, d'Avannes begged and beseeched her that as pledge of her word she would grant him a kiss. But she refused, saying that for his sake she would not break the custom of her people. As he thus pressed her, the husband arrived, and d'Avannes turned to him, saying, 'My dear father, I am so beholden to yourself and to your wife, that I would like to ask you to think of me as your son for ever.'

The good man replied warmly that gladly he would, and d'Avannes went on: 'As a token of this bond of affection, allow me, I beg you, to kiss you.' They embraced, and d'Avannes went on again: 'If I were not afraid of contravening the law, I should request the same of my dear mother, your wife.'

So the husband ordered his wife to kiss d'Avannes, which she did without showing in any way whether her husband's order was to her liking or not. But, at the touch of that kiss, [so long desired, so hard sought and so cruelly refused,] the fire that mere words had kindled in the young lord's heart, began to grow ever hotter.

After this d'Avannes went back to the château to see the King, his brother, and there he told all sorts of stories about the journey he was supposed to have made to Montserrat. But he learned that his brother was planning to go to Olite and Tafalla, and he became very downcast at the thought, because he would have to go as well and he feared that the journey would be a long one. So downcast was he that he resolved to try to find out whether the wise lady was not perhaps after all more favourably inclined towards him than she had allowed herself to appear. What he did was to take lodgings in a house in town, situated in the same street. It was a tumbledown old place, built of wood, and about midnight he set fire to it. The news soon spread round the town and eventually reached the house of the rich man, who leaned out of the window to ask where the fire was. On learning that it was at Monseigneur d'Avannes' house, he went straight there, taking all his servants with him. He found the young man standing in the street in his nightshirt and felt so moved by the sight that he took him in his arms, wrapped him in his robe and led him back to his house with all possible haste. When they arrived, he said to his wife, who had remained in bed: 'I have a prisoner here, my dear! Be his gaoler and treat him just as you would treat me!'

No sooner was he out of the room than d'Avannes, who would have liked nothing better than to be treated like the husband, leapt nimbly into the bed, hoping that an opportunity like this would make the wise lady change her tune. But not so! As he jumped in at one side, she got out at the other, grabbing her tunic and covering herself up in it.

'Monseigneur,' she began, as she approached the head of the bed, where d'Avannes had landed, 'did you imagine that a chaste heart can be changed by opportunity? For you should know that just as gold is tested in the furnace, so a chaste heart proves itself stronger and more virtuous in the midst of temptation, and the more it is beset by its contrary, the cooler it grows. You may be quite sure, therefore, that if my wishes were otherwise than I have told you, I would certainly have found ways and means of satisfying them – ways and means to which, having no desire to use them, I have given no consideration. If you wish me to retain such feelings as I have for you, then I would ask you not only to rid yourself of the desire to make me other than I am, but also to rid yourself of the very idea that by some deed or other you could ever accomplish such a goal.'

While she was speaking her serving-women came in, and she ordered them to bring a collation of preserves. But d'Avannes did not in the circumstances feel like either eating or drinking, so wretched did he feel at having failed in his attempt. Not only that, but he was fearful lest his demonstration of desire should cost him such intimacy as he had previously enjoyed.

Having seen that the conflagration was dealt with, the husband came back and prevailed upon d'Avannes to stay the rest of the night. And so he did, but his eyes spent that night in weeping and did not close for sleep. Early the next morning he went to bid his hosts farewell in their bed. As he kissed the lady, he knew that she felt more pity than resentment at what he had done. Thus was one more coal piled upon the fire of his love. After dinner he joined the King, to accompany him to Taffalla, but before he left he went once more to say goodbye to his good father and to his lady, who since she had been so instructed by her husband, no longer raised objections to kissing d'Avannes as her son. However, you may take my word for it, the more virtue prevented the hidden flame from showing itself in her eyes and in the expression on her face, the hotter it grew and the more unbearable it became. In the end, she was unable to endure the war in her heart between love and honour. It was a war that she had, however, resolved never to reveal, and, deprived of the consolation of being able to see and speak to the man who was life itself to her, she fell into a continuous fever due to a melancholic humour. Her extremities became quite cold and internally she burned incessantly. The doctors – not that they have any final say in the matter of human health – began to be concerned about her illness. They suspected an internal obstruction as the cause of her acute melancholy, and they were so worried that they told the husband to warn his wife to take care of her conscience and to realize that she was in the hands of God – as if you are not in the hands of God when you are healthy. The husband loved his wife dearly, and was so upset to hear the doctors' pronouncements that he wrote to d'Avannes for consolation, begging him to take the trouble to come to see them and expressing the hope that the sight of him would do the patient good. D'Avannes did not lose a moment when he received the letters but came post-haste. On entering the house, he found all the servants going about as if in a state of mourning for their beloved mistress, and he was so shocked that he stood at the door as if paralysed. His good father came to him, embraced him and, weeping so bitterly that he could not speak, led him to his poor sick wife's room. She turned her languishing eyes towards the young man, looked at him, held out her hand and with all the strength [left in her enfeebled body,] drew him towards her. She kissed him, embraced him, and gave voice to this woeful lament:

'Oh Monseigneur, the hour has come when all dissimulation must cease, and I must confess the truth that till now I have striven so hard to hide from you. Know then that if you have felt deeply for me, I have felt none the less deeply for you. But the pain I have endured has been greater, for I have had to hide my suffering against all that I wished and all that I desired. For God and my honour forbade me ever to declare it to you lest I should encourage in you that which I sought to diminish. Yet, though so often I said no to you, I confess that it has hurt so much to pronounce the word that it is now the cause of my death. But I am content that it should be so, for it is by God's grace that I die before the violence of my love should stain my conscience and my name. Lesser fires than mine have ruined greater, stronger buildings. I depart full of joy that before I die I have been able to declare to you my feelings, feelings that are the match of yours, save only that in men and women honour is never the same. And I beseech you, Monseigneur, that you should not henceforth shrink from addressing yourself to the highest and most virtuous ladies in the land, for it is in hearts such as these that the greatest passions dwell, and hearts such as these who conduct their great passions with prudence and sobriety. Your grace, your beauty and your nobility are such that they will never let the toils of love go fruitless. I shall not ask you to pray for me, for I know that the gate of Paradise is not closed to true lovers, and I know that love is a fire that punishes lovers so sorely in this life that they are exempt from the bitter torments of Purgatory in the next. So, adieu, Monseigneur. Take care of your good father, my husband. Tell him the truth, I beg you, so that he will know how truly I have loved God and loved him. Come no more now before my eyes. For henceforth I wish only to think of how I shall receive the promises that were made to me by God before the creation of the world.'

So saying she embraced him and kissed him with all the strength that remained in her weak arms. D'Avannes, stirred to the depths of his soul by this spectacle, and no less sick at heart than his suffering lady, could not summon the strength to utter a single word. He withdrew from her sight and collapsed in a deep faint on a bed that was in the room.

Then the lady called her husband to her side. After many a noble exhortation, she commended d'Avannes to him, declaring that next to himself it was d'Avannes whom she had loved most in all the world. So saying, she kissed her husband, and bade him her last farewell. Then, after extreme unction, they brought her the holy sacrament of the altar, and she received them joyously, as one who is sure of her salvation. Her sight began to grow dim and her strength ebbed from her. She started to repeat the *In manus tuas* in a loud voice. Hearing her cry out, d'Avannes raised himself on his bed. Overwhelmed with pity he watched as with a gentle sigh she rendered her glorious soul unto Him from whom she had come. When he realized that she was dead, he sprang up, and though he had never approached her living body except in fear and trembling, he now threw himself upon her lifeless corpse. Clasping it in his arms, he covered it in kisses, and it was only with the utmost difficulty that they were able to remove it from his grip. The husband, who had never supposed that d'Avannes felt so deeply about his wife, was overwhelmed. 'This is too much, Monseigneur!' he said. They left the room together and wept long, [the one for his wife, the other for his lady.] Then d'Avannes told the husband the whole story of his love, and how until her death his wife had given no sign that he could have read as anything other than coldness and reserve. It pleased the husband to hear these words, though they increased too the pain of his loss, and for the rest of his days he devoted himself to the young man's service. D'Avannes himself, however, who at this time was only eighteen years of age, made his way straight to court. There he remained for many years, refusing to speak to any other woman, refusing even to see any other woman. And for ten whole years he dressed himself in black.

*

'Well, Ladies, that shows you the difference between a wanton woman and a wise one, two women who demonstrate the different effects of love. In the one it led to a glorious death that we should all admire; in the other it led to disgrace, shame and a life that was all too long. For as much as the death of a saint is precious before God, the death of a sinner is nothing worth.'

'Indeed, Saffredent,' said Oisille, 'you have told us a most beautiful story. And anyone who knows the person in question, as I do, will think the more highly of it. I have never seen a finer, more handsome gentleman in all my life than the Seigneur d'Avannes.'

'But just consider,' said Saffredent. 'Here we have a wise woman, who, for the sake of showing herself outwardly more virtuous than she was in her heart and for the sake of covering up a passion which the logic of Nature demanded she should conceive for this most noble lord, goes and allows herself to die just because she denies herself the pleasures that she covertly desires!'

'If she really had felt such desires,' said Parlamente, 'she had plenty of opportunities to show it. But so great was her virtue, that her desire never went beyond her reason.'

'You can dress it up as you please,' said Hircan, 'but I know that when one devil's been chased out it's always replaced by a worse one, that where women are concerned it's pride that ousts desire much more than fear, or love of God, and also that those long skirts they wear are nothing more than a fabric woven from lies and deception, preventing us knowing what's hidden beneath! For, if their honour were unstained by the fact as ours is, you would find that Nature has no more forgotten anything where women are concerned than she has where we men are concerned. They impose on themselves the constraint of not daring to help themselves to pleasures they desire, and in the place of this vice they put another vice, one which they regard as more honourable: namely, cruel hardness of heart and vainglorious concern for reputation, by means of which they hope to acquire immortal renown. Thus, glorying in their resistance to the law of Nature, as if Nature were vicious, not only do they make themselves no better than cruel and inhuman beasts, but they turn into veritable demons, and take on the arrogance and malice of demons!'

'It's a great pity that your wife is such a good woman,' said Nomerfide, 'seeing that you not only want to discredit virtue but also want to prove it to be a vice!'

'I'm very glad,' Hircan replied, 'to have a wife who gives no ground for scandal, and neither would I myself wish to cause scandal. But as far as chastity of the heart is concerned, I believe that she and I are both children of Adam and Eve. So if we look at ourselves properly, we shall have no need to cover our nakedness with fig-leaves, but rather to confess our frailty.'

'I accept,' said Parlamente, 'that we are all in need of God's grace, since we all incline to sin. Yet the fact is that our temptations are not the same as yours, and if we sin through pride, no one suffers for it, and neither our body nor our hands are tainted by it. But all your pleasure is derived from dishonouring women, and your honour depends on killing other men in war. These are two things that are expressly contrary to the law of God.'

'I admit what you say,' said Geburon, 'but God has said: "Whosoever looks on a woman to lust after her hath committed adultery with her already in his heart" and "Whosoever hateth his brother is a murderer." In your opinion, are women any more exempt from this than we are?'

'It is God who is the judge of hearts,' said Longarine, 'and He will pass His sentence. But if men are unable to accuse us, that is in itself a good thing. For the goodness of God is so great that He will not judge us without an accuser, and the frailty of our hearts is so well known to Him that He will love us still for not acting openly in accordance with that frailty.'

'Come now,' said Saffredent, 'let's drop this disputation – it smacks more of sermonizing than story-telling. I pick Ennasuite to tell the next tale, and I hope she'll take good care to make us laugh.'

'Don't worry,' she replied, 'I shan't disappoint you. I did have a very uplifting story for today, but as I was on my way here, somebody told me a very funny one about two men in the service of a certain princess, and I laughed so much that I forgot all about the tragic and melancholy tale I had intended to tell. I'll leave that one till tomorrow, because I'd never be able to make it sound convincing if I told it with a smile on my face!'

STORY TWENTY-SEVEN

In the town of Amboise there lived a certain man who served the princess in question in the capacity of chamberlain. He was an honourable man and enjoyed entertaining anyone who came to visit him, especially his own colleagues. Now, not long ago one of these colleagues, a man who acted as secretary to the princess, came to stay with him, and remained for ten or twelve days. This secretary was so ugly, that to look at him, you'd have thought he was king of the cannibals rather than a Christian! And he did something that showed not merely that he had forgotten what honour was, but that honour had never had the smallest place in his heart, and he did it in spite of the fact that his host had treated him most honourably, indeed, had treated him as a true friend and brother. What he did was to pursue his colleague's wife, just to satisfy his own dishonourable and illicit desires, regardless of the fact that there was nothing in the slightest desirable about her. In fact she was the very antithesis of sensual desire, and as respectable a woman as any in the town of Amboise. She realized what the evil intentions of the secretary were, and decided to expose his vicious ways by means of subterfuge rather than cover them up by refusing him from the outset. So she pretended to welcome his advances. As for him, he thought he had her where he wanted her. He never left off pestering her and was not in the slightest concerned about her age (she was around fifty), or the fact that she was not exactly beautiful, let alone the fact that she had the reputation of being a respectable woman who loved her husband dearly. One day they found themselves in a room together, while the husband was in some other part of the house. The wife, continuing her pretence, said that the only thing they needed was a safe place to have a little tête-a-tête, just as he wanted. To which he replied that all they had to do was to go up to the attic. So up she got, and told him to go first and wait for her. He trotted off up the stairs, grinning all over his face like a performing monkey. Listening intently for the longed-for footsteps on the stairs, he awaited the object of his desire. His passion burned within him – not with the pure bright flame you get with juniper wood, more like a smouldering coal from a smoky old forge! But instead of the discreet footsteps he hoped for, what he heard was the lady's voice calling out: 'Just wait a second, Monsieur le secrétaire, I'll go and ask my husband if he minds if I come up and join you!'

Just imagine! The secretary was an ugly man when he was laughing – think what he must have looked like when he was snivelling! Well, up he jumped and ran downstairs, tears in his eyes, begging and beseeching her that for the love of God she would not say anything to upset the good relations he had with his colleague.

'I'm quite sure,' she replied, 'that you are too good a friend of his to want to say anything to *me* which you wouldn't want repeated to *him*! So I'll just go and have a word with him.'

And that is just what she did, notwithstanding the man's attempts to dissuade her. All he could do was take to his heels, as mortified by this humiliation as the husband was satisfied by his wife's virtuous little trick. Indeed, so satisfied was the husband with his wife's great virtue that he overlooked his colleague's vicious streak. After all, he had been punished enough by having the disgrace he had tried to visit on his colleague's family rebound on to his own head.

*

'In the light of this story it seems to me that decent people ought to learn not to detain in their houses those whose consciences, hearts and minds are ignorant of God, of honour and of true love.'

'Although your tale was a short one,' said Oisille, 'it was as amusing as any I've heard, and what is more, it was to the honour of an honest woman.'

'Good Lord!' exclaimed Simontaut. 'There's not much honour involved when an honest woman merely turns down a man as ugly as you say this secretary was. If he'd been handsome and honourable, then there'd have been some evidence of virtue. Actually, I think I know who the man was, and if it were my turn, I'd tell you another tale every bit as funny as the one we've just heard.'

'That's no problem,' said Ennasuite. 'I appoint you as the next storyteller.'

So Simontaut began: 'People who are used to residing at court or in the big towns have such a good opinion of [their own] cleverness that they think everyone else is nothing compared with them. It does not however [follow] that there are not always plenty of clever, cunning people in all countries and all walks of life. But because those who think they're the world's cleverest are so puffed up, one gets much more fun from laughing at them when they make some mistake, as I hope now to demonstrate in a story about something that took place quite recently.'

STORY TWENTY-EIGHT

It was while King Francis I, accompanied by his sister, the Queen of Navarre, was staying in Paris. The Queen had brought one of her secretaries with her, a man called Jean. He was not the sort of man to let a good opportunity slip through his fingers. There was not a single president or councillor with whom he was not acquainted, and not a single merchant or man of means with whom he did not have an understanding and whose house he did not frequent. Now it so happened that at about the same time there was also in Paris a certain merchant from Bayonne by the name of Bernard du Ha. This man approached the *lieutenant-criminel*, partly because he was a native of the same region, and partly because he wanted his professional help and advice on a piece of business. But it so happened that the Queen's secretary, devoted servant that he was to his master and mistress, was also in the habit of visiting the lieutenant.

One fine day, when everyone was enjoying a public holiday, the secretary went round to the lieutenant's house, and on arriving there found neither the lieutenant nor his wife at home. Instead, there was Bernard du Ha playing a hurdy-gurdy or something of the sort, and teaching the lieutenant's chambermaids how to dance a Gascon *branle*! When the secretary saw this he tried to make him believe that he was committing a terrible crime, and warned him that if the lady of the house and her husband found out, they would be extremely displeased. He painted so lurid a picture of what might happen that the man begged him to keep quiet about it. Seeing his chance, the secretary then said, 'What will you give me not to breathe a word about it?' Bernard du Ha, however, was not so scared as he pretended. He knew full well that the secretary was trying to trick him, but he promised in return to present him with the best [Basque] ham pie he had ever tasted in his life. The secretary was very pleased with this offer and asked him to bring the pie the following Sunday after dinner. This Bernard du Ha promised to do.

Counting on this promise, the secretary then went off to see a certain lady whom he passionately desired to marry, and said to her: 'Mademoiselle, I will come to supper with you on Sunday, if I may, but there's no need to worry about preparing anything. All we need is some good bread and wine – because I've just tricked some stupid fellow from Bayonne into providing the rest of the meal at his own expense! In fact, thanks to this little trick I've played on him, I shall serve you the best [Basque] ham that has ever been eaten in the whole of Paris!'

Taking him at his word, the lady invited two or three of her most respectable friends from the neighbourhood and promised to treat them to an entirely new dish that they had never tasted before.

Sunday came and the secretary went in search of his merchant friend. Eventually he found him on the Pont au Change.

'The devil take you!' said he, greeting him in his most ungracious manner. 'The trouble I've had trying to find you!'

To which Bernard du Ha replied that there were people who had had an even worse time and not been rewarded with such gastronomic delights for their pains. As he spoke he produced the pie from beneath his cloak. It was big enough to feed an army! The secretary was overjoyed. He pursed up his ugly great mouth so small in anticipation that he looked as if he would never be able to open it again to taste the object of his delight. Then, greedily grabbing hold of it, he [left the merchant standing where he was,] without even bothering to invite him, and dashed off to join his lady, who could hardly wait to see whether the dishes of Guienne were as good as those of Paris. When supper-time came, and they were all sitting eating their soup, the secretary said: 'Let's not bother with this tasteless stuff. Let's sharpen our palates on something a little more tasty!'

So saying, he opened up the enormous pie, and tried to [cut into] the ham. It was so hard that the knife made not the slightest impression! After several desperate attempts, it dawned on him that he had been fooled. It was not a ham at all, but a wooden clog, the kind they wear in Gascony! A bit of charred wood had been stuck in one end, and the whole thing had been sprinkled with [soot], flakes of iron, and spices to give it a pleasant smell. Well, if anyone was ever crestfallen, it was our secretary. Not only had he been made a fool of by the very person he had tried to fool himself, but he had also made his lady look foolish – the very person to whom he wanted to tell the truth and to whom indeed he had thought he *was* telling the truth! And on top of all that he had to content himself with a bowl of soup for his supper. The guests, who were also somewhat vexed, would have accused him of being behind the trick, had it not been perfectly plain from the expression on his face that he was even more put out than they were! When he had finished this now rather slender supper, the secretary went off in high dudgeon. As Bernard du Ha had not kept his promise, he was not going to keep his either. So he went straight to the lieutenant's house, fully intending to tell him the worst possible things he could about the aforementioned Bernard. However, Bernard had beaten him to it. He had already told the lieutenant the whole story, and the lieutenant was ready to deliver his judgement on the secretary. All he had to say to him was that he had now been taught a lesson for playing tricks on Gascons! So there was no consolation there for the poor secretary. All he got out of it was his own humiliation!

*

'That sort of thing often happens to people who think they're too clever and forget themselves in their cleverness. So you see, there's nothing like doing by others as you would be done by!'

'I assure you,' said Geburon, 'that I've often seen things like that happen – people you'd have thought village idiots making fools of people who think they're clever. For there's nothing more foolish than a man who thinks he's clever, and nothing more wise than the man who knows that he is nothing.'

'And the man knows something,' said Parlamente, 'who knows that he does not.'

'Well, I'm afraid we wouldn't have enough time to do justice to what you have to say,' said Simontaut, 'so I call upon Nomerfide to tell the next story. I'm sure she's not one to hold us up with a lot of rhetoric!'

'All right, I shall tell you just the kind of story you desire,' she replied. 'It's not surprising to me, Ladies, that love should inspire princes [and people brought up in noble circumstances] with the means to escape from danger. After all, such people are brought up surrounded by learned people, and I'd be more surprised if there was anything they were ignorant of. No, the resourcefulness that comes from being in love shows all the more clearly when the person is lacking in native wit. To demonstrate this, I shall tell you a tale about a trick perpetrated by a priest – a priest whose only teacher was love, for the man was so ignorant in all other matters that he was scarcely capable of reading his masses!'

STORY TWENTY-NINE

In a village called Carrelles in the county of Maine, there once lived a rich farmer, who late in life had married a beautiful young woman. He had had no children by her, but she consoled herself for this disappointment by having several lovers. When she ran out of men of gentle birth and other worthy individuals, she turned to her last resource – the Church. As her accomplice in sin she chose the very man who could absolve her from it – the local parish priest, who paid many a visit to this member of his flock. The dull old husband never suspected a thing, but he was a sturdy man with rough ways and the wife preferred to play her little game with as much secrecy as possible. She was afraid her husband would kill her if he found her out. One day, when he was out of the house and she did not expect him back for some time, she sent for her priest to come and confess her. And they were having a good time together, when the husband unexpectedly comes back home. There was no time for the priest to get away, and he looked round desperately for somewhere to hide. On the wife's suggestion he climbed up into a loft and covered the trap-door with a winnowing basket. Meanwhile the husband had come in, and his wife, afraid lest he should suspect anything, was doing her best to be nice to him over his dinner. She gave him plenty to drink, and he consumed so much that what with this and being worn out after working in the fields he began to feel sleepy as he sat in his chair by the fire. Meanwhile, the priest was getting bored up in the loft. When he heard everything had gone quiet in the room below, he leaned out over the trap-door, craning his neck as far as he could until he saw the old man fast asleep. But as he peered, he accidentally leaned on the winnowing basket. Down they fell, both priest and basket in a heap right by the sleeping man! The good fellow woke with a start at the noise, but the priest was on his feet before the husband had even seen him.

'Ah, here's your winnowing basket, neighbour,' he said, 'and many thanks for lending it me!'

And without more ado, off he went. The poor farmer was astonished and said to his wife:

'What's all that about?'

'It's the winnowing basket which the curé borrowed, my dear,' she replied. 'And he has just called to return it.'

'Very rough way of returning something you've borrowed,' he growled. 'I thought the house was falling down.'

And so it was that the curé escaped scotfree at the expense of the good old farmer, whose only complaint was the abrupt manner in which his winnowing basket had been returned!

*

'So, Ladies, the master he served saved him on that occasion, but only so that he could possess and torment him the longer in the future.'

'You should not think that simple folk of low station in life are any more exempt from evil intent than the rest of us,' said Geburon. 'On the contrary, they're a good deal worse. Just look at the thieves, murderers, sorcerers, counterfeiters and people of that kind. Their criminal minds never have a moment's rest. And they're all poor people and artisans.'

'I don't find it strange that such people should exhibit more evil intent than others,' observed Parlamente, 'but I do find it strange that love should trouble them when they have their energies taken up by so many other things. It's extraordinary that so noble a passion can find its way into such vulgar hearts!'

'Madame,' said Saffredent, 'you know that Maître Jean de Meung said in the *Roman de la Rose* that

Whether frieze or lawn you wear,
Love's fancies free do linger there!

Besides, the love in your story isn't exactly of the kind that brings trials and tribulations. True, poor folk don't have the wealth or the same marks of distinction that we do, but they do have freer access to the commodities of Nature. Their food may not be quite so delicate, but they have better appetites, and they get more nourishment on coarse bread than we do on our delicate diets. They don't have fine beds and linen like we do, but they have better sleep and deeper rest than we. They don't have fine ladies with their make-up and elegant clothes like the ones we idolize, but they have their pleasure more often than we do, and they don't need to worry about wagging tongues, except perhaps for the birds and animals who happen to see them. [In short], everything that we have, they lack, and everything we lack, they have in abundance.'

'Come along, let's leave the peasant and his lass,' said Nomerfide, 'and finish the day before vespers. Hircan will tell the final tale.'

'Well, I've been saving one for you. It's the strangest and most piteous story you've ever heard. And although I'm reluctant [to speak ill of any lady], knowing as I do that men are malicious enough to draw conclusions from the misdeeds of one woman in order to cast blame on all the rest, yet the story is so extraordinary that I suppress my reluctance. In any case, it may be that bringing the ignorance of one woman into the open may make the others wiser. So I shall not be afraid to tell you my story.'

STORY THIRTY

During the reign of King Louis XII, at the time when the Legate at Avignon was one of the d'Amboise family, in fact the nephew of Georges d'Amboise, who was Legate of France, there lived in Languedoc a certain lady whose name, for the sake of her family, I shall not reveal. She had an income of more than four thousand ducats, had been widowed at an early age, and had been left with one son. Whether out of sorrow at the loss of her husband or whether out of her love for her child, she had vowed never to remarry. To avoid any situation that might lead to her doing so, she insisted on having nothing to do with anyone except people who were devout. She thought that it is opportunity that leads to sin, and did not realize that it is the reverse: sin manufactures opportunity. This young widow gave herself up entirely to attending divine service. She shunned all worldly gatherings – to such an extent that she even made going to weddings and listening to the organ in church a matter of conscience. When her son was seven years of age, she took on a man of saintly ways as the boy's tutor, so that he might be instructed in all devotion and sanctity. But when he was between fourteen and fifteen years old, Nature, that most secret of teachers, found that this well-grown lad had nothing to occupy him and began to teach him lessons somewhat different from those of his tutor. He began to gaze upon and to desire the things that seemed to him full of beauty. And amongst these things there was a young lady who slept in his mother's room. No one suspected anything, since he was regarded as no more than a child, and in any case, in that household nothing was heard but godly conversation. Well, the young gallant started making secret advances to the girl, and the girl came to complain to her mistress. The boy's mother loved her son so much and had such a high opinion of him that she thought the girl was making the complaint simply in order [to turn her against him]. But the girl persisted in her complaints, and in the end her mistress said:

'I will find out if what you say is true, and if what you say is indeed true, I will punish him. But if your accusation is false, it will be you who shall pay the penalty.'

In order to establish the truth of the matter, then, she instructed the girl to make an assignation with her son. He was to come at midnight and join her in the bed where she slept alone by the door of her mistress's chamber. The girl dutifully obeyed, but when the evening came, it was the mother who took her place. If the accusation was true, she was resolved to give her son such a chastising that he would never in the whole of his life get in bed with a woman without remembering it. Such were her angry thoughts, when her son appeared and climbed into the bed with her. But, even though he had actually got into the bed, she still could not believe that he would do anything dishonourable. So she did not speak immediately, waiting till he gave some clear sign that his intentions were bad, for she could not believe on such slender evidence that his desires might go as far as anything criminal. She waited to see what he would do. So long did she wait, and so fragile was her nature, that her anger turned to pleasure, a pleasure so abominable, that she forgot she was a mother. Even as the dammed-up torrent flows more impetuously than the freely flowing stream, so it was with this poor lady whose pride and honour had lain in the restraints she had imposed upon her own body. No sooner had she set her foot on the first rung down the ladder of her chastity, than she found herself suddenly swept away to the bottom. That night she became pregnant by the very one whom she had desired to prevent getting others with child. No sooner had the sin been committed than she was seized with the most violent pangs of remorse, remorse so deep that her repentance was to last her whole life long. She rose from her son, who still believed he had lain with the young girl, and in bitter anguish withdrew to a room apart, where, going over in her mind how her good intentions had come to such wicked fruition, she spent the rest of the night in solitary weeping and gnashing of teeth. Yet, instead of humbling herself and recognizing how impossible it is for our flesh to do otherwise than sin unless we have God's help, she tried to give satisfaction for past deeds through her own means, through her tears and through her own prudence, to avoid future evil. Her excuse for her sin was the situation she had been placed in, never evil inclination, for which there can be no remedy but the grace of God. She thought it would be possible in the future to act in such a way as to avoid slipping again into such unfortunate circumstances, and, as if there were but one kind of sin that can damn us, she bent all her efforts to avoiding this one alone. But the root of pride, which external sin should cure, only grew and increased, with the consequence that by avoiding one kind of evil she merely fell in the way of several others. For the very next morning, as soon as day broke, she sent for her son's tutor and said to him:

'My son is growing up now, and it's time he left home. I have a relative who is away beyond the mountains with the Grand-Maître de Chaumont. His name is Captain Montesson, and he will be very pleased to enlist my son. So, take him at once, and to spare me the pain of parting, tell him not to come to bid me farewell.'

So saying, she gave him the necessary money for the journey. That very morning the young man departed for the wars, and, having as he believed spent the night with his paramour, there was nothing better that he could have wished for. The lady remained for a long time plunged into a deep sadness and melancholy. Had it not been for her fear of God, there was many a time when she would gladly have wished that the unhappy fruit of her womb should perish. She pretended to be ill, so that she could wear an outer garment to conceal her fault. When the time of her confinement was near, she turned to the one man in whom she could place her trust, a bastard brother, to whom she had in the past given a great deal. She told him what had befallen her, without telling him about her son, and asked him to help her save her honour, which he gladly agreed to do. A few days before she was due to give birth, he came and invited her to have a change of air, saying that it would help her recover her health if she came to stay in his house for a while. So, accompanied by a small group of attendants, she went with him. Waiting for them they found a midwife who had been told it was the brother's wife she was to attend. One night, without the midwife's realizing who she was, the lady was delivered of a beautiful baby girl. Her brother had the child fostered with a wet-nurse, pretending that it was his own child. The lady stayed one month, and then, fully recovered, returned to her own house, where she began to live a more austere life than ever, subjecting herself to fasts and other disciplines.

When the wars in Italy were over, the lady's son, who by this time had grown to full manhood, sent word to his mother, asking if he might return to her house. But she was afraid of falling into the same sin again, and refused to give her permission. The son persisted, until in the end she could no longer find any reason to continue in her refusal. However, she sent a message to him to the effect that he was never to appear before her unless he was married to somebody he loved deeply. It did not matter who she was; her fortune was not important; so long as she was a girl of gentle birth, that would be sufficient. During this time, the lady's bastard brother saw that his adopted daughter had grown up into a beautiful young girl, and decided that she should be placed in a household in some far-off region where she would not be known. On the advice of her mother she was placed with Catherine, the Queen of Navarre. At the age of twelve or thirteen the girl had indeed grown so beautiful and noble in her ways that the Queen came to hold her very dear, and was anxious that she should be married to someone of high estate. But though the girl had many men to pay her court, because she was poor, she had none to be her husband. One day, however, the noble lord who was her unknown father came back from over the mountains and arrived at the house of the Queen. No sooner had he caught sight of his daughter than he fell in love with her. Having received permission from his mother to marry whom he pleased, all he desired to know about the girl was whether she was of gentle birth, and on hearing that indeed she was, he asked the Queen for her hand. The Queen, who knew that he was rich, and not only rich but handsome, noble and good, gladly gave her consent.

Once the marriage had been consummated, the noble lord wrote to his mother again, saying that she could surely no longer refuse to have him, for now he could bring with him a daughter-in-law as perfect as anyone could ever desire. His mother asked further about the match he had made, and on realizing that her son's wife was their own daughter, she sank into a state of such utter desperation that she thought her end was near. For the harder she tried to place impediments in the way of disaster, the more she became the instrument whereby ever new catastrophes overcame her. Not knowing what else she could do, she went to the Legate at Avignon, confessed the enormity of her sin, and asked for his advice on what she should now do. [In order to satisfy] her conscience the Legate summoned several doctors of theology, to whom he explained the whole affair, without revealing the names of the persons involved. In the light of their counsel he concluded that the lady should never say anything to her children, for they had acted in ignorance and consequently had not sinned. But she, their mother, was to do penance for the rest of her life without giving the slightest indication of it to them. The poor lady returned to her house, and not long after that her son and her daughter-in-law arrived. They were very much in love. Never was there such love between husband and wife, never were a husband and wife so close. For she was his daughter, his sister, his wife. And he was her father, brother and husband. They endured for ever in this great love, while the poor lady, their mother, in the extremity of her penitence, could not see them show their love but she would withdraw to weep alone.

*

'There, Ladies, that is what becomes of those women who presume by their own strength and virtue to overcome love and nature and all the powers that God has placed therein. Better were it to recognize one's weakness, better not to try to do battle with such an enemy, but turning to the one true lover, to say with the Psalmist*: "Lord, I am oppressed; answer thou for me."'

'One could not possibly hear a stranger story than that,' said Oisille, 'and I think that every man and woman here should bow their heads in the fear of God, to see how, as a result of presuming to do good, so much evil came about.'

'Be you assured, the first step man takes trusting in himself alone is a step away from trust in God,' said Parlamente.

'He is a wise man,' said Geburon, 'who recognizes no enemy but himself, and who distrusts his own will and counsel [, however good and holy they may appear to be.'

* Actually Isaiah 38:14.

'And no matter how good a thing it might appear to be,' said Longarine,] 'nothing should induce a woman to risk sharing a bed with a male relative, however close he may be to her. It's not safe to set a naked flame near tinder.'

'Without a doubt she was one of those foolish, vainglorious women who had had her head filled with nonsense by the Franciscans,' said Ennasuite, 'and thought she was so saintly that she was incapable of sin, as some of them would persuade us to believe that through our own efforts we actually can be, though this is an extreme error.'

'Is it possible, Longarine,' said Oisille, 'that some of them are so foolish as to believe that view?'

'They do better than that!' replied Longarine. 'They even say that it's necessary to habituate themselves to the virtue of chastity, and in order to put their strength to the test, they converse with the most beautiful women they can find, with women whom they particularly like. Then by means of fondling and kissing they test themselves to see if they have achieved mortification of the flesh. If they find that they are aroused by these little pleasures, they go into solitude and subject themselves to fasts and austere disciplines. And when they have overcome the desires of the flesh to the point where a conversation and a kiss no longer [arouse] them, they try out the ultimate temptation of going to bed with a woman and embracing her without lustful desire. However, for every one who survived this test, there were many who did not, and the consequences were so unfortunate that the Archbishop of Milan, where these particular religious practices were rife, was obliged to separate the men from the women, putting the women in women's convents and the men in monasteries of their own.'

'Really,' said Geburon, 'it's the extreme of folly to want to put oneself through one's own efforts above sin, and then actually to go looking for situations where a sin may be committed!'

'Some people do the opposite, however,' said Saffredent, 'and avoid such situations as much as they can – but even then their concupiscence goes with them. The good Saint Jerome, even after he had flagellated himself and hidden himself away in the wilderness, confessed that he could not get rid of the fire that burned in the marrow of his bones. So we should commend ourselves to God, for if He does not hold us in His grip, we stumble and take great pleasure in so doing.'

'But you're not taking any notice of what I can see!' interrupted Hircan. 'While we've been telling our stories, the monks have been listening behind the hedge! They didn't even hear the bell for vespers, but now that we've started talking about God they've run off and they're ringing the second bell!'

'We will do well to follow them,' said Oisille, 'and go to render thanks to God for having spent this day so happily.'

At this, they rose and made their way to the church, where they all devoutly heard vespers. Afterwards, when they went for supper, they discussed the things that had been said during the day and recounted many things that had happened in their time, in order to see which were worthy of note. After passing the evening in this happy way, they all retired peacefully to bed, looking forward to continuing on the next day the pastime which they found so agreeable. And so the third day came to its close.

END OF THE THIRD DAY

FOURTH DAY

PROLOGUE

The next day Madame Oisille rose long before the others as was her wont, and passed the time meditating on her Bible until they had all assembled. The laziest amongst them excused themselves with an allusion to the words of the Bible, saying 'I have a wife, and therefore I could not come so early'! When Hircan and his wife Parlamente arrived, they found the daily lesson was well under way. But Oisille knew how to find the passage in which Scripture reproaches those who are negligent in listening to the sacred word. She not only read them the text, [but] she also gave such sound and devout expositions that no one could possibly find it boring. Once the reading was over, Parlamente said to her:

'I was angry with myself for being lazy when I arrived, but as my failing has led you to speak so excellently, my laziness has yielded twice the profit – I have rested my body by sleeping longer, and given repose to my mind by listening to your excellent words.'

Oisille replied, 'Well, as penance let us go to mass to pray to Our Lord to give us the will and the means to carry out His commandments, and that He will command that which is His pleasure.'

As she said these words, they entered the church where they devoutly heard mass. Afterwards, they sat down at table, and Hircan did not overlook the opportunity to tease his wife for her laziness. Having eaten, they each retired so that they could study their scripts. At the appointed time, they went to their usual meeting place. Oisille asked Hircan whom he would choose to start the day.

'If my wife had not started yesterday,' he replied, 'I would have picked her, for although I've always known she loved me more than all the men in the world, she showed this morning that she loved me even more than she loved God and His word, by the way she neglected your reading to stay with me! However, seeing that I can't choose the wisest woman amongst us,

I'll choose the wisest man, who is Geburon. And I would ask him not to spare the monks!'

To which Geburon replied: 'You have no need to ask me – I already had them in mind, for not long ago I heard a story about monks told to Monsieur de Saint Vincent, the Emperor's ambassador. It's a story that ought not to be allowed to slide into oblivion, so I shall tell it to you forthwith.'*

* De Thou gives the following variant for Geburon's reply: 'So this is how Geburon began: "Ladies, I had decided not to tell you any more stories concerning the misdeeds perpetrated by members of the religious orders, being aware that those who have their honour at heart in this world ought to be more afraid of offending them than of offending all the princes of Christendom, considering the power to speak and do evil which they possess. All this has been much better expounded than I could ever do by Jean de Meung in his chapter about False-Seeming, where he gives them such power so to act that, after reading the *Romance of the Rose*, I am as much desirous of gaining their friendship and staying in their good books as I am of winning worldly honour and glory. However, I have recently heard told to Monsieur de Saint Vincent, the Emperor's ambassador, a story which is so extraordinary that it ought not to be allowed to slide into oblivion."'

STORY THIRTY-ONE

In the lands subject to the Emperor Maximilian of Austria there was a Franciscan monastery highly esteemed by all. Nearby there lived a certain gentleman who had become so friendly with the friars that there was nothing he had which he would not gladly give them in order to be able to share in their good works, their fasts and their disciplines. Now one of the good brothers – a handsome strapping fellow he was – had been taken on by this gentleman as his confessor and had as much authority in the gentleman's household as the gentleman himself. Well, having observed that the man's wife was as good and beautiful as it was possible to be, our Franciscan friend fell so much in love with her that he lost all appetite for food and drink, and with it his natural reason.

One day, he made up his mind that the deed must be done. He went alone to the house, and finding the gentleman out he asked the lady of the house where he had gone. She replied that he had gone to one of his estates, that he would be staying there two or three days, but that if the good brother wanted to see him on business, she would send a man specially to fetch him. The friar replied that that would not be necessary, and started to go about the house as if he had some affair of great importance on his hands. When he had left the room, the lady said to one of her two maids: 'Go after the good father and find out what he wants, because it appears from the expression on his face that he is not at all happy.' The chambermaid went out into the courtyard to ask if he required anything. He replied that indeed he did, and dragging her into a corner, he took a dagger from his sleeve with which he proceeded to slit her throat. No sooner had he done this than a servant rode into the courtyard on horseback, having been to collect rent from one of his master's farms. As soon as he had dismounted he greeted the Franciscan, who embraced him, cut his throat from behind, and closed the castle gate after him.

When her chambermaid failed to reappear, the lady, puzzled

that she was such a long time with the monk, said to her other maid, 'Go and see what is keeping your companion.' The maid went off and as soon as the monk saw her, he drew her into a corner and dealt with her as he had with her companion. Now that he was completely alone in the house, he came to the lady and told her that he had been in love with her for a long time and that the time had come when she must obey him. The lady, who had never had the slightest suspicion of this, replied, 'Father, I think that if I were ever to desire anything so wicked, you would be the first to want to reprimand me.'

To which the monk said, 'Go outside into the courtyard and you'll see what I've done.'

When she saw her two maids and her servant lying dead, she was so terrified that she stood there like a statue, motionless and speechless. Then the evil man, who certainly had no intention of letting her go after a [mere] hour of pleasure, decided not to take her by force, but said instead, 'Mademoiselle, do not be afraid. You are in the hands of a man who loves you more than anyone in the world.' So saying, he stripped off his habit and presented to the lady a smaller habit which he had on underneath, telling her that if she did not put it on, he would send her to join the corpses lying on the ground in front of her.

The lady, more dead than alive, decided to pretend to obey him, as much to save her life as to gain time, in the hope that her husband would return. So, she did as he ordered and started to let her hair down, taking as long over it as she could. Once her locks were loose, the friar, without a thought for their great beauty, hastily hacked them off. Then he made her strip to her shift and put on the small habit he had brought with him, while he got back into his own. This done, he set off with all possible speed, leading behind him his little Franciscan whom he had desired for so long. But God, who has pity on the innocent in distress, saw the tears of the poor lady. The husband, having concluded his business sooner than expected, was riding back along the same road. However, when the friar saw him in the distance, he said to the lady:

'Here's your husband coming! If you look at him, he'll try to take you from me. So walk right in front, and don't turn your head in the direction he's going, because if you make any sign to him, my dagger will be in your back before he can do a thing to save you.'

As he spoke, the gentleman approached and asked him where he was coming from, to which the friar answered, 'From your house, where I have left Madamoiselle, who is very well and is waiting for you.'

The gentleman went on his way, without noticing his wife. But one of the servants who was with him was in the habit of chatting with the Franciscan's usual companion, whose name was Brother John, and thinking that that was who it was, he called across to the cowled figure who was really his own mistress. The poor woman, not daring to turn her head towards her husband, did not reply. But the manservant crossed the road to have a look at her face, and without saying anything the lady signalled to him with her eyes, which were full of tears. The manservant went after his master and said:

'Monsieur, when I crossed over, I had a close look at the Franciscan's companion, and it's not Brother John at all! It looks just like Mademoiselle, your wife, and she looked at me in the most piteous way, with her eyes full of tears!'

The gentleman told him he must be dreaming and took no notice. But the manservant insisted, begged leave to follow the pair, and requested that his master wait at the road to see if it was as he suspected. The gentleman agreed, and waited to see what his servant would find out. But when the Franciscan heard the manservant behind him calling Brother John, he guessed that the lady had been recognized and came at him with a great studded stick which he carried. He dealt the man such a blow in the side that he knocked him off his horse on to the ground. In a flash he jumped on top of him and cut his throat. The gentleman had seen his servant fall, and thinking he must have had an accident, rode after him to help him up. When the friar saw him, he turned on him with his studded stick, just as he had turned on the servant, knocked him to the ground and leapt on top of him. But the gentleman, who was well-built and powerful, got his arms round the monk in such a way as to prevent him doing him any harm and sent his dagger flying out of his hand. His wife picked it up immediately, handed it to her husband, and at the same time seized hold of the friar by his hood, holding on to it with all the strength in her body. The husband stabbed him several times with the knife, until he begged for mercy and confessed his wickedness. The gentleman had no desire to kill him. Instead he asked his wife to go to the house to fetch his servants, and a cart to take the friar away in. This she did, stripping off her habit, and running, shift and shorn head for everyone to see, all the way back to the castle. Immediately the whole household came running to their master to help him bring in the wolf he had caught. They found the friar on the road, seized him, bound him, and carried him back. The gentleman subsequently had him led before the court of the Emperor in Flanders, where he confessed his evil intents. And it was discovered as a result of his confession and an inquiry at the scene by special commissioners that in this particular monastery a large number of noblewomen and other good-looking girls had been abducted by the same method that the Franciscan had attempted to use – a method in which he would have succeeded, were it not for the grace of our Lord, who always helps those who place their hope in Him. The monastery was deprived of its spoils and of the beautiful girls who were there, and the monks were locked in and burned along with the monastery building as a perpetual memorial to the crime. Thus one can see that there is nothing more dangerous than love when it is founded on vice, just as there is nothing more human and laudable than love when it dwells in a heart that is virtuous.

*

'I am sorry, Ladies, that the truth does not bring us as many stories to the Franciscans' advantage as to their disadvantage, for I am very fond of the order and it would give me great pleasure to hear some tale that would give me occasion to praise them. But we've sworn so firmly to tell the truth that having heard the accounts of reliable people, I am obliged not to conceal it. I assure you that when monks do something memorable that is to their credit, I will take pains to place them in a better light than I have in telling you this particular story, true as it is.'

'Indeed, Geburon,' said Oisille, 'this is a case of love that should really be called cruelty.'

'I'm amazed,' said Simontaut, 'that he had the restraint not to take her by force, when he saw her standing there in her underclothes, and in a spot, too, where he had the upper hand.'

'He wasn't interested in titbits,' said Saffredent. 'He was a glutton! He wanted to have his fill of her every single day, not just amuse himself with one little nibble!'

'That's not the point,' said Parlamente. 'In fact a violent man is always a scared man. He was afraid of being discovered and that someone would take away his prey, so he had to carry off his little lamb like a wolf, in order to be able to devour her at his leisure.'

'All the same,' said Dagoucin, 'I cannot believe he [loved] her, or that in a heart as base as his the god of love [could] find a dwelling place.'

'Be it as it may,' said Oisille, 'he received his just deserts. I pray God that the outcome of all such deeds may be a similar punishment. But who do you choose to tell the next story?'

'You, Madame,' said Geburon. 'You will not fail to give us a good story.'

'As it is my turn,' she replied, 'I shall tell you a good one, and I shall tell it because it happened during my time and because it was told to me by the very man who witnessed it. I am sure you are all aware that at the end of all our woes is death, but that since death puts an end to all our woes, it can be called our joy and repose. Man's greatest woe, therefore, is to desire death and not to be able to have it. Consequently, the greatest punishment that can be meted out to an evil-doer is not death but continuous torture, torture severe enough to make him desire death, yet not so severe that it causes death. This is just what one husband did to his wife, as you shall now hear.'

STORY THIRTY-TWO

King Charles VIII sent to Germany a gentleman by the name of Bernage, Seigneur of Sivray, near Amboise. This Bernage, seeking to expedite his mission, rested neither night nor day, and late one evening he came to a castle, where he asked for a night's lodging, which with great difficulty he was able to obtain. However, when the master of the house learned that he was in the service of so great a king, he went straight to him and begged him not to be annoyed at the discourtesy of his servants. The reason was that his wife's parents bore a grudge against him, and he was obliged to keep his house closed up. So Bernage told him the purpose of his mission, and the gentleman, offering to do everything in his power for his master the King, took him into the house, where he lodged and entertained him with due honour.

It was suppertime, and the gentleman led him into a beautiful room draped with magnificent tapestries. When the food was brought onto the table, he saw emerge from behind the tapestry the most beautiful woman it was possible ever to behold, though her hair was cropped and the rest of her body clad in black in the German style. After Bernage and the gentleman had washed together, the water was taken to the lady, who washed in her turn and went to sit at the end of the table without speaking to anyone and without anyone speaking to her. The Seigneur de Bernage looked at her closely. She seemed to him to be one of the most beautiful women he had ever seen, except that her face was very pale and her expression very sad. When she had eaten a little, she asked for something to drink, and a servant of the house brought her a most remarkable drinking-cup made of a skull, the [apertures] of which were filled in with silver. From this she took two or three draughts. When she had finished the meal and washed her hands, she curtseyed to the master of the house, and went back behind the tapestry without speaking. Bernage was taken aback at such a strange spectacle, and became quite melancholy and pensive. Seeing this, the gentleman said to him:

'I see you are surprised by what you've seen over this meal, but I perceive that you are an honourable man, and I do not want to hide the truth of the matter from you, lest you should think I am capable of such cruelty without good cause. The lady you saw is my wife, whom I have loved more than any man ever could, so much so that in order to marry her I left fear behind me and brought her here against her parents' wishes. She too showed me so many signs of affection that I would have risked ten thousand lives to bring her here and give her the happiness that was also my happiness. Indeed, for a long time we lived a quiet, contented life, and I considered myself the happiest gentleman in Christendom. But while I was away on a journey that for honour's sake I was obliged to undertake, she so forgot her conscience, her own honour and her love for me, that she became enamoured of a young gentleman whom I had brought up in this house. On my return I believed that I had detected their liaison, but I loved her so much that I could not bring myself to doubt her, until the moment when my eyes were opened and I saw for myself what I had feared more than death itself. So my love turned to fury and desperation. I kept a close watch on her, and one day, having told her I was going out, I hid in the room where she now lives. Not long after I had disappeared, she came into the room and sent word for the young man to join her there. I saw him come in with the kind of familiarity to which I alone have the right. But when I saw he was intending to climb on to the bed with her, I jumped out from my hiding-place, seized him while he was still in her arms and slew him. And since my wife's crime seemed to me to be so heinous that a similar death would hardly suffice, I imposed a punishment which I think she finds more painful than death. I decided to lock her up in the very room where she used to go to wallow in her pleasures, and keep her there in the company of the man she loved more than she had ever loved me. In a cupboard in the room I hung her lover's skeleton like some precious object in a private gallery. And so that she should never forget him even when eating and drinking, I made her sit [in front of me] at table and had her served from the man's skull instead of a cup, so that she would have before her both the living and the dead, both him whom through her sin she had transformed into a mortal enemy and [him whose love she had preferred to mine.] Thus when she takes dinner and supper she sees the two things that must distress her most, her living enemy and her dead lover, and all by her own sin. For the rest I treat her as myself, except that she has her hair shorn, for the crowning glory of woman no more becomes an adulteress than the veil becomes a harlot. So her head is shaved to show that she has lost her modesty and the honour of [chastity.] If you would care to see her, I'll take you to her.'

Bernage gladly accepted. They went downstairs and found her in a beautiful room, seated in front of a fire. The gentleman drew a curtain in front of an alcove to reveal hanging there the skeleton of a dead man. Bernage wanted very much to talk to the lady, but dared not do so because of the husband. Realizing this, the gentleman said: 'If you would like to say something to her, you'll see how graciously she speaks.'

So Bernage said to her: 'Madame, your resignation matches your suffering. I think you are the unhappiest woman in the world.'

Tears came to the lady's eyes, and she spoke with the greatest possible grace and humility: 'Monsieur, I confess that my sins are so great that all the suffering that is inflicted upon me by the lord of this house, whom I am not worthy to call my husband, is as nothing compared with the remorse I feel in having wronged him.'

As she spoke she began to weep bitterly. The gentleman took Bernage by the arm, and drew him away. The next morning he left in order to carry out the mission entrusted to him by the King. But as he bade farewell to the gentleman he could not resist adding:

'Monsieur, the affection I bear you and the honours and kindness which you have shown me in your own house oblige me to say to you that as your poor wife's remorse is so deep, it is my belief that you should show some compassion towards her. Moreover, you are young and you have no children. It would be a great shame to let so fine a house as yours slip from your hands and permit it to be inherited by people who may be far from being your friends.'

The gentleman, who had resolved never again to speak to his wife, thought for a long time about the things Bernage had said to him. Finally he realized that Bernage was right, and promised that if his wife continued to live in such humility, he would one day have pity on her. So Bernage went off to complete his mission. On his return to court he recounted the whole story to his master the King, who found upon inquiry that it was even as it had been told him. And having heard [tell] also of the lady's great beauty, he sent his painter, Jean de Paris, to bring back her living likeness. This the painter did, with the approval of the husband, who, because of his desire to have children, and because of the compassion he felt for his wife in her humble submission to her penance, took her back, and subsequently had many fine children by her.

*

'Ladies, if all the women who behaved like this one were to drink from cups like hers, I fear that many a golden goblet would be replaced by a skull! From such things may God preserve us, for if His goodness did not restrain us, there is not one of us here who is not capable of doing things worse by far. But if we place our trust in Him, He will guard those women who confess that they cannot guard themselves. And women who trust in their own strength and virtue are in great danger of being tempted to the point where they have to confess their weakness. [I can assure you that there have been many whose pride has led to] their downfall in circumstances where [humility] saved women thought to be less virtuous. As the old proverb says, "That which God guards is guarded well."'

'I find the punishment extremely reasonable,' said Parlamente. 'For just as the crime was worse than death, so the punishment was worse than death.'

'I don't agree,' said Ennasuite. 'I would far rather be shut up in my room with the bones of all my lovers for the rest of my days than die for them, since there's no sin one can't make amends for while one is alive, but after death there is no making amends.'

'How could you make up for loss of honour?' said Longarine.

'You know that nothing a woman can do after such a crime can ever restore her honour.'

To which Ennasuite replied: 'Tell me, I beg you, whether the Magdalene does or does not have more honour amongst men than her sister, who was a virgin?'

'I admit,' said Longarine, 'that she is praised for her great love for Jesus Christ and for her great penitence, but even so she is still given the name of Sinner.'

'I don't care,' said Ennasuite, 'what names men call me, only that God pardons me and my husband. There is no reason why I should wish to die.'

'If the lady in the story had loved her husband as she should have done,' said Dagoucin, 'I am amazed she did not die of grief when she looked at the bones of the man whose death she had caused by her sin.'

'What, Dagoucin,' said Simontaut, 'do you still have to learn that women possess neither love nor regrets?'

'Indeed, I have still to learn,' said Dagoucin, 'for I have never dared try out their love, for fear of finding less than I desired.'

'So you live on faith and hope,' said Nomerfide, 'like a plover on the wind? You're easy to feed!'

'I am satisfied,' he replied, 'with the love I feel within me, and with the hope that in the hearts of ladies such love also resides. But if I knew for certain that it was even as I hoped, my joy would be too intense to bear, and I should die!'

'You should rather watch out for the plague,' said Geburon, 'because there's no need to worry about that sickness, I can assure you! But I'd like to see whom Madame Oisille will choose next.'

'I choose Simontaut,' she said, 'who will not, I know, spare anyone.'

'In other words, you accuse me of having a somewhat malicious tongue! Well, I shall nevertheless show you that those who have been called malicious have in fact spoken the truth. I don't think, Ladies, that you are foolish enough to believe all the stories people tell you, however pious they might appear, unless you have such firm proof that they are beyond all doubt. Similarly, behind what may appear as miracles there are often abuses. This is why I wanted to tell you a story about a supposed miracle which in the end is no less to the credit of a certain faithful prince than it is to the discredit of a certain corrupt minister of the Church.'

STORY THIRTY-THREE

Count Charles of Angoulême, father of Francis I, a faithful, God-fearing prince, was in Cognac, when someone told him that in the nearby village of Cherves there was a girl who lived a life so austere that everyone marvelled at her; yet, although still a virgin, she had been found to be pregnant. She made no attempt to hide the fact, assuring everyone that she had never known a man and that she had no idea how it happened, if it was not the working of the Holy Spirit. The local people believed this without question and treated her as a second Virgin Mary, for it was known to all that she had from childhood been so wise and good that never once had she shown any sign of worldliness. Not only did she fast on the days prescribed by the Church, but in addition she fasted several times a week of her own accord, and she was never away from the church whenever there was a service. Her way of life was so much respected by local folk that they all came to visit her, thinking a miracle had been wrought on her, and anyone who came close enough to touch her dress would consider himself blessed indeed. The parish priest was her brother, an elderly man, who himself lived an austere life and was loved and respected by his parishioners, who regarded him as a very holy man. But he was so strict with his sister that he had her shut up in a house. This greatly displeased the villagers, who complained so loudly that the affair eventually reached the ears of the Count himself. When he saw how people were being deceived, his immediate desire was to disabuse them, so he sent a referendary and a chaplain, both honest men, to find out the truth of the matter. They went to the village, made the most careful inquiries they could and approached the priest himself. The man was so upset by the whole affair that he begged them to be present the next day at a special ceremony which he hoped would prove the matter once and for all.

Early the next morning, then, the priest sang mass. His sister was there, kneeling the whole time, and looking very pregnant.

At the close of the service the priest took the *Corpus Domini*, and before the whole congregation said to his sister:

'Wretched woman that you are, behold Him who for your sake suffered death and passion. Before Him I charge you to tell me whether you be a virgin, as you have always assured me.'

To which she boldly replied that she was.

'And how then is it possible that you are with child, yet still a virgin?'

She replied: 'I cannot explain it unless it be the grace of the Holy Spirit who performs in me what he pleases. But neither can I deny the grace which God has granted me to keep myself a virgin. Nor did I ever have any desire to marry.'

Then her brother said: 'I will give you the most precious body of Jesus Christ, which you take to your damnation if the truth is other than you say. And let the gentlemen here present, sent by Monseigneur the Count, be witnesses to your oath.'

Then the girl, who was aged [sixteen], swore the following oath: 'I take the body of Our Lord present here, before you, Messieurs, and before you my brother, to my damnation, if ever a man touched me any more than you.'

So saying, she received the body of Our Lord. Having seen this, the Count's referendary and the chaplain went off, thoroughly abashed, and feeling that no one could lie on an oath like that. So they told the the Count what had happened, and tried to convince him. But the Count was a wise man, and after thinking carefully he asked them to repeat the exact words used in the oath. Having considered them closely, he said:

'She said that no man had ever touched her, *any more than her brother had*. I think the truth is that it's her brother who has made her pregnant, and that he wants to cover up his wickedness under this enormous piece of deception. And we who believe that one Christ has already come to this earth ought not to be expecting a second. So fetch the priest, and throw him into prison! I am sure he will confess the truth.'

His orders were duly carried out, but not without considerable criticism from those who thought that an unnecessary scandal was being created around a good man. However, as soon as he was taken prisoner, he confessed to his crime. He also admitted that he had counselled his sister to speak as she had in order to cover up the life they had been leading together, not just by means of the tenuous explanation she had given but also by means of her ambiguous form of words, which they had hoped would permit them to remain in public esteem. And when the priest was accused of going so far in his wickedness as to make her swear on the body of Our Lord, he replied that he did not have the temerity to go as far as that – he had used bread which was not consecrated or blessed! This was reported to the Count of Angoulême, who ordered the courts of law to do what was proper. They waited till the girl had been delivered of a fine little boy, then they burnt her and her brother together. The local people were extremely shocked to discover such a hideous monstrosity under the cloak of sanctity, to discover, concealed behind such a holy and commendable life, vice that was so detestable.

*

'So that, Ladies, is how the faith of the good Count remained firm against outward signs and miracles, for he knew that we have but one Saviour, who, when He said *Consummatum est*, showed that he was leaving no way open for any successor to bring us salvation.'

'What an extraordinary outrage, and what utter hypocrisy,' said Oisille, 'to cloak so heinous a crime under the mantle of God and of true Christian people!'

'I've heard,' added Hircan, 'that people who use royal authority as an excuse to commit acts of cruelty and oppression receive double punishment, because they've used the King's justice as a cover for their own injustice. So you see that although hypocrites may prosper for a time under a cloak of godliness, God eventually unmasks them and reveals them in all their nakedness. And then their nakedness, filth and corruption is seen to be the more ugly, the more their cover [was] worthy of respect.'

'Nothing's more agreeable than to speak simply and frankly, straight from the heart!' said Nomerfide.

'Because one profits by it,' said Longarine, 'and I think you give your opinion in accordance with your disposition.'

'Let me tell you this,' replied Nomerfide. 'I notice that the foolish live longer than the wise – so long as they're not murdered, that is. And there's only one reason, as far as I can see – they don't disguise their emotions. If they're angry, they lash out; if they're happy, they laugh; and those who think themselves wise disguise their shortcomings to such an extent that their hearts become full of poison.'

'I think that what you say is the truth,' said Geburon, 'and that hypocrisy, whether towards God, towards men or towards Nature, is the cause of all the evils we have.'

'It would be a fine thing,' said Parlamente, 'for our hearts to be so filled, through faith, with Him who is all virtue and all joy that we could freely show it to everyone.'

'That,' said Hircan, 'will come the day when we're mouldering in the grave and the flesh has dropped from our bones!'

'But,' Oisille said, 'the spirit of God is stronger than death and can mortify the heart without changing or destroying the body.'

'Madame,' said Saffredent, 'you refer to a gift from God which is [scarcely] shared by all men.'

'It is shared,' said Oisille, 'by those who have faith. But this is a matter beyond the understanding of those still bound to the flesh, so let us see who Simontaut will choose to speak next.'

'I choose Nomerfide,' said Simontaut, 'because she has a cheerful spirit, and her story won't be a sad one.'

'Well,' said Nomerfide, 'since you want to laugh, I'll give you something to laugh at, and to show you how much harm fear and ignorance can do, and how much damage can be done through misunderstanding something, I'll tell you what happened to two Franciscans from Niort who nearly lost their lives because they misunderstood the language of a butcher in whose house they were staying.'

STORY THIRTY-FOUR

Between Niort and Fors there is a village called Gript belonging to the Seigneur de Fors. One day two Franciscan friars on their way from Niort arrived in the village of Gript late one evening, and stayed in the house of a butcher. As their room was only separated from that of their host by a badly jointed screen of planks, they decided they would like to listen to what the husband would say to his wife when they were in bed. So they put their ears to the partition close to the head of the husband's bed. The husband, not suspecting what his guests were up to, started to talk to his wife about his business.

'I've to get up early tomorrow, my dear,' he said, 'to have a look at our little friars. There's a big fat one needs slaughtering. We'll salt him right away and make quite a bit on it.'

Although he was only talking about his pigs, which he habitually called his 'little friars', the poor brothers were convinced they had overheard a murder conspiracy of which they themselves were to be the victims! They waited until daybreak in fear and trembling. One of them was in fact very fat, while the other was rather thin. The fat one decided to make his last confession to his companion, saying that a butcher who had lost all love and fear of God would no more hesitate to slaughter him than an ox or any other beast. And since they were shut up in their room unable to get out except by passing through their host's room, they could only wait, certain of death, and recommend their souls to God. But the younger one, who was not so paralysed by fear as his companion, told him that as the door was locked they would have to try to get out through the window – whether they stayed or whether they jumped, death was the worst that could befall them. So the fat one agreed. The younger one opened the window and seeing that it was not too far down, jumped out and landed lightly on the ground. He wasted no time waiting for his friend, but ran off as fast and as far as he could. Then the fat one made the jump, but fell so heavily that he hurt his leg badly and was obliged because of his weight to stay put. When he saw that his young friend had abandoned him and realized he could not possibly catch him up, he looked round for somewhere to hide. The only place he could see was a pigsty, into which he crawled as best he could. As he opened the door, two large pigs ran out, leaving just enough space for the poor friar. He closed the door behind him, intending to call out for help if he heard anyone passing by. As soon as morning came, the butcher got his big knives ready and asked his wife to go with him to slaughter his fat pig. When he arrived at the pigsty where the friar was hidden, he began to shout in a loud voice, as he opened the door: 'Come on out, my plump little friar, come on out! I'm going to make sausage-meat of you today!'

The poor Franciscan, not being able to stand up on his injured leg, crawled out of the sty on all fours, shouting for mercy at the top of his voice. The butcher and his wife were no less terrified than he was, for they thought Saint Francis was angry with them for calling their pigs 'friars'. They got down on their knees in front of the poor monk, begging Saint Francis and his order to have mercy on them. So, there they were, the friar crying for mercy from the butcher, the butcher and his wife crying for mercy from the friar. This went on for a good quarter of an hour before any of them calmed down. Eventually, the good father, realizing that the butcher did not mean him any harm, explained why he had hidden in the sty. Their fright immediately gave way to laughter – except that the poor Franciscan with his injured leg was not really in any state for merriment. However, the butcher took him back home and dressed his wounds. As for his brother who had left him in his hour of need, he ran all night long until he came in the morning to the house of the Seigneur de Fors. There he protested loudly about the butcher, who, he supposed, must by now have caught and killed his missing companion. The Seigneur de Fors immediately sent someone to Gript to make inquiries. When the truth of the matter was revealed there was clearly nothing to cry about – on the contrary. And the Seigneur de Fors made a special point of recounting the story to the Duchess of Angoulême, who was the mother of Francis I.

*

'That then, Ladies, shows that you shouldn't listen to other people's secrets without being asked and so misunderstand their words.'

'Wasn't I right in thinking that Nomerfide wouldn't make us cry,' said Simontaut, 'but make us laugh instead? And I think we've all acquitted ourselves well, as far as laughing's concerned!'

'And why is it,' said Oisille, 'that we are more inclined to laugh at foolish acts than at deeds which are wise?'

'Because,' replied Hircan, 'folly is more amusing in so far as it resembles our own nature, which in itself is never wise. And everyone takes pleasure in things that resemble himself: fools like folly, the wise like wisdom. I think nobody, whether wise or foolish, could stop himself laughing at this story.'

'There are people,' Geburon said, 'whose hearts are so devoted to the love of wisdom that whatever they heard, no one could make them laugh, for they have joy in their hearts and contentment so full of moderation that no accident can change them.'

'And [who] are these people?' said Hircan.

'The philosophers of ancient times,' said Geburon, 'by whom sadness and joy were hardly felt at all. At least, they did not show their feelings, so great a virtue was it in their eyes to overcome the self and the passions.'

'I think, as they do, that it's a good thing to overcome vicious passions,' said Saffredent, 'but to overcome a natural passion that has no tendency to evil, that seems to me to be a useless victory.'

'Even so,' said Geburon, 'the ancients considered it to be a great virtue.'

'That doesn't mean they were *all* men of wisdom,' said Saffredent. 'On the contrary, it was more a matter of the appearance of sense and virtue than of actual effects.'

'Nevertheless,' said Geburon, 'you [can see] that they condemn anything that is evil. Diogenes even trampled on Plato's couch, [because] he thought him too much concerned with luxury, and in order to show that he despised and wished to trample underfoot Plato's vainglory and desire for possessions, saying "I [trample] on Plato's pride.'"

'But you're not telling the whole story,' said Saffredent. 'Plato replied immediately that Diogenes was indeed trampling on his pride, but that he was doing so with pride of another sort.'

'If the truth be told,' said Parlamente, 'it's impossible to overcome the self by our own means, without extraordinary arrogance on our part. And arrogance is a vice we should fear above all others, because it is born of the death and destruction of all the virtues.'

'Have I not read to you this morning,' said Oisille, 'of how those who think themselves wiser than other people and who by the light of reason have come to know God, who created all things, only to attribute that glory to themselves and not to Him from whom it comes, how such people, believing that it is their own effort that has brought them such knowledge, have become not only more ignorant and unreasonable than other men but more ignorant and unreasonable even than the beasts? For, allowing their minds to go astray, attributing to themselves that which belongs to God alone, they have shown their errors by the disorder of their bodies, forgetting and perverting their sex, as Saint Paul has written in his epistle to the Romans.'

'There's not one of us,' said Parlamente, 'who doesn't admit on reading that epistle that all external sins are the fruit of an inner [lack of faith], which, the more it is covered by virtue and miracles, the more dangerous it is to root out.'

'We men,' Hircan said, 'are [therefore] closer to our salvation than you, for since we do not disguise our fruits, we more easily recognize the root which bears them. But you women, who do not dare to bring them into the open and who do so many seemingly fair deeds, only with great difficulty will you recognize that deep-rooted pride which goes on growing beneath such a fair exterior.'

'I admit,' said Longarine, 'that if the word of God does not by faith show us the leprosy of faithlessness hidden within our hearts, God's grace is great indeed when we stumble and commit some visible fault which makes us see clearly the plague hidden within us. And blessed are they whom faith has so humbled that they have no need of external effects to have their sinful nature demonstrated to them.'

'But look how far we've come,' said Simontaut. 'We started

with folly and we end up with philosophy and theology! Let's leave such disputes to those better able to muse on such matters than we, and ask Nomerfide who she will choose as the next storyteller.'

'I choose Hircan,' replied Nomerfide, 'but I would ask him to be considerate of the honour of the ladies.'

'You could not ask for anything more appropriate,' replied Hircan, 'since the story I have prepared is just what is required to obey your command. Even so, when you hear it, you will admit that both men and women are by nature inclined to vices of all kinds, unless they are preserved by Him to whom honour for any victory is due. And in order to humble the pride you women feel whenever you hear a story that does you credit, I shall give you an example that is very true.'

STORY THIRTY-FIVE

In the town of Pamplona there was once a lady who was widely esteemed, not only for her great beauty, but also for her virtue. Indeed, she was considered to be the most chaste and the most devout lady in the land. She loved her husband, and was so obedient to him that he confided everything in her. She spent her whole life attending divine service and sermons, and had managed to persuade her husband and children to do likewise. Now one Ash Wednesday, when she was in her thirtieth year, that is, at a time of life when ladies usually want to be known for their wisdom rather than for their beauty, this lady went to church to receive the ashes. She arrived to find the sermon being preached by a particular Franciscan friar who was regarded by everybody as a holy man because his austere and saintly life made him look so pale and thin – not *so* pale and thin, however, that he was not regarded also as one of the handsomest men in the world. The lady devoutly listened to his sermon, her eyes firmly fixed on this venerable individual and her ears hanging on his every word. Thus the sweetness of the preacher's words penetrated her ears and reached her heart, and the sight of his handsome face entered by her eyes and wounded her spirit so sorely that she was as someone in a state of ecstasy. After the sermon she took care to note which chapel the preacher was going to say mass in, and made sure she was there to take the ashes from his hands, hands which were as fine and white as any lady's. And upon these hands the devout lady meditated rather than upon the ash they proffered. Firmly believing that spiritual love and whatever pleasurable sensations it aroused could not hurt her conscience, she made a point of attending the friar's sermons every single day, taking her husband with her. They both admired the preacher so much that when they were at table, and even when they were not, they would talk of nothing else. The fire of her passion beneath its spiritual guise was carnal to such a degree that the flames raging in the poor lady's heart spread throughout the whole of her body. Being slow to feel the heat, she caught fire all the more quickly and experienced the pleasure of passion before she had even realized that it was passion that had her in its grip. The enemy had caught her by surprise. She could offer no resistance to Love's demands. But even worse for her was that the man who could cure her suffering knew nothing of her malady. So putting aside all the misgivings she ought to have felt at exposing her folly before such a good man, her wicked vice to a man so virtuous and wise, she began to write to him of her love, at first in veiled tones. A young page was entrusted with the letters, and instructed what to do. In particular he was to be careful not to let the husband see him going to the monastery. But the page, taking a short cut, went down a street where his master happened to be sitting in a shop. When the husband saw him passing by, he came out to see where he was going. The lad was scared and hid in a nearby house. At this, his master went after him, grabbed him by the arm, and asked him where he thought he was going. The page merely stammered some vague excuses and looked terrified, upon which the master threatened to give him a good beating if he did not say where he was going. The poor page replied: 'Alas, Monsieur, if I told you, Madame would kill me!' The gentleman thought his wife was making some purchase behind his back. He assured the page that he would come to no harm, that he would be well rewarded if he told the truth, but that he would be put into prison for good if he lied. The page, thinking he would avoid trouble and might even make some gain, told him the whole story and showed the letters his mistress had written to the preacher. The husband was amazed and distressed, for he had been sure all his life that his wife was faithful to him and had never known any fault in her. But being a wise man he disguised his anger, and in order to find out exactly what were his wife's designs he decided to write a reply in the preacher's name, thanking her for her kind sentiments and declaring that he for his part felt no less well inclined. Having sworn to carry out this mission as secretly as he could, the page took the letter straight back to his mistress. She was, of course, overjoyed – so much so that her husband could see immediately that her expression had changed, for instead of looking thin from the Lenten fast, she was even more beautiful and fresh than she had been at Shrovetide.

Mid-Lent arrived and the lady was still writing to the preacher about her wild passion. Even at Passiontide, and during Holy Week, she persisted. It seemed to her that every time the man looked in her direction, or talked about the Love of God, he did it for love of her, and she did her best to express her thoughts in her eyes. Throughout this time her husband went on writing the replies to her letters. After Easter he wrote her a letter, in the name of her preacher, in which he begged her to tell him how he might meet her in secret. She could not wait. So she suggested to her husband that he go and inspect some lands they owned in the country outside Pamplona. This he promised to do, but instead stayed behind and lay low at the house of a friend. The lady wrote at once to the preacher, to tell him he could come, as her husband had left for the country. The gentleman wanted to test his wife's heart to the bitter end, so he himself went to the preacher and begged him in God's name to lend him his habit. But the preacher, who was a good man, told him that their rule forbade such a thing and that he had no intention of letting him have his habit to use for fancy dress. However, the gentleman assured him that he would not abuse it and that it was for a matter essential to his good and his salvation. So in the end, knowing him to be a good and devout man, the Franciscan agreed. The gentleman put on the habit, completely covering his face so that his eyes could not be seen. Then he put on a false beard and nose to make himself look like the preacher, and a piece of cork in his shoes to make himself taller. Thus attired he went that very evening to his wife's bedroom, where, immersed in her devotions, she was waiting. The poor silly woman did not even wait for him to approach her, but like someone out of her senses ran up to him and threw her arms round him. The husband kept his head bowed to avoid recognition, made the sign of the cross and pretended to back away, saying over and over again the words: 'Temptation! Temptation! Temptation!'

The lady said: 'Oh, Father, how right you are! The strongest temptation is that which comes from love, and you have promised to cure me of love. I beg you, now that we have the chance, have pity on me!'

So saying, she struggled to embrace him, while he ran round the room, waving his arms about in the sign of the cross, and continuing to shout 'Temptation! Temptation! Temptation!' But when she got too close, he took out a big stick he had under his habit, and beat her so soundly that he soon got rid of her temptation for her! Then, without having been recognized by her, he went straight to the preacher to give him back his habit, assuring him that it had brought success.

The next day he returned to the house, pretending he had just come back from his journey. He found his wife in bed, and as if he did not know what was ailing her, he asked what was the matter. She answered that she had a cold in the head and could not use her arms or her legs. The husband nearly burst out laughing, but pretended to be very upset, and as if to cheer her up, told her the same evening that he had invited the saintly preacher to eat with them. At this she burst out: 'My dear, whatever you do, don't invite people like that! They bring trouble to every house they go into.'

'What!' said her husband. 'You've told me such a lot of good things about him. As far as I'm concerned, if ever anyone were a saint, it is he!'

The lady replied: 'They're good in church and when they preach sermons, but when they get inside a house they are Antichrists! I beg you, my dear, let me not have to see him, for with my present illness it would be sufficient to bring me to my deathbed!'

To this the husband replied: 'Since you don't want to see him, then you shan't see him. But I'm going to invite him to supper all the same!'

'Do as you please,' she said, 'so long as I do not have to see him. I detest these people as if they were the Devil himself!'

When he had served supper to the good father, the husband said: 'Father, I look upon you as so favoured by God's love, that He will not refuse you any request. I beg you to take pity on my poor wife, who for the past week has been possessed by some evil spirit which makes her want to bite and scratch anyone who comes near her. Crosses and holy water make no impression on her. I believe that if you were to place your hands on her, the devil would leave her. I beg you with all my heart to do this for me.'

The good father replied: 'My son, to the believer all things are possible. Do you not firmly believe that God in His goodness never refuses His grace to anyone who asks for it in faith?'

'I do, Father,' said the gentleman.

'Be you then also assured, my son,' said the friar, 'that God can do what He wills, and that He is as powerful as He is good. Let us go forth firm in faith to resist this roaring lion, let us wrest from him the prey which God has made His own by the blood of His son Jesus Christ!'

Thereupon the gentleman took the good man to his wife, who was lying on a couch. She was horrified to see him, thinking that it was he who had given her the beating. Inwardly she was seething with rage, but as her husband was present, she lowered her eyes and kept quiet. The husband said to the holy man: 'When I'm with her the devil hardly troubles her. But the moment I leave the room, sprinkle her with holy water, [and] you'll see the evil spirit in action right away!'

The husband then left him alone with his wife and waited outside the door to see what would happen. When she found herself alone with the good father, she started to scream like someone out of her mind, calling him evil, wicked, murderer and deceiver. The good father, thinking she really was possessed by an evil spirit, made to take her head in his hands in order to pray over her, but she scratched and bit him so hard that he was obliged to stand back and speak to her from a distance. He then said a lot of prayers, showering her with holy water as he did so. When the husband felt the friar had sufficiently fulfilled his purpose, he went back into the room and thanked him for his trouble. The moment he appeared, his wife stopped screaming her curses, and meekly kissed the cross, fearing her husband might find her out. But the holy man, who only a moment previously had seen her in a state of uncontrollable rage, firmly believed that as a result of his prayers Our Lord had cast out the devil, and he went off giving thanks to God for the great miracle that had been wrought! When the husband saw that his wife had been duly punished for her wild infatuation, he decided not to tell her what he had done. He contented himself instead with the knowledge that by means of his own good sense he had brought about a change of heart, so that she now felt nothing but hatred for the man for whom she had before felt nothing but passion. So it was that she came to hate her folly, [declaring that she would give up all superstitious ways,] and devoted herself to her husband and home more earnestly than before.

*

'In this story, Ladies, you can see the good sense of a husband and the fragility of a [reputedly] good woman. It is, as it were, a mirror, and once you've looked into it, I think you will learn to turn to Him in whose hands your honour lies, instead of relying on your own powers.'

'I'm glad to see,' said Parlamente, 'that you have started to preach for the ladies. I'd be even happier if you would kindly continue to preach these fine sermons to *all* the ladies you address!'

'I assure you,' said Hircan, 'that whenever you wish to listen to me, that is the way I'll speak.'

'In other words,' said Simontaut, 'when you're not there he'll have other things to say!'

'He will do what he likes,' said Parlamente, 'but I prefer to believe for my peace of mind that he always speaks as he just has. At least, the example he's given us will be of use to women who think that spiritual love isn't dangerous. It seems to me that it's the most dangerous kind of love there is.'

'But it seems to me,' said Oisille, 'that love for a good, virtuous, God-fearing man is not something to be despised, and that one can only be the better for it.'

'Madame,' replied Parlamente, 'believe me, there's no one more stupid, no one more easily taken in, than a woman who's never been in love. Love by its very nature is a passion which seizes the heart before one realizes it. It's a passion that provokes such pleasurable sensations that if it can disguise itself under the cloak of a virtuous exterior, it's hardly ever recognized before something unfortunate ensues.'

'What could ever go wrong,' said Oisille, 'if one loves a good man?'

'Madame,' replied Parlamente, 'there are plenty of men who

are good by repute. But I don't think that these days there is a single man alive who is genuinely good with regard to ladies, and who can be trusted with a lady's honour and conscience. Women who believe it is otherwise, and accordingly act in complete confidence, end up by being deceived! They enter into such liaisons by way of God, and often get out of them by way of the Devil. I know many women who, under the guise of talking about God, embarked on a liaison which they later wanted to break but couldn't, because they were caught up in their own cloak of respectability. You see, vicious love disintegrates of its own accord, and is unable to survive in a heart that is pure. But "virtuous" love has such subtle bonds that one gets caught before one notices them.'

'From what you say,' said Ennasuite, 'no woman would ever want to be in love with a man. But your law is so harsh that it cannot endure.'

'I know,' said Parlamente, 'but in spite of that, I still think it desirable that every woman should be content with her own husband, as I am with mine!'

Ennasuite felt that these words were aimed at her and coloured: 'I don't think you should assume the rest of us are any different at heart from yourself,' she said, 'unless you regard yourself as more perfect than we are.'

'Well,' said Parlamente, 'so as not to get into an argument, let's see who Hircan will pick to speak next.'

'I choose Ennasuite,' he said, 'to make up for what my wife has said.'

'Well, since it's my turn,' said Ennasuite, 'I shall spare neither men nor women, in order to make everything equal. And seeing that you can't bring yourselves to admit that men can be good and virtuous, I'll take up the thread of the last story, and tell you one that is very similar.'

STORY THIRTY-SIX

It is about a man who was president of the Parlement of Grenoble – a man whose name I can't reveal, although I can tell you he wasn't a Frenchman. He was married to a very beautiful woman, and they lived a happy and harmonious life together. However, the President was getting on in years, and the wife began an affair with a young clerk who was called Nicolas. Every morning, when her husband went off to the Palais de Justice, Nicolas would go to her bedroom to take his place. This was noticed by one of the President's servants, a man who had been in his household for thirty years, and who, being loyal to his master, could not do otherwise than tell him. The President was a prudent man, and was not prepared to believe the story without further evidence. He said that the servant was merely trying to sow discord between his wife and himself. If it was true, he said, then he ought to be able to show him the living proof. If he could not do so, then he would conclude that the man had been lying in order to destroy the love which he and his wife had for one another. The servant assured him that he should see with his own eyes what he had described.

One morning, as soon as the President had left for the courts and Nicolas had gone into the bedroom, the servant sent one of his fellow-servants to tell the master to come, while he stayed by the door to make sure Nicolas did not leave. When the President saw the servant give him the signal, he pretended he was feeling unwell, left the court, and hurried back home, where he found his other faithful old servant by the bedroom door assuring him that Nicolas was inside and that he had indeed only just gone in.

'Do not move from here,' said the President. 'As you know, there is no way in or out except through the small private room to which I alone have the key.'

In went the President and found his wife and Nicolas in bed together. Nicolas, who had nothing on but his shirt, threw himself at the President's feet, begging forgiveness, while the wife started to weep.

'Your misdemeanour is a serious one, as you well know,' said the President to his wife. 'However, I do not wish to see my household dishonoured or the daughters I have had by you disadvantaged. Therefore, I order you to cry no more and to listen to what I mean to do. And you, Nicolas, hide in my private room and make no noise.'

Then he opened the door, called his old servant, and said:

'Did you not tell me that you would show me Nicolas and my wife in bed together? I came here on the strength of your word and might have killed my poor wife. I have found nothing to bear out what you have told me. I have looked all over the room and there is no one here, as I now desire to demonstrate to you.'

So saying, he made the servant look under the beds and everywhere else in the room. When he found nothing, the old man was amazed, and said to his master: 'The Devil must have carried him off! I saw him come in, and he didn't come out through the door – yet I can see that he is not here!'

Then his master replied: 'You are a miserable servant to try to sow discord between my wife and myself. Therefore I give you leave to depart. For the services that you have rendered I shall pay what I owe you and more. But leave quickly and take care not to be found in this town when twenty-four hours have passed!'

The President gave him five or six years' wages in advance, and knowing how loyal he was, said that he hoped to reward him further. So the servant went off in tears, and the President brought Nicolas out of his hiding-place. After telling his wife and her lover what he thought of their wicked behaviour, he forbade them to give any hint of it to anyone. He then instructed his wife to dress more elegantly than usual and to take part in all the social gatherings, dances and festivities. He ordered Nicolas too to make merry more than before, but added that the moment he whispered in his ear the words 'Leave this place!', he should take care to be out of town within three hours. So saying, he returned to the Palais de Justice without the slightest hint that anything had happened.

For the next fortnight he set about entertaining his friends and neighbours – something he had not at all been in the habit of doing. After the banquets which he gave, there were musicians with drums for the ladies to dance to. On one occasion he noticed that his wife wasn't dancing, and told Nicolas to be her partner. Nicolas, thinking the President had forgotten what had happened, danced with her quite gaily. But after the dance was over, the President, on the pretext of giving him some instructions about domestic duties, whispered into Nicolas's ear: 'Leave this place and never return!'

Now Nicolas was sorry indeed to leave his lady, but none the less glad to escape with his life. The President impressed upon all his relatives, friends and neighbours how much he loved his wife. Then, one fine day in the month of May, he went into his garden and picked some herbs for a salad. After eating it, his wife did not live more than twenty-four hours, and the grief that the President showed was so great that nobody suspected that he was the agent of her death. And so he avenged himself on his enemy and saved the honour of his house.

*

'It is not my wish, Ladies, to praise the President's conscience, but rather to portray a woman's laxity, and the great patience and prudence of a man. And do not take offence, Ladies, I beg you, because the truth sometimes speaks just as much against you as against men. Both men and women have their share of vice as well as of virtue.'

'If all those women who've had affairs with their domestics,' said Parlamente, 'were obliged to eat salads like that one, then I know a few who wouldn't be quite so fond of their gardens as they are, but would pull up [*all*] their herbs to avoid the ones that restore the honour of families by taking the lives of wanton mothers!'

Hircan, who guessed full well why she said this, replied angrily, 'A woman of honour ought never to accuse [another] of doing things she herself would never do!'

'Knowing something is not the same as making foolish accusations,' said Parlamente. 'The fact remains that this poor woman paid a penalty which not a few deserve. And I think that the husband, considering that he was intent on revenge, conducted himself with remarkable prudence and good sense.'

'And also with great malice,' said Longarine, 'as well as vindictiveness that was both protracted and cruel – which shows that he had neither God nor conscience in mind.'

'And what would you have wanted him to do, then,' asked Hircan, 'to avenge himself for the worst outrage a woman can perpetrate against a man?'

'I would rather,' she said, 'that he had killed her out of anger, for the learned doctors say that such a sin is remissible, because the first movements of the soul are not within man's powers. So if he had acted out of anger he might have received forgiveness.'

'Yes,' said Geburon, 'but his daughters and his descendants would have borne the stigma for ever.'

'He shouldn't have killed her,' said Longarine, 'for once rage had subsided, she could have lived with him as an honourable woman and the whole thing would have been forgotten.'

'Do you really think,' said Saffredent, 'that he had really calmed down, just because he had managed to conceal his anger? I think that the day he made the salad he was just as angry as at first, because there are people whose first movements never subside till their passion is put into effect. And I'm glad to say the theologians regard this kind of sin as readily pardonable. I share their view on this.'

'One needs to watch one's words with people as dangerous as you,' said Parlamente, 'but what I said was meant to apply to cases where the passion is so great that it suddenly overwhelms the senses, and does so to such an extent that reason cannot operate.'

'Taking that point further,' said Saffredent, 'I would argue that a man who is deeply in love does not commit a sin, or only commits a venial sin, whatever he does. Because I'm certain that if he is in the grip of perfect love, he will not hear the voice of reason, either in his heart or in his understanding. And, if we're truthful about it, there's not one among us who's not experienced this wild passion, which, I believe, is readily pardonable. What is more, I believe that God is not even angered by sin of this kind, since it is one step in the ascent to perfect love of Him, to which one cannot ascend without passing up the ladder of worldly love. For St John says: "How shall you love God, whom you see not, unless you love him whom you see?"'

'There is not a single text in Holy Scripture, however beautiful,' Oisille said, 'that you would not turn to your own ends. But take care lest, like the spider, you turn wholesome meat into poison. Be you assured that it is indeed dangerous to draw on Scripture out of place and without necessity.'

'Do you call telling the truth "out of place" and "without necessity"?' said Saffredent. 'Do you mean to say, then, that when we're talking to you unbelieving ladies and call God to our aid, do you mean that we're taking His name in vain? But if there's any sin in *that*, it's you who should take the blame – because it's *your* unbelief that obliges us to look for all the oaths we can possibly think of. And even then we can't kindle the fire of charity in your icy hearts!'

'That just shows,' said Longarine, 'that you're all liars – for the truth is so mighty that we could do no other than believe you, were truth in the words you spoke. But the danger is that the daughters of Eve are too ready to believe this serpent.'

'I can see, Parlamente, that women are invincible,' replied Saffredent. 'So I shall keep quiet, to see who Ennasuite will choose to speak next.'

'I shall ask Dagoucin,' she said, 'because I do not think he will speak against the ladies.'

'Would to God,' he said, 'that they responded as much in my favour as I desire to speak in theirs! And to show how I have striven to honour virtuous ladies by recounting their good actions, I shall now tell you about one such action. I do not deny, Ladies, that the gentleman of Pamplona and the President of Grenoble showed great patience, but they also showed no less vindictiveness. When one wants to praise a virtuous man, one should not exalt a single virtue to such an extent that one also has to make that one virtue a cloak for some great vice. A virtuous person is one who performs virtuous acts solely for the love of virtue – as I hope now to show you, with the example of [the virtue and patience] of a lady whose good deed had no other end than the honour of God and the salvation of her husband.'

STORY THIRTY-SEVEN

There was once a lady of the house of Loué, who was so good and virtuous that she was loved and admired by all her neighbours. Her husband quite properly entrusted all his affairs to her, and she conducted his business so prudently that through her efforts his house came to be one of the richest and best appointed in the lands of Anjou and Touraine. She lived happily with her husband for many years, and bore him several fine children. But all happiness must come to an end, and hers too began to fade, for her husband became dissatisfied with their quiet, respectable life and abandoned her to seek excitement elsewhere. He adopted the habit of getting up as soon as his wife was asleep, and not returning till morning was close. The lady of Loué was distressed by his behaviour, and so much so that, having sunk into a state of jealousy which she desired to conceal, she neglected her domestic affairs, herself and her family. It was as if she felt that she had lost the fruit of all her labours in losing her husband's love, and would have willingly suffered anything to keep it. However, she saw clearly that it was lost, and became so neglectful of everything else in the household that the ill-effects of the husband's absences soon became obvious. On the one hand he began to spend recklessly, and on the other she no longer attended to the domestic affairs. So it was not long before the household became so disorganized that they started felling the timber on their estates and even mortgaging the land. One of her relatives, who knew what was ailing her, reproached her and told her that even if she would not consider the family fortunes for love of her husband, then she ought at least to think of the poor children. She was moved by this appeal to rally her spirits and to bend all her efforts to winning back her husband's love. So, one night, she waited for him to get up, and after he had done so, she rose also and put on her dressing-gown. Then she had the bed made, and said her devotions while waiting for his return. When eventually he came in, she went up to him and gave him a kiss. At the same time she presented him with a bowl of water, so that he could wash his hands. He was amazed at this unaccustomed behaviour, and told her that he had only been to the privy and had no need of a wash. But her reply was that although it was not of any great importance, still it was only decent to wash one's hands when one had been somewhere foul and dirty, thereby wishing to bring him to acknowledge and abhor his wicked ways. In spite of this he did not amend his life, and the lady went on with this ritual for a good year. She realized that it was all to no purpose, and one day, having waited for her husband longer than usual, she had a sudden desire to go and fetch him. So she went from room to room until she found him in an obscure closet asleep in bed with the ugliest, dirtiest and foulest chambermaid in the house. She would teach him to leave an honest woman for this foul and dirty creature, she thought. And she set fire to some straw in the middle of the room. But as soon as she saw that the smoke was as likely to kill him as wake him, she grabbed hold of his arm, shouting 'Fire! Fire!' If the husband was overcome with shame and deeply distressed to be discovered by his virtuous wife in bed with such filth, it was not without good reason. The wife then said:

'Monsieur, I have been trying for the past year to save you from your wicked ways. I have tried to exercise patience and kindness, to show you that in washing the outside, you should be also inwardly cleansed. But when I saw that it was all to no avail, I decided to employ that element which shall bring an end to all things. And I assure you, Monsieur, that if you do not thereby amend your life, then I do not know if I shall have it in my power a second time to save you from danger. I beg you to remember that there is no greater despair than love, and if I had not constantly had my eyes on God, I could not have endured what I had to endure.'

The husband, glad to escape so lightly, promised never again to give her cause to suffer on his account. The lady willingly took his word for it and, with his consent, cast out that which offended her. And from that time on, they lived together in such great affection, that past misdeeds only increased their happiness by the good that had come of them.

*

'Ladies, I beg you, if God has given you such husbands, do not finally despair until you have tried all possible means of bringing them back. For there are twenty-four hours in a day in which a man may change his mind. A woman should consider herself more fortunate to have won her husband through patience and long-suffering than to have been provided with a more perfect one by parentage and fortune.'

'That was an example of which all married women should take note,' said Oisille.

'Anyone who cares to may follow that example,' said Parlamente, 'but as far as I'm concerned, it would be impossible to be so patient, because although patience may be a fine virtue in all other situations, it seems to me that in marriage it must lead to ill-feeling. The reason is that if one suffers because of one's partner, one is obliged to separate oneself from him or her as far as possible, and this estrangement gives rise to contempt for the one who has been unfaithful, and contempt leads in turn to diminution of love, since one's love for a person depends on one's estimation of his worth.'

'But,' said Ennasuite, 'there's a danger that the impatient wife will have a violent husband, who would give rise to suffering rather than patience.'

'And what worse could a husband do than what we've just heard in the story?' said Parlamente.

'What?' replied Ennasuite. 'He might beat her, make her sleep in the servant's bed and put the woman he loves in his own bed!'

'I believe,' said Parlamente, 'that any woman of honour would be less distressed at being beaten in a fit of rage than at being despised because of someone who is not of equal worth. Once a wife has borne the pain of separation after such affection, there's nothing a husband can do that could distress her further. That is why the story says that the efforts she made to draw him back were out of love for her children, and I think this is true.'

'And do you consider it was patience and long-suffering to go and light a fire under his bed?' asked Nomerfide.

'Yes,' said Longarine, 'because when she saw the smoke, she woke him up – and that perhaps was her great mistake. Husbands like that ought to be burnt and their ashes used for the washing!'

'You are cruel, Longarine,' said Oisille, 'but you did not live thus with your own husband.'

'No,' said Longarine, 'because, thank God, he never gave me occasion. On the contrary, I shall miss him for the rest of my life, not complain about him.'

'And supposing he *had* treated you like that,' said Nomerfide, 'what would you have done?'

'I loved him so much,' she replied, 'that I think I would have killed him and myself afterwards. For vengeance and death would be preferable to living faithfully with a man who had been unfaithful.'

'It seems to me,' said Hircan, 'that you only love your husbands for your own sakes. If they're the way you want them, you love them well enough, and if they commit the slightest error, it's like losing a week's pay just because you fail to work on Saturday! You always want to be in command, and this I accept for my part, but let other husbands agree to it!'

'It's reasonable that the man should govern us as our head,' said Parlamente, 'but not that he should abandon us or treat us badly.'

'God has so wisely ordained,' said Oisille, 'both for men and for women, that, provided one does not abuse it, marriage is, I believe, the finest and surest state in this world; and I am sure that all of us here, whatever impression they may wish to give, are of the same opinion. And as the man claims to be wiser than the woman, so he will be the more severely punished if the fault is on his side. But enough has been said. Let us see who Dagoucin will choose to speak next.'

'I call on Longarine,' said Dagoucin.

'I accept with pleasure,' she said, 'and have a tale that is worthy to follow yours. Since we are praising virtue and patience in women, I shall give you an even more laudable case than the one we've just discussed, a case that is all the more admirable as it concerns a townswoman, for townswomen are not usually so virtuously brought up as other women.'

STORY THIRTY-EIGHT

In the town of Tours there was once a virtuous and beautiful woman. She was loved by her husband, but also admired and respected by him for her virtuous qualities. However, such is the fragility of men that they soon tire of bread which is good and wholesome, and this husband was no exception. He fell in love with a woman who farmed his land.* He took to making trips to the country to inspect his farm, and staying there for a day or two. But when he returned to Tours, he always had such a bad cold that his poor wife had her work cut out to get him on his feet again. As soon as he recovered he would be off again to his farm, where the pleasures he enjoyed made him forget all his ills. His wife cared above all things about his life and his health, and when he kept coming back in such bad shape she went to the farm herself, where she found the young woman who was the object of her husband's affections. She did not lose her temper, but said in the most gracious possible way that she knew that her husband often came to see her. What worried her, however, was that he appeared to be so poorly cared for during his visits that he always came home with a bad cold. The poor woman, partly because she was overawed by the presence of her landlady, partly because she could not deny the truth, made no protestation, and begged forgiveness. The lady demanded to see the room and the bed her husband slept in. She found the room so cold, dirty and ill-kept that she felt sorry for him, and immediately sent away for a good bed with sheets and counterpane – just the kind her husband liked. She had the room decorated and hung with tapestries. She provided decent crockery for him to eat and drink from, a cask of good wine, and a supply of sweetmeats and preserves. Then she requested the woman kindly not to send her husband back so run-down in future. It was not long before he went as usual to see his *métayère*, and was astonished to find her humble dwelling so well

* In the *métayage* system the owner provides stock and seed and takes a proportion of the produce as rent.

appointed. He was even more surprised when she gave him a drink in a silver cup! He asked her where all these belongings had come from, and the poor lass burst into tears, saying that it was his wife who had furnished the house because she was worried about him, and had asked her to keep an eye on his health. The husband realized how good his wife was to do all this for him after the rotten tricks he had played on her, and had to admit to himself that his behaviour was no less wicked than hers was virtuous. So he gave a sum of money to his *métayère*, begged her in the future to live like a decent woman, and then went back to his wife. He confessed his debt, saying that if she had not acted with such goodness and kindness, he would never have been able to give up the kind of life he had been leading. And leaving the past behind them they lived from that time on in harmony together.

*

'Believe me, Ladies, there are few husbands who cannot be won round by a wife who is patient and loving. If they cannot, then they must be harder than rock, for even rock is in the end worn down by the soft, gentle flow of water.'

To this Parlamente replied: 'That woman had no heart and no backbone!'

'What do you mean?' said Longarine. 'She was practising God's command to do good to those who wrong you.'

'I think,' said Hircan, 'that she was in love with some Franciscan who'd ordered her by way of penance to make things nice for her husband when he was in the country, so that while he was there she had the chance to stay in the town and be nice to the friar!'

'Come now, you are just showing how malicious you really are,' said Oisille, 'to judge ill of what was a worthy act. I believe that she was so purified by divine love that her sole concern was to save her husband's soul.'

'It seems to me,' said Simontaut, 'that he would have had more reason to go back to his wife when he was shivering with cold on his farm than when she made him comfortable there.'

'Apparently you're not of the same opinion as a certain wealthy Parisian,' said Saffredent, 'who was incapable of taking off his costly garments without catching cold when he went to bed with his wife! Yet when he went to see the chambermaid in the cellar in the depths of winter, wearing neither hat nor shoes, he never came to any harm at all – even though the wife was very beautiful and the servant very ugly!'

'Haven't you heard,' said Geburon, 'that God is good to fools, lovers and drunkards? The man in the story might have been all three at once!'

'Do you mean by that,' said Parlamente, 'that God is not good to the wise, the chaste and the sober?'

'Those who can help themselves don't need help from anywhere else,' said Geburon, 'for He who said that He came not to help the healthy, but the sick, came by the law of His mercy to heal our infirmities and to repeal the harsh decrees of His justice. He who would be wise is a fool before God. But to bring our sermon to a close, who will Longarine choose to speak next?'

'I'll choose Saffredent,' replied Longarine.

'Well then,' Saffredent said, 'I hope to show you, by means of an example, that God does *not* favour lovers. For, Ladies, although it has been said earlier that vice is equally shared by men and women, it is in fact women rather than men who will the more eagerly and craftily devise acts of cunning. I shall give you my example.'

STORY THIRTY-NINE

There was once a Seigneur de Grignols, a chevalier d'honneur in the household of Anne of Brittany, Queen of France, who on returning home after an absence of more than two years found his wife living on a neighbouring estate. On asking her the reason for this, she replied that there was a ghost in the house, which had been tormenting them so much that no one could stay there any longer. Monsieur de Grignols, who was not a man to believe such fabrications, told her that he at least was not afraid, even if it was the Devil himself, and took his wife straight back to the house. That night he lit a lot of candles so that he could see the ghost. After he had waited up a long time without hearing anything, he finally fell asleep. He was woken up immediately by a great slap on his cheek, and heard a voice crying out 'Brenigne! Brenigne!' which had been his grandmother's name. He called out to [the woman] who slept close by to light another candle, because the ones he had lit earlier had all gone out. But she did not dare to move. Then the Seigneur de Grignols felt the counterpane pulled off him, and could hear tables, trestles and stools falling around the bedroom. The clatter went on until morning, but the Seigneur was more worried about losing his sleep than about the ghost, since he was not in the slightest inclined to believe it really was one. The next night he made up his mind to catch it, and, shortly after getting into bed, he started to snore loudly, keeping his hand at the ready by his face. After a while, he felt something coming up to him. So he snored louder than ever. This made the ghost bolder, and it gave him an even harder slap than before. Instantly the Seigneur de Grignols grabbed its hand as it landed on his face, and shouted to his wife, 'I've got the ghost!' She jumped out of bed, lit some candles and saw that the ghost was the chambermaid who slept in their room. The girl fell on her knees and begged their forgiveness, promising to tell the truth. She had for a long time been having a love affair, she said, with another servant of the house, and it was this that had led her to put on this act, in order to drive the master and mistress out of the house. The pair had hoped they would be left in sole charge, so that they could make merry all on their own together – which was exactly what they had done. Monsieur de Grignols, who was a rough sort of fellow, gave orders for both of them to be given such a beating that they would never forget their ghost, and when this had been duly carried out, he threw them out of the house once and for all. Thus was the house of the Seigneur de Grignols delivered of the ghosts by whose antics for two whole years it had been haunted!

*

'It's a marvellous thing, Ladies, when one thinks how the great god Love banishes all fear from women's hearts and shows them how to torment us men to reach their ends. However, if the maid's intentions were despicable, the master's good sense was worthy of praise, because he knew perfectly well that once departed, spirits never come back.'

'True,' said Geburon. 'Love didn't show any favours to the servant and his maid on that occasion, and I agree, the master's good sense stood him in good stead.'

'All the same,' said Ennasuite, 'the girl's cunning got her what she wanted for quite a long time!'

'Pleasure which is based on sin, and which ends only in punishment and humiliation, is wretched indeed,' said Oisille.

'That is true, Madame,' said Ennasuite, 'but there are a lot of people who cause themselves a great deal of pain and suffering in order to live a righteous life, and who don't have the sense to get as much pleasure from life as the pair in the story.'

'But it is my opinion,' said Oisille, 'that there can be no perfect pleasure, if the conscience is not at ease.'

'What?' replied Simontaut. 'The Italian maintains that the greater the sin the greater the pleasure!'

'Truly,' said Oisille, 'the man who produced that remark is the Devil himself! So let us leave it at that, and ask Saffredent who he will choose to speak.'

'Who I will choose?' said Saffredent. 'There is only Parlamente left, but if there were a hundred people waiting their turn, I would still pick her out as someone from whom we are all bound to learn something.'

'Well, since it's up to me to close the day,' said Parlamente, 'and since I promised you yesterday that I would tell you why Rolandine's father had that castle built in which he kept her locked up for so long, that is the tale I shall now tell.'

STORY FORTY

Rolandine's father, the Comte de Jossebelin, had several sisters, some of whom had made wealthy marriages, and some of whom had entered religious orders. But there was one who stayed at home and never married. She was incomparably more beautiful than the others, and was so loved by her brother that he put her even before his wife and children. Many eligible men sought her hand in marriage, but because of the brother's fear of losing her, and because he was too fond of his money, they were always turned down. Consequently, she remained unmarried for a great part of her life, living respectably in her brother's house. Now in the same house there lived a handsome young gentleman, who had been brought up there since early childhood, and who had grown up to be a person of such handsome appearance and such excellent qualities that he had acquired a certain influence in his master's house. Thus when the Count wished to send messages to his sister, he always did so by means of this young gentleman. He even gave him the authority to visit her alone, with the result that, seeing her morning and evening as he did, the visits blossomed into deep affection. But the young gentleman feared for his life if his master should be offended, and the lady feared likewise for her honour. So their love went no further than words, until the Seigneur de Josselin started remarking to his sister that he only wished that the young gentleman was from as good a family as she. There was, he said, nobody he would rather have as a brother-in-law. He said this so often that after discussing the matter carefully, the couple thought that if they were to marry, the brother would forgive them. Those blinded by love believe what they wish to believe and, vainly thinking that nothing but good could come of it, they were married, without anyone but the priest and some female companions knowing.

For several years they enjoyed those pleasures that a married man and woman may take together. They were the handsomest couple in Christendom, and the most deeply and perfectly in love. But Fortune, unable to see two people so happy together, became envious, and roused against them an enemy, who spied on the young lady, and who, though ignorant of her marriage, became aware of her happiness. This enemy came to the Seigneur de Josselin and told him that the young gentleman whom he trusted so much was going too often to his sister's room, and at times of the day when gentlemen ought not to. At first the Count did not believe this, because of the great confidence he had both in his sister and in the gentleman. But after much persuasion he was induced in the name of his family's honour to ensure that a watch was placed on them, with the result that the poor couple, who suspected nothing, were discovered. One night the Seigneur de Josselin was informed that the gentleman was in his sister's room. He went at once and found the poor love-blind couple in bed. He was speechless with rage, and drawing his sword, chased the gentleman out with the intention of killing him. But the gentleman, who was an agile man, got away, still wearing his nightshirt. Unable to escape by the door, he jumped from a window into the garden. The poor lady, who was also still in her night attire, fell on her knees before her brother, saying:

'Spare my husband's life, Monsieur, I am married to him, and if we have done wrong, then punish me alone, for all that he has done was done at my request.'

The brother was beside himself with anger and could only reply: 'Even if he were a hundred thousand times your husband, still I would punish him as a bad servant and as one who has deceived me!'

So saying, he leaned out of the window and shouted orders for him to be killed – orders that were instantly carried out, even as they watched. Having witnessed this piteous spectacle, the lady addressed her brother like someone bereft of her senses:

'Brother, I have neither mother nor father, and I am old enough to marry as I please. I have chosen to marry a man of whom you have said again and again that you wished I could have married him. And because I have followed your advice in doing something that I could quite legally have done without it, you kill the one man in the world you loved above all others! So since my pleading could not save him from death, I beg you, in the name of all the love you have ever had for me, make me his companion in death, even as I have been his companion in all his fortunes. So satisfy the demands of your cruel and unjust anger, grant rest to the body and soul of one who will not and cannot live without her spouse!'

Although the brother was overwrought to the point of losing his reason, he had pity on his sister, and without either granting or refusing her request, he walked away and left her standing there. After pondering his deed and ascertaining that the dead gentleman had in fact been married to his sister, he wished that he had never committed the murder. Being afraid that his sister would seek revenge or would appeal to law, he had a castle built in the middle of a forest in which he shut her up, forbidding anyone to speak with her.

After a time, in order to appease his conscience, he tried to regain her confidence and even had the subject of marriage raised. But she sent word back that he had already given her such an unpleasant foretaste that she had no desire to feed further on such fare, and that she hoped to live in such a manner that her own brother would not become the murderer of a second husband. For she could hardly believe that, after committing so vicious a crime against the man he loved best in all the world, he was likely to be merciful to someone else. She also said that in spite of being unable in her weakness to avenge herself, she placed her hope in Him who was the true judge, who left no evil unpunished and in whose love she wished to abide in the lonely castle that was now her hermitage. She was true to her word, for there she remained until she died, living a life of such long-suffering and austerity that after her death people from far and wide visited her remains as if she had been a saint. From then on, the brother's family declined until of his six sons only one was left. They all died miserably. In the end it was his daughter Rolandine who remained sole heiress, as you heard in the earlier story, and inherited the prison which had been built for her aunt.

*

'Ladies, I pray God that you will take note of this example, and that none of you will wish to marry merely for your own pleasure, without the consent of those to whom you owe obedience. For marriage is an estate of long duration, and one which should not be entered into lightly or without the approval of our closest friends and relatives. Even then, however wisely one marries, one is bound to find at least as much pain as pleasure.'

'That is indeed true,' said Oisille, 'and if there were no God or laws to teach girls to behave themselves, Parlamente's example would be enough to make them show more respect for their parents and relatives than to take it into their heads to make marriages of their own choosing.'

'But, Madame,' said Nomerfide, 'if one has only *one* good day in the year, one can't say one is miserable for the *whole* of one's life! She *did* have the pleasure of seeing, and being able to speak to, the one person she loved best in the world. What is more, she was able to enjoy it through marriage, without having anything on her conscience. I consider that this satisfaction must have been so great that it makes up for the sorrow she had to bear.'

'What you mean,' said Saffredent, 'is that women derive more pleasure from going to bed with their husbands than displeasure from seeing them murdered under their noses?'

'That's *not* what I meant,' said Nomerfide; 'that would go against what I know of women. What I mean is that an *unusual* pleasure, such as marrying the man one loves most in the world, must be greater than the pain of losing him through death, which is a common occurrence.'

'Yes,' said Geburon, 'but through a natural death, whereas the death in question was excessively cruel. It seems very strange to me that the Seigneur de Josselin should dare to go to such extremes of cruelty, seeing that he was neither her husband nor her father, merely her brother, and seeing that she was of an age at which the law allows daughters to marry [as they think fit].'

'I don't find it strange at all,' said Hircan, 'since he didn't kill the sister, whom he loved so much, and over whom he had in any case no authority, but punished the gentleman he had brought up as his son and loved as his own brother. He heaped privileges on him, advanced him in his service and then the man goes and seeks the hand of his master's sister in marriage! He had no right at all to do that.'

'Quite,' said Nomerfide. 'It isn't any common, ordinary

pleasure, when a lady of such high birth marries for love alone a gentleman of her household. You may have found his death "strange", but the pleasure too must have been rare – and all the greater, since it runs counter to the views expressed by all wise men, and has in its favour the fact that a loving heart found satisfaction and that a soul found true repose. For there was nothing in all this to offend God. And as far as his death is concerned, which according to you was so cruel, it seems to me that since death is inevitable, the swifter it is the better. If one thing is certain, it is that we all must pass from this life. I think the fortunate ones are those who do not have to linger on the outskirts of death, and who soar out of the one state in this world that can be called bliss straight into the bliss that is eternal.'

'What do you mean by "lingering on the outskirts of death"?' asked Simontaut.

'I mean those people who suffer torments of the mind,' answered Nomerfide, 'and those who have been ill a long time, and who, because of the extreme nature of their bodily or mental suffering, no longer fear death, but rather find it slow in coming. I mean those people who have journeyed through the outskirts and can tell you the names of inns where they have wept rather than rested. It was inevitable that the lady in question should at some time lose her husband, but she was, thanks to her brother's violence, spared the experience of seeing her husband suffer from long sickness or distress. Moreover, she could count herself happy indeed in converting the happiness she had enjoyed with her husband to the service of our Lord.'

'Do you give no consideration to the humiliation she suffered, and the imprisonment?' said Longarine.

'I believe,' said Nomerfide, 'that if one loves perfectly, with a love rooted in God's commandments, then one will not experience humiliation or dishonour, provided one does not go astray and fall from the perfection of one's love. For the glory of loving truly knows no shame. And though her body was imprisoned, her heart was free and united with God and her husband, so that I believe she did not experience her solitude as imprisonment but regarded it rather as the highest liberty. For when one can no longer see the person one loves, one's greatest pleasure is to think about that person incessantly. Prison walls are never confining when the mind is allowed to wander as it will.'

'Nothing could be more true than what Nomerfide says,' said Simontaut, 'but the man who in his fury brought about the separation of the couple ought to consider himself miserable indeed, having offended as he did against God, against Love and against Honour.'

'In all truth,' said Geburon, 'I am amazed by the varied nature of women's love. It seems clear to me that women who love most are the most virtuous, but that those who love to a lesser degree cover up what love they have, because they wish to appear virtuous.'

'It's quite true,' said Parlamente, 'that a heart which opens itself virtuously to both God and men is capable of stronger love than a sinful heart, and is not afraid of anyone seeing into its true feelings.'

'I've always heard it said,' said Simontaut, 'that men should not be condemned for pursuing women, since it was God who put love in men's breasts in the first place and gave them the boldness to do the asking, while He made women timid and chaste, so that they would do the refusing. If a man is punished for having used the powers implanted in him, he suffers an injustice.'

'But,' said Longarine, 'it was extraordinary that the brother should have sung the young gentleman's praises over such a long period of time. It seems to me that it's either madness or cruelty if the keeper of a fountain praises the beauty of its waters to someone dying of thirst, only to kill him when he wants to drink from it!'

'Without doubt,' said Parlamente, 'it was the brother with his fair words who kindled the fire, and he had no right to put it out with his sword.'

'It astonishes me,' Saffredent said, 'that anyone should so disapprove of an ordinary *gentilhomme*, who after all used neither subterfuge nor coercion other than devoted service, merely because he succeeded in marrying a woman of high birth. For all the [ancient] philosophers assert that the lowliest of men is worth far more than the highest born and most virtuous woman in the world.'

'The reason is,' said Dagoucin, 'that in order to maintain peace in the state, consideration is given only to the rank of families, the seniority of individuals and the provisions of the law, and not to men's love and virtue, in order that the monarchy should not be undermined. Consequently, in marriages between social equals which are contracted according to the human judgement of the family concerned, the partners are often so different in the feelings of the heart and in temperament that far from entering into a state leading to salvation, they frequently find themselves on the outskirts of Hell.'

'Equally,' said Geburon, 'there have been many couples who are extremely close in their feelings and in their temperament, couples who marry for love without considering differences of family and lineage, and who have never stopped regretting it. Great but indiscreet love of this kind frequently turns into violent jealousy.'

'In my opinion,' said Parlamente, 'neither of these kinds of marriages is praiseworthy. If people submit to the will of God, they are concerned neither with glory, greed, nor sensual enjoyment, but wish only to live in the state of matrimony as God and Nature ordain, loving one another virtuously and accepting their parents' wishes. Even though there is no condition in life that is without some tribulation, I have seen couples like this live together with no regrets. Indeed we are not so unfortunate that in our present gathering we have no such couples at all!'

Hircan, Geburon, Simontaut and Saffredent affirmed that they had all been married in this way, and swore that they had never regretted it. True or not, the ladies concerned were so pleased at this, that, feeling they could wish to hear nothing better, they got up to go and give thanks to God for it, and found the monks were ready to say vespers. After the service they all had supper, returning to the subject of their own marriages, with the men going on to talk the whole evening about their experiences when wooing their wives. But they all kept interrupting one another, and it has been impossible to memorize their tales in full, tales which would have been no less delightful to record than the ones they told in the meadow. They enjoyed themselves so much that bedtime arrived without their noticing. Madame Oisille retired, and the others, still in merry mood, followed her. So happy were they all that I think the married couples amongst them did not do quite so much sleeping as the rest – what with talking about their love in the past and demonstrating it in the present. Thus the night passed sweetly till morning broke.

END OF THE FOURTH DAY

FIFTH DAY

PROLOGUE

When morning came they broke their fast with a spiritual meal prepared for them by Oisille, a meal so nourishing that it sufficed to fortify both body and soul. The whole company was very attentive, and it seemed to them that they had never heard a sermon so much to their profit. Hearing the last bell ringing for mass, they went to exercise their souls in contemplation of the holy words to which they had just been listening. When they had heard mass and had taken a short walk, they sat down to eat, looking forward to what would no doubt be a day every bit as agreeable as those which had gone before. Saffredent declared that he wished the bridge would take another month to build, so much was he enjoying himself. But the Abbot of the place took no consolation from living amongst so many honourable people, because he did not dare to entertain his lady pilgrims in the way he was wont. Consequently he had the work on the bridge continued with all possible haste. They rested a little after dinner, and then returned to their customary diversions. Once they were all sitting in the meadow, they asked Parlamente to pick the next storyteller.

'I think,' she said, 'that Saffredent will start the day well – from the expression on his face he won't be wanting to tell us stories to make us cry!'

'Ladies,' he began, 'you'll be very hard-hearted if you don't feel sorry for this Franciscan friar I'm going to tell you a story about. Some of the stories about monks that we've already heard might have led you to think that they concern things happening to young ladies only because no great obstacles were placed in the way of their execution, and because the perpetrators of these deeds were not scared off at the outset. However, I want to show you that what really happens is that their blind lust deprives them of all fear and circumspection, and in order to convince you, I'm going to tell you about something that took place in Flanders.'

STORY FORTY-ONE

It was the year that Madame Margaret of Austria came to Cambrai on behalf of her nephew the Emperor in order to negotiate the peace treaty between him and our most Christian King, who was represented by Madame Louise of Savoy. Now in the retinue of Margaret of Austria was the Countess of Egmont, who had the reputation among her companions of being the most beautiful of all Flemish women. After the peace conference the Countess returned to her home, and as it was the season of Advent, she sent a request to a Franciscan convent for a competent, honest man who could preach, as well as hear confessions from herself and her whole household. The Superior of the convent, being the beneficiary of the house of Egmont as well as of the house of Fiennes, to which the Countess belonged, sought out the best man he had for the job. Being more concerned than any other order to curry favour with the big noble families, the friars sent the most renowned preacher they had. Throughout Advent he carried out his duties very well, and the Countess was greatly pleased with him. On Christmas Eve she wished to make her communion and receive her Creator, so she first called for her confessor. When she had finished her confession, which for the sake of privacy she made in a chapel behind closed doors, she was followed by her maid of honour, who, after making her own confession, sent her daughter in to take her turn. The girl told him everything, and the details of her private life made our good father think he would like to risk an unusual kind of penance. So he said to her:

'Your sins are great, my daughter, so great that as a penance I order you to wear my cord against your bare flesh.'

The girl, reluctant to disobey, replied, 'Give it to me, father, and I will wear it.'

'My daughter,' answered the good father, 'it would not be right for you to tie it on yourself. It is necessary that my own hands, these same hands which will give you absolution, should first fasten the cord around you. Then you will be absolved from all your sins.'

The girl burst into tears, and said she would not let him do anything of the kind.

'What!' said the confessor, 'are you a heretic, refusing to do penance, against the orders of God and Holy Mother Church?'

'I make my confession just as the Church commands,' said the girl, 'and earnestly desire to receive absolution and do penance, but not at your hands. So I am indeed refusing your penance!'

'If that be the case,' said the confessor, 'I cannot give you absolution.'

The young lady got up and went out with a troubled conscience, for she was indeed very young and afraid lest she had done wrong in refusing the priest. When the end of the mass came, the Countess of Egmont received the *Corpus Domini*, and the lady-in-waiting, whose turn was next, asked her daughter if she was ready to follow her. The girl started to cry, and said that she had not made her confession.

'What were you doing all that time with the preacher, then?' asked her mother.

'Nothing,' said the girl, 'because I refused to carry out the penance, and so he refused to give me absolution.'

The mother discreetly inquired a little further, and found out the strange nature of the penance which the good father wanted to impose on her daughter. She had the girl confessed by another priest, and they then made their communion together. As soon as the Countess returned from church, the lady-in-waiting registered her complaint about the preacher. The Countess was surprised and extremely angry, for she had always had a high opinion of the man. All the same her anger did not prevent her laughing at the originality of the penance. But neither did her laughter prevent her having him soundly beaten in the kitchens until under the hail of blows he confessed the truth. Finally she sent him bound hand and foot back to his Superior with the request that next time more respectable people should be appointed to the preaching of God's word.

*

'So, Ladies, you see that even in a household as exalted as this one these men aren't afraid of giving vent to their passions. Just imagine what they are capable of in the more humble places where they go asking for offerings, and where so many opportunities present themselves that it's a miracle they ever get away without causing a scandal. It is all this, Ladies, which leads me to beg you not to think ill of them any more, but to be compassionate. Remember, the passion that blinds Franciscans doesn't spare women either when it decides to strike!'

'Well,' said Oisille, 'that particular Franciscan was wicked indeed! His sin is all the worse because he was a monk, a priest and a preacher, and yet he could still do an evil thing like that, on Christmas day, in church and under cover of the confessional!'

'To hear you talk,' said Hircan, 'it would seem that Franciscans ought to be angels, or somehow better behaved than other men. But from the examples you've heard you should expect them to be even worse than the one we've just heard about. Indeed, it seems to me that this man was very much to be excused, given the fact that he found himself in a situation where he was alone, at night, with a pretty young girl.'

'Yes,' said Oisille, 'but after all it was Christmas night.'

'And that excuses him all the more,' said Simontaut, 'because he was in the same situation as Joseph – in the company of a beautiful virgin, and he wanted to beget a child so that he could truly play his part in the mystery of the Nativity!'

'If he'd really been thinking of Joseph and the Virgin Mary,' said Parlamente, 'he wouldn't have had such evil intentions. But the fact is that he was a thoroughly bad character – or he would not, without any provocation whatsoever, have tried such an evil trick.'

'It seems to me,' said Oisille, 'that the Countess punished him as he deserved, and in a way that should serve as a warning to his companions.'

'But the question is,' said Nomerfide, 'whether she did right to shock people like that, I mean, whether it might not have been better if she had gently reproached him for what he had done rather than expose a fellow creature in such a fashion.'

'I think what she did was right,' said Geburon, 'since it is required that we correct our fellow-men privately before telling anyone else or referring it to the Church. [In any case, when a man has no sense of shame at all, it's very difficult for him ever to reform,] since it's shame that keeps people from sin, just as much as conscience itself.'

'I believe,' said Parlamente, 'that we should indeed follow the teaching of the Gospel – except towards people who themselves preach the word of the Gospel yet practise the opposite. We shouldn't hesitate to make a public scandal of people whose scandalous behaviour affects everybody. It seems to me to be to one's credit to let these people be seen as they really are, so that a cheap imitation doesn't get mistaken for the precious stone, [and so that young girls who are not always alive to the dangers may be put on their guard.] But who will Saffredent choose to speak next?'

'Since it is you who ask me,' replied Saffredent, 'it is you whom I choose. Could any man of understanding do otherwise?'

'Well, since you have chosen me, I'll tell you a story whose truth I can myself testify to. I've always heard it said that when virtue resides in a weak and frail person, when it is assailed by some strong and all-powerful antagonist, it is then that virtue is most to be praised, and then that it shows itself as it truly is. If strength can defend itself against strength, that is not surprising, but if the weak defeats the strong, then the weak is extolled by the whole world. The people in my story are known to me personally, and I would, I think, be doing an injustice if I did not recount to you how I have seen great virtue hidden beneath the most humble garments and ignored by everyone. The deeds of the person I have in mind are so noble and so good that I feel obliged to tell you about them.'

STORY FORTY-TWO

In one of the best towns in Touraine there lived a lord, a lord of high and noble birth, who had been brought up there from his early childhood. I shall say nothing of the perfections, of the grace and beauty of this young prince, except that in his day there was no one to equal him. At the age of fifteen he derived more pleasure from horses and hunting than from looking at the ladies. But one day, when he was in a church, he caught sight of a young lady who had been brought up in the château which was his home. This girl was called Françoise. Her father had remarried after her mother's death and she had moved to Poitou with her brother. She also had an illegitimate half-sister, of whom her father was extremely fond, and who had been married to a butler in this young prince's household, with the result that she was as well-placed as anyone else in the family. The father died and left everything he possessed to Françoise, who went to live in her newly inherited property, just outside the town. But being marriageable, and only sixteen years old, she preferred not to remain alone in her house, and instead went to board with her sister, the butler's wife. Now the young prince saw that for a girl with light brown hair she was rather attractive and that her graceful manner was unusual for one of her station, to the point that she looked more like a noblewoman or a princess than a townswoman, and he took a long look at her. He had never before been in love, but now he felt within his heart an unaccustomed glow of pleasure. When he returned to his chamber he made inquiries about the girl whom he had seen in church, and realized that when he had been small she had come to the château to play with her dolls with his sister, who, once reminded of her childhood friend, sent for her, gave her a warm welcome and invited her to come to see them often. This the girl gladly did, whenever there was a wedding feast or some other gathering. On these occasions the young Prince derived such pleasure from the sight of her that he took it into his head to be in love with her. As he knew she was of poor family and of low birth, he expected to get what he wanted without any difficulty. Having no way of speaking to her personally, he sent one of the gentlemen of his chamber to make the necessary approaches. But she was a sensible, God-fearing girl, and said she did not believe that the messenger's master, this prince, who was so handsome and so noble, should want to look twice at an ugly creature like herself, especially as there were so many beautiful women in the château that he had no need to go looking for them in the town. What was more, she said, she thought the man had made it all up, and that his master had not given him any such orders. But when love meets resistance it becomes all the more persistent, and when the young Prince heard about the girl's response, he merely pursued his end all the more ardently. He wrote her a letter begging her to believe all the messages that the gentleman brought her. The girl could read and write very well, so she was able to read the letter from beginning to end. But however much the gentleman pleaded with her, she still refused ever to reply to it, saying that it was not right for someone of her humble station to write to such a great prince. She begged the gentleman not to think her so silly as to believe that he should regard her highly enough to love her as much as he said. And if he thought that he could do as he pleased with her, just because she was poor, then he was quite wrong. No princess in the whole of Christendom, she declared, had a heart more noble than hers, and there was nothing in the world more precious to her than honour and a clear conscience. She begged him, therefore, not to try to prevent her preserving this treasure for the rest of her life. Nothing would make her change her mind, not even death.

The young prince did not find this reply to his liking. But he loved her all the more for it, and never failed to have his seat set up in the church where she was accustomed to go to hear mass. During the service it was to her image that he always turned his eyes. As soon as she noticed, she would move to another chapel – not so much to avoid seeing him, for it would have been unreasonable of her not to want to be able to see a man like him, but rather to avoid being seen by him, because she did not consider herself elevated enough for him to love her honourably or with the intention of marrying her. And she did not wish him to love her for the sake of wanton pleasure. When she realized that whichever side-chapel she moved to the Prince followed her and had mass said right next to her, she refused to go to that particular church any more, and went instead to the most distant one she could find. Moreover, although she was repeatedly invited by the prince's sister to the festivities that took place at the château, she always declined on the grounds that she was not well. The prince realized that he was not going to be able to talk to her on her own, so he turned to his butler, and offered him a handsome reward in return for his help. The butler readily agreed – as much to please his master as in the expectation of profit. Every day he told the prince what she talked about and what she did, and in particular he reported that she avoided any circumstances which might lead to her seeing him. So the prince, desperately anxious to speak to her, was led to seek alternative measures. What he did was to take his thoroughbreds (which he was beginning to learn to handle with great skill) to be exercised in a big square in the town opposite the butler's house, where Françoise lived. He put them through their paces right in front of the house, so that she could see. Then he deliberately fell off his horse into a large patch of mud, taking care to hit the ground gently, so as not to hurt himself. Howling loudly, he asked if there was not some house where he could go to change his clothes. Everybody round the square offered, but someone said that the butler's house was the closest and the most respectable. So that was the house he chose. The room into which he went was well-appointed. His clothes were all muddy, so he stripped to his shirt, since the rest of his clothes were covered in mud, and got into a bed. When he saw that everyone except his gentleman had gone off to fetch some fresh clothes for him, he called for his host and hostess and asked them where Françoise was. They had a good deal of difficulty finding her, because as soon as she had seen the young prince come in, she had gone off to hide in the furthest corner of the house. However, her sister found her in the end, and begged her not to be afraid of coming to speak to so honourable and worthy a prince.

'What!' replied Françoise. 'I've always thought you were like a mother to me, and now you're telling me to go and speak to this young lord, when you know as well as I do what it is he wants!'

But her sister protested with her, and firmly promised not to leave her on her own with him. So in the end Françoise went to speak to him, but her face was so pale and dejected that she looked more an object of pity than of desire. When the young prince saw her come up to his bed, he took hold of her hand, which was cold and trembling, and said:

'Françoise, do you think I'm so wicked, so cruel, so monstrous that I eat the women I look at? Why are you so frightened of a man who is only concerned for your honour and advancement? You know that I've tried to speak to you at every available opportunity, but have failed. To spite me more, you've avoided going to the places where I used to be able to see you at mass, so that my eyes, no less than my tongue, are denied satisfaction. But it has availed you nothing, because I have stopped at nothing to come here, as you have seen, and have risked breaking my neck by falling deliberately from my horse, so that I could have the pleasure of speaking to you freely. Françoise, I have taken such pains to have this opportunity, I beg you, do not make my efforts worthless. I implore you, since I love you so much, give me your love in return!'

He waited a long time for her reply, but she stood with tears in her eyes, looking down at the ground. So he pulled her as close as he could, thinking he would be able to put his arms round her and kiss her. But she said:

'No, Monseigneur, no! What you seek cannot be. Even though I am no more than a worm in comparison with you, my honour is precious to me, and there is no pleasure in this world for which I would damage it. I would rather die! And what makes me tremble is the fear that the people who saw you come in here doubt that those are my true feelings. Since you do me the honour of coming to speak to me, I am sure you will forgive me if I reply as honour itself requires. Monseigneur, I am neither so blind, nor am I so foolish, that I cannot see that God has endowed you with grace and beauty, and that the woman who shall possess the body and love of such a prince will be the happiest woman in the world. But of what good is all that to me? It's not for me, nor for anyone of my station in life. It would be madness even to long for it. What other reason can I think you have for coming to me, if it is not that the ladies of your household (whom you must surely love if you have any love for beauty and for grace) are so virtuous that you do not dare to ask from them or even hope from them that which because of my low station you think you can have from me? I am sure that if you had what you wanted from people like me, it would be just one more thing to keep your mistress amused for an hour or two, telling her about your conquests at the expense of those weaker than yourself. But I beg you, Monseigneur, to accept that I am not like that. I was brought up in your house, and that is where I learnt what love is. My mother and father were both good servants of yours. So I beg you, since God has not made me a princess who could marry you, nor even of a rank where I could be your beloved mistress, do not try to lower me to the rank of those poor and wretched women who have succumbed. For I regard you as the happiest and most fortunate prince in Christendom, and would not wish it otherwise. And if you really wish to amuse yourself with women of my station, then you will find plenty in this town who are far more attractive than I, and who won't put you to the trouble of all these entreaties. Be satisfied with those women who will be only too glad to have you buy their honour, and don't go on tormenting the one person who loves you more than she loves herself. If it came about today that God should demand either my life or yours, I would consider myself blessed indeed to offer mine to save yours. It is not lack of love that makes me shun your company. Rather it is because I care too well for my conscience and for yours. My honour is dearer to me than life itself. If it is your wish, Monseigneur, I shall remain in your good graces, and pray my whole life long for your health and for your prosperity. It is true that this honour which you do me will make me more highly esteemed among people of my own kind – for they will say, what man of her own station will she deign to consider now? So my heart will be free, except for one obligation, which I shall ever willingly accept – that of praying for you. No other service can I ever render you.'

Although this honourable reply was not what he had wanted, the young prince respected it none the less when he heard it. He did everything he could to convince her that he would never love anyone else. But she had too much sense for anything so unreasonable to take hold in her mind. During this dialogue he received repeated messages that his change of clothes had arrived from the château, but he was so contented where he was that he sent word that he was still asleep, and delayed until supper-time, when, because of his mother, who was one of the most virtuous ladies in the world, he dared delay no longer. So he left his butler's house imbued with greater respect than ever for the girl's virtue. He talked about her often to the gentleman who slept in his bedchamber, and the gentleman, being of the opinion that money was more effective than love, recommended him to offer the girl a respectable sum of money [in order to make her condescend] to do as he desired. The young prince's mother was in charge of his finances, and he only received small sums to spend on his own amusement. But he saved these, and putting them together with what he was able to borrow, he managed to raise the sum of five hundred écus. This he instructed his gentleman to take to the girl with the request that she should now change her mind. However, when she saw the gift, she said to the young prince's gentleman:

'Kindly tell Monseigneur that my heart is pure and honourable, and that if I felt compelled to obey his commands, I would have already been conquered by his grace and beauty. But if grace and beauty have no power over my honour, then all the money in the world will be useless. So take it back to him, for I prefer to live in poverty with my honour intact than to possess all the riches that could ever be desired!'

Hearing this blunt reply, the gentleman began to think that the only way to possess her would be to employ intimidation, so he resorted to threatening her with his master's power and authority. But she only laughed at him and said:

'You can try frightening women who don't know him, but I know that he is too virtuous and too good to say such things himself, and I am sure he will disclaim them when you tell him. But even if what you say were true, even torture and death could not make me change my mind. For as I have already said, since love has not led my heart astray, there is no threat, no gift in the world that could make me stray from my chosen path.'

The gentleman, who had promised his master that he would win her over, reported what she had said with considerable irritation, and tried to persuade him that he should continue to press her by all the means available, arguing that it [would be a great dishonour] to fail to vanquish a woman of this kind. The young prince, however, only wanted to make use of honourable means, being also afraid that if the story reached his mother's ears she would be extremely angry with him. So he did not dare take any further steps until the gentleman eventually presented him with such an easy plan that when he heard it, he felt that the girl was already as good as in his arms. What he had to do was to have a word with the butler, who was ready and willing to serve his master in whatever way was required. So one day the butler asked his wife and his young sister-in-law to go to inspect the grape harvest at a house he had close by the forest, and this the two women promised to do. When the appointed day came, the butler sent word to the young Prince, whose intention it was to meet them there, alone except for his gentleman. His mule was ready, waiting in secret for the moment of departure. But as God willed, that was the day on which the Prince's mother was engaged in the decoration of a private gallery, the most beautiful in the world, and she had all her children helping her. So there the Prince had to stay until the agreed time came and passed. It was scarcely the butler's fault, for he had dutifully taken his sister-in-law on his horse to the house by the forest, having first made his wife pretend she was ill and say, just as they were setting out, that she would not be able to accompany them. When he saw that it was getting past the time when the prince was to appear, he said to his sister-in-law, 'I think we can go back to town now.'

'And who's been stopping us?' asked Françoise.

'Monseigneur the Prince had promised to come,' replied the butler, 'and I was waiting for him.'

Hearing this and realizing the base intention behind it, she said, 'Don't wait any longer for him, brother. I know he won't be coming today.'

Her brother-in-law accepted this, and took her back home. Once in the house she gave vent to her anger, telling him that he was the servant of the Devil and that he was going a lot further than he had been ordered. She was certain that what he had done was entirely his and the gentleman's work, and not the work of the young prince himself. All her brother-in-law wanted, she said, was to get his fingers on the prince's money by encouraging him in his weaknesses, rather than acting as a good servant should. And now that she knew what he was like, she would not stay in his house a moment longer. Thereupon, she sent for her brother to take her to his own part of the country, and moved out of her sister's house immediately.

The plan having failed, the butler went off to the château to find out why it was the young prince had not come. [Scarcely had he arrived] when he saw the prince on his mule, alone except for the gentleman who was his confidant.

'Well, is she still there?' asked the young prince.

The butler told him what he had done and what had happened. The prince was extremely upset at the failure of this plan. which he had regarded as absolutely his last hope of [possessing her]. So, seeing there was nothing more he could do about it, he set about looking for her and eventually found her with some people from whose company she could not easily escape. He burst out in anger when he saw her, accusing her of being harsh and cruel towards him and of deserting her brother-in-law's house. Françoise replied that she had never come across a worse or a more dangerous man than her brother-in-law. The prince was indebted indeed to his butler, she went on, seeing that the man not only gave his body and possessions in his master's service, but also his very soul and conscience! When the prince realized that this time there was really nothing more he could do, he decided to press her no further, and for the rest of his life he regarded her with great respect. One of his servants wanted to marry the girl when he saw how virtuous she was, but she would not accept before the prince, to whom she had given all her affection, had approved the marriage and given his orders for it. She had the matter brought to his attention, and it was finally thanks to his goodwill that the marriage took place. For the rest of her days she lived a life of blameless reputation, and the young prince bestowed great benefits upon her.

*

'Well, Ladies, what are we to make of that? Are our hearts so base that we allow our servants to become our masters? The girl in the story could not be overcome either by the force of love or by the torment of importunity. My appeal to you is that we should all follow her example, that we should be victorious over ourselves, for that is the most worthy conquest that we could hope to make.'

'There is only one thing I would regret,' said Oisille, 'and that is that the virtuous actions of this young girl didn't take place in the time of the great [Roman] historians. The writers who praised Lucretia so much would have left her story aside, so that they could describe at length the virtue of the heroine of your story. Indeed, [I find your heroine's virtue so great, that were it not for the fact that we have solemnly sworn to tell the truth in our stories, I would find it incredible.']

'I don't find her virtue quite so great as you do,' said Hircan. 'For just as in certain illnesses the patient sometimes loses his taste for good wholesome food and prefers food that is bad and dangerous to his health, so it could be that this girl had some gentleman or other of her own rank who made her disdain nobility.'

But to that Parlamente replied that the girl's life and end showed that no man alive found a place in her heart save the man whom she loved more than her life, though not more than her honour.

'You may put notions like that out of your mind,' intervened Saffredent, 'and let me tell you about the origin of the term "honour" as it's used by women. Perhaps those women who are always talking about it don't know how the word came into being. You see, in the beginning, when ill-will was not quite so widespread amongst men as it is now, love was so naturally open and so vigorous that there was no need at all for any kind of dissimulation, and the more perfectly you loved, the more you were praised. But then greed and sin came and took hold of [men's hearts,] drove out both God and love, and in their place put love of self, hypocrisy and deceit. Now, seeing that their hearts [lacked] the virtue of genuine love, and that the term "hypocrisy" incurred odium, women dubbed it "honour" instead. Then those who were incapable of true and honourable love said that it was "honour" which was forbidding them! And in fact they made it into such a harsh and rigid law that even women who *are* capable of perfect love dissemble, because they regard what is really virtue as a vice. But women of good sense and sound judgement never fall into this error. They know the difference between black and white. They know that true honour lies in purity of heart, which should live by love alone and not pride itself on its capacity for the vice of dissimulation.'

'Even so,' said Dagoucin, 'people say that it is the most secret love that is the most admirable.'

'Yes,' added Simontaut, 'secret from those who might criticize it, but openly acknowledged at least by the two people concerned.'

'That is what I mean,' replied Dagoucin, 'indeed it would be better for it to go unknown by one of the two than for it to be known to a third, and it is my view that the girl's love was all the greater because she did not reveal it.'

'Be that as it may,' said Longarine, 'one should always give due respect to virtue, and the greatest manifestation of virtue is to overcome one's emotions. Considering the opportunities which this girl had when she might have been tempted to override her conscience and forget her honour, considering her virtue in overcoming her heart and her desires, and considering the way she resisted the man she loved above all else, I declare that she was worthy to be truly called a woman of strength and honour.'

'Since you take the degree of self-mortification as the measure of virtue,' [Saffredent said,] 'I declare that the prince in the story was even more to be praised than the girl, because in spite of his love for her he still refrained from utilizing his power, although he had ample opportunity to do so. He refused to contravene the rules of true love, according to which prince and pauper are equals, and the methods he used remained within the bounds of honour and decency.'

'There are many men who would have behaved quite differently,' said Hircan.

'All the more reason to admire him,' said Longarine, 'because he managed to overcome the evil common to all men. Blessed is the man who has the power to do wrong and yet does not do it.'

'All this reminds me of a woman,' said Geburon, 'who was more afraid of causing offence in the eyes of men than she was of displeasing God or of acting against love and conscience.'

'Then tell us the story,' said Parlamente. 'I nominate you to speak next.'

'There are people,' Geburon began, 'who have no God at all, or if they do believe in a God, they think He is so remote from them that He can't see or hear the bad things that they do. And even if they do think He can see them, they think He doesn't care and that He won't punish them because He isn't bothered about the things that go on down on earth. Now there was once a young lady (whom for the sake of her family I shall simply call Jambique) who held such views. She often remarked that one was extremely fortunate if one only had God to worry about and was able to preserve one's honour in the eyes of men. But, Ladies, neither her prudence nor her hypocrisy could stop her intimate secrets being revealed – as you will see from my story, in which the whole truth will be told, with the exception of the names of people and places, which will be altered.'

STORY FORTY-THREE

In a beautiful château there once lived a great and powerful princess. In her retinue she had a young lady called Jambique, a rather haughty girl by whom she was so taken in that she did nothing without first consulting her, for she regarded her as the most sensible and virtuous lady of her day. This Jambique was always condemning illicit love, and if she came across any men enamoured of her companions she used to reproach the lovers sharply and make such a damning report to the princess that often they would receive a severe reprimand. Not surprisingly, therefore, Jambique was more feared than loved. She herself never spoke to men at all, except in a loud, arrogant voice, and she had acquired the reputation of being the mortal enemy of love – although in the depths of her heart she was the very opposite. For there was a certain gentleman in the service of her mistress with whom she had fallen so much in love that she could scarcely bear it. But she was so infatuated with the idea of her honour and reputation that she was obliged to conceal her love for the man entirely. She suffered her passion for a good year, but refused to be like other women in love and obtain relief by means of a glance here and a word there. The fire of passion was so intense within her breast that she was driven to resort to the ultimate remedy. And she settled the matter by telling herself that it was better to satisfy her desire and have God alone know what was in her heart, than to tell a mere mortal who might reveal all.

Having reached this conclusion, it happened that one day, when she was in her mistress's chamber gazing out idly on to the terrace, she saw the object of her affections taking a walk in the garden. She watched him there until evening fell and it was too dark to see. Then she called one of her little page-boys and pointed the gentleman out to him.

'Do you see that gentleman,' she said, 'with the crimson satin doublet and the robe edged with lynx fur? Go and tell him that there's a friend of his who wants to speak to him in the arcade in the garden.'

While the page did this, she went out through her mistress's private room into the garden, with a mask covering her eyes and her cap pulled down over her face. When the gentleman appeared she quickly closed the doors, so that no one should find them, and whispered as quietly as she could:

'For a long time, my love, the love that I bear you has made me desire a time and a place to see you. But my fear for my honour was so great that against my will I was constrained to hide my passion. Yet in the end the power of love has overcome my fears. I know you are an honourable man, and so, if you will promise to love me and never tell a soul, nor ask me who I am, I will promise in turn to be a good and faithful mistress to you and never to love another man. But I cannot tell you who I am, for I would rather die.'

The gentleman promised everything she asked, and so she in turn was ready to do the same for him – to let him have whatever he might wish. It was five or six on a winter's evening, and he could see nothing, but as he touched her clothes, he found they were of velvet – and in those days it was not every day one wore velvet, unless one was of high birth and had an important position. And as he felt what lay beneath, he found that there too everything was of high quality, firm and generally in good shape! So he made it his business to give her of his best. She did likewise. And so the gentleman also learned that the lady was married.

Afterwards, she wanted to go back the way she had come as quickly as possible, but the gentleman said to her: 'I value highly the favour you have granted me, a favour that I have not merited. But even more highly would I value a favour granted at my request. Your graciousness towards me gives me such pleasure that I beg you to tell me whether I may not hope for further favours and how it would please you that I should act, for not knowing who you are, I do not know how I may seek such favours.'

'Do not worry,' replied the lady, 'but be assured that I shall send for you every evening before my mistress dines, provided that you are on the terrace where you were earlier. I shall merely send word that you are to remember your promise. Then you will know that I am waiting for you here in this arcade. But if what you hear is that I am about to eat, then you may retire for that day or come to our mistress's chamber. But above all I beg you never to seek to know who I am if you do not wish to destroy our love.'

The gentleman and the lady then withdrew and went their separate ways. But they continued to meet in this fashion for a long time without the gentleman ever discovering who she was. He was overcome by curiosity and wondered over and over again who she could be. He could not imagine that any woman would not want to be seen and loved, and so began to think she might be some kind of evil spirit, having heard some stupid preacher say that nobody would love the Devil if he ever saw his face uncovered! To dispel his doubts he decided to find out once and for all who this woman was who was regaling him with such favours. What he did was to take with him a piece of chalk the next time she sent for him, and while he was in her arms he made a mark on the back of her shoulders without her noticing. As soon as she left him, he dashed into the Princess's chamber and stood by the door where he could see the ladies from behind as they entered. Along with the others he saw Jambique come in, so haughty that he hardly dared look at her. He was sure that she could not be the one, but just as she turned her back towards him he caught sight of the chalk mark. He was so astonished he could scarcely believe his eyes. However, he looked at her figure and realized it was the one he had felt, and his sense of touch told him that the features of her face were the same. He knew for certain that she was the one, and felt most gratified that he alone should have been chosen by a woman who had never been known to have any man devoted to her service and who had indeed refused a good many worthy gentlemen. But he could not remain content with this for long. Love is a restless force.

He became so confident in his prowess and his prospects that he made up his mind to declare his love, feeling sure that once he had made it known it would receive all the more encouragement. One day when the princess was out strolling in the garden, lady Jambique went to walk down another path. The gentleman, seeing her alone, approached her, and pretending that he had had no other contact with her, said:

'Mademoiselle, for a long time I have loved you, loved you with all my heart, but have been afraid to tell you, lest I offend you. I have suffered so much that I will die if I have to continue in this fashion. There is no man alive, I think, who could love you as much as I do . . .'

Lady Jambique did not even let him finish, but interrupted with anger and indignation:

'Have you ever heard of my having a lover, of my having any man devote himself to my service? I am sure that you have not, and I am amazed that you can have the insolence to address such remarks to me, a virtuous woman. You have seen enough of me here to know that I shall never love anyone but my husband. So think twice before speaking to me like that again!'

The gentleman could not restrain himself from laughing at this extraordinary act. 'Madame,' he said, 'you have not always been quite so severe with me. What is the use of such dissimulation? Would it not be better to accept a perfect love than to love imperfectly?'

'I love you neither perfectly nor imperfectly!' replied Jambique. 'I think no more nor less of you than of any other man in my mistress's service. But if you continue to speak to me in this manner I am likely to conceive such a hatred for you that you will suffer grievously!'

But the gentleman persisted: 'What has happened to the passionate welcome which you usually give me on those occasions when I cannot see you? Why do you deny it to me when the light of day reveals the perfection of your grace and beauty?'

Jambique crossed herself ostentatiously, and said: 'You have lost all reason or else you are the greatest liar in the world! I have never in my life welcomed you either any more or any less than I welcome you now. I beg you to tell me what you mean!'

The poor gentleman, thinking he could lead her on from here, described their meeting place, and told her about the chalk. Beside herself with rage, she told him that he was the most evil man in the world, and that he had fabricated so vicious a lie about her that she would not rest till she had made him regret it. He knew that Jambique had great credit with the princess, and was anxious to appease her. But in vain. In a fury Jambique left him standing there and ran straight to her mistress. The princess, who loved Jambique as she loved herself, left her entourage to come to talk to her, and seeing that she was angry about something, asked her what the matter was. Jambique had no intention of hiding it, and told her everything the gentleman had said, presenting the poor man in such a bad light that the princess ordered him that very evening to return home immediately without speaking to anyone, and to stay there till he was sent for. He obeyed with alacrity, for fear that anything worse should happen to him. And for as long as Jambique remained in the princess's household he never came back, nor did he hear any more of this lady, who, after all, had sworn that he would lose her if he ever tried to discover her identity.

*

'So, Ladies, you see how this woman, who placed her worldly reputation higher than her conscience, lost both. For the story I've told today has revealed to everyone what she tried to keep from the eyes of her lover. She wanted to avoid being laughed at by one person, and now she is laughed at by everybody. And you can't excuse her on the grounds that she was naïve and her love sincere – if that were so, we all ought to have pity on her. No, she stands doubly accused, on the one hand of masking her low desires with a veil of honour and pride, and on the other hand of making herself out to be other than she really was, both in the eyes of God and in the eyes of men. But honour belongs to God alone, and He, by tearing aside the veil, has placed her in double disgrace.'

'Indeed,' said Oisille, 'her wickedness was inexcusable. How could anyone defend her, when she stands accused by God, by honour and even by love?'

['How could anyone defend her?'] said Hircan, 'Well, by appealing to pleasure and folly, both of which constitute considerable pleas in the defence of the feminine cause!'

'If those were the only grounds we had for you to plead on our behalf,' said Parlamente, 'then our case wouldn't stand up very well in court. Women who are dominated by pleasure have no right to call themselves women. They might as well call themselves men, since it is men who regard violence and lust as something honourable. When a man kills an enemy in revenge because he has been crossed by him, his friends think he's all the more gallant. It's the same thing when a man, not content with his wife, loves a dozen other women as well. But the honour of women has a different foundation: for them the basis of honour is gentleness, patience and chastity.'

'You're talking about those women who are wise,' said Hircan.

'Of course,' replied Parlamente, 'because I do not wish to recognize any others.'

'If there really weren't any foolish women at all,' said Nomerfide, 'those men who want all the world to believe everything they say and do in their attempts to lead women astray in their simplicity would be a long way from achieving their ends.'

'Well, Nomerfide,' said Geburon, 'let me invite you to speak next so that you may tell us a story on that subject.'*

'Since I'm bound by our agreement to tell the truth, and since you ask me to speak next, I'll tell you what I know. I've not heard a single one amongst us mention the friars without putting them in a bad light. But I feel sorry for them, so in the story I'm going to tell you I shall say something good about them.'

* The passage from 'If there really weren't . . .' to '. . . that subject' is based on the Gruget edition.

STORY FORTY-FOUR

A Franciscan came to the house of the Seigneur de Sedan, asking Madame de Sedan, who belonged to the Croye family, for the pig she used to give every year as alms. And the Seigneur de Sedan, who was a man with a lot of good sense, and very witty, had the good father stay to dine with him. While they were chatting, he said to him, in order to provoke and discompose him: 'Father, it's clever of you to come round asking for your alms before people get to know you. I'm very much afraid that if your hypocrisy becomes known, you won't any longer be able to get your hands on the bread of the children of the poor earned by the sweat of their fathers!'

The Franciscan was not at all taken aback by this, and simply said: 'Monseigneur, our order has a sure foundation, and it will endure for as long as the world endures. Never, as long as there are men and women on this earth, will the foundation on which our order rests fail us.'

Monseigneur de Sedan was anxious to know upon what foundation their life really was built, and pressed the friar to tell him. After several attempts to evade, he said: 'As you insist, I'll tell you. The fact is that we found our lives upon female foolishness, and so long as there exist foolish or stupid women in the world, we shall not die of hunger!'

At this, Madame de Sedan, who was a rather hot-tempered woman, flew into a rage, and was so angry that if her husband hadn't been there she would have made the friar suffer for it. She swore that he would certainly not have the pig which he had been promised. The Seigneur de Sedan, however, swore that he would give him *two* pigs, and had them taken to the monastery – because he realized that the Franciscan had at least made no attempt to conceal the truth!

*

'And that, Ladies, is how the Franciscan, being confident that offerings would be forthcoming from women, managed to obtain goodwill and alms from men – by not concealing the truth! If he'd told a lot of flattering lies, he would no doubt have been more pleasing to the ladies, but he would have done himself and his brethren much less good.'

The story made everyone laugh, especially those who knew the lord and lady of Sedan. And Hircan commented: 'So the Franciscans ought never to use their sermons to try to make women more wise, since it's more useful to them if women remain foolish!'

But Parlamente replied: 'They don't preach to them because they want them to *be* wise – they merely want them to *think* they are! For women who are totally foolish and worldly do not give very much in the way of alms. But the ones who think they are the most wise because they frequent the monasteries and wear rosaries with little death's heads dangling from them and pull down their hoods lower than the other women – those are the ones who are the most foolish. For their hope of salvation is based on their blind trust in the saintliness of men who are truly iniquitous but whom they believe to be demigods because they're impressed by their external appearances.'

'But who,' said Ennasuite, 'could prevent herself from believing in them, since they're appointed by our prelates to preach the Gospel and admonish us for our sins?'

'I'll tell you who,' said Parlamente. 'Anyone who can see that they're hypocrites, and who knows the difference between the doctrine of God and the doctrine of the Devil!'

'Holy Jesus!' said Ennasuite. 'Do you really think those men would dare to teach bad doctrine?'

'Think? I know for certain that the Gospel's the last thing they believe in,' said Parlamente. 'I mean the bad ones, of course, because I do know a lot of good people who preach the Scriptures in their simplicity and purity, who conduct their lives accordingly, without scandal, without ambition and without envy, and whose chastity and purity is not false or forced. But the streets aren't exactly paved with them – in fact the streets are full of their very opposites! The good tree is known by its fruits.'

'But I thought,' said Ennasuite, 'that we were bound on pain of mortal sin to believe what they preach to us from the pulpit?'

'Only when they speak of what is in Holy Scripture,' [said

Oisille,] 'or adduce the expositions of the divinely inspired holy doctors.'

'As far as I am concerned,' said Parlamente, 'I can't overlook the fact that there have been some men of very bad faith among them. I know for a fact that one of them, a doctor of theology called Colimant, who was a well-known preacher and a Provincial of [his] order, tried to persuade several of his brethren that the Gospel was no more credible than Caesar's *Commentaries* or any other histories written by [pagan authors.] Ever since I heard that, I have refused to believe these preachers, unless what they say seems to me to conform to the word of God, which is the only true touchstone by which one can know whether one is hearing truth or falsehood.'

'Be assured,' said Oisille, 'that whosoever reads the Scriptures often and with humility will never be deceived by human fabrications and inventions, for whosoever has his mind filled with truth can never be the victim of lies.'

'Even so,' said Simontaut, 'it seems to me that a simple-minded person will always be easier to deceive.'

'Yes,' replied Longarine, 'if you think that simplicity is the same thing as stupidity.'

'What I mean is,' said Simontaut again, 'that a nice, gentle, simple woman is easier to deceive than one who is cunning and crafty.'

'It sounds to me,' said Nomerfide, 'as if you know someone who had too much of that kind of goodness, so I ask you to be the next storyteller, and tell us about her.'

'Since you have guessed correctly,' replied Simontaut, 'I won't disappoint you, but you must promise me not to weep when you hear it. People who say of you, Ladies, that you are more wickedly cunning than men would find it very hard to find an example to counter the one I'm about to tell you. It's a story in which I shall reveal not only how extraordinarily cunning a certain husband was, but also how simple and good his wife was.'

STORY FORTY-FIVE

In the town of Tours there was once a sharp, quick-witted fellow, who was a tapestry-maker to the late Duke of Orléans, son of Francis I. Although he had become deaf through illness, his wits were in no way dulled. There was not a cleverer tapestry-maker in the trade – and he knew how to use his wits in other ways, too, as you will hear. He had married a decent, respectable woman, with whom he lived quietly and contentedly. He was greatly afraid of upsetting her, while she for her part sought only to obey her husband in all things. But he was a charitable man as well as being an affectionate husband – so charitable that he quite often donated to his neighbours' wives what rightfully belonged to his own, though he was always as discreet as could be about it! Now there happened to be a buxom young chambermaid in the household, of whom our tapestry-maker became enamoured. Afraid that his wife might find out, he was in the habit of pretending to scold the girl, saying she was the laziest wench he had ever seen and that he was not in the least surprised she was idle, because her mistress never beat her. One day he was chatting to his wife about whipping the girls out of bed on the morning of the feast of the Holy Innocents,* and he said: 'It would be a great act of charity to whip that idle hussy of yours on Innocents' day. But it would be better if it wasn't you who did it – your arms aren't strong enough and you're too soft-hearted. It would be preferable if I did it, and then we might get better service from her.'

His poor wife suspected nothing. She asked him to go ahead with his proposal, agreeing that she was not strong enough and had not the heart in any case to give the girl a beating. The husband agreed willingly to perform the deed, and proceeded to act the harsh executioner. He bought the springiest canes he could find, and to make it look as if he had no intention of letting the

* The custom was supposed by theologians to commemorate the slaughter of the innocents celebrated on 28 December. It was also a feast of fools and in sixteenth-century France had become a notorious excuse for sexual pranks.

girl off lightly, he had the canes hardened in brine. This made the poor wife more sorry for the maid than suspicious of her husband's intentions.

When the day of the Holy Innocents came, the tapestry-maker got up early, and went to the room at the top of the house where the chambermaid slept. There he performed the Innocents' Day custom – though rather differently from the way he had told his wife he would! The girl started to cry, but to no avail. Just in case his wife came and found them, he beat the canes he had brought against the bedstead until they were frayed and splintered. Then he went back to his wife, carrying the broken canes, and said: 'I don't think your maid will forget the Holy Innocents in a hurry after that, my dear!'

But when he had gone out of the house, the wretched chambermaid came down, and threw herself at her mistress's feet, protesting that the master had done to her the greatest wrong that [was ever done] to a chambermaid. But the lady of the house interrupted, thinking the girl was referring to the beating she believed her husband had given her. 'My husband acted very properly,' she said. 'I've been asking him to do it for over a month now. And if it hurt, I'm very pleased. He's not given you half what he ought!'

When the maid saw that her mistress approved, she concluded that it was not such a great sin as she had thought. It must surely be all right if her mistress, who was regarded as a respectable woman by everyone, was behind it all. So she did not dare raise the matter again. When the master of the house saw that his wife was just as happy to be deceived as he was to do the deceiving, he decided to try and make her happy more often, and so completely won the maid over that she no longer wept when he 'performed the Innocents' with her. Things went on like this for quite a time without the wife finding out, until the winter snows began. The tapestry-maker had been in the habit of 'doing the Innocents' on the grass in his garden, and he fancied continuing this practice in the snow. So one morning, before anyone was up, he took the girl outside in her shift to perform his little passion play in the snow. The pair romped about and threw snowballs at one another – and did not neglect of course to 'play the Innocents'. All this was noticed by a neighbour who had got up to look through her window at the weather. The window overlooked the garden, and when the woman saw the disgraceful goings-on next door, she was so angry that she made up her mind to tell her good neighbour all about it in order to save her from being further deceived by such a wicked husband, and from being waited on by such a good-for-nothing creature. Looking up from his little games, the tapestry-maker glanced round to see if anyone could see them, and caught sight of the neighbour at her window. He was somewhat annoyed at this, but he was just as clever at embroidering the truth as he was at embroidering tapestry – so clever in fact, that he ended up by tricking both the next-door neighbour and his wife. This is what he did. He went straight back to bed and promptly made his wife get up and go out into the garden with him in her nightdress. He had a good game of snowballs with her, as he had done previously with the maid, and finished by 'giving her the Innocents' too! Then they both went back to bed.

Next time the good lady went to mass, she was met by her neighbour, who in her concern for her friend earnestly advised her, without going into details, to dismiss her maid, who, she said, was an immoral and vicious little slut. The tapestry-maker's wife first wanted to know why her neighbour had such a low opinion of the girl, and in the end she was told how the maid had been seen in the garden one morning with her husband. At this she only started to laugh loudly, and said: 'Heaven help me, neighbour, it was me!'

'What?' said the other. 'But she was in a nightdress and it was about five o'clock in the morning!'

'I swear to you, my dear, it was me!' said the wife. But the neighbour persisted.

'They were throwing snowballs at one another, and then he put his hand in her bosom, and then somewhere else, as intimate as they possibly could be!'

'Oh dear,' giggled the tapestry-maker's wife, 'it was me!'

'But listen!' said the neighbour. 'I saw them afterwards on the snow doing things that didn't seem either very nice or very respectable to me!'

'My dear,' replied the other, 'I've said it once, and I'll say it again, it was *me* you say you saw doing all those things! That's what we do in private, my good husband and myself. There's no need to be so shocked. You know that wives have to humour their husbands.'

In the end the neighbour went off, rather wishing that she had a husband like that herself. When the tapestry-maker arrived back home, his wife told him at length everything the neighbour had said.

'Well, my dear,' he replied, 'if you weren't such a good, sensible woman, we would have left one another a long time ago. But I hope God will continue to preserve us in our mutual affection, to the glory of His name and for the continuation of our happiness together!'

'Amen to that,' said the good woman. 'I hope that you will never find me to fail you!'

*

'After hearing a story like that, a story, Ladies, which is perfectly true, one would have to be really incredulous not to maintain the view that there is as much wickedness in you as there is in men – though without wishing to malign anyone, one can't help feeling that neither the man nor the woman really deserved very much in the way of praise.'

'The man in the story was an extremely bad character,' said Parlamente, 'because he deceived both his wife *and* the chambermaid.'

'You haven't understood the story properly,' said Hircan. 'The point is that the man satisfied them both in one morning! *I* think that he showed great prowess, both mentally and physically, considering that he managed to act in such a way as to satisfy conflicting interests.'

'It is merely doubly reprehensible,' answered Parlamente, 'to satisfy the simple heart of one woman with a lie, and to pander to the immorality of the other with vice. But I am well aware that sins of that sort will always be excused when judgement is passed by people like you.'

'I assure you all the same that I myself would never undertake such a risky operation as the man in the story,' said Hircan, 'for as long as I can make you content I shan't think I've been wasting my time!'

'If mutual love doesn't bring contentment into a person's heart,' replied Parlamente, 'then nothing else will.'

'Truly,' said Simontaut, 'I think nothing in the world is so painful as to love and not be loved in return.'

'If one wants to be loved,' Parlamente said, 'one must turn to someone who is disposed to give such love. But very often, women who are loved and won't love in return are the most loved, and men who are the least loved love most ardently.'

'You remind me of a story I hadn't intended to include among the good ones,' said Oisille.

'Please tell it to us,' said Simontaut.

'I shall do so gladly,' she replied.

STORY FORTY-SIX

In the town of Angoulême, where Charles, Count of Angoulême, the father of King Francis, often resided, there was a certain Franciscan friar, De Vale by name, who was highly thought of as a scholar and a preacher. So highly thought of was he indeed that one Advent he was invited to preach before the Count himself, and he acquired such prestige as a result that everyone who heard about him besieged him with invitations to dinner. Amongst these people was one of the Count's judges of exempts, a man who had married a good-looking and respectable woman. Now the friar was passionately in love with this woman, but could not summon up the courage to declare himself. She was fully aware of his feelings and found him highly ridiculous. He made his lecherous intentions apparent on several occasions, until one day he caught sight of the judge's wife going up into the attic, and thinking he would catch her alone, he went up after her. But she heard him making a noise behind her, so she turned round and asked him where he was going.

'I'm following you up,' he replied. 'I have a secret to tell you!'

'Don't come up here, father,' said the judge's wife. 'I'd rather not be on my own with people like you. If you come one step further, you'll be sorry!'

But the sight of her all alone was too much for him, and ignoring her warning, he scrambled up. Being a woman of spirit, she gave him a kick in the stomach as soon as he appeared at the top of the stair, shouting after him:

'Up hill and down dale, Mr De Vale!'

And she knocked him all the way down the stairs. The friar was so humiliated that he did not even stop to lick his wounds, but fled from the town as fast as he could, fully expecting her to tell her husband what had happened. He was quite right. She did tell her husband, and the Count and Countess as well. To crown it all, he demonstrated his evil nature by going off and insinuating himself into the household of a certain lady who had a predilection for the Franciscans. After he had preached a sermon or two for her, he clapped eyes on her daughter, who was extremely beautiful. And he would often reprimand her in front of her mother for not getting up in the morning to come to his sermons.

'Oh father,' said the mother, 'I wish to God she had had a taste of the discipline that you and your good brothers submit yourselves to!'

So the good friar promised her that if the girl went on being lazy, he would give her a taste of that discipline – and the girl's mother warmly encouraged him to do so. A day or two later he went into the lady's room, and as he did not see the daughter there, he asked where she was. The lady replied: 'She has such little respect for you that I think she's stayed in bed.'

'Make no mistake,' said the friar, 'it is a very bad habit for young girls to stay in bed. Not many people take the sin of sloth seriously. But *I* regard it as one of the most dangerous of all the sins, both for the body and for the soul. So you should punish her – or if you will give *me* the responsibility, I'll soon stop her staying in bed when she should be up saying her prayers to God!'

The poor lady, who took him for an honest man, pressed him to teach her daughter a lesson. Well, he lost no time. He ran up the little wooden staircase leading to the girl's room, found her all alone in bed, and raped her as she slept. The wretched girl woke up not knowing whether it was a man or a devil, and screamed for her mother to come to save her. But the mother just stood at the bottom of the stair, calling up to the friar: 'Don't let her off lightly! Give it her again! Teach the wicked girl a lesson!'

When the friar had satisfied his evil desires, he went downstairs to the lady of the house, and said, with his face all on fire: 'I think, Madame, that your daughter won't forget the lesson I've just given her!'

The girl's mother thanked him and went upstairs to her daughter, who was greatly distressed, as well she might be, after being the victim of such a crime. As soon as she heard the truth, she had the Franciscan searched for everywhere, but he was already a long way off. And he was never seen again in the kingdom of France.

*

'So you see, Ladies, just how safe you are in giving such responsibilities to people who have no intention of carrying them out honourably! Corporal punishment should be administered to men by men, and to women by women. For women would be as lenient to men, if they were charged with punishing them, as men would be cruel, if they were charged with punishing women.'

'Holy Jesus!' exclaimed Parlamente. 'What a vile and vicious friar, Madame!'

'Nearer the truth to say that the mother was a silly fool,' said Hircan, 'for being so deluded by the false colours of hypocrisy that she allowed into her house the sort of man you should only ever see in church!'

'True,' said Parlamente. 'I admit that she was one of the stupidest mothers there ever was. If she'd had as much sense as the judge's wife she'd have thrown him down the stairs, not sent him up! But what can you expect? The devil who appears as half angel is the most dangerous of the lot, because he's so good at transforming himself into an angel of light that it makes you feel guilty if you suspect them of being what they really are, and in my opinion it's praiseworthy not to be suspicious.'

'All the same,' said Oisille, 'one should be ready to suspect the kind of wickedness one ought to avoid, especially when people in positions of responsibility over others are involved. It's better to suspect something bad, even though it doesn't exist, than to fall prey to an evil that does exist by being foolish and credulous. I've never seen any women fall victim to deception as a result of being reluctant to believe what men say, but I *have* seen many taken in because they've been too ready to take lies at their face value. That is why I say that the possibility of some evil occurrence cannot be too strongly suspected [by those] who have charge over men, women, towns and states. For however much on one's guard one is, the world is full of treachery and wickedness, and the shepherd who is not vigilant will be deceived by the wiles of the wolf.'

'Nevertheless,' commented Dagoucin, 'if a person is suspicious, he will never be able to preserve [true affection.] Indeed, many true friendships have been broken because of suspicion.'

'Well, if you can prove your point by means of an example,' said Oisille, 'then you may tell the next story.'

'I know a story,' said Dagoucin, 'which is so true that I'm sure you will enjoy it. And I'll tell you what it is that is most likely to destroy true affection, Ladies. It is when the certainty of affection starts to give way to suspicion. For just as trusting a friend is the greatest honour one can do him, so mistrusting him is the gravest dishonour, because that means that one believes him to be other than one would like him to be. It is this that causes the destruction of many true affections, and turns friends into enemies, as you will see from my story.'

STORY FORTY-SEVEN

Not far from Perche there were once two gentlemen who had from their childhood grown up together as such good and true friends that, as they were one in heart and mind, so in house, bed, board and purse they were as one. For a long time they lived together in this state of perfect friendship, and never once was there in word or wish any sign of difference between them. They were even more than brothers. They lived as if they were one man. Then one of them married, but this did not prevent him continuing his friendship and continuing to live with his friend just as he had before. If they ever had to stay in cramped quarters, he did not hesitate to let him sleep in the same bed as himself and his wife – though it is true that he slept in the middle. Their belongings were held in common, and nothing, neither marriage nor anything else, could put a stop to their perfect friendship. But in this world happiness never lasts for long. Perhaps the three were too happy. Anyway, after a certain length of time the husband began to lose the confidence he had had in his friend, and, [without any justification, became extremely suspicious both of him and of his own wife.] Unable to hide his feelings from her, he spoke to her sharply about his suspicions. She was extremely surprised, because he had always commanded her to treat his friend, in all things but one, just as affectionately as she treated him, yet now he was telling her not to speak to him at all unless she was in company. She conveyed this to the friend, who found it hard to believe, for it had never occurred to him to do anything that would offend the husband. Not being in the habit of concealing anything from him, he told him what he had heard, and begged him not to conceal the truth. For the last thing he wanted to do for that or any other reason was to give cause to end the friendship between them that had lasted so long. The husband replied that nothing of the kind had ever entered his head, and that whoever had been spreading such a rumour was a malicious liar. To this his friend said:

'I know well enough that jealousy is a passion which is as

impossible to bear as love itself and if you are jealous, and jealous of me of all people, I shall not criticize you for it, because you cannot help it. But there is one thing that you could help, and which I can legitimately complain about, and that is that you have tried to cover up your sickness, when never before have you hidden your ideas, your feelings and your opinions from me. In the same way, if I had been in love with your wife, you should not condemn me for it as if it were a deliberate crime, because love is like fire – it is not something which I can pick up in my hands and do what I please with. But if I were to hide my feelings from you and try to demonstrate my love to your wife – then I would be the most treacherous friend the world has ever seen. However, I can assure you that although she is a good and honest woman, I never saw anyone less likely, even if she were not your wife, to arouse amorous thoughts in me. However, even though there is no cause for concern, I urge you to tell me if you have the slightest suspicion, so that I may set the matter right and so that we do not permit our friendship to be destroyed for the sake of a woman. For even if I loved her more than anything else in the world, I would never speak a word to her, because I would put your [love] before that of any other person.' Again the husband solemnly swore that nothing of the kind had ever entered his head, and insisted that the friend should go on living in his house in exactly the same way as before. His friend replied.

['Since that is what you want], then I shall do so, but I beg you to remember that if after this you ever think badly of me again and hide it from me, I shall stay with you no longer.'

They lived together as before for a while, but then the husband became even more suspicious and ordered his wife to stop treating his friend in the fashion she did. She told the friend about this, asking him not to speak to her any more, as she had been ordered not to speak to him. Hearing this, and also guessing from the expression that sometimes came over his face that the husband had not kept his word, the friend spoke to him in great anger:

'If you are jealous, my friend, that is only natural. But after the promise you made, I am distressed that you have hidden it from me so persistently. I always thought that nothing would ever come between us or get in the way of our friendship. But to my great sorrow and through no fault of my own, I see that the opposite is the case. Not only are you jealous of your own wife and of me, but you want to cover your feelings up in order that your disease lasts so long that it is eventually transformed entirely into hatred. Just as our friendship has been the greatest friendship of our time, so shall our enmity be the deadliest. I have done what I could to prevent this unfortunate turn of events, but since you suspect me of being so corrupt, and the very opposite of what I've always been, I swear on my oath that henceforth I shall be what you think I am. I shall not rest till I have had from your wife that which you believe I have pursued. From now on, beware! For as your suspicion has destroyed my love for you, now your love for me will be destroyed by my anger!'

And although the husband tried to make him believe it was all a mistake, the other man would have none of it. He moved out his share in the goods and chattels which they had previously held in common. With this division of their property the union of their hearts was finally dissolved, and as he had promised, the unmarried gentleman did not rest till he had cuckolded his friend.

*

'And may such a fate befall all those, Ladies, who wrongly suspect their wives of misbehaving. Husbands often actually make their wives do what they suspect, because a good woman is more likely to be overcome by despair than she is by all the pleasure in the world. And I would contradict anyone who claims that suspicion is the same as love. Suspicion may come from love, just as ashes come from fire – but like ashes, suspicion stifles the flame.'

'I think that nothing brings greater grief either to a man or to a woman,' said Hircan, 'than to be suspected of being the opposite of what one really is. And as far as I'm concerned there's nothing else that would be more likely to make me end a friendship.'

'Nevertheless,' said Oisille, 'that is not a reasonable excuse for a woman to take vengeance for her husband's suspicions at the expense of her own honour. It is like running oneself through with one's own sword because one can't kill one's enemy, or like biting one's own fingers because one can't scratch one's opponent's face. She would have done better not to speak to the friend, so that she could demonstrate to her husband how unjust he was to suspect her. Then, in time, they would both have been appeased.'

'But she did show she was a woman of character by the way she acted,' said Ennasuite, 'and if more women acted in the same way their husbands would not be as offensive as they are.'

'Be that as it may,' said Longarine, 'it is long-suffering that in the end makes women victorious and chastity which makes them worthy to be praised. There we must stop.'

'But,' Ennasuite went on, 'women can be unchaste without sin.'

'What do you mean?' asked Oisille.

'If a woman were to mistake someone else for her husband,' replied Ennasuite.

'She would be a fool,' said Parlamente, 'if she didn't know the difference between her husband and some other man, however well he might be disguised.'

'There have been some in the past, and no doubt there'll be some in the future, who have been deceived, while remaining innocent and not guilty of any sin.'

'If you know of a case of this kind,' said Dagoucin, 'then I invite you to tell the next story, because I find it very strange to think that sin and innocence can exist together.'

'Well, listen,' said Ennasuite. 'In case, Ladies, the tales you have already heard have not warned you sufficiently that it is dangerous to give lodging in one's own home to those men who call us worldly while regarding themselves as saintly and superior, I have decided to offer yet another example. We're always hearing about the mistakes people make when they trust these people too much, and I would like to recount a tale about them that will show you that not only are they ordinary men like all the others, but that there's also something diabolical about them which goes beyond the ordinary wickedness of men.'

STORY FORTY-EIGHT

At a village inn somewhere in the Périgord a wedding feast was being held for a girl of the household, and all the friends and relations were doing their best to enjoy themselves as much as possible. During the festivities two Franciscans appeared, and as it did not suit their status to join in the wedding celebrations, they were given supper in their room. However, the leader of the pair, who not only had more authority but also more inclination to evil, thought to himself that since he was being kept separate from the feast he would show them one of the tricks of his trade and help himself to a share in the bridal bed! When evening came and the guests started dancing, the friar had a long look at the bride through the window and found her very beautiful and very much to his taste. He carefully inquired of the chambermaids which room she was to sleep in, and discovered to his delight that it was quite near to his own. He kept a close watch until he saw the bride quietly leave the gathering, led away by the old women, as is the custom. Because it was still very early the husband preferred not to leave the dancing, which he was so much enjoying that he seemed to have forgotten all about his wife. But the friar hadn't. As soon as he heard that the bride had climbed into bed, he stripped off his grey habit and went to take the place of the bridegroom. But he was afraid of being caught, and had not been in bed very long before he jumped out and ran to the end of the passage, where his companion was keeping watch for him. Having been given the sign that the husband was still dancing, the Franciscan, who had not yet had time to satisfy his evil desires properly, ran back and got into bed again with the bride. There he intended to stay till his companion gave him the sign to leave. Eventually the husband came to bed. His wife, who had already been so tormented by the friar that all she wanted was a little rest, could not restrain herself from saying: 'Have you decided not to go to sleep at all and to do nothing but torment me?'

The poor husband, who had only just arrived, was somewhat

taken aback, and asked her what she meant, since he had been dancing all evening. 'Dancing!' said the poor girl. 'What a way to dance! This is the *third* time you've come to bed tonight! I think it'd be better if you went to sleep!'

The husband was amazed at this, and forgetting everything else, insisted on finding out the truth of the matter. When he had heard the whole story, he suspected immediately that it was the Franciscans who had been given rooms at the inn. He got up at once and rushed into their room, only to find that they had disappeared. He shouted for help at the top of his voice. His friends came flocking round, and when they had heard what had happened they all went off to search for the friars with candles, lanterns and all the dogs of the village. When they did not find them in any of the houses, they searched and searched until they caught them in the vineyards. There they gave them what they deserved. They beat them, cut off their arms and legs, and left them in the vines in the care of Bacchus and Venus, for they were better disciples of the god of wine and goddess of love than of Saint Francis.

*

'Now don't be surprised, Ladies, that people like this, who are cut off from ordinary life, do things that any brigand would be ashamed of. In fact, we should be surprised that they don't do far worse things, when God withdraws his guiding hand from them. It's far from the truth to say that the habit makes the monk; on the contrary, they become so arrogant because of it that it often *un*makes them. For myself, I prefer the sort of piety preached by Saint James: to have a heart pure and undefiled before God, and to do all in one's power to be charitable to one's neighbour.'

'Merciful God!' exclaimed Oisille. 'Shall we never cease hearing stories about these tiresome Franciscans?'

'If princes, noble ladies and gentlemen are not spared in our stories,' said Ennasuite, 'it seems to me that the Franciscans should feel honoured that anyone deigns to talk about them at all. They're so useless that no one would ever mention them if they didn't do noteworthy deeds of evil, for it's better, so it's said, to do evil deeds than to do nothing at all! And the more variety we have, the better our bouquet of stories.'

'Well, if you all promise,' said Hircan, 'not to be angry with me, I'll tell you a story about a certain lady of high birth – a story so scandalous that you'll be only too ready to excuse that poor Franciscan for satisfying his needs when he could. For the lady I'm going to tell you about had, unlike the friar, quite enough to satisfy her appetite, but indulged herself in illicit morsels in the most disreputable fashion!'

'We have all sworn to tell the truth,' said Oisille, 'and we have sworn also to listen. Therefore you may speak freely, for when we recount the evil doings of the men and women in our stories, we are not doing it in order to bring shame upon individuals, but in order to remove the esteem [and] trust placed in the mere creatures of God, by means of displaying the sorrows to which those creatures are subject, to the end that our hope may come to rest upon Him who alone is perfect and without whom all men are but imperfection.'

'Well then,' replied Hircan, 'I shan't be afraid to tell you my story.'

STORY FORTY-NINE

At the court of King Charles – I won't say which Charles for the sake of the honour of the lady in question, nor will I refer to the lady in question by her real name – there was a certain Countess. She came from a high-ranking family, but she was foreign. People are always attracted by novelties, and when this lady first arrived they could not take their eyes off her, partly because the style of her clothes was new to them and partly because their magnificence betokened great wealth. Not that she was one of the most beautiful women in the world, but she had a certain grace combined with the most disdainful manner you can imagine, and a manner of speaking so dignified and overbearing that there was nobody at court who was not afraid of addressing her – with the exception of the King who was extremely fond of her. So that he could have her to himself he sent her husband, the Count, on some piece of business which kept him absent for a considerable length of time. Meanwhile the King enjoyed himself with the Countess. Now there were several gentlemen in the King's service who knew that the King was receiving her favours, and they made bold to approach her themselves, One of these was called Astillon, a man of fine bearing and fearless temperament. Her first reaction to him was to stand on her dignity and threaten to tell the King. But the fiercest warrior on earth would not have intimidated Astillon, and he persisted until she eventually agreed to see him alone and told him the best way of getting into her room. He followed her instructions, but so that the King would not suspect anything, he first of all asked him for leave of absence. So he made his departure from the court, but left his attendants after the first day and returned by night to receive the favours that the Countess had promised him. She kept her word, and Astillon was so satisfied that he was content to stay there for [seven or eight] whole days, shut up in her dressing-room and living on nothing but light, nourishing food. During the course of the week one of his companions, a man by the name of Durassier, also came along to make advances to the Countess. She started off in exactly the same way as before, with a brusque and disdainful rebuff, only to soften as the days went by. And on the day she dismissed her first prisoner, she duly installed a second one to serve her in his place. And while *he* was there, a third one came along – this time a man called Valnebon – and went through the same ritual as the first two. And after them two or three more came along and did *their* spell in this far from unpleasant captivity. This went on for some time, and the Countess managed it so shrewdly, that none of the men knew anything at all about the others. They each knew of course that all the others were equally enamoured, but each one of them thought that he was the only one to have his wishes granted, and each one secretly laughed at the others for having failed to win such a prize.

One day, however, these gentlemen happened to be together enjoying themselves at a banquet, and the conversation turned to their adventures and experiences as prisoners during the wars. Valnebon had been finding it unbearable to keep quiet all this time about his good fortune and could not resist saying to the others:

'I don't know what it's like in the prisons *you* were in, but for my part, I liked so much being in one of the prisons I was in that I shall for the rest of my days have nothing but praise for all the rest. I think there's no pleasure in the whole world that comes anywhere near the pleasure of being a prisoner!'

But Astillon, who had been the first of the 'prisoners', had a good idea what 'prison' he was talking about, and replied:

'Valnebon, who was this gaoler who gave you such good treatment that you actually liked being in prison?'

And Valnebon replied: 'Whoever the gaoler was, the prison was so enjoyable that I wish I could have stayed there longer, because I've never been so well treated, and never more satisfied!'

Now Durassier, not normally a very talkative man, [strongly suspecting] that they were referring to the 'prison' that he too had been in, said to Valnebon: 'What sort of food did you receive in this prison which you praise so highly?'

'What sort of food?' answered Valnebon. 'The King himself doesn't have anything better, nor anything more nourishing!'

'But I still need to know,' said Durassier, 'if the person who kept you prisoner made you work for your bread?'

Valnebon guessed that they had seen through him, and could not stop himself bursting out with an oath: 'God Almighty! Could it be that I've had comrades in this? I thought I was the only one!'

Seeing that here was a dispute in which he was as much involved as the others, Astillon laughed and said: 'We all of us serve the same master. We've been friends and comrades since our youth. So if we are now comrades in this [misfortune], then we should find cause for laughter. But in order to be sure that what I suspect is true, I ask your permission to put some questions and request that you confess the truth. For if what I believe has happened to us really has happened, then I think it will make one of the funniest stories you could find within a thousand leagues!'

So they all swore they would tell the truth, if it turned out that it could not be denied.

'I will tell you what happened to me,' said Astillon, 'and you will say whether or not the same thing happened to you.'

They all agreed on this, and Astillon said: 'I asked the King for leave of absence.'

'We did the same!' responded the others.

'Then, when I was a couple of leagues away from court, I left my attendants and went to give myself up as prisoner.'

'We did exactly the same!'

'I stayed about seven or eight days, I slept in a dressing-room, and I was given nothing but light, nourishing food to eat and other things to consume, the best I've ever tasted. When the week was up my gaoler let me go, and I left a good deal weaker than when I'd arrived!'

They declared, every one of them, that the same had happened to them.

'And my spell in this prison started on such-and-such a day, and I was released on such-and-such a day,' said Astillon, naming the day on which he was released.

'I started my stretch on exactly the day you finished,' said Durassier, 'and stayed till such-and-such a day!'

Valnebon, who was losing his patience, began to curse. 'By the blood of Christ! It looks as if I'm the third person to think I was the first one and the only one because that was the day *I* went into prison!'

He told them what day he had been let out, and the remaining three men who were at table with them swore that they too had followed, one after the other in a row.

'Well,' said Astillon, 'since that is the case, I shall venture to say what our gaoler's status is: she's married and her husband is away!'

'That's the one!' they replied together.

'Now to put us all out of our misery,' Astillon continued, 'I'll be the first to say who she was, since I was the first on the lady's rota: it's the Countess – the Countess who's so proud and arrogant that when I thought I'd won her love I felt as if I'd conquered Julius Caesar himself! To the Devil with the miserable woman for making us work so hard for what we wanted and making us feel so pleased with ourselves when we got it! There has never been such a wicked woman! While she kept one man hidden away, she was enticing the next one so that she would never be without some amusement! I'd rather die than see her go unpunished!'

[They all asked Astillon what punishment he thought she deserved,] assuring him that they were all ready to carry out whatever he might recommend.

'It seems to me,' he replied, 'that we should tell our King, since he treats her like a goddess.'

'No,' [they all replied.] 'There are enough ways of taking revenge without appealing to our master. Let's all meet together tomorrow and wait for her as she goes to mass. We'll all wear an iron chain around our necks and as she goes into church we'll all greet her in a suitable manner.'

Everybody thought that this was a good idea, and they all went off to provide themselves with iron chains. The following morning they arrived dressed in black with their iron chains wound round their necks and stood in wait for the Countess on her way to church. No sooner had she seen them in this strange accoutrement than she burst out laughing and said: 'Where are all these miserable-looking people off to?'

'Madame,' said Astillon, 'we are your humble prisoners, your slaves, and we are duty-bound to serve you.'

The Countess, pretending that she did not understand, replied: 'But you are not my prisoners, and I see no reason why you should serve me any more than any other men!'

Valnebon stepped forward and said: 'But we have eaten your bread for so long, Madame, that it would be most ungrateful of us not to do you service.'

She retained her composure, however, thinking that a dignified manner would disconcert them. But they were so persistent that she realized that the whole affair had been uncovered. So she quickly found a way of outdoing them, for she had lost her honour, she had no conscience left and she certainly had no intention of being put to shame in the way they intended. No, being a woman who preferred her pleasure to all the honour in the world, she did not become angry or change her behaviour in any way. The men were so abashed at this that the shame they had desired to bring down on her fell upon them and remained in their hearts.

*

'Now, Ladies, if you don't think *that* story's enough to show that women are as wicked as men, I can find plenty more to tell you. But it seems to me that the one I've just told you ought to be quite enough to persuade you that when a woman becomes completely shameless she's a hundred times worse in the extent of her misdeeds than a man would be.'

After listening to Hircan there was not a single woman in the party who did not start making the sign of the cross. One would have thought they had suddenly had a vision of all the devils in Hell! But Oisille turned to them and said:

'Ladies, let us humble ourselves after listening to this terrible account, and let us do so because the person who is abandoned by God comes to resemble him with whom she is joined. For even as they who cling to God have with them the spirit of God, so they who cling to God's adversary are imbued with the spirit of evil. Nothing more resembles a brute than a person deprived of the spirit of God.'

'Whatever this poor woman did,' said Ennasuite, 'I would not have anything good to say about these men who boasted about "being in prison".'

'In my opinion,' said Longarine, 'it costs no less effort for a man to keep quiet about something when he's got it, than it does for him to chase after it in the first place. For there is no hunter who does not take pleasure in sounding his horn when the quarry is caught, nor lover who does not glory in his conquest.'

'That is an opinion,' said Simontaut, 'which I would argue to be heretical before all the Inquisitors of Christendom! Many more men than women are capable of being discreet, and I know that one can find men who would rather not be received kindly at all by a lady, [if] it meant that any living creature should hear of it. That is why the Church, as a good mother, has ordained that priests, not women, should be confessors, because women are incapable of concealing anything.'

'That,' said Oisille, 'is not the real reason. The real reason is that women are such great opponents of vice that they would not grant absolution as easily as men, and the penances they imposed would be more severe.'

'If women were as severe in imposing penances as they are in their replies,' said Dagoucin, 'then they would throw more sinners into the depths of despair than they would ever draw to salvation. So whatever the case may be, mother Church has provided well. But for all that I don't wish to condone the gentlemen who boasted about their "prison", for a man never deserved honour for speaking ill of ladies.'

'Since they shared a common misfortune,' said Hircan, 'I think that they did right to console one another.'

'But,' replied Geburon, 'for the sake of their honour they should never have confessed. The books of the Round Table tell us that it is not honourable for a knight to vanquish an unworthy opponent.'

'I'm surprised,' said Longarine, 'that the poor woman didn't die of shame when she saw her "prisoners" in front of her.'

'Women who have lost their shame,' Oisille replied, 'recover it again only with great difficulty, unless it be that some great love caused it to be temporarily forgotten. Amongst those women who lost their shame for love I have seen many turn back to the path of virtue.'

'I believe,' said Hircan, 'that you have indeed seen women in love turn back. For great love in women is not easy to find.'

'I do not agree with you,' said Longarine, 'because I believe there are women who have loved until death.'

'I am so anxious to hear your story,' said Hircan, 'that I invite you to be the next to speak, so that we can find out about this love in women, which I personally never thought they had.'

'You'll believe it when you've heard the story,' Longarine said, 'and you'll accept that love is the strongest passion there is. Love makes people undertake things that are virtually impossible, in order to achieve some happiness in life. But, equally, it is love which more than any other passion leads men and women to despair when they lose all hope of attaining their desire – as you shall now see from my story.'

STORY FIFTY

Not long ago in the town of Cremona there lived a gentleman by the name of Messire Jean-Pierre, who had for a long time been in love with a certain lady who lived close by. But no matter how he approached her he could not obtain the answer he desired, although the lady really loved him with all her heart. So the poor gentleman, distressed and frustrated as he was, withdrew into himself and stopped going out. He resolved no longer to pursue in vain his heart's desire and waste his life away. Thinking that he could divert his mind from his love, he went for several days without seeing her, but fell into such a melancholic state that people could scarcely recognize his face. His parents sent for the doctors, and the doctors, seeing his face had gone yellow, considered he was suffering from an obstruction in the liver, and prescribed a bleeding. Now the lady who up till then had been so hard-hearted, knew very well that his illness was entirely due to the fact that she had spurned him, and sent an old woman whom she trusted to give him a message. This old woman was to say to him that the lady now recognized that his love was true, that she had decided to grant him that which she had for so long refused. She had found a way of leaving the house and going to a place where he could meet her alone. The gentleman, who had been bled from the arm that morning, was restored to health far more effectively by this message than any medicine or blood-letting. He sent word that he would not fail to appear at the appointed hour, and that she had performed a manifest miracle, for by uttering a single word she had cured a man of a disease for which all the doctors had failed to find a remedy.

When the night came which he had so long desired, the gentleman went to the appointed place. His happiness was complete, so complete that it could not increase but only come to an early end. Having arrived, he did not have long to wait before the lady whom he loved more than he loved his soul came to join him. He did not waste time making speeches. For the fire burning within him drove him on to seek that which he scarcely believed was within his power. Love and pleasure intoxicated him beyond all bounds, and fondly believing that in his reach he had a remedy to save his life, he merely brought about his early death. In his passion for his mistress he was oblivious of himself, and did not notice that the bandages of his arm were coming undone. The recent wound opened and the blood gushed forth so profusely that the poor gentleman was soaked in it. Feeling himself overcome by weakness, he thought it must be due to his excesses, and decided to return home. Then Love, who had united them too closely together, brought about their separation, for as the gentleman departed from his mistress, his soul departed from his body. The flow of blood was so great that he fell dead at the feet of his lady. And she, beside herself with grief, stood aghast as she pondered the loss of so perfect a lover whose death she alone had caused. [She considered too the shame] which would remain upon her if the body was found in her house, and in order to conceal what had happened she carried the corpse into the street with the aid of a trusted chambermaid. There, unable to leave the dead man, she took his sword, determined to share his fate. The cause of the disaster had been the heart, and the heart it was that she punished as she plunged the blade into her breast and fell dead upon the body of her lover. The next morning her mother and father came upon this pitiful spectacle as they left the house. And after mourning their loss in the fashion it deserved they buried the couple in one and the same grave.

*

'So you see, Ladies, that the extremes of love lead to [extremes of misfortune].'

'It gives me great pleasure,' said Simontaut, 'to hear about a love which is so equal that when one partner dies the other no longer desires to live. And if God had given me the grace to find such a lady, then I believe no man would have loved more perfectly than I.'

'Nevertheless,' said Parlamente, 'I'm quite sure that love has never blinded you so much as it did the young man in the story. You would have bandaged your arm better than he did! The time has passed when men give up their lives for ladies.'

'But not the time when ladies give up the lives of their servants for the sake of their own pleasures!' said Simontaut.

'I think,' said Ennasuite, 'that there is not a woman in the world who would derive pleasure from seeing a man die, even if he were a mortal enemy. But if men actually want to kill themselves, there's nothing ladies can do to stop them.'

'Nevertheless,' said Saffredent, 'if a lady refuses to give bread to some poor wretch dying of hunger, then she is regarded as a murderess.'

'If your requests were as reasonable as those of the poor begging bread in their hour of need,' said Oisille, 'then a lady would indeed be extremely cruel to refuse them. But the malady *you* are talking of only kills those, thank God, who would die anyway within the year!'

'Madame,' answered Saffredent, 'I cannot think that a man can have any greater need than that which makes him forget all other needs. Indeed, when love is truly great, a lover knows no other bread, knows no other meat, than a glance, a word from his beloved.'

'You would soon change your mind,' Oisille said, 'if anyone ever left you without anything to eat but that kind of food!'

'I grant,' he replied, 'that the body might grow weak, but the heart and the will, never.'

'In that case,' said Parlamente, 'God has been very gracious to you – since He has led you to love a lady who gives so little satisfaction that you are obliged to console yourself with food and drink, an obligation you fulfil very well, it seems to me. So you really ought to give thanks to God for such sweet cruelty!'

'I am so used to feeding on sorrow, that I am beginning to count as blessings sufferings that others complain about!' said Saffredent.

'But perhaps,' said Longarine, 'it is in fact [your] moans and complaints which keep you away from the very company where, were you contented, you would be perfectly welcome. Nothing is so irritating as an importunate lover!'

'As a cruel lady, you should say!' said Simontaut.

'It appears to me,' said Oisille, 'that if we wanted to listen till Simontaut had given us all his arguments on this subject which so concerns him, we might find ourselves here till compline instead of vespers. So let us go and thank God that this day has passed without more serious dispute.'

Oisille rose first and the others followed her. Simontaut and Longarine went on arguing, with the greatest civility, until Simontaut, without drawing his sword, prevailed and demonstrated that the greater the force of passion, the greater the need of the victim. On this note they all went into the church, where the monks were waiting for them.

When vespers were over they went to supper, just as hungry for conversation as for food. Their discussions continued till they were all seated around the table, and went on through the evening until Oisille suggested that they should all retire to give their minds a rest. The first five days had been filled with so many excellent stories, she said, that she feared the sixth day may not be the same, for even if they were to invent some stories, it would be impossible to tell better stories than the true ones which they had already told to one another. However, Geburon assured her that as long as the world endured there would be plenty of things worth recounting. 'For the wickedness of evil men is the same now as it always has been. So too is the goodness of good men. As long as good and evil reign on the earth, the earth will be filled with new deeds, even though it is written that there is nothing new under the sun. For [we], who have not been called to God's privy council and who are ignorant of the first causes of things, [find all things new, and the less we are able or willing to do them ourselves, the more wonderful we find them]. Therefore have no fear that the days that are left will not be as good as those that have passed, and think only of doing your duty as best you can.'

Oisille said that she commended herself to God, and in His name bade them a good night. Thus the whole company retired, bringing the fifth day to a close.

END OF THE FIFTH DAY

SIXTH DAY

PROLOGUE

The next morning Oisille rose earlier than usual to prepare her reading in the hall. The rest of the company, having been told of this, and anxious to hear her excellent teaching, dressed themselves with such haste that they kept her waiting hardly at all. Oisille knew the fervour in their hearts, and read to them the Epistle of Saint John the Evangelist, an Epistle full only of love, because every morning till then she had been reading the Epistle of Saint Paul to the Romans. The assembled ladies and gentlemen found this such sweet nourishment that although they listened for half an hour longer than usual, it seemed to them that they had been there no more than a quarter of an hour. Afterwards they went to the contemplation of the mass, where they commended themselves to the Holy Spirit in order that they might that day satisfy those who would listen to them. After they had eaten, and rested for a while, they went off to spend their day in the accustomed manner. Madame Oisille asked them who should begin the day's stories. Longarine replied: 'I call upon Madame Oisille. The lesson she read us this morning was so beautiful that she cannot fail to tell us a story worthy to complete the glory she won this morning.'

'I regret,' replied Oisille, 'that I cannot this afternoon tell you anything as rewarding as what I told you this morning. But at least the intention of the story that I shall tell you will not be out of keeping with the teaching of Holy Scripture, where it is written "Trust not in princes, nor in the son of man, in whom there is no salvation." And, so that you will not forget this truth for want of an example, I am going to give you one which is true and so fresh to the memory that those who witnessed the pitiful sight I shall recount have hardly yet dried their tears.'

STORY FIFTY-ONE

The Duke of Urbino, called the Prefect, who had married the sister of the first Duke of Mantua, had a son of eighteen to twenty years of age, and this young man was in love with a girl from a good and noble family. She was the sister of the abbé de Farse. Since he did not have the freedom to speak with her as he would have liked (such was the local custom), the young man drew on the help of a gentleman in his service. This gentleman happened to be in love with a beautiful and virtuous young woman in the service of the Duchess, and it was through this young woman that the Duke's son declared his great love to his beloved. The poor young woman saw no wrong in acting as messenger, and was glad to be of help, since she believed the young man's intentions to be so good and noble that he could not possibly have desires which she could not honourably convey. But the Duke himself was more concerned with furthering the interests of his family than with pure and noble love. He was afraid lest his son run the risk of a commitment to marriage. So he had a keen watch put on him, and it was reported to him that the Duchess's lady-in-waiting was involved in the carrying of letters on behalf of his son to the girl with whom he was so much in love. The Duke was so enraged that he resolved at once to put a stop to it. But he could not hide his anger sufficiently to prevent the Duchess's lady-in-waiting hearing about it. She was overcome with terror, for she knew the extent of the Duke's wickedness and that it was as great as his conscience was small. So she approached the Duchess to beg her for permission [to retire to a place away from court until the Duke's fury had subsided. But the Duchess told her that she would try to discover her husband's mood before giving her permission.] However, the Duchess very soon discovered how the Duke felt from the malevolent way he spoke of the affair, so not only did she grant permission to her lady-in-waiting, but also advised her to withdraw to a convent till the storm had passed. This the girl did with as much secrecy as possible, but not with sufficient secrecy to prevent the Duke finding out. Putting on a good-humoured air, he approached his wife and asked her where the young woman had gone. She, thinking that he knew all about it, told him what he wanted. When he heard, he pretended to be distressed, and said that there was no need to go to such lengths. He did not mean the girl any harm, and his wife must call her back, because the gossip would not do them any good. She replied that since the poor girl was so miserable because she had lost favour, then it would be better for the moment if she did not appear in his presence. But he would not listen to any of her objections, and ordered her to have the girl brought back at once. Accordingly the Duchess made the Duke's wishes known. But the girl was not reassured, and begged her mistress not to make her take the risk. She knew very well, she said, that the Duke was less inclined to grant pardons than he pretended. Nevertheless, the Duchess assured her that she would not come to any harm, and vouched for it on her life and honour. The girl knew that her mistress was very fond of her and would not readily deceive her, so she took her promise on trust, feeling, moreover, that the Duke would never go against a promise pledged on his wife's life and honour. Thus it was that she went back with the Duchess. But immediately the Duke was informed, he came into his wife's room. No sooner had he set eyes on the girl than he said to his wife, 'How can this creature dare to come back?' Thereupon he turned to his gentlemen, and ordered them to arrest the girl and throw her into prison. The poor Duchess, who had persuaded the girl on her word to come out of her place of refuge, was overcome by despair and threw herself on her knees in front of him. She besought him for the sake of his own honour and for the sake of his family not to do such a thing, for it was she herself who, in order to obey him, had brought the girl back from her safe hiding-place. But none of her pleas, nor any of the arguments she could think of, were able to soften his hard heart, or overthrow his stubborn desire to avenge himself upon her. Without so much as a word in reply, he left the room, and ignoring all legal forms, God and the honour of his house, he had the girl cruelly put to death by hanging.

I could not begin to describe the distress of the Duchess. I can only say that it was such as befitted a lady of honour and of noble heart who was obliged to witness the death of a person whom she had wished only to save and to whom she had pledged her word. Even less could one express the grief of the young man who had been her devoted servant. He took it upon himself to do everything in his power to save his beloved's life, even offering to sacrifice his own in her place. But nothing could move the Duke's heart to pity. His sole pleasure was to wreak vengeance on the people he hated. And so it was that this innocent young woman was put to death by this cruel Duke, against all laws of honour and justice, and to the great sorrow of all who knew her.

*

'Ladies, observe the effects of wickedness when combined with power.'

'I had heard,' said Longarine, 'that the Italians are subject to three vices above all others, but I wouldn't have thought that cruelty and the spirit of revenge would have gone so far as to put someone to death in such a cruel manner for such a trivial reason.'

Saffredent said to her, laughing: 'Longarine, you've mentioned one of the three vices. We must be told about the other two.'

'If you don't know what they are, then I'll tell you. But I'm sure that you do know what they are, all of them.'

'Do you mean by that,' said Saffredent, 'that you think I'm full of vice myself?'

'Not at all,' she replied. 'Just that you know all about the ugliness of vice, so you are able to avoid it better than anyone else.'

'There's no need to be surprised by this act of cruelty we've just heard of,' said Simontaut. 'People who've travelled through Italy have seen the most incredible things, things which make this a mere peccadillo by comparison.'

'Yes, indeed,' said Geburon. 'When Rivolta was taken by the French there was an Italian captain whom everybody regarded as a valiant comrade-at-arms and who came across a man lying dead, a man who was only an enemy in the sense that he had been a Guelph, while the captain was a Ghibelline. He tore the dead man's heart out of his chest, roasted it over a charcoal fire, and ate it. When some people asked what it tasted like, he replied that he had never tasted a more delicious or enjoyable morsel. Not content with this fine deed, he killed the dead man's wife, who was pregnant, tore out the fruit of her womb and dashed it against the battlements. He then filled the corpses of both husband and wife with oats and gave them to his horses. So judge for yourselves whether a man like that would be capable of hanging a girl whom he suspected of doing something he didn't like.'

'It would seem,' said Ennasuite, 'that the Duke of Urbino was more worried about his son marrying somebody poor than about finding him a wife to his liking.'

'One cannot doubt, I think,' answered Simontaut, 'that it is the nature of Italians to love things created merely for the service of nature more than nature itself.'

'It's even worse than that,' said Hircan, 'because they make their God out of things that are against nature.'

'Those are the sins I was referring to,' said Longarine. 'Everyone knows that to love money, unless one is using it to some end, is idolatry.'

Parlamente said that Saint Paul had not been unaware of the Italians' vices, nor indeed of the vices of all those who regard themselves as rising so high above their fellows in honour, wisdom and human reason, upon which they rely so heavily, that they fail to render to God the glory that is His due. Consequently the Almighty, jealous of His honour, makes all those who think themselves better endowed with sense than others more insensate than maddened beasts, causing them to show by acts against nature that they are reprobate.

Longarine interrupted to point out that that was the third sin the Italians were subject to.

'Now that comment gives me a great deal of satisfaction,' said Nomerfide, 'because it means that the people we usually think of as being the greatest and most subtle speakers are punished by being made more stupid than the beasts. So one must conclude that people like myself who are lowly, humble and of little ability are filled with the wisdom of the angels.'

'I can assure you,' said Oisille, 'that your view is not far removed from my own. For no one is more ignorant than the person who thinks he knows.'

'I have never seen,' said Geburon, 'a mocker who was never mocked, nor a deceiver who was never himself deceived, nor arrogance that was never in the end humiliated.'

'That reminds me of a practical joke I once heard of, which I would have been pleased to tell you about, if it were decent,' said Simontaut.

'Well, since we're here to tell the truth,' said Oisille, 'whatever it may be, I nominate you to tell it to us for our next story.'

'Then since it is my turn,' answered Simontaut, 'I will tell you.'

STORY FIFTY-TWO*

Near to the town of Alençon there lived a gentleman by the name of the Seigneur de Tirelière. One morning he walked from his house into town. It was not far, and as it was freezing extremely hard, he thought the walk would warm him up. So off he went, not forgetting to take with him the heavy coat lined with fox fur which he owned. When he had carried out the business he had to do in town, he met a friend of his, an advocate named Antoine Bacheré. After chatting for a while about business matters, he said that he felt like getting a good dinner – provided that it was at someone else's expense. As they were talking this over, they sat down in front of an apothecary's shop. Now in the shop was a serving lad, who, overhearing what they were saying, thought it would be a splendid idea to give them a dinner they would not forget. So he went out of the shop into a side-street where everyone went to relieve their natural needs, and found a large lump of excrement standing on its end, frozen solid and looking just like a little sugar loaf. He quickly wrapped it up in a nice piece of white paper, just as he did in the shop to attract customers. Then he hid it in his sleeve, and as he was going past the gentleman and his lawyer friend, he pretended to drop it near them. Then he went into a house, as if he had been going to deliver it. The Seigneur de Tirelière lost no time in picking up what he believed to be a nice little sugar loaf. Just as he was doing so, the apothecary's lad came back, looking around and asking if anyone had seen his piece of sugar. Our gentleman, thinking he had properly outwitted the lad, hurried off to a nearby inn, saying to his comrade as they went: 'We'll pay for our dinner at the lad's expense!' When they got inside he ordered some good meat, some bread, and a good wine, thinking he now had adequate means to pay. As he ate and warmed himself by the fire, his sugar loaf began to thaw out.

* The de Thou manuscript has a version of this tale which is different in style and narrative organization, although the events described are essentially the same.

The stench filled the whole room. The gentleman, from under whose coat the foul smell was issuing, started to get angry with the serving wench: 'You are the most disgusting people in this town I've ever seen! You or your children have littered the whole room with shit!'

The wench replied: 'By Saint Peter, there's no muck in this house, unless it's you that brought it in!'

At this point, not being able to stand the smell any longer, they got up and went over to the fire. The gentleman got out his handkerchief – now stained with the thawed out sugar loaf! He opened his coat – the one lined with fox fur. It was ruined! All he could say to his companion was: 'It's that wretched apothecary's lad! We thought we'd tricked him and he's well and truly got his own back!'

And, after paying the bill, they left somewhat less pleased with themselves than when they had come.

*

'Well, Ladies, that is the sort of thing that often happens to people who enjoy playing tricks like the Seigneur de Tirelière. If he hadn't wanted to eat at someone else's expense, he wouldn't have ended up having such a disgusting meal at his own. I'm afraid my story wasn't a very clean one! But you did give me leave to tell the truth. And that is what I've done, my aim being to show that when a deceiver is himself deceived, no one is very sorry.'

'People generally say that words themselves never stink,' said Hircan, 'but those about whom they were uttered didn't get off so lightly as far as smell was concerned!'

'It is true,' said Oisille, 'that words like that do not smell, but there are other words, words referred to as disgusting, which have [such] an evil odour that the soul is far more disturbed than is the body smelling something like the sugar loaf in your story.'

'Tell me, I beg you,' said Hircan, 'what these words are, which you know to be so foul that they make an honest woman sick in her heart and in her soul.'

'It would be a fine thing,' said Oisille, 'if I uttered words which I would advise no other woman to say!'

'By these very words,' said Saffredent, 'I know what these terms are which women who want to appear modest don't generally use! But I would like to ask everyone here why it is that if they daren't actually speak about such things, they are so ready to laugh when they hear others speaking about them?'

'It isn't that we laugh because we hear these fine words,' replied Parlamente. 'But the fact is that everyone is inclined to laugh when they see somebody fall over or when somebody says something unintentional, as often happens, even to the most modest and best spoken of ladies, when they make a slip of the tongue and say one word instead of another. But when you men speak amongst one another in a disgusting fashion, out of sheer wickedness and in full knowledge of what you are doing, I know of no decent woman who would not be [so] horrified that not only would she not want to listen, but would want to avoid the very company of such people.'

'It's true,' said Geburon. 'I've seen women make the sign of the cross when they hear [such] words, and go on doing so until the speaker stopped repeating them.'

'Yes,' said Simontaut, 'but how many times do they hide behind their masks, so that they can have the freedom to laugh just as much as they pretend to complain?'

'Even that would be better,' said Parlamente, 'than letting everyone know that they found such language amusing.'

'So you would praise hypocrisy in ladies, just as much as virtue itself?' said Dagoucin.

'Virtue would be better,' said Longarine, 'but when it is lacking, one must use hypocrisy, just as people wear high shoes to cover up the fact that they are not very tall. If we can hide our imperfections, even that is something worth doing.'

'On my oath,' said Hircan, 'it would be better to show a little imperfection sometimes, rather than to cover it up so carefully under a veil of virtue!'

'True enough,' said Ennasuite. 'Honour can be put on like a borrowed garment, but the borrower will be dishonoured when he has to give it back. I could mention a certain lady who, precisely because she made too much effort to conceal a trivial fault, ended up falling into a much more serious one.'

'I've a good idea who you mean,' said Hircan, 'but at least don't give her name away.'

'Ah! You have permission to speak next,' said Geburon, 'on

condition that after telling us the story you will tell us the names of those involved, and we will swear never to reveal them.'

'I give you my word,' said Ennasuite, 'for there is nothing that cannot be recounted in an honourable fashion.'

STORY FIFTY-THREE

King Francis I was staying at a certain fine château. He had gone there accompanied by a small party in order to do some hunting and to relax. In the party was the Prince de Belhoste, a man as noble, virtuous, wise and handsome as any at court. He had married a woman who was not from one of the great families.* But he loved her and treated her as well as any husband can treat a wife, and placed such trust in her [that] when he fell in love with other women he made no attempt to conceal the fact from her. For he knew that he and she were of one will. Now this Prince entered into rather too intimate a friendship with a widow called Madame de Neufchâtel, a lady who had the reputation of being the most beautiful woman a man could ever wish to behold. If the Prince loved her greatly, his wife loved her none the less. Indeed she often invited her to eat with her, and found her so modest and honourable that, far from being upset that her husband should be so fond of her, she was glad to see him addressing his attentions to someone so well endowed with honour and virtue. This friendship lasted for a long time, and the Prince was as active in managing the affairs of Madame de Neufchâtel as he was in managing his own, and the Princess, his wife, did likewise. But Madame de Neufchâtel's beauty attracted many great lords and noble gentlemen, all of whom made great efforts to obtain her favour. Some did so out of love for her and for no other reason, and some sought her hand in marriage because she happened to be very rich as well as very beautiful. Amongst these suitors was a young man named the Seigneur de Chariots. He pressed his suit so hard that he spent all the time he could by her side, staying near her the whole day long, and never failing to be present at her levee and her *couchée*. The Prince de Belhoste was not at all pleased by this, as it seemed to him that a man who was of such poor origins and such inelegant appearance did not merit such a courteous and gracious reception. He frequently reproached the lady on

* De Thou has: *was not of great beauty*.

this score, but she was a duke's daughter, and excused herself by saying that she was accustomed to speak to everybody, whoever they might be, and that their own friendship would be all the better concealed if she did not speak to any man more than to another. But after a certain length of time, this [Seigneur] de Chariots advanced so far in his suit that, more because of his persistence than because of any love between them, Madame de Neufchâtel promised to marry him on condition that he would not press her to make the marriage public until her daughters too were married. Thereafter, without any scruple of conscience, the Seigneur started going at all hours to the lady's room, and there was never anyone there except a woman attendant and another man who knew of the affair. When the Prince saw that the gentleman was becoming a more and more frequent visitor to the house of the woman with whom he himself was in love, he found it so distasteful that he could not help saying to her:

'I have always treasured your honour as that of my own sister. And you know that I have always addressed myself honourably to you, and that it gives me great pleasure to love a lady who is as modest and virtuous as you are. But if I thought that somebody else, without meriting it, had by his importunity obtained that which I myself would never ask for against your will – then it would be unbearable for me, and none the less dishonourable for you. I say all this to you because you are young and beautiful, and because hitherto you have enjoyed such a good reputation. But you are beginning to be the subject of very unpleasant rumours, for even though this man is not your equal in power, knowledge and grace, it would have been better for you to marry him than to make everyone suspect you of misconduct. So, tell me, I beg you, if you intend to grant him your love, for I do not wish to be his associate. If such is indeed your intention, then I shall leave him entirely to you and shall give up the goodwill which hitherto I have borne you!'

The poor lady began to weep, fearing that she would lose his friendship. She swore that she would rather die than marry the gentleman. But he was, she said, so importunate that she could not prevent him coming to her room at the hour everybody else came.

'I am not talking about the times when everyone else comes,' replied the Prince. 'I could go then as well, and everyone can see what you are doing. But I have heard that he comes to your room after you have gone to bed. I find this so extraordinary that if you continue such behaviour and do not announce your marriage to him, you are the most dishonoured woman I have ever heard of!'

She swore on all the oaths she knew that she regarded him neither as a husband nor as a lover, but as the most importunate gentleman there ever was.

'Since it seems to be the case,' the Prince said, 'that the man is annoying you, I promise that I shall get rid of him for you!'

'What!' she exclaimed. 'You mean you'll kill him?'

'No, no,' said the Prince, 'but I shall let him know that the royal household is no place for ladies to be brought into dishonour. I swear, by the bond of love that binds me to you, that if after I have spoken with him he does not mend his ways, then I shall punish him so severely that he will be an example to the others.'

So saying, he went, and as he left the room, he met the Seigneur de Chariots who, not unexpectedly, was on his way in. He told him exactly what you have just heard him promise to tell him, assuring him that the very next time he was found there outside the hours when it is proper for gentlemen to visit ladies, he would give him a fright he would never forget. Furthermore, he warned, the lady in question was of too good a family to be played with in this fashion. The young nobleman insisted that he had only ever been to visit her in the same way as all the other men, and gave him leave to do his worst, if he should find him there for any other end.

Some days later, thinking that the Prince would have forgotten all about his threat, the young man went along in the evening to see his lady and stayed quite late. The same evening the Prince remarked to his wife that the Dame de Neufchâtel had a bad cold. His good wife asked him to go and visit her on behalf of them both and to send her apologies for not going herself, as she had some urgent matter to see to. The Prince waited till the King was in bed, and then went to pay his respects to his lady. But he was just going up the staircase to her room, when he met a valet de chambre coming down, who, on being asked what his mistress was doing, swore that she was in bed and fast asleep. The Prince went down again, but strongly suspected that the valet was lying; so he glanced behind him and saw the fellow making his way back upstairs in great haste. He walked round in the courtyard at the bottom of the stairs to see if he would return. A quarter of an hour later he saw him come down and look all round to see who was in the courtyard. The Prince now concluded that the Seigneur de Chariots was in his lady's room and that he did not dare come down for fear of being seen. This just made him go on walking round longer still. It occurred to him that there was a window in his lady's room, overlooking the garden. It was not very high, and he remembered the old proverb, 'If you can't get out by the door, get out by the window.' So he immediately called one of his own valets de chambre, and said: 'Go into that garden round the back, and if you see a young nobleman climbing out of the window, wait till he gets one foot on the ground, then draw your sword, rattle it against the wall and shout "Kill him! kill him!", but take care not to touch him.'

The valet went off as he had been ordered, and the Prince went on walking round in the courtyard till about three hours after midnight. When the Seigneur de Chariots was told that the Prince was still outside, he decided to climb out through the window. Having first thrown out his cloak, he jumped, with the help of his friends, into the garden. As soon as the Prince's valet de chambre caught sight of him, he made a great clatter with his sword, as he had been instructed, and shouted 'Kill him! kill him!' At this, the poor young gentleman, who thought it was the Prince himself, was so terrified that he ran off as fast as he possibly could, without even remembering to pick up his cloak. The archers on watch were astonished to see him running off like this, but he did not dare explain to them. All he could do was beg them to open the gates for him, or to let him stay in their quarters till day came. And since they did not have the keys to the gate, it was in the archers' quarters that he stayed.

Then at last the Prince went home to bed, and finding his wife asleep, woke her up. 'Guess what time it is, dear wife,' he said.

'I haven't heard the clock strike since I came to bed,' she replied.

'It's after three o'clock in the morning!'

'Holy Jesus!' she exclaimed. 'And where have you been all this time, Monsieur? I do hope it's not going to damage your health!'

'Staying up will never make me ill, my love,' said the Prince, 'so long as I stop people who try to deceive me from getting *their* sleep!'

As he spoke he broke into such a hearty laugh that his wife begged him to tell her what it was all about. So, showing her the wolf-skin cloak his valet had brought back with them, he explained the whole story. Then, after laughing together for a while at the young man's expense, they went to sleep, and slept sweetly and restfully, while the other two in their fear and anxiety lest their affair be revealed, spent the night in toil and turmoil. The next day, however, the young gentleman presented himself at the Prince's levee in order to beg him not to expose him and to ask him to have his cloak returned. The Prince merely pretended that he had no idea what he was talking about, and kept up the pretence so convincingly that the young man did not know where he stood. But he learnt a lesson he had not been expecting, for the Prince assured him that if he was ever found in the lady's room again, he would tell the King and have him banished from court.

*

'Ladies, I ask you to judge whether it would not have been better for this poor lady to have been completely honest with the man who did her the great honour of loving and respecting her, than to force him by her dissimulation to find her out in a way that brought so much shame on her own head.'

'She knew,' said Geburon, 'that if she confessed the truth, she would forfeit his good opinion entirely, and this was the last thing she wanted to do.'

'It seems to me,' said Longarine, 'that since she had freely chosen a husband to suit her whim, she shouldn't have been concerned about losing the friendship of other men.'

'I really think,' said Parlamente, 'that if she had dared to announce the marriage, she would have been quite contented with her husband. But, because she wanted to keep it secret until her daughters were married, she didn't want to lose such an honourable means of covering it up.'

'It wasn't that at all,' Saffredent replied. 'The fact is that women are so ambitious that one man isn't enough for them. I've heard that the wisest of them like three: one for honour, one for profit and one for pleasure! All three of them think they are the most favoured, but the first two are only retained for the benefit of the third!'

'You're speaking of those women who possess neither love nor honour,' said Oisille.

'Madame,' came the reply, 'there exist women who are as I have described, women whom *you* regard as the most honourable women in the country.'

'You may rely upon it,' said Hircan, 'a cunning woman will always find a way of surviving when everyone else would die of hunger.'

'But when their cunning is found out, the discovery is death to them,' said Longarine.

'Not at all,' said Simontaut. 'It is life itself for them, because it's no small distinction in their eyes to be regarded as more cunning than their sisters. And the reputation of being "cunning" which they earn themselves at men's expense will more readily attract men into obedient servitude than will their physical beauty. For to conduct their liaison with cunning is one of the greatest pleasures lovers can have.'

'What you're talking about,' said Ennasuite, 'is base love, because true love does not need to be covered up.'

'Oh! I beg you, put that notion out of your head,' said Dagoucin. 'The more precious the drug, the less it should be exposed, for one must beware of the malice of those who take account solely of external signs, signs that are the same, be one's love [base] or be it true. One must hide these signs just as much when one's love is virtuous as when it is not, in order not to risk being wrongly judged by those who cannot believe that a man can love a lady honourably. For, being slaves to pleasure themselves, they believe everyone else is also. But if we were all of good faith, neither words nor glances would be disguised, at least not from those who would rather die than think evil thoughts.'

'Your philosophy, Dagoucin, I can tell you, is so high-flown that there isn't a single man here who either understands it or believes it,' said Hircan. 'It seems that you would have us believe that men are either angels, devils or made of stone!'

'I know indeed,' replied Dagoucin, 'that men are men and subject to all the passions. Nevertheless, there are some who would rather die than that for their pleasure the lady whom they love should do anything against her conscience.'

'To say they would rather die is saying a lot,' said Geburon, 'and I wouldn't believe it, even if I heard it coming from the most austere monk in the world!'

'I'm quite sure,' said Hircan, 'that there isn't a single man in this world whose desires are not in fact exactly the opposite of what Dagoucin says. It's just that they cry sour grapes when the object of their desires is beyond their grasp!'

'But,' said Nomerfide, 'I think this Prince's wife must have been pleased that her husband found out what women are really like.'

'I assure you that wasn't the case,' said Ennasuite. 'On the contrary she was very distressed, because of her affection for the lady in question.'

'I'd rather have the lady who laughed when her husband kissed her chambermaid,' said Saffredent.

'You shall tell us that story,' said Ennasuite. 'You may take my place.'

'Although it's a short story,' began Saffredent, 'I'll tell it to you, because I'd rather make you laugh for a brief while, than make you weep at length.'

STORY FIFTY-FOUR

Somewhere between the Pyrenees and the Alps there once lived a nobleman by the name of Thogas. He had a wife, children, a fine house and so much wealth and pleasure that he had every good reason to be content with life. Apart from one thing. He was subject to great pain beneath the roots of his hairs. The pain was so severe that the doctors advised him to stop sleeping with his wife. She agreed to this willingly, concerned as she was solely for the health and well-being of her husband. So she had her bed placed in the other corner of the room, directly opposite her husband's, so that neither of them could put their heads out without seeing one another. Now this lady had two chambermaids, and when she and the Seigneur de Thogas had gone to their beds, these two maids would often hold a candle for them while they each read some bedside book. To be more precise, the young one held the candle for the master of the house and the other one held the candle for his wife. Noticing that his chambermaid was younger and more attractive than his wife, Thogas began to take great delight in looking at her, and would interrupt his reading in order to talk to her. His wife could hear them talking, but considered it a good thing that the servants provided her husband with some entertainment, being sure that he loved nobody but her. However, one evening, when they had been reading for longer than usual, the lady of the house glanced along the side of her husband's bed where the maid was holding the candle. She could only see the girl from behind, and her husband she could not see at all. But the side of the chimney, which came out in front of his bed, was white, and reflected the light from the candle. On this wall were clearly cast the shadows of the faces of her husband and the maid, and the wife could distinguish quite plainly what the two were doing – whether they were moving apart, getting closer together, or laughing. The husband, all unawares, and quite sure his wife could not see them, kissed the girl. The first time, the wife put up with it without saying anything. But when she saw that the shadows were coming together rather frequently, she was afraid that there was some reality hidden behind them. So she started to laugh out loud, with the result that the two shadows, startled by the laughter, separated from one another. The husband asked her what she was laughing about and would she kindly share the joke.

'My dear,' she replied, 'I'm such a silly thing that I laugh at my own shadow!'

Question her as he might, the husband could not persuade her to say any more. But he gave up kissing the shadowy face on the wall, all the same.

*

'And that is what you reminded me of, when you were talking about the wife who was so fond of the lady adored by her husband.'

'On my honour,' exclaimed Ennasuite, 'if my chambermaid had done such a thing, I would have got up and put the candle out on her nose!'

'You're very ruthless,' said Hircan. 'But it would not have done much good if your husband and the maid had turned round on you and given you a thorough beating. It's not worth making a fuss about a kiss. And the wife would have done better to have said nothing, and let her husband have a little amusement. It might have cured him of his ailment.'

'But,' said Parlamente, 'she was afraid that his little diversion would lead to something that would only aggravate his condition.'

'She was not,' said Oisille, 'one of those against whom Our Lord speaks, saying "We have mourned to you, and you have not wept. We have sung unto you and you have not danced." For, when her husband was sick she wept, and when he was happy she laughed. Thus should all women share equally the good and the bad, the joy and the sorrow, that befalls their husbands, and love, serve and obey him, even as the Church serves and obeys Jesus Christ.'

'So it follows, Ladies,' said Parlamente, 'that our husbands should be towards us as Christ is towards his Church.'

'And so we are,' replied Saffredent. 'What is more, we go

further, if such a thing is possible. Christ only died once, but we die every day for our wives!'

'Die!' exclaimed Longarine. 'It seems to me that you and the rest of you here are worth a good deal more now than you were when you were married!'

'And I know why,' said Saffredent. 'It's because our worth is put to the test so often. And our shoulders certainly feel the strain after being in harness for so long!'

'If you had been obliged,' said Ennasuite, 'to wear armour for a whole month and sleep on the bare ground, you'd be only too glad to get back to your good wife's bed and wear that "harness" you're complaining about now. But they say that people can put up with anything except comfort, and that no one appreciates peace and quiet until they lose it.'

'This [good] woman, who laughed when her husband was happy, had learnt to find peace everywhere,' [said Oisille].

'I think she liked peace and quiet better than she liked her husband,' said Longarine, 'seeing that whatever he did, she didn't take it to heart.'

'But she did take to heart anything that could have damaged his health or weighed on his conscience,' said Parlamente, 'though at the same time she didn't care to waste time about things of little importance.'

'You make me laugh when you mention conscience,' said Simontaut. 'Conscience is something I would rather a woman never troubled herself about.'

'It would serve you right,' said Nomerfide, 'to have a wife like the one who, after her husband's death, turned out to be more concerned about his cash than his conscience.'

'Then will you tell us the story,' asked Saffredent, 'if I invite you to be the next speaker?'

'I hadn't intended to tell such a short story,' replied Nomerfide, 'but since it is to the point, I will do so.'

STORY FIFTY-FIVE

In the town of Saragossa there was a rich merchant. Seeing that his death was near, and that he could not take his wealth with him – wealth which perhaps he had not acquired altogether honestly – he thought that he might make some amends for his sins by making some little donation or other to God. As if God grants his grace in return for money! Anyway, he made arrangements regarding his house, and gave instructions that a fine Spanish horse of his should be sold, and the proceeds distributed to the poor [mendicants]. It was his wife whom he requested to carry out these instructions as soon as possible after his death. No sooner was the burial over and the first few tears shed, than the wife, who to say the least was no more stupid than Spanish women in general, approached her servant, who had also heard her husband's wishes.

'I think I've lost enough,' said she, 'in losing my husband whom I loved so dearly, without losing his property as well. Not that I want to disobey his instructions. In fact, I want to carry out his wishes even better than he intended. You see, the poor man was so taken in by those greedy priests. He thought he would make a sacrifice to God after his death by giving away a sum of money, not a single écu of which he would have given away during his lifetime, however great the need, as you know. So I've made up my mind that we shall do what he instructed us to do after his death – indeed we shall do better, and do what he *would* have done himself, had he lived a fortnight longer. Only not a soul must hear of it!'

The servant gave his word, and she went on: 'You will go and sell his horse, and when they ask you how much you want, you will say one ducat. But I also have an excellent cat that I want to sell, and you will sell it at the same time, for ninety-nine ducats. Together the horse and the cat will fetch a hundred ducats, which is what my husband wanted for the horse alone.'

So the servant promptly went off to do as his mistress requested. As he was leading the horse across the square, carrying the cat in his arms, he was approached by a certain nobleman who had seen the horse before and was interested in acquiring it. Having asked the price, the nobleman received the answer: 'One ducat!'

'I should be obliged if you would be serious,' said the man.

'I assure you, Monsieur, that the price is one ducat. You have to buy the cat with it, of course. I can't let the cat go for less than ninety-nine ducats!'

The nobleman thought this was a fair enough bargain. On the spot he paid one ducat for the horse, and ninety-nine for the cat, as requested, and led his purchases away. The servant took the money back to his mistress, who was extremely pleased, and lost no time in giving away the proceeds from the sale of the horse to the poor mendicants. As for the rest, that went to provide for the wants of herself and her children.

*

'Well, what do you think of her? Wasn't she wiser than her husband, and wasn't she just as much concerned about his conscience as she was about doing well for her family?'

'I think she loved her husband,' said Parlamente, 'but realized that most men's minds wander when they're on their deathbeds, and knowing what his real intention was, she wanted to interpret his wishes for the benefit of their children, and I think it was very wise of her to do so.'

'What!' exclaimed Geburon. 'Do you not think it a grave error to fail to execute the last will and testament of deceased friends?'

'Indeed I do!' replied Parlamente. 'Provided the testator is sound of mind and not deranged.'

'Do you call it deranged,' replied Geburon, 'to give away one's goods to the Church and to the poor mendicants?'

'I do not call it deranged,' she replied, 'if a man distributes to the poor that which God has placed within his power. But to give away as alms what belongs to other people – I do not think that shows great wisdom. It's all too common to see the world's greatest usurers putting up ornate and impressive chapels, in the hope of appeasing God for hundreds of thousands of ducats' worth of sheer robbery by spending ten thousand ducats on a building! As if God didn't know how to count!'

'Indeed, I am frequently astonished,' said Oisille, 'that they presume to be able to appease God by means of the very things, which, when He came to earth, He condemned – things such as fine buildings, gilded ornaments, decorations and paintings. But, if they had rightly understood what God has said of human offerings in a certain passage – that "the sacrifice of God is a troubled spirit: a broken and contrite heart, O God, shalt thou not despise" – and again, in another passage, what Saint Paul has said – that "ye are the temple of the living God, in which He will dwell" – if they had rightly heard these words, I say, they would have taken pains to adorn their conscience while they were yet alive. They would not have waited till a time when man can do neither good nor evil. Nor would they have done what is even worse and placed upon those who remain the burden of dispensing their alms to those upon whom, during their lifetime, they did not even deign to look. But He who reads men's hearts will not be deceived, and He will judge them not only according to their works, but according to the faith and charity that they have shown towards Him.'

'Why is it, then,' said Geburon, 'that the Franciscans and Mendicants talk of nothing else when a man's dying but of how we ought to make bequests to their monasteries, with the assurance that they will send us to Paradise whether we want or not?'

'What, Geburon!' broke in Hircan. 'Have you forgotten your story about the Franciscans, that you're asking how men like that can possibly lie? I'll tell you, as far as I'm concerned, there's no one on this earth tells lies like they do. It may be that those who speak for the good of their community as a whole aren't to be criticized; but there are some who forget their vow of poverty in order to satisfy their own greed.'

'Hircan,' said Nomerfide, 'it sounds to me as if you have a particular instance in mind. Will you tell us about it, if it's worthy of the ladies and gentlemen here?'

'Certainly,' he replied, 'although it distresses me to have to talk about these people. I think they belong with those Virgil was referring to when he said to Dante, "Let us not speak of these; but look and pass." But to show you that they don't put aside their passions when they relinquish their worldly attire, I'll tell you what happened.'

STORY FIFTY-SIX

A French lady was passing through the town of Padua. Hearing that there was a Franciscan friar in the episcopal prison, and that everyone treated it as a great joke, she asked what it was all about. She was told that the friar in question was the elderly confessor of a highly devout and respectable widow with an only daughter. This lady was so fond of her daughter that she was prepared to do anything to provide her with a fortune and find her a good match. Seeing that her daughter was growing up, her constant concern was to find her someone who would live with them quietly and peacefully – in short, a person of as good a conscience as she considered herself to be. Now she had heard some foolish preacher say that it was better to do something wrong on the advice of the doctors of the Church, than to do a good act in the belief that one was inspired by the Holy Spirit. So she addressed herself to her fine father confessor, an already elderly man, who was a doctor of theology, and well regarded by the whole town as being a man of blameless reputation. She was sure that through his advice and through his prayers on her behalf she could not fail to find the security she desired for her daughter and herself. So she earnestly asked him to choose a husband for her daughter, the kind of husband he knew a God-fearing woman who cared for her honour ought to wish for. He replied that first of all he must seek the grace of the Holy Spirit through prayer and fasting, and that then, with God's guidance, he hoped to be able to find her what she requested. So off went the Franciscan to think it over.

Now he had been told by the good lady that she had saved five hundred ducats to give to the girl's future husband, and also that she would provide the couple with a house and furnishings, and keep them in food and clothing. And it occurred to him that among his younger brethren there was a good-looking, well-built fellow to whom he could give the pretty girl, the house, the furnishings, the food and the clothing, while he himself could take the five hundred ducats to assuage his own burning greed.

So he spoke to the young brother, and finding him in agreement, he went back to the girl's mother.

'I truly believe,' he announced, 'that God has sent His angel Raphael to me, even as He sent him to Tobias, so that he may find a perfect husband for your daughter. For I am able to tell you that I have [at hand] the most respectable young man in all Italy. He has on occasions seen your daughter, and is so much in love with her that, this very day, as I was at prayer, God sent him to me, and made known to me how much he desired this marriage. And I, who know his parents and family, and know that he is of distinguished lineage, have myself promised to speak to you on his behalf. There is, however, just one difficulty, which is known to me alone. It is that, desiring to save a friend whom another man was threatening to kill, this young man drew his sword to part them; but as fortune would have it, his friend killed the other man, so that the young man, although he himself struck not a single blow, has had to flee from his home town, because he was at the scene of the murder and had drawn his sword. On the advice of his parents he has sought refuge in this town, disguised as a student, and here he will remain until his parents have settled the affair, which he hopes they will have done very soon. For these reasons it is necessary that the marriage be concluded in secret, and that you should not object to his going out during the day to public lectures and returning in the evening to eat and sleep.'

'Monsieur,' the lady replied, 'I find that what you have to say is greatly to my advantage, for, at least, I shall have by me that which I love most in all the world.'

So the Franciscan acted as they had agreed and duly produced the young man for her, all dressed up in a crimson satin doublet. She was very pleased with what she saw. Indeed, no sooner had he arrived than they celebrated the betrothal, and no sooner had midnight sounded than they had mass said and the couple were married. Then they went to bed, and stayed there till the break of day, when the husband turned to his bride and said that to avoid being recognized he had to go back to his college. After putting on his crimson satin doublet, his long robe and of course his black silk cap, he came to say goodbye to his wife, who was still in bed. He assured her that he would come every evening and eat supper with her, but told her that she must not expect him for dinner. And so he went off for the day, leaving his wife thinking herself the happiest woman in the world for having found such a good match. The newly-wed young friar thus returned to his older brother, taking with him the five hundred ducats, as agreed in the marriage contract. And in the evening he went back to the poor girl who thought he was her husband. Indeed, she, and her mother, came to love him so much, that they would not have exchanged him for the greatest prince in the world.

They lived happily together in this way for some time. But God in His goodness takes pity on those who in all good faith have been deceived, and by His grace and goodness it came to pass one morning that the good lady and her daughter were overcome by a fervent desire to hear mass at the Franciscan church, and to visit the good father confessor, who in their eyes had been responsible for providing them with such a fine husband and son-in-law. As it happened, neither the confessor nor anyone else they knew was to be found on their arrival, so they contented themselves with listening to high mass, which was just beginning, while they waited to see if he would come. The young wife followed the divine service and its sacred mystery attentively. When the priest turned round to say his *Dominus vobiscum*, she was dumbfounded. It was her husband, or else someone very like him! However, she kept quiet for the time being, waiting for him to turn round again, so that she could get a better look. The second time there was no doubt, and she nudged her mother, who was plunged into meditation.

'Mother, alas! [what] do I see?'

'What is it that you see?' asked the mother.

'It is he, my husband, saying the mass, or somebody who is exactly like him!'

Her mother, who had not looked very carefully, replied:

'You should not let such ideas enter your head, my daughter. It is quite impossible that such holy people should commit such a fraud. You would be sinning greatly against God to entertain such an idea!'

All the same, the mother took care to have a good look, and when it came to the *Ite missa est*, she could see plainly enough that no two twin brothers were ever more alike. Even then, she was so simple-minded that she would readily have prayed, 'My God, keep me from believing my own eyes!' But as it was a matter which affected her daughter, she could not leave it without getting to the bottom of it, and she made up her mind to find out the truth. Just before the husband, who had not seen them in the church, was due to arrive home, the mother said to her daughter:

'If you agree, we can find out the truth about your husband. As soon as he's in bed, [I'll come in to him], and you will pull off his cap from behind before he knows what's happening. Then we shall see if he is tonsured like the one who said mass.'

The plan was carried out just as they had arranged. As soon as the wicked husband came to bed, the old lady came in, and took hold of both his hands as if in jest. The daughter immediately pulled off the cap. There he sat, his crown completely bald! The two women were as horrified as it was possible to be. Without more ado, they called the servants and had him seized and tied up till the morning. Excuses and fine words were to no avail. When day came the lady sent for her confessor, pretending that she had something urgent to confide in him. He came in haste, and was immediately seized and bound like his young companion. Accusing him of fraud, she called in the Law, and handed them both over. And if they had honest men for judges, one must presume that they did not get off lightly.

*

'There you are, Ladies. That's to show you that the men who make vows of poverty are not exempt from the temptations of avarice – a fact which gives rise to so much evil.'

'On the contrary,' said Saffredent, 'to a lot of good! Because, thanks to those five hundred ducats which the old woman wanted to hoard up, a great deal of pleasure was procured. And the poor girl, who had waited so long to have one husband, stood to have a second one and, in all truth, [to be able] to speak better about all kinds and conditions of men!'

'You always express the most false opinions,' said Oisille, 'for you seem to think that all women have the same temperament as yourself.'

'Madame, pardon me, but that is not so,' he replied. 'I dearly wish that they were as easily satisfied as we men are!'

'That is wicked talk,' said Oisille, 'for there is no one here who does not know that the truth is the opposite of what you say. And that it is not true is clear from the story we have just heard, which shows how simple and innocent we poor women are, and how wicked are those men normally considered above the rest of you, for neither the old lady nor her daughter would ever do anything they wanted simply because they wished to, but always submitted their wishes to higher advice.'

'Some women are so difficult to please,' said Longarine, 'that they seem to think only an angel will do for them.'

'And that is why,' said Simontaut, 'they often end up with devils – especially women who do not place their trust in God's grace, and imagine that their common sense or someone else's will serve to achieve happiness in this world, whereas true happiness is given by, and can come from, God alone.'

'Well, Simontaut!' said Oisille. 'I did not know that you were capable of such good thoughts!'

'Madame,' he replied, 'it is a pity I am not tried out more often, for I can see that for want of knowing me better you have already formed a low opinion of me. After all, if a friar can turn his hand to my trade, why shouldn't I turn my hand to his?'

'So,' said Parlamente, 'you would say that your trade is deceiving women, would you? You condemn yourself out of your own mouth!'

'Had I deceived a hundred thousand women,' he replied, 'I would still not have had my revenge for the suffering caused me by one woman alone!'

'I know that you're always bemoaning the treatment you receive from ladies,' said Parlamente, 'yet you always look so fit and cheerful, it's hard to believe you've suffered as much as you say. But then, according to the *Belle Dame sans Mercy*, it is well to say it's so, for such comfort as you may gain.'*

'The celebrated doctor you are quoting,' said Simontaut, 'is not only disagreeable in himself, but causes the ladies who follow his doctrine to be disagreeable also.'

'Nevertheless,' she replied, 'his doctrine is of greater value to young ladies than any other I know.'

* See p. 164. Allusion to the poem by Alain Chartier, quoted in story 12.

'If it were the case,' he went on, 'that all ladies were "sans mercy", we might as well put our horses to grass and let our armour go rusty till the next war comes along, and think about nothing but domestic affairs. Is it, I ask you, to any lady's good name to be known for being without pity, without charity, without love, in fact "sans mercy"?'

'Charity and love,' replied Parlamente, 'she should not be without. But this word "mercy" has an unpleasant ring among women. They can't use it without offending their honour, because *mercy* really means granting the favour that one is asked. And one well knows what favours men desire.'

'Yet with all respect, Madame,' he answered, 'some men are so reasonable that they ask nothing more than the word.'

'You remind me,' said Parlamente, 'of a man who was happy with nothing more than a lady's glove.'

'We must find out who this gracious lover was,' said Hircan. 'May I invite you to tell us the story?'

'With pleasure,' she replied, 'for it is a chaste and noble tale.'

STORY FIFTY-SEVEN

King Louis XI sent to England as his ambassador the Seigneur de Montmorency, who was so well received there, so loved and so admired by the King and all his princes, that his advice would often be sought on the most secret matters. One day he was at a banquet given in his honour by the King and was sitting next to an English lord, a man from one of their most distinguished families. This man had attached to his cloak a small glove, a lady's glove. It was fastened with gold hooks, and the fingers were covered with diamonds, rubies, emeralds, and pearls. The value of that glove was thought to be very high. The Seigneur de Montmorency kept looking at this object, and the English lord realized that he was curious to know why it was so extravagantly decorated. And thinking that the story which lay behind it could only redound to his praise, he launched into it.

'I can see,' he began, 'that you find it strange that I have decorated a mere glove so richly. I am even more anxious to explain it to you, for I know you to be an honourable man who knows the power of the passion of love. I know you will applaud me if I have acted rightly. If not, you will, I know, excuse me for submitting to Love, who holds sway over every noble heart. I must tell you, then, that all my life I have loved a certain lady. I love her still, and even after death I shall love her. But my heart was bolder in choosing the object of its love than was my tongue in declaring it, and for seven years I did not dare give the slightest hint of it, for fear that if she perceived my love, I should lose such opportunities as I then had of being in her company – a possibility that was more dreadful to me than death itself. But one day, in a meadow, as I was gazing upon her, I was overcome by such a violent fluttering of the heart that I quite lost my colour and my composure. I collapsed. She noticed, and asked me what the matter was. I replied that I was sick at heart. Unbearably. She, not realizing that I was sick for love, expressed her concern for me. This made me beg and beseech her to place her hand upon my heart, so that she might know how fast it was beating. This she did, more out of kindness than affection. As I held her gloved hand upon my heart, it began to race and jump, and she saw that I had spoken the truth. Then, pressing her hand to my side, I said, "Alas! Madame, take this heart which strives to break my sides, so that it may leap into the hand of her from whom I hope for mercy, for pardon and for life. It is this heart that constrains me now to declare the love which for so long I have kept hidden, for neither my heart nor I are masters of this powerful god." Taken aback by these words, she tried to withdraw her hand. But I held it tight, and as she pulled away her cruel hand, her glove remained. And because I had never before been so close to her – nor have I since – I affixed this glove as a sticking plaster, the most fitting I could find, to my wounded heart! I have adorned it with the richest rings in my possession, though the riches I receive from the glove itself I would not exchange for the crown of England. There is nothing in the world more precious to me than to feel it as it presses against my side.'

The Seigneur de Montmorency, who would have rather had the hand than the glove, told him he admired his great chivalry. He was, he assured him, the truest lover he had ever come across, and deserved better treatment for prizing so little so much – although, he added, if he had got any further than the glove, he might in view of the magnitude of his love have expired in ecstasy. The English lord agreed with Montmorency on this point without the slightest suspicion that he was being mocked.

*

'If all the men in the world were so pure and noble in their intentions, then ladies could certainly trust them, since a glove is all it would cost them!'

'I know Montmorency well enough,' said Geburon, 'to know that *he* wouldn't have wanted to adopt English habits in these matters. If *he*'d satisfied himself with so little, he wouldn't have had the good luck in love which he did have. As the old song says,

Faint praise is all the part
Of lovers faint in heart.'

'You can just imagine the poor lady snatching her hand away when she felt his heart thumping,' said Saffredent. 'She must have thought he was about to die, and there's nothing women hate more, so they say, than to touch a corpse!'

'If you'd spent as much time around hospitals as you have around taverns,' said Ennasuite, 'you'd have seen the *women* laying out the dead, while *men*, however bold they may claim to be, are afraid to touch.'

'It's quite true,' said [Simontaut], 'that there's no one who's had penance imposed on them who doesn't do the reverse of the action which in the past has given them the most pleasure. For example, I once saw a young lady in a distinguished house making up for the pleasure she'd had from kissing a man she was in love with. She was found at four o'clock in the morning kissing the corpse of some nobleman who'd been killed the previous day, and for whom she had never had any particular affection. Everyone knew immediately that she was doing penance for past pleasures.'

['That,' said Oisille,] 'is precisely the way in which men malign the good works that are done by women. And that is why I am of the opinion that men should not be kissed, alive or dead, unless it be according to God's command.'

'As far as I'm concerned,' said Hircan, 'I feel so little interest in kissing any other woman but my own wife that I'm quite ready to accept any laws anyone cares to mention. But I do feel sorry for young people – you're taking away from them a harmless source of happiness, and nullifying the command of Saint Paul, who said that we should kiss *in osculo sancto*.'*

'If Saint Paul had been a man like you,' said Nomerfide, 'we should have certainly demanded first-hand evidence of the spirit of God which spoke in him!'

'In the end you would rather doubt Holy Scripture,' said Geburon, 'than fail to observe a single one of your petty ceremonies!'

'Heaven forbid,' exclaimed Oisille, 'that we should doubt Holy Scripture, for we are far from believing in your lies. There is not one woman here who does not know what she should

* Romans 16:16: 'Salute one another with an holy kiss.

believe: never cast doubt on the word of God, and even less give credence to the word of men.'

'I believe,' said [Dagoucin], 'that more men are deceived by women than [women] by men. They show us so little love that they are prevented from believing us, truthful as we are. On the other hand, the love we bear them inclines us to place complete trust in the lies which they tell, with the result that we allow them to deceive us, rather than admit the possibility that they could do such a thing.'

'It seems to me,' said Parlamente, 'that you have heard some stupid man complaining about being duped by some frivolous woman. What you say carries so little weight that it requires reinforcing by means of an example. So if you have one in mind, I invite you to take my place and to tell it to us. That doesn't mean that we're obliged to believe you on the strength of just one story. Even if you do speak ill of us, our ears will suffer no pain, for we know the truth of the matter.'

'Well, since I am asked to speak,' said Dagoucin, 'I shall do so.'

STORY FIFTY-EIGHT

At the court of King Francis I there was a certain lady of lively wit, whose grace, refinement and pleasant tongue had won the hearts of several devoted gentlemen. She was capable of amusing herself with them while keeping her honour intact, and conversing with them so agreeably that none of them knew quite what to expect from her. The most self-assured despaired and the most despairing took heart. However, although most of them she did not take seriously, she could not help feeling great affection for one particular gentleman, whom she referred to as her cousin to give her an excuse [to see more of him.] But nothing in this world remains stable. Often their love would turn to resentment, but only to be [renewed] and grow stronger than before, so that the court could scarcely fail to notice it. One day the lady decided to play a trick on the gentleman, partly to make it plain that she was not to be moved by anyone or anything, and partly to punish him [a little] for what she had had to put up with through her love for him. So the next time she saw him she put on a more encouraging front than she ever had before. Now the man in question was no coward, either in war or love, and he set about pursuing [the favours] that he had so often before sought from her. She, pretending that she felt so sorry for him that she could resist no longer, told him that she would grant his request and that to this end she would go up to her room, which was at the top of the building, where she knew nobody else would be. As soon as she went out, he was to follow her immediately, for he would find her alone, [with no other company than her tender thoughts for him.] The man, who believed every word, was so pleased that he went off to amuse himself with the other ladies, while he waited for the moment when she would leave the room and he would follow her. The lady, who was certainly not short of female cunning, went over to Madame Marguerite, the King's daughter, and to the Duchess of Montpensier.

'If you wish,' she said, 'I will show you the most amusing thing you have ever seen.'

The Princess and the Duchess, who were certainly not looking for something to be melancholy about, eagerly asked her what she had in mind.

'There is a certain gentleman,' she said, 'who is known to you as the most honourable man there ever was, and who is no less daring and brave. You know how many unkind things he has done to me, and how at the time when I loved him most he left me for the love of other women. His behaviour caused me more unhappiness than I allowed myself to show. Well, God has given me the chance to take my revenge. What I am going to do, is go up to my room, which is just overhead, and if you would keep your eyes open, you will see him immediately follow me. As soon as he is through the galleries and about to go up the stairs, may I ask you both to go over to the window and shout "Help! Thief!" along with me? You'll see how angry he'll be. I think he'll provide us with no mean performance! And if he doesn't openly shout curses at me, I fully expect that he'll think them to himself!'

These words caused not inconsiderable amusement, for no other gentleman at court was so relentless in laying siege to the ladies. He was also highly regarded, much sought after by everyone, and not the sort of man one risked being mocked by. So the two ladies felt they would be sharing in any triumph their companion might have over him. As soon as the instigator of the plot had left the room, they kept a close watch on her pursuer's movements. It was not long before he left his place, and as he went out of the room, the ladies followed him into the gallery, so as not to lose sight of him. Suspecting nothing, he pulled his cloak up around his neck to hide his face and went down into the courtyard. Then he started to come back up the stairs. However, he met someone by whom he did not wish to be seen, so he went down again and came back in by another entrance. All this the ladies saw without his noticing a thing. The moment he arrived at the foot of the staircase which gave him the safest way of reaching his lady's room, her two accomplices went straight across to the window. They could see the lady in the upstairs room and heard her start to shout 'Help! Thief!' at the top of her voice. They joined in, and made such a noise between them that their shouting could be heard all over the castle. I leave you to imagine the man's anger and frustration as he fled back to his quarters. But his rage was not so well hidden that it was not apparent to the two ladies who were party to the plot, and they have often since taunted him with it. The lady who perpetrated the unkind trick often taunted him with it too, and told him how she had enjoyed her revenge. But he was quick with his answers and his defence, and tried to convince them that he had accepted the lady's invitation to go to her room simply to give them a little amusement! After all, he claimed, he would not have gone to such lengths out of love, because for a long time there had been no question of his being in love with her. But the ladies did not accept the truth of that, and there is still some doubt about the whole business. However, if it were the case that he had believed the lady (as is likely, for he was so brave and good that there were [few, if any,] of his generation who surpassed him, as was shown by his most brave and chivalrous death), then it seems to me that you must admit that the love of valiant men is such that through believing too much in the truth of ladies they are often deceived.'

*

'In all honesty, I applaud this lady for playing the [trick] she did,' said Ennasuite. 'For when a man is loved by a lady and abandons her for someone else, she can never avenge herself too much.'

'Yes, if she is loved by him to begin with,' said Parlamente. 'But there are women who love men without being sure that their feelings are returned, and when they discover that the man is in love with someone else, they say that he is fickle. So wise women are never deceived by [words.] They pay attention to, and believe, only men who tell the truth, in order to avoid falling prey to liars, for truth and falsehood speak the same language.'

'If all women were of your opinion,' said Simontaut, 'we men might as well pack away our fine speeches and humble supplications. But whatever you and those who are like you say, we shall never believe that women are as unbelieving as they are beautiful. And convinced of this, we shall live content, however much you try to disconcert us with your reasonings.'

'I know who the lady in this story is,' said Longarine, 'and really, she's so shrewd there's nothing I could not believe her capable of. After all, she made no exception for her husband, so why should she make an exception for her devoted servant?'

'What, her husband?' said [Dagoucin.] 'So you know more than I. I give you my place so that you may tell us.'

'If you wish, then I obey,' replied Longarine.

STORY FIFTY-NINE

The lady in the story you have just told was married to a rich man from a fine old family. They had married out of deep affection for one another. She was a lady who spoke as agreeably as any woman in the world, and did not hide from her husband the fact that she had gentlemen devoted to her service – servants whom she teased for her own amusement. He found this amusing enough himself for a while, but eventually it began to irritate him. For one thing he did not like the way she conversed at great length with people he did not consider to be either relatives or friends. For another, he was worried by the expense he was obliged to incur in order that she could follow the court and maintain her elegant style of life. So whenever he could he withdrew to his own house. But so many people went to visit her there that his expenditure was hardly reduced at all. Wherever his wife went she always found some way of putting on dances, games and all the other kinds of entertainment that young women may, quite respectably, indulge in. When her husband said to her jocularly that they were spending too much, she would reply that she might give him beggars' rags, but never a cuckold's horns. For she was so fond of finery that she insisted on having the most beautiful and most extravagant attire at the court, and did her utmost to attend as often as possible – while he, of course, did his utmost to avoid taking her at all. In order to have her own way, the lady would humour her husband, with the result that he generally found it easiest to comply.

One day, however, when none of her wiles were succeeding in persuading him to take her to court, she happened to notice that he was being extremely attentive to one of her chambermaids. It occurred to her that here was an opportunity she could turn to her advantage. She took the girl on one side, and questioned her so cunningly, that eventually, by dint of threats and [promises,] she confessed that not a day had gone by since she had been in the house without her master making amorous overtures. But, she would sooner die, she declared, than do anything to offend God and her honour, especially as Madame had been so gracious as to take her into service – that would make it doubly bad. The lady was at once angry and pleased to learn of her husband's disloyalty. She was angry to see him professing to love her, yet secretly doing his best to insult her under her very nose by pursuing this girl, who in her view was without question her inferior in beauty and refinement. But she was pleased, because she now hoped to catch her husband out, and place him so much in the wrong that he would never again criticize her for her devoted servants or the time she spent at court. To this end she asked the girl to come round little by little to her husband's demands, on certain conditions which she laid down. At first the girl was reluctant, but once assured that her life and honour were safe, she agreed to do anything her mistress desired.

The husband, who continued to pursue the girl as before, suddenly found that her manner had completely changed. So he pressed her more passionately than ever. She, however, had learnt her part off by heart, and pointed out to him that she was very poor, and that if she obeyed him, she would be dismissed by her mistress, with whose help she had expected to acquire a good husband. To this came the reply that she was not to worry her head about such things – *he* would find her a better husband, and a better-off one, than her mistress ever could. In any case, he would manage their love-affair with such secrecy that no one would ever be able to talk about it. And so they came to an agreement. As for the most suitable place for doing this fine deed, the girl declared that the best place, and the place least likely to be suspected, was a little house in the park, where there was, conveniently enough, a room with a bed in it. The husband, for whom anywhere would have been acceptable, was perfectly happy with this proposal. He could not wait for the day to come.

The girl, for her part, kept her promise to her mistress. She told her all about the arrangement she had made with her husband – how she was to meet him the following day after dinner, and how she would go as planned, but would first give her mistress a warning. She was most anxious that Madame should be on the alert, and that she should not fail to go along to the house at the right time to protect her from the danger to which, out of obedience, she was exposing herself. The lady told her not to be afraid. She would never let her down, and would protect her from her husband's fury.

The next day came, and after dinner the man was more agreeable with his wife than he had ever been. Although by no means pleased at this, she put on such a good act that he noticed nothing. When she asked him how he would like to spend the evening, he replied that he would like nothing better than to have a game of *cent*, and he got out the cards. His wife, however, said she preferred not to play, and would enjoy herself just as much watching the others. So he sat down to play, and as he was doing so he whispered to the girl not to forget her promise, and she, once he was immersed in the game, slipped out of the room giving the sign to her mistress as she did so that she was about to embark on her little pilgrimage. The lady duly took note, but the husband noticed nothing.

An hour later, one of his valets motioned to him across the room, and he turned to his wife to say that he had a slight headache and would have to take a rest and then go out for some fresh air. She knew as well as he did what was the matter with him, and asked if he would like her to play his game. He replied that he would be glad if she would, and that he would be back soon. But she assured him that he should not worry – she would be quite happy to take his place for a couple of hours. So off he went, first to his room, and then down a path screened by trees to the park. His wife knew a quicker route, and waited a little. Then, pretending she had a sudden attack of colic, she gave her hand to one of the other players. Once out of the room, she took off her high pattens and ran as fast as she could. She did not want business to be concluded before she arrived! But she was there in plenty of time, so went into the room by another door. Her husband was only just arriving. Hiding herself behind the door, she was able to overhear the fine, high-flown phrases he started to produce for the benefit of her chambermaid. As she saw him approach the criminal act, she seized him from behind, saying, 'I'm too close to you for cheating this time!' Needless to say, he was mad with rage, not only because he had just been frustrated of his pleasure, but also because his wife obviously knew more about him than he cared for. He was terrified lest he lose her love for ever. But ignoring his wife, he flew wildly at the girl, thinking that she was the one who had planned the trap. He would have killed her, if his wife had not pulled her free. He called her the most brazen creature he had ever met, and said that if his wife had only waited, she would have seen that he was merely trying to catch her out! Far from being about to do what she thought he was about to do, he was really intending to give the girl a good beating by way of punishment! But his wife knew what to make of excuses like that, and berated him there and then with such vehemence that he was afraid she was going to desert him. He promised her everything she wanted, said that her angry rebukes were entirely justified and admitted that he had been wrong all along to object to her having devoted gentlemen. For a beautiful and honest woman is none the less virtuous because she is loved by men, [provided] that she does nothing and says nothing to sully her honour. But when a man deliberately pursues a woman who does not even love him, in order to wrong both his wife and his own conscience, then he deserves to be punished. So he would, he said, never stop her from going to court again, nor would he complain about her devoted servants, [for he knew that she spoke to them more to mock them than because she had any affection for them]. The lady was not displeased with the way he spoke, because she realized that she had scored a point. However, she pretended to be the very opposite of pleased, saying that she no longer cared to go to court, since obviously he did not love her any more. She could not bear to go into society if he did not love her. It was only if a woman was truly loved by her husband and loved him in return, as she did, that a woman could feel she had a safe-conduct to speak with everyone without fear of being mocked. The poor man did everything he could to convince her that he still loved her, and eventually they went away good friends. To avoid any further mishaps of this kind, however, he asked her to dismiss the chambermaid who had caused him so much trouble. This she did – but not before she could see the girl respectably married at her husband's expense. And he, in order to make his wife forget his foolish aberration, lost no time in taking her to court – and in such high style that she had every reason to be satisfied.

*

'And that, Ladies, is what led me to say that I wasn't surprised at the trick she played on one of her devoted servants considering what she had done to her husband.'

'You've depicted a very shrewd woman, and a very stupid husband,' said Hircan. 'Seeing he'd got as far as he had with the girl, he shouldn't have given up following such a promising trail.'

'And what *should* he have done?' inquired Longarine.

'What he'd set out to do,' replied Hircan. 'When his wife found out what he was intending to do, she was every bit as angry as if he'd actually done it. Perhaps she'd have thought more of him, if she'd seen he was bolder and more of a man!'

'All very well,' said Ennasuite, 'but where are you going to find a man who can force two women at once? Because the wife would have defended her rights and the girl her virginity!'

'True enough,' replied Hircan, 'but a man who is bold and strong isn't afraid of attacking two weaker people and achieving his end!'

'I can quite see,' said Ennasuite, 'that if he'd drawn his sword, he might have killed them both, but otherwise I don't see how he could have escaped. So I should like to know what *you* would have done.'

'I'd have picked my wife up in my arms and carried her outside, then gone back in to do what I pleased with the chambermaid, by love or by force!'

'Hircan,' said Parlamente, 'it is sufficient that you know how to do evil deeds!'

'I'm sure I'm not shocking the innocent by what I say, Parlamente. Nor do I mean to defend foul deeds. I would praise neither the deed itself, which was certainly not good, nor the man behind it, who failed in the event to carry it out – because he gave up more through fear of his wife than through love for her. I would praise a man who loves his wife according to God's law, but if he doesn't love her, I don't respect him for being afraid of her.'

'In all truth,' said Parlamente, 'if love didn't make you a good husband, then I should set no great store by what you would do out of fear!'

'You need not worry, Parlamente,' he replied, 'for the love I bear you makes me more obedient to you than would fear of death or Hell.'

'You may say what you like,' said Parlamente, 'but I am content with what I have seen of you already, and what I already know about you. As for what I've not known, I've not felt disposed to be suspicious, and even less to inquire.'

'I always think it is great folly for husbands to pry too much into what their wives do, and equally great folly for wives to pry into what their husbands do,' said Nomerfide. 'Sufficient unto the day is the evil thereof, without taking so much care for the morrow.'

'Yet sometimes,' said Oisille, 'it is necessary to inquire into things that may concern family honour – in order to restore order, but not in order to speak ill of particular individuals. For there is no one who [at some time or another] is not liable to err.'

'It does sometimes happen,' said Geburon, 'that people get into difficulties precisely because they don't inquire sufficiently into what their wives are doing.'

'If you know an example,' said Longarine, 'please do not keep it from us.'

'I do know of an example,' replied Geburon, 'and since you wish me to, I will tell it to you.'

STORY SIXTY

In the town of Paris there once lived a man who was so good-natured that even if he had before his very eyes seen someone else in bed with his wife, it would have gone against his conscience to believe it. The poor man had in fact married the most unbridled creature you could imagine, but he never noticed what she was really like, and treated her as if she was the best wife in the world. One day, while King Louis XII was in Paris, she abandoned herself to one of his cantors. When she found out that the King was leaving town and that she would no longer be able to meet her cantor, she made up her mind to go with him and leave her husband. The cantor agreed, and took her away to a house he had near Blois, where they lived together for some considerable time. When the poor husband discovered that his wife had disappeared, he looked for her high and low, until eventually someone told him that she had gone off with the cantor. Anxious to find the lost ewe he had guarded so badly, he wrote to her again and again, begging her to return, and promising to have her back if she would be an honest woman. She, however, was so enjoying her cantor's song that she had quite forgotten the voice of her husband, and took no notice whatsoever of his fine words – indeed, she laughed at them. This angered the husband, and he informed her that since nothing else could persuade her to come back to him, he would seek her return through the Church courts. Frightened that if the law intervened, she and her cantor would both pay dearly for it, the woman devised a plan in keeping with her character. Pretending to have fallen sick, she sent word for some of the honest women of the town to come and visit her. This they willingly did, in the hope that her illness would lead her to abandon her wicked life. They each made the most eloquent speeches urging her to mend her ways, upon which she, feigning to be grievously ill, pretended to weep and admit her sins, with the result that all these good ladies, who thought she was speaking from the depths of her heart, were moved to pity.

Seeing her so penitent and humble, they tried to console her, telling her that God was not so fearsome as many preachers portrayed Him, and that He would never refuse her His mercy. Then they sent for a good priest to hear her confession, and the next day the local curé appeared to administer the holy sacrament, which she received in such a pious manner that all the good ladies of the town who were standing round her bed wept to see such devotion, and gave thanks to God for having pity in His goodness upon this poor creature. After that she pretended that she could no longer swallow food, and the curé came again, this time to bring her extreme unction. This she received in silence, but with much sanctimonious gesticulation, for she had now made them believe that she had lost the power of speech. And so she went on, gradually losing her sight, her hearing, and the other senses – which had them all wailing 'Jesus! Jesus!' By now night was approaching, and the ladies, who had a long way to go, prepared to leave. As they were going out of the house they were told the news that she had died. So, saying the *De profundis* for her as they went, they made their way back home.

The curé asked the cantor where he wanted her to be buried, and he replied that it had been her wish to be laid in the cemetery, and that it would be best to take the body there during the night. So the much pitied and much lamented lady was laid out for burial – by a chambermaid who took very good care that she did not come to any harm! She was carried forth by torchlight to a grave that the cantor had had prepared for her. The ladies who had seen her receive holy unction came out of their houses as the cortège passed by, and accompanied the coffin to its resting-place. Once the priest and the women had disappeared into the distance, the cantor, who had remained behind together with the maid, immediately dug up the grave – and out came his mistress more alive than ever! He took her back to the house, where he kept her in secret for a long time.

Meanwhile the husband was continuing his search, and arrived at Blois intending to seek satisfaction at law, only to be told that his wife was dead and buried. The ladies of Blois assured him of the fact, and told him how beautiful her end had been. The good fellow was rather glad to be able to believe that his wife's soul had gone to Paradise, and that he was now rid of her troublesome bodily presence on earth. And so, with gladness in his heart, he returned to Paris, where eventually he married a beautiful and virtuous young woman, who proved a thoroughly good wife and housekeeper, and by whom he had several children. They lived happily together for fourteen or fifteen years. But rumour keeps nothing hidden for long, and he came to hear that his first wife was not dead after all, but alive and living with the wicked cantor. He tried to hide it for as long as he could, pretending to know nothing of the rumour, and hoping with all his heart that it was false. But his second wife, who was a virtuous woman, heard the rumour as well, and became so distressed that she nearly died of her sorrow. Had she been able conceal it with a clear conscience, she would have done so, but that in any case was impossible. For the Church was anxious to regulate the matter immediately, and as a first measure insisted that the two should be separated until the truth was established. Then the poor man was obliged to leave his good wife in order to go and look for his bad one. He arrived in Blois, shortly after the accession of King Francis I. Queen Claude and the Regent were in residence there, and [he brought his case before them], seeking restitution of the woman whom in his heart he would far rather never have seen again. But there was no other way, and the whole assembly felt great pity for him. When his wife was found and brought to him, she insisted for a long while that he was not her husband – which, had he been able, he would have gladly believed. She went on, more indignant than ashamed, to tell him that she would rather die than go back to him. This he was only too relieved to hear. But the noble ladies who were listening to this shameful and dishonest speech sentenced her to return to her husband. They also harangued the cantor, until he was obliged under threat to tell his odious mistress that he no longer desired to see her and that she must go back to her husband. Hounded on all sides, the wretched woman went home with her husband, there to be treated far better than she ever deserved.

*

'So that, Ladies, is why I say that if the poor husband had been a little more vigilant over his wife, he wouldn't have lost her in the first place. If you look after things properly they don't easily go astray. But neglect them, and you only encourage the thief.'

'It's a strange thing how strong love is when it seems least reasonable!' said Hircan.

'I've heard it said that it's easier to break up a [hundred] marriages,' said Simontaut, 'than to break up a liaison between a priest and a chambermaid!'

'Quite so,' said Ennasuite. 'Those who tie people together in matrimony are so good at tying knots that only death can put an end to it! The doctors of the Church maintain that spiritual language is greater than any other; consequently spiritual love surpasses any other kind.'

'If a lady abandons a worthy husband or lover for a priest, however handsome and worthy he might be, that is one thing for which I could never pardon her,' said Dagoucin.

'Do not presume, Dagoucin, to discuss our holy mother Church,' said Hircan. 'You may rest assured that women who are rather quiet and timid derive much pleasure from sinning with a man they know can absolve them. A lot of women are more ashamed of confessing a deed than of the deed itself.'

'You are speaking,' Oisille intervened, 'of women who have no knowledge of God whatsoever, who believe that the things they try to keep secret will not one day be revealed before the whole company of Heaven. I do not think that these women pursue confessors in order to make their confession. They are blinded to such a degree by our enemy the Devil, that what they are really looking for is the opportunity to sin in secrecy and security rather than the opportunity to seek absolution for sins of which they do not in the least repent.'

'Repent!' exclaimed Saffredent. 'They actually think they're more saintly than other women! I'm quite sure there are women who think it is to their honour to persist in that sort of love-affair.'

'You speak as if you have some particular person in mind,' said Oisille. 'I beg you to tell us what you know tomorrow, to begin the day. The last bell for vespers is ringing already, for our friends the monks went as soon as we had finished the tenth story and left us to finish our discussion on our own.'

Thereupon they all rose and went to the church, where the monks were waiting for them. After they had heard vespers they ate together, speaking as they did so of many fine tales. After supper they went, as was their wont, to the meadow to disport themselves a little, and then to their rest, in order that their memories would be fresh for the next day.

END OF THE SIXTH DAY

SEVENTH DAY

PROLOGUE

The next morning Oisille did not fail to administer to the whole company the saving nourishment which she drew from her reading of the Acts, and the righteous deeds of the glorious knights and apostles of Jesus Christ according to Saint Luke, telling them how these tales should be sufficient to make them long to live in such an age, and weep for the corruption of the present. When she had thoroughly read and expounded the opening chapters of this noble book, she exhorted them all to go into church, in the union and fellowship in which the apostles themselves prayed together, and to seek God's grace, which is never refused to those who seek it through faith. This sentiment was found good by all, and they arrived at the church to find the mass of the Holy Spirit about to begin. This seemed most appropriate, and made them listen to the service in great d votion. Afterwards they dined, recalling the apostolic life. So much pleasure did they have in this, that they almost forgot their story-telling venture. Nomerfide, the youngest, was the first to remember, and said: 'Madame Oisille has plunged us so deep into devotion that it will soon be past the time when we usually go to our rooms to prepare ourselves for our stories.' Her words brought everybody to their feet, and after they had each spent some time in his or her own room, they duly went out to the meadow, just as they had the day before. Once they had made themselves comfortable, Madame Oisille said to Saffredent:

'Although I am quite sure you will say nothing that would be to any woman's advantage, nevertheless I must call upon you to tell the story which you promised us yesterday evening.'

'I declare, Madame,' he replied, 'that I shall not acquire a [dishonourable] reputation as a malicious gossip merely because what I tell you is the truth, nor forfeit the favour of all virtuous women, merely because I tell of the misdeeds of those who are foolish. For I know from experience what it is just to be banished from their sight – indeed, had I been [thus] deprived of their good grace, I should not at this moment be alive.'

And as he spoke he turned his gaze away from her who was the cause both of his joys and of his sorrows, towards Ennasuite, who blushed, as if it was she herself to whom he was referring. His remark went home none the less to the person for whom it had been intended. Madame Oisille assured him that he might tell the truth freely at the expense of whomsoever his story might concern. So Saffredent began.

STORY SIXTY-ONE

Not far from the town of Autun there lived an extremely beautiful woman. She was tall, fair-skinned, and had the loveliest face I ever saw. She had married a man apparently younger than herself, who loved and cherished her so dearly that she had every reason [to return his love] and to be perfectly contented. Not long after they were married he took her into Autun, where he had some business to attend to. While he was engaged in the law-courts with a claim he had to make, she would go into a church to pray to God for him. During their stay in the town she went so often to this sacred place that she was noticed by a certain canon, a very wealthy man, who fell in love with her. He pressed his suit so hard that in the end the poor unfortunate woman gave in. The husband suspected nothing. He was preoccupied more with protecting his property than his wife. When the time came to return to their home, which was seven good leagues away, she was overwhelmed by grief at the prospect. But the canon promised to visit her often. He was as good as his word, and could always find an excuse to make a journey that would take him by way of her house. The husband, however, was not so stupid that he did not realize why the canon kept calling, and so arranged things that when the canon came his wife was never to be found. In fact he kept her so well hidden that the canon never once managed to speak to her. As for the wife, she was well aware of her husband's jealousy, but gave no hint of her annoyance. Instead she quietly went ahead and laid her own plans, for it was very Hell for her to be deprived of the vision of her God! One day, while her husband was out, she managed to keep her manservants and chambermaids occupied and out of the way, so that she was alone in the house. She swiftly collected together some essentials, and, unaccompanied by anything but the senseless passion that swept her along, she set out on foot for Autun. She arrived late, but it was still light enough for her canon to be able to recognize her.

For over a year, in spite of the warnings and excommunications that the husband had thrown at him, the canon managed to keep her living with him in secret. In the end, the husband realized that his only recourse was an appeal to the Bishop himself. The Bishop's archdeacon, a man as good as any man in France, went round all the canons' houses personally, and so thoroughly, that he eventually found the woman, who by then was beginning to be given up for lost. She was duly thrown into prison, and the canon himself was condemned to severe penance. Once the husband heard that the efforts of the archdeacon and of several other worthy people had led to the recovery of his wife, he expressed his willingness to take her back. She swore to him that in the future she would lead the life of a respectable lady, and he, loving her as he did, was only too ready to accept her word. And so he brought her back to his house, and treated her as kindly as before, the only difference being that he now provided her with two elderly chambermaids, one of whom always remained with her whenever she was left alone. But however well he treated her, her base passion for the canon persisted and the quiet life she now led was torment to her. Moreover, beautiful though she was, and strong, healthy and active though *he* was, they never had any children. For her mind was always seven good leagues away from her body. She concealed her feelings so well, however, that her husband believed she had, like himself, completely buried the past.

But that was far from true – she was too far gone in wickedness for that. Just as her husband was growing to love her more and more, and suspect her less and less, she made up her mind to pretend to be ill. She kept up the act so well that the poor man became deeply distressed and spared nothing to try to find a cure for her. But she played her part so well that not only he but the whole household were convinced that she was becoming steadily weaker and coming close to death. He should have been overjoyed! But seeing that he was on the contrary greatly upset, his wife asked him to authorize her to make a will – which with tears in his eyes he gladly did. Having the right to make a will, although she had no children, she gave to her husband what she could, begging his forgiveness for the things she had done to him in the past. Then she called for the curé, made her confession, and received the holy sacrament of the altar so devoutly that all around her were moved to tears to see such a glorious end. Towards evening she begged her husband to have extreme unction administered, saying that she was sinking so fast that she feared she might not live to receive it. With all haste he had the priest sent for. Then in deep humility she received unction, and inspired everyone to sing her praises. When she had finished acting out this farcical ritual, she said to her husband that since God had granted her His grace to receive all the sacraments that the Church commands, she felt her conscience in a state of great peace and would like now to rest a little. She begged him to do likewise, for had he not need of rest, after watching and weeping by her bedside? Out went the husband, and the manservants, and the two poor old ladies who had guarded her so closely and so long while she had been well, and who now no longer feared to lose her, unless it be through death. Off they all went to bed, and could soon be heard snoring loudly. At once, the dying lady was out of her bed, creeping out of the bedroom in her night-dress, listening carefully for noises. When she was sure that the coast was clear, she went out through a little garden gate which was never locked.

All through the night she walked, barefoot, and clad only in her nightdress, in the direction of Autun and the saint who had kept her from death. But the road was long, and daylight overtook her before she arrived. Looking round, she saw in the distance two horsemen riding hard. Suspecting it was her husband in hot pursuit, she hid herself in a swamp by the road, her head concealed between the reeds, and the rest of her in the mud. As her husband rode by she could hear him say to one of their servants, like a man at his wits' end: 'Ah! the wicked creature! Who would have thought that she could have done such a base and abominable deed under the disguise of the holy sacraments of the Church!'

And the servant replied: 'If Judas could betray his master in such a way, then do not be surprised at the treachery of a woman!'

So saying, they passed by. And his wife was a good deal happier to have outwitted him as she lay there among the reeds, than she had been to remain at home, in servitude, where her bed was warm and dry. As for the husband, he rode on to

Autun, where he searched for her everywhere. But he soon realized that she had never even entered the town, and he retraced his steps, cursing her as he went, bemoaning his loss and threatening her with nothing less than death if he found her. Not that fear of death entered *her* mind, any more than her body felt the cold – though being in a place like that at that time of the year ought to have been quite enough to make her repent of having ever undertaken such a damnable journey. And anyone who did not know how the fire of Hell warms those who are filled with it, would marvel at how this poor woman, who had just jumped out of a nice warm bed, could remain for a whole day in such extreme cold. Yet she did not lose heart, nor did she abandon the journey, for as soon as night fell she set off once again. Arriving at Autun just as the town gates were about to be locked, the pilgrim made her way straight to the body of the saint who was the object of her devotion. He was so astonished to see her that he could scarcely believe his eyes. However, when he had had a good look at her and examined her all over, he found that she possessed bones and flesh, which a spirit does not. Thus he satisfied himself that she was indeed no ghost, and from that moment on there was such harmony between them that they lived together for some fourteen or fifteen years.

For a while she was kept hidden, but as time went by she became less timid, and, what was worse, actually began to pride herself on having a lover who was so highly placed. So proud of herself was she, that she went to church, and assumed precedence over most of the other respectable women of the town, [whatever their station]. She had children by the canon, and one of her daughters was married to a rich merchant. The wedding was most elegant, and the ladies of the town muttered amongst themselves, but had no power to put matters right. Now it was around this time that Queen Claude, the consort of King Francis, was passing through Autun in the company of the Regent, the King's mother, and of her daughter, the Duchess of Alençon. One of the Queen's chamber women, a person by the name of Perrette, came to the Duchess and said: 'Madame, I beg you, listen to me, and you will perform a far greater work than going to hear all the services of the day.' The Duchess willingly agreed to listen, knowing that nothing but good counsel could come from her. Perrette went on to explain how she had engaged a small girl to help soap the Queen's washing. When she had asked the girl for news of the town, she had been told how upset the respectable ladies living there had been at the way the canon's wife took precedence over them. She had also been told something of the woman's past history. The Duchess went at once and told this story to Madame the Regent and the Queen. Without further formality they had the unfortunate woman sent for. She made no attempt to conceal herself. Far from being ashamed, she had become proud of the distinction of being mistress in such a rich man's household. So without the least sign of surprise or shame she presented herself to the ladies of the court, who were so shocked at this effrontery that at first they did not know what to do or to say. But Madame the Regent eventually addressed to her such a severe reprimand that any right-thinking woman would have been reduced to tears. Not so this poor woman. With extraordinary audacity she replied:

'Ladies, I beg you not to let my honour be attacked, for I have lived so respectably and virtuously with the reverend canon that nobody alive could reproach me, and I thank God for it! Let no one imagine that my way of life contradicts the will of God. It is three years now since there was anything between us and we live as chastely and lovingly as two dear little angels without either of us ever uttering a word of disagreement or even wishing to disagree with the other. And it would be a sin to make us part, for the good canon is nearly eighty years old, while I am only forty-five, and he would not live for long without me!'

You can imagine what the ladies [had to say to this stubborn creature], and the rebukes that each laid before her, when they saw that her obstinacy was in no way diminished by the words that had been addressed to her, or by her mature years, or by the noble company in which she found herself. And in order to humble her further, they sent for the good archdeacon of Autun, who sentenced her to a year's prison on bread and water. They sent also for her husband, who agreed readily, as a result of their exhortations, to take her back once her penance was completed. But realizing that she was to be thrown into prison, and learning also that the canon had made up his mind never to have her back, she expressed thanks to the noble ladies for getting a veritable devil off her back, and was overcome by such profound and perfect penitence that her husband, instead of waiting for a year to go by, waited no longer than a fortnight before going to the archdeacon to ask for her return. And ever since they have lived together happily and peacefully.

*

'Thus, Ladies, are the chains of Saint Peter turned by corrupt ministers of the Church into the chains of Satan, chains so hard to break that the sacraments which cast devils from the body are for such people as these the means whereby devils are kept in their conscience even longer. For the best things are those which, when one abuses them, may be turned to evil ends.'

'She was indeed an unfortunate woman,' said Oisille, 'but it was an appropriate punishment to be brought for judgement before the ladies whom you have mentioned. For so powerful and so full of virtue was the very gaze of Madame the Regent that there was no decent woman who did not fear to come into her presence, lest she should feel herself unworthy. And any woman who found herself looked on with favour considered it a great honour, for everyone knew that this noble lady could not look kindly on any woman who was other than virtuous.'

'It would be a fine thing,' observed Hircan, 'if we were to stand more in awe of a woman's eyes than of the holy sacraments – which, if they are not received in faith and charity, [are received] to one's eternal damnation.'

'Women who aren't inspired by God,' replied Parlamente, 'go more in fear of temporal than of spiritual power, I can promise you. And I think the poor creature in the story was more chastened by being thrown into prison, and by the prospect of not seeing her canon, than she was by all the speeches of condemnation.'

'But,' said Simontaut, 'you're forgetting the main reason why she went back to her husband. The canon was eighty years of age, whereas the husband was younger than she was. So the good lady profited in all her transactions. If the canon had been young, she wouldn't have been so ready to give him up. The ladies could have made as many speeches of condemnation as they liked – it would have had no more effect than the sacraments she had received.'

'Even so,' said Nomerfide, 'it seems to me that she was right to be so reluctant to admit her guilt, because sins of this sort should be confessed humbly before God, and denied strenuously before men. Even if the accusation is true, by lying and swearing to the contrary, it is always possible to cast doubt on its truth.'

'It's difficult nevertheless,' said Longarine, 'for a sin to be kept so secret that it's never revealed – unless God in His mercy grants concealment to those who truly repent for love of Him.'

'Well, what do you say,' said Hircan, 'about the sort of women who no sooner commit some folly or other than they go off and tell somebody?'

'I find it astonishing,' replied Longarine. 'It's a sign that the sin they committed was not altogether unpleasant. As I've already said, it's impossible for someone whose sin is not covered by God's grace to deny it before men. There are a lot of women who derive some kind of pleasure from talking about such things, and feel some kind of pride in making their vices public. And there are also a lot of women who give themselves away by a slip of the tongue and make themselves their own accusers.'

'If you know a story about such a woman,' said Saffredent, 'then I give you my place and beg you to tell it to us.'

'Then listen carefully,' said Longarine.

STORY SIXTY-TWO

There was, in the reign of Francis I, a certain lady of royal blood, endowed with honour, virtue and beauty, who was well-known for her ability to tell a good story in an elegant style, as well as for her ability to laugh at a good story told by others. On one occasion, while staying in one of her houses, she was being visited by her neighbours and dependants, for she was as much loved as any lady could be. Amongst the visitors was a young woman, who, hearing that everyone was in the habit of recounting tales for the royal lady's amusement, decided that she would do likewise, and said: 'Madame, I can tell you a fine story. But you must promise not to talk about it afterwards.'

[Her request having been granted, she began thus:] 'Madame, this is a true story. I vouch for it on my conscience. It is about a certain noblewoman, who was married, and who led a very respectable life with her husband, in spite of the fact that he was old and she was young. A young nobleman who was her neighbour, realizing she had married an old man, fell in love with her. He pressed her for several years, but received no response other than that which it behoves a lady in those circumstances to give. One day the man thought to himself that if he could catch her at a moment when he had the advantage over her, she might not be quite so cold. For a long time he weighed the risks, but in the end his love for the lady banished all fear, and he set about picking the right time and place. He kept his eyes open until an opportunity presented itself. One summer morning, the lady's husband went away to one of his other houses, and set off at daybreak to avoid the heat. The young gallant then betook himself to the young lady's house, where he found her asleep in bed, and noticed that the chambermaids had gone out of the room. Without even thinking to shut the door behind him, he jumped straight into bed with her, still wearing spurs, boots and leggings! When she woke up, she was as distressed as it was possible for anyone to be. But protest as she might, he took her by force, saying that if she told anyone about it he would say that she had sent for him. The lady was so terrified at this that she did not dare scream. Then some of the maids came in, and he scrambled out of bed as fast as he could. No one would have noticed a thing, if it had not been for the fact that his spur had caught on the top sheet, pulling it right off, and leaving the lady lying on the bed stark naked!'

Although the lady had been telling the story as if about another person, she could not stop herself saying at the end: 'No woman has ever been as embarrassed as I was, when I found myself completely naked!'

The royal lady, who had been listening to this story, had so far followed without a smile, but when she heard this, she could not help laughing.

'I can see,' she said, 'that you can indeed vouch for the truth of the story!'

The poor woman did her best to try to retrieve her honour – but too late, the bird had flown and there was no calling it back!

*

'I can assure you, Ladies, that if this kind of act had been distasteful to her, she would have wanted to erase it completely from her memory. But as I've already said, a sin like hers would be revealed by the sinner herself sooner than it was discovered by other people, unless it were covered with that covering [which makes man blessed, so that with David we may truly say.

O happy he whose sins committed
Are through His grace at last remitted:
Whose wickedness sees not the light
And covered hides before God's sight.]'

'Upon my honour,' said Ennasuite, 'of all the fools I've ever heard of, she was the biggest, to make others laugh at her own expense!'

'I don't find it in the least strange that after committing the act, she went on to talk about it,' Parlamente said, 'for words come more easily than deeds.'

'Good Heavens! What sin did she commit anyway?' exclaimed Geburon. 'There she was, asleep in bed, and this man threatens her with death and public humiliation! She only did the same as Lucretia herself, who is usually praised for it!'

'It is true, I admit,' said Parlamente, 'that no one is so righteous that he or she may not lapse. But when one experiences disgust at some action, one also experiences disgust at the memory of it. That is why Lucretia killed herself, whereas the silly woman in the story we've just heard wanted people to find it amusing.'

'All the same,' said Nomerfide, 'it does seem that she was a virtuous woman, since the man had several times made overtures to which she had never once succumbed – indeed, she was so firm that the man had to resort to deception and violence.'

'What!' exclaimed Parlamente. 'It is your view that provided a woman has refused two or three times already, she can give in without endangering her honour? In that case we ought to consider as women of honour a great many women who are not usually so regarded. We've all seen women who have rejected the advances of men to whom they have in reality already abandoned their hearts. Sometimes they reject them in order to protect their honour, sometimes to make themselves all the more ardently loved and admired. So it follows that one should not give credit to a woman, unless she holds firm to the very end.'

'What if a man were to reject a beautiful girl?' asked Dagoucin. 'Would you regard that as a great virtue?'

'I should indeed find it praiseworthy,' said Oisille, 'if a healthy young man were to make such a refusal, but none the less difficult to believe.'

'But I have known some young men who *have* refused to indulge in the sort of escapade that other young men of their age will deliberately look for,' he replied.

'Then I invite you to take my place,' said Longarine, 'and to tell us about it – only remember that here the truth must be told.'

'I promise,' he replied, 'to tell the truth so purely that there will be no embroidery to disguise it.'

STORY SIXTY-THREE

There were once four girls living in Paris. Two of them were sisters, and all four of them were so young, fresh and beautiful that they were constantly besieged by would-be lovers. Now there was also a certain gentleman, who had recently been made Provost of Paris by the King. Aware that his royal master was young and of an age to find the company of four such beautiful girls highly desirable, he talked them all round so cleverly that each of them thought that the King was interested in her alone, and agreed to whatever the Provost suggested. What he proposed was that they would all go to a banquet, to which he would invite his master. The King had been told of the plan and wholeheartedly approved, as did also two other [high-born] lords of the court. All three agreed to take a share in the venture. As they were seeking a fourth person to join them, along came another noble lord, handsome, honourable, [and about ten years younger than the others], and he too was invited to the banquet. He accepted with good grace, although in his heart he had no desire to do so. For one thing he had a wife who had borne him fine children. He was very contented and would not for anything in the world have wanted to give her grounds for suspicion. For another thing, he was devoted to the service of one of the most beautiful women in France at that time, and he admired and loved her so greatly that all other women seemed plain beside her. From his earliest youth, even before his marriage, no one had been able to persuade him to frequent other women, however great their beauty. He derived more pleasure from seeing his lady and loving her in the perfection of true love than he could have ever derived from all the favours of other women. This young lord went home to his wife and told her in secret what his master was planning, and how he for his part would as soon die as carry out the promise he had made. For, unless he was driven by the violent extremes of passion that can blind the most virtuous of men, he would rather die than break his marriage for the sake of someone else's carnal appetites – just as, although there was no man alive whom he would not dare attack in anger, he would rather die than commit a premeditated and unprovoked murder, unless compelled by honour. Seeing such virtue and nobility in one so young, his wife felt more love and admiration for him than ever. She asked him how he could decline to participate, in view of the fact that high-born princes are in the habit of taking exception to those who do not applaud everything that they themselves enjoy, and he replied:

'I have heard it said that the wise man always has some urgent journey or some indisposition up his sleeve to which he can resort when necessary. So I have decided that four or five days in advance I shall pretend to be seriously ill; and if you too would adopt a becoming bearing, my purpose would be well served.'

'That is the kind of hypocrisy which one can rightly call good and holy,' said the wife, 'and I shall not fail to give you support with the most sorrowful countenance I can contrive. Blessed is he who can avoid offending God and avoid the wrath of the monarch!'

They acted exactly as they had planned. The King was very distressed to hear from the wife of the young lord's illness. It did not have to last very long, however, for the King, faced with some piece of pressing business, sacrificed pleasure to duty, and unexpectedly left Paris. But some time later he remembered that their venture had been left unfulfilled, and he said to the young lord: 'We were foolish to have left in such haste, without seeing the four girls who were promised to us as the most beautiful in our kingdom.'

The young man replied: 'I am most pleased that you were unable to attend, for I was afraid that through my illness I alone would miss such an excellent opportunity.'

From these words it never occurred to the King that he was dissembling. And the young lord was loved more dearly by his wife than ever before.

*

At this point Parlamente burst out laughing, and could not resist saying: 'He'd have shown even greater love for his wife, if he'd done what he did for her sake alone. All the same, whatever the reasons, what he did was highly praiseworthy.'

'In my opinion,' said Hircan, 'there's nothing very praiseworthy about a man keeping his chastity out of love for his wife. For there are so many reasons why he should keep his chastity that he is almost compelled to do so. First, God commands it, secondly, his marriage vow binds him, and then fully satisfied natural appetites, unlike unfulfilled needs, are not in any way subject to temptation and craving. But consider the sort of love that a man gives freely to a lady who grants no favours in return, indeed grants no satisfaction at all other than permitting him to see her, speak to her and, more often than not, receive a sour reply for his pains. If a man's love for a woman in those circumstances is so unswervingly loyal that right through the most tempting opportunities it never wavers – then I say that such chastity is not just praiseworthy, it's nothing short of miraculous!'

'It is no miracle,' said Oisille, 'for when the heart is true, nothing is impossible to the body.'

'For bodies already transformed into angels, maybe!' Hircan replied.

'I do not only mean the bodies of those who through God's grace have been transmuted into Him,' she went on, 'but also those bodies that belong even to the basest spirits we see here on earth among men. If you look closely at the matter, you will find that those who have given their heart and affections to the pursuit of the perfection of knowledge, have not only forgotten the pleasures of the flesh, but even the most basic needs, such as eating and drinking. For, as long as the soul is by affection within its body, the flesh remains as if it were insensible. Thus it is that those men who love beautiful, honourable and virtuous women find such contentment in seeing them and hearing them speak. Thus it is that their minds are so contended that the flesh finds peace and is rid of all desires. Those who cannot experience such contentment are men of carnal natures, who, being too much enveloped in their flesh, do not even know whether they have a soul or not. But when the body is subject to the spirit it is almost insensible to the imperfections of the flesh, so much so that the strong conviction of such people may render them insensible. I once knew a man of noble birth, who, in order to demonstrate that he had loved his lady more deeply than anyone else, had given proof to his comrades by holding a candle in his bare fingers [for three whole nights]. As he did so, he fixed his gaze upon his beloved, and held firm, until his flesh was burnt away to the bone. Moreover, he said that he had felt no pain.'

'It seems to me,' said Geburon, 'that the devil who martyred him ought to have made him a second Saint Lawrence! There are very few men so consumed with the fire of passion that they do not fear even the smallest candle. If a lady made me endure so much for her sake, I'd demand adequate compensation, or I'd withdraw my affections!'

'So,' said Parlamente, 'you would insist on having your moment, once your lady had had hers? That sounds rather like a certain nobleman from Valencia in Spain about whom I was once told a story by a Knight Commander, a thoroughly worthy man.'

'Then may I ask you to take my place,' said Dagoucin, 'and to tell us your tale? For I am sure that it will be a good one.'

'This, Ladies,' began Parlamente, 'is a tale that will teach you to think twice before you refuse something. It will teach you not to place trust in the present, hoping that things will remain the same for ever, [but] to recognize that the present is in constant change and to have thought for the future.'

STORY SIXTY-FOUR

In the city of Valencia there was a man of gentle birth who for five or six years had loved a lady so perfectly and so well that his honour and conscience, and the honour and conscience of his beloved, remained intact. For his intention was to take her as his wife – an entirely reasonable ambition, for he was handsome, rich and of good family. This being so, he did not enter her service and pay court to her, without first seeking out her own wishes in the matter. She said that she would agree to the marriage subject to the desires of her friends [and relations]. They all assembled to discuss it, and found the marriage a very reasonable proposition, [provided that the girl herself was in agreement.] But the girl then started finding all kinds of objections, perhaps because she hoped for a better match, or perhaps to hide the love she felt for the man. Whatever the reason, the result was that the assembled friends and relations had to depart, regretting that they had been unable to bring what they knew to be an advantageous marriage on both sides to a satisfactory conclusion. The most distraught was of course the poor suitor, who would have been better able to bear the rejection if it had come from the family rather than from the girl. But that was the fact of the matter, and knowing it made his suffering worse than death. Without speaking a word to her or to anyone else, he went home and shut himself away. Then, after making a few necessary arrangements, he went away to an isolated spot and did his utmost to forget his love. He converted it entirely into the love of Our Lord, a love to which he was more beholden. Throughout this entire time he heard nothing either from his beloved or from her relatives. So, since he now felt that he had lost all prospect of leading the happy life he had hoped for, he resolved to enter upon the most austere and difficult way of life he could imagine. And, in this sorry state of mind – it could be called despair – he went and entered a Franciscan monastery which was situated not far from where several of the girl's relatives lived. As soon as they learned of his desperation, they spared no efforts to try to restrain him, but his resolve was so firm that there was no possible means of turning him from it. They knew well what had brought about his malady, and in their search for the cure, they turned to the young woman who was the cause of this sudden access of devotion. She was overcome with sorrow when she heard about the unfortunate turn of events. She had thought that a temporary rejection would serve merely to test the sincerity of his intentions. It had not entered her mind that she would lose him for ever – a possibility that she could plainly see was imminent. So she sent him a letter, which, badly translated, ran like this:

Man's love can never be approved
Unless its truth be truly proved
And so I wished to test by Time
That thing which I desired as mine –
To wit a husband good and true,
Who should not fail his whole life through.
So urgently I begged and prayed
That yet a while should be delayed
This bond that unto death must reign
And doth to many bring great pain.
My true desire was your affection,
It was not a real rejection!
For no one else could I adore
As lord and master ever more!
Oh wretched Fate! Now have I learned
That you have taciturnly turned
Unto the cloister cold and bleak.
It rends my heart and I must speak,
My tongue must sing a different song,
The song you sang and did no wrong,
To seek the one who come and sought,
To catch the one who has me caught.
My love, my life, if you depart,
I cannot live with broken heart,
So turn again, Alas! Alack!
Lest it's too late, turn back, turn back!
Turn from the robe so rough and rude,

Turn back to her you long have wooed
And take the bliss that you desire,
For Time stills not nor lulls Love's fire.
To you alone myself I give,
For without you I cannot live.
So turn again, and if you care
To seal the memories we share,
Then take me, tie the marriage knot,
And trust in me alone. Trust not
The dictates of your stricken mind.
'Twas not my thought to be unkind
But happiness and love the best
To grant you when you'd passed the test.
And now you've truly demonstrated
Faith and love, though long you waited
And constancy shines bright and true,
Myself I wholly give to you,
So take me, love, take what is thine,
As I am yours, so you be mine!

This epistle, along with all other conceivable exhortations, was delivered by a friend. As the gentleman, now a Franciscan friar, read the letter, a deep sorrow crept over his face. He sighed ardent sighs enough to consume the piteous words and wept tears enough to drown them in their flood. He made no reply, except to tell the messenger that the mortification of his extreme passion had cost him so dear that the will to live had left him, and that he no longer feared to die. To her who was the cause of his woe he sent word that, since she had not wished to gratify his passionate desires, she should not, now that he was free from them, seek to torture him further, but should content herself with what pain she had already occasioned him. His only remedy was to choose a life so austere that continual penance allowed him to forget his sorrows, to choose a life of fasting and chastisement which so weakened the body that the thought of death was his supreme consolation. Above all, he begged her, let him never hear from her again, for the mere memory of her name was an unbearable Purgatory.

The messenger returned with this sad reply. The chagrin she

felt when she received it was almost too much to bear. But Love does not allow the spirit to be utterly cast down, and she conceived the notion that if she could only see him, she would have more effect on him by speaking to him face to face than she had had by writing to him. So, accompanied by her father and her closest relatives, she went to the monastery. She spared no artifice to enhance her beauty, assuring herself that if he could but see her and hear her speak, the fire that had so long smouldered in both their breasts must inevitably be rekindled stronger than ever. It was almost the end of vespers when she arrived at the monastery, and she waited in a little chapel in the cloisters until he arrived. He had no idea who had called to see him. Unforewarned, he was about to enter the hardest battle of his life. He appeared, pale and worn, almost beyond recognition, yet full of a certain grace that rendered him no less worthy to be loved than before. Love overcame her, and she opened her arms to embrace him. But so overwhelmed was she, so sick at heart, to see him in the state he was, that she collapsed and fainted. The poor friar, who was not bereft of fraternal charity, lifted her up and placed her on a bench in the chapel. In reality, he was as much in need of help as she was. He affected not to notice the evidence of the girl's passion and fortified his heart in the love of his God against the great opportunity now at his fingertips. He seemed unaware of what was going on before his very eyes. When she recovered from her faint, she looked at him with her beautiful eyes, full of pity, and sufficient to soften the hardest rock. She began to speak, saying everything she could think of which seemed likely to persuade him to leave the monastery. And he replied, in the most virtuous terms he could devise. But eventually the poor friar [felt] his heart softened by the tears poured forth by his lady. It was as if he saw Love himself, that heartless bowman, at whose hand he had so long suffered, draw his golden dart, ready to inflict a new and yet more deadly wound. Flight was his only recourse. He fled from Love, he fled from his beloved.

Once he was back in the seclusion of his room, he was reluctant to let her depart without a more fitting end. He wrote a few words in Spanish – words which seem to me so full of meaning that I prefer not to diminish their grace by translating them.

They were taken to her by a young novice, who found her still sitting there, sunk in the depths of despair. Indeed, had it been legally possible, I believe she would have stayed there and become a Franciscan herself. But she opened the note and read:

Volvete don venesti, anima mia,
*Que en las tristas vidas es la mia.**

At this she realized that all hope was gone. She resolved to follow the advice of her friends. And so to her own house she returned, there to lead a life as melancholy as the life now led by her cloistered suitor.

*

'So, Ladies, you see,' concluded Parlamente, 'how the man wrought revenge on his harsh lady. She had meant to try him out, but threw him into a state of despair, with the result that when she wanted him back, it was too late.'

'I'm sorry he never abandoned the monk's habit to marry her,' said Nomerfide. 'I'm sure it would have been a perfect marriage.'

['In all truth,' said Simontaut, 'I think he was very wise. Anyone who has gone into the burdens of marriage] will agree that the matrimonial state is every bit as irksome as the austere religious life. This man was already weakened by abstinence and fasting, and he was afraid of taking on a burden which would be lifelong!'

'I think it was wrong of her,' said Hircan, 'to tempt him with marriage. That's too much to bear, even for the strongest man in the world. On the other hand, if she had proposed a liaison free of any obligation, other than that voluntarily entered into, there's no cord that could not have been unloosed, [no knot that could not have been untied.] As it was, she was offering Hell as an alternative to Purgatory, so in my view he was quite right to reject her and make her feel what he had felt when she had rejected him.'

'It is indeed true,' said Ennasuite, 'that there are many people who, thinking they can do better than others, end up worse off or with the opposite of what they wanted.'

* Return whence you came, my soul, so hard are the trials of my life.

'It's not altogether to the point,' said Geburon, 'but what you say reminds me of a certain woman who ended up with something she hadn't intended. It caused a great stir in the church of Saint John in Lyons.'

'Then take my place, I beg you,' said Parlamente, 'and tell us the story.'

'It will not be as long,' said Geburon, 'nor will it be as sad, as the tale told by Parlamente.'

STORY SIXTY-FIVE

In the church of Saint John in Lyons there is a rather dark side chapel. Inside this chapel there is a stone tomb, on which there are sculpted life-size figures. Around the bottom of the tomb there are figures of soldiers in sleeping postures. One summer's day a soldier was strolling about inside the church. It was very hot outside, and he suddenly felt like taking a nap. He noticed the chapel, and seeing that it was dark and cool inside, thought it would not be a bad idea to join the other figures guarding the tomb. So he went and lay down beside them. Then, while he was fast asleep, along came a devout old woman. She muttered her devotions, clutching a burning candle. When she had finished, she wanted to stick her candle on the tomb, and it happened to be the sleeping soldier who was within her reach. Thinking he was a stone statue, she placed the candle on his forehead. But the wax would not stick, so, thinking it was because the stone was cold, she tried to warm it with the flame, in order to make the candle hold. But this was no insensible statue, and it began to shout. The old woman was terrified out of her wits. 'A miracle!' she shrieked. 'A miracle!' All the people in the church came running up at once. Some went into the chapel to see the miracle. Some went and started to ring the bells. The old woman took them all to see the statue that had moved, and a lot of people had a good laugh about it. But the [priests] were not too pleased. They had already made up their minds that they should turn their tomb to account and make as much money out of it as they had from their crucifix – the one that hangs over the rood-screen and is supposed to have spoken. However, it only needed one woman's stupidity to become known for *that* farce to come to an end!

*

'If everyone recognized their stupidity, they would not be thought so saintly, nor would their miracles be taken for the truth. Henceforth then, Ladies, take care which saints you offer your candles to!'

'It's worth noting,' observed Hircan, 'that whatever the circumstances, women always have to do wrong!'

'Is it doing wrong,' asked Nomerfide, 'to place candles on a tomb?'

'Yes,' he replied, 'when you burn men's foreheads with them! You can't call a good action good if it turns out bad. Just imagine, the poor woman thought she was giving God a magnificent present by offering a bit of a candle!'

'I do not look to the value of the present,' said Oisille, 'but to the heart that presents it. It may be that this good woman had greater love of God than those who light huge torches, for, as the Gospel says, she gave of her penury.'

'Even so,' said Saffredent, 'I do not think that the stupidity of women is pleasing to God, who is supreme wisdom. For although it is true that He looks with favour on simplicity, I note from my reading of Scripture that He scorns ignorance. And if He bids us be as simple as the dove, He also bids us none the less strongly to be as wise as the serpent.'

'For my part,' said Oisille, 'I do not think a woman ignorant for bringing her lighted candle before God, if she does so to make amends, kneeling upon the ground, taper in hand, before her sovereign Lord, confessing to Him her sins, begging with firm hope for mercy and salvation.'

'Would to God,' said Dagoucin, 'that everybody acted with the same intention as you. But I fear that such is not the case with these poor stupid women.'

But Oisille replied: 'The women who are the least able to talk about it are often the ones who feel more deeply the love and will of God. For this reason one should not judge anyone but oneself.'

'There's nothing very out of the ordinary about waking up a sleeping soldier,' said Ennasuite, laughing. 'There are low-born women who've done better than that – some have scared the highest princes of the realm, without putting burning candles on their heads!'

'It sounds to me,' said Geburon, 'as if you know a good story on the subject. So I invite you to take my place and to tell it to us.'

'It's not a long story,' she began, 'but if I can express it as it really happened, it's certainly not one that'll make you cry!'

STORY SIXTY-SIX

It was the year when the Princess of Navarre and the Duke of Vendôme were married. After the bride's parents and the King and Queen had been regaled at Vendôme, they all went off together to the Guienne. They were entertained *en route* at the house of a nobleman, where many refined and beautiful ladies were assembled, and where the whole company danced till the early hours. The newly married couple were exhausted and retired to their bedroom, where they collapsed fully clothed upon the bed, and fell asleep. They were quite alone and the doors and windows were closed. Shortly, however, they were awakened from the depths of their slumber by the sound of someone opening their door from the outside. Monsieur de Vendôme, suspecting it might be one of his friends trying to catch him unawares, drew back the curtain to have a look. But it was an old chambermaid of theirs. She walked straight up to the bed, and although it was too dark for her to see who it really was, she could just make out the two figures lying very close together. She began to shout:

'You wicked, shameless good-for-nothing! I've suspected you for a long time, but I couldn't prove it, and didn't dare go and tell my mistress! But now I've caught you, I'm not going to keep quiet any longer! And as for you, you degenerate apostate! Do you know what shame you've brought on this house, to undo this poor lass like this? If I weren't a God-fearing woman, I'd give you a thorough beating here and now! Get up! Are you still not ashamed of yourself? In the Devil's name get up, won't you!'

The Duke and the Princess were speechless with laughter, and hid their faces against one another, to make the old woman go on a bit longer. Seeing that for all her angry words the couple gave no sign of moving, she went closer and made to grab hold of them by the arms. It was then she realized, recognizing first the clothes and then the faces, that she had made a mistake. She was down on her knees in an instant, begging them both to forgive her for disturbing their sleep. Monsieur de Vendôme, however, had not yet heard all he wanted, and, jumping up, asked the old woman to tell him who she had mistaken them for. She was reluctant at first, but once he had assured her on his oath that he would tell no one, she told him that she had thought it was a young lady of the house, and a certain individual who bore the office of protonotary apostolical, and who was in love with the girl. She said that she had had her eye on the pair of them for a long time, because she did not like to think that her mistress should place her confidence in a man who brought such shame on the house. So saying, she went out and left the Duke and Princess alone again, as she had found them. They laughed long and heartily at what had happened, and although they told everybody about it subsequently, they never actually named the people for whom they had been mistaken.

*

'And that, Ladies, is how the good lady, thinking she would give two illicit lovers their just deserts, revealed to two princely strangers something that the other servants of the house knew nothing at all about.'

'I think,' said Parlamente, 'that I know whose house this happened in. And I think I know who the protonotary was, too. He's already wielded his influence in a good number of ladies' houses, and when he doesn't manage to win the favour of the mistress of the house, he manages to ingratiate himself with one of the young women. Apart from that, he's a good and honourable man!'

'Why do you say "apart from that"?' asked Hircan. 'I think he was a good man precisely because he did what he did!'

To which Parlamente replied: 'I see you recognize the patient and what he was suffering from, and if he needed a defence, you wouldn't fail to act as his advocate! All the same, I wouldn't trust a man who can't manage even his own intrigues without the chambermaids finding out.'

'And do you think,' said Nomerfide, 'that men care whether anyone knows, so long as they achieve their ends? Believe me, [if nobody else talked about it, they would have to go and make it public knowledge themselves]!'

Hircan was angry at this, and retorted: 'There's no need for men to talk about everything they know!'

'Perhaps,' said Nomerfide, blushing, 'it would not be to their advantage if they did.'

'To hear you speak,' Simontaut intervened, 'one would think that men took pleasure in hearing ill of ladies. I'm sure you think that I do. So, lest all the other [ladies] think me a slanderer as well, I should very much like to tell you something good about one!'

'Then I give you my place,' said Ennasuite, 'and urge you to restrain your natural inclinations in order that you may honour us as you are duty bound.'

And this is how Simontaut began:

['It is so unexpected to me, Ladies, to hear of you performing any virtuous deed, that when such a deed does occur, it seems to me that it should not be concealed but rather written in letters of gold, in order to serve as an example to women and as a source of wonderment to men.] Seeing in the weak sex that which weakness itself opposes, I am led to recount what I have heard from Captain Robertval and several of his crew.'

STORY SIXTY-SEVEN

It happened during the aforementioned Captain Robertval's voyage to the island of Canada. He had been appointed leader of the expedition by the King, and, provided the climate was favourable, his orders were to stay in Canada and establish towns and forts. You all probably know how he took the first steps in carrying out these orders. In order to populate the land with Christians, he took with him artisans of all types. Amongst these people there was a certain individual who was low enough to betray his master, and almost caused him to be taken prisoner by the natives. But by God's will the plot was uncovered before it could harm Captain Robertval, who had the wicked traitor seized, with the intention of punishing him as he deserved. And he certainly would have punished him, had it not been for the man's wife, who had braved all the perils of the sea with him, and could not now bear to see him die. She wept and pleaded with the Captain and the whole crew, until, partly out of compassion, partly because she at least had served faithfully, they granted her request. The couple were to be left together on a little island inhabited only by wild animals, and with them they would be allowed to take only a few basic necessities.

Finding themselves alone with only the ferocious beasts of the island for company, these unfortunate people had no help but in God, who had always been the sure hope of the poor wife. She was a woman who placed all her trust in Him, and for her preservation, nourishment and consolation she had brought the New Testament, in which she read unceasingly. But she also laboured alongside her husband to build as best they could a little hut in which to live. When the lions and other wild animals came close to devour them, they defended themselves so well, he with his arquebus and she with stones, that not only did they succeed in repelling them, but they were often also able to kill them for food. With the meat of the animals they killed and the herbs they gathered, they were able to live for a while, even [after] the bread they had brought with them had run out. [But] as time went on the husband found it increasingly difficult to take this diet. Eventually, he fell ill from the water they had to drink, and his stomach became distended. He died in a very short space of time, without any rites or any consolation other than those provided by his wife, who served him both as physician and as confessor. And thus he passed joyously from this desolate island into the regions of Heaven. All alone, the poor woman buried the body as deeply in the ground as she was able. But the lions at once caught the scent and came looking for the decaying corpse. From the protection of her little house, determined that her husband's mortal remains should have a decent resting-place, she fought off the wild animals with shots from his arquebus. And so she lived on, her bodily existence no higher than that of the beasts, but her soul in the sphere of the angels. For she spent her time in reading the Scriptures, in contemplation, prayer and other devotions. Her soul, within her emaciated and half-dead body, was joyous and contented. But He who will never abandon his people, He who shows His strength in the midst of man's despair, did not suffer that the virtue He had bestowed upon this woman should remain hidden from men, but willed that to His glory it should be made known. And after a certain time had elapsed He brought it to pass that one of the ships of Robertval's fleet should sail by the island. The crew, catching sight of smoke, were reminded of the couple who had been left there, and decided to go and see how God had dealt with them. The poor woman saw the ship approach, and dragged herself to the water's edge, where the sailors found her as they landed. Giving thanks to God, she led them into her humble abode, and showed them how she had been living. They would have found it beyond belief, without the knowledge that God is almighty to nourish His servants in the barren desert even as in the finest banquets in the world. Unable to remain there any longer, they took the poor creature with them on their [long] voyage back to La Rochelle. When they had arrived and told the inhabitants of the town of her fidelity and steadfastness, she was received with great honour by all the ladies, who were glad to send their daughters to her to learn to read and write. In this worthy manner she earned her livelihood for the rest of her days and her sole desire was to exhort all people to love Our Lord and place their trust in Him, holding forth as an example the great mercy He had shown to her.

*

'Now, Ladies, will you not admit that I have fairly praised the virtues that the Lord has endowed you with – virtues which are all the worthier to be praised as their recipients are the weaker?'

'Far be it from us,' replied Oisille, 'to be sorry that you praise the graces of Our Lord in us, for in truth all goodness flows from Him; but it must be avowed that neither man nor woman is favoured in the work of God, for in their endeavours, both do but plant, and God alone gives the increase.'

'If you've read Scripture properly,' said Saffredent, 'you will know that Saint Paul wrote that Apollos planted and that he watered, but he says nothing about *women* lending a hand in God's labour!'

'You're as bad as all the other men who take a passage from Scripture which serves their purposes, and leave out anything that contradicts it. If you had read everything Saint Paul says, you would find that he commends himself to those women who have laboured with him in the Gospel.'

'Be that as it may,' said Longarine, 'the woman in the story certainly deserves praise, both because she loved her husband and risked her life for him, and because she loved God, who, as we've seen, never abandoned her.'

'As to the first point,' came in Ennasuite, 'I think there is not a woman amongst us who would not do the same to save her husband's life.'

'And I think,' said Parlamente, 'that some husbands are such stupid beasts that women who live with them should not find anything odd about living with their wild cousins!'

Ennasuite took this remark to be aimed at her, and could not resist replying: 'Provided they didn't bite, I'd prefer the company of wild beasts to the company of men who are bad-tempered and unbearable! But as I was going to say, if my husband were in danger, like the man in this story, I would not leave him, no, not if it cost me my life.'

'You should be careful not to love him too much,' said Nomerfide. 'Too much love could lead you both astray. There's a happy medium for everything. If there's a failure of understanding, love may engender hatred.'

'I don't think you would have made that point,' said Simontaut, 'if you weren't intending to confirm it with some example. So if you have one, I invite you to take my place and tell it to us.'

'Well then,' she answered, 'I shall make it short and sweet, as is my wont.'

STORY SIXTY-EIGHT

In the town of Pau, in the Béarn, there was once an apothecary by the name of Étienne. He was married, and his wife was a good woman, an excellent housewife and attractive enough to keep him contented. But just as he had an expert taste for the different types of drugs he dispensed, so it was with women. He liked to try out the various kinds, so as to be more knowledgeable about their different constitutions, and this so vexed his wife that she was beginning to lose all patience. For he took no notice at all of her – except in Holy Week, by way of penance. One day while the apothecary was in his shop, his wife hid behind the door to listen to what he was saying to the customers. A woman came in who was a close friend and neighbour. She happened to be suffering from the same trouble as the apothecary's wife.

'Oh dear! neighbour,' she began, 'I'm the most miserable woman in the world. I love my husband more than myself! I can think of nothing but how to serve and obey him. But all my efforts are in vain, because he'd rather have the nastiest, foullest, filthiest female in town than me. So I was wondering, neighbour, if you might have some medicine that might change him . . . If you have, could you let me have some? I promise I'll pay you back in any way I can, if he treats me well again.'

To console her he replied that he did know of a certain powder. If she put it in her husband's soup or on his roast, like *poudre de duc,** he would give her the biggest treat in the world. The poor woman was only too eager for this miracle to come about, and she asked what the powder was and if she could get hold of some. There was nothing in it but Spanish fly powder, he replied, and he had plenty of that in stock. Before leaving, she persuaded him to prepare the powder properly, and took with her the quantity he prescribed for what she wanted. Later she had occasion to thank him profusely for his trouble. Her hus-

* An aid to digestion made with cinnamon and sugar.

band, who was a strong, well-built man and had not taken too large a dose, felt none the worse for it – [and she felt considerably better]!

The apothecary's wife had heard her husband serving their neighbour, and it occurred to her that she had need of this prescription herself. So she took careful note of where he put what was left of the powder, intending to make use of it when she had the chance. Her opportunity arrived three or four days later, when her husband began to feel a chill in the stomach, and asked her if she would make him a broth. She told him a roast sprinkled with *poudre de duc* would be better for him and was promptly ordered to take some cinnamon and sugar from the shop and get one ready. This of course she did, not forgetting to help herself to the remainder of the powder that had been given to the neighbour but giving no thought whatsoever to weight, measure or dosage. The husband ate his roast, and at first thought it very good. But he soon began to feel the effects – which he tried to alleviate with the aid of his wife. To no avail! He felt as if his insides were on fire. He did not know which way to turn. Then he accused her of poisoning him, and demanded to know what she had put in the roast. She admitted the truth – that she was as much in need of a potion as the neighbour. The poor man would have beaten her if he could, but he was in such torture that he could only manage curses. He ordered her to go out and fetch the Queen of Navarre's apothecary, who eventually came and administered the remedies necessary to cure him. It was not long before he recovered, and the royal apothecary reprimanded him [so severely for recommending drugs he would not take himself that he inwardly passed judgement on himself for committing a reckless act, and admitted that his wife had only acted properly, seeing that she had merely wished to make him love her.

Thus the poor man was obliged to accept his foolishness and acknowledge that God had justly punished him in turning upon him the trick that had been intended for someone else.]

*

'It seems to me, Ladies, that this woman's love for her husband was no less indiscreet than it was deeply felt.'

'Do you call it loving her husband,' demanded Hircan, 'when she made him suffer merely for the sake of the pleasure she hoped to have?'

'I think she only wanted to win her husband's love back,' replied Longarine, 'when she thought she had lost it. There is nothing a woman would not do for such a treasure.'

'Nevertheless,' said Geburon, 'a woman ought not to cook for her husband, whatever the reason, unless she knows from her own experience or from the experts that it won't be harmful to him. [But if ignorance has to be excused, then I suppose this woman must be excused.] For the most blinding passion of all is love, and the blindest person of all is the woman who can't bear the burden wisely and well.'

'Geburon, you are departing from your customary excellent sentiments,' said Oisille, 'and joining the ranks of your companions. But I insist that there are women who have borne the burden of love and jealousy with patience and restraint.'

'Yes, and they enjoy themselves at the same time,' said Hircan, 'for the wisest ones are the ones who have as much fun laughing at their husbands' antics, as their husbands have in trying to go behind their backs. If you will permit me to speak next, so that Madame Oisille may follow me with the closing story of the day, I'll tell you one about a man and a wife who are well known to all of you.'

'Then begin,' said Nomerfide.

And, with a laugh, Hircan began his story.

STORY SIXTY-NINE

In the château of Odos, in Bigorre, there lived an equerry of the King, one Carlo by name, an Italian, who had married a noble and virtuous lady. Unfortunately she had now aged somewhat, having borne him a number of children. Not being all that young himself, he was content to live with her on peaceable and friendly terms. However, from time to time he would chat to her maids. She never made a fuss about this, but just quietly dismissed them whenever they seemed to be getting too friendly with [him]. One of the maids she took on was a very good, well-behaved young girl, and she decided to tell her what her husband was like, warning her that she was in the habit of turning girls out if she found them misbehaving. The maid wanted to stay in her mistress's good books and not lose her position, so she made up her mind to be an honest woman. The master often accosted her, of course, but she would turn a deaf ear and run straight off to tell her mistress. They used to laugh together about his silly behaviour.

One day the chambermaid was sifting grain in a room at the back of the house. She was wearing her smock over her head as they do in that part of the world – it's a garment like a hood, but it covers the shoulders and falls full length at the back. Well, along comes the master, and seeing her in this attire, he eagerly starts to make overtures. She would not for a moment have given in, but she led him on by asking if she could first of all go to make sure that his wife was busy – so that they should not be caught, she said. He agreed, and she suggested that he put her smock over his own head, and get on with the sifting in the meantime, so that the mistress would not wonder why the noise had stopped. He was only too eager to agree to this plan. At last he was going to have what he wanted. But the girl, who was certainly not devoid of a sense of humour, ran off at once to the lady of the house. 'Come and have a look at that husband of yours,' she said, 'I've shown him how to sift, to get rid of him!' They hurried back to see this newly acquired servant. When the wife saw him, with the hood of the smock over his head and the sieve in his hands, she burst out laughing, and clapped her hands in glee. She eventually managed to say: 'Well, lass, how much a month do you want me to pay you?' The husband recognized the voice and realized he had been tricked. He threw his smock and his sieve to the ground in a rage, and turned on the maid, calling her all the names under the sun. If his wife had not intervened he would have paid her her due and turned her out then and there. However, in the end everyone calmed down, and from then on they lived under the same roof without a cross word.

*

'What do you say about that woman, Ladies? Wasn't it sensible of her to have fun when her husband was trying to have fun too?'

'I don't see that he had much fun,' commented Saffredent, 'if he failed in his intentions.'

'I would think,' said Ennasuite, 'that he had more fun laughing at it with his wife, than he would have had if he *had* managed to have his way. It could have killed him at his age!'

'Even so,' said Simontaut, 'I would have been extremely annoyed to be found with my chambermaid's smock over my head!'

'I've heard,' said Parlamente, 'that it was only thanks to your wife that you were *not* caught out in some such attire, in spite of your cunning, and she's not had a moment's peace ever since.'

'Stick to stories about your own household,' said Simontaut, 'without prying into mine – though I would add that my wife has no cause to complain about me. And even if what you say about me *were* true, she would never notice. There's no reason why she should – she has all her needs satisfied.'

'Honest women need nothing,' said Longarine, 'but their husband's love, which alone can content them. And women who seek nothing but animal satisfaction never find it within the limits prescribed by honour.'

'Do you call it animal satisfaction, when a woman wants from her husband what she is entitled to?' demanded Geburon.

'What I say is this,' she answered, 'that a chaste woman whose heart is filled with true love has more satisfaction from being loved perfectly, than she possibly could from all the pleasures that the body could desire.'

'I am entirely of your opinion,' said Dagoucin, 'although the noble lords here would never accept it or admit it. I believe that if a woman is not contented by mutual love in the first place, there is nothing at all a husband can do on his own to content her. I mean, if she does [not] live in accordance with what is honourable for women in matters of love, then she is bound to be tempted by infernal animal concupiscence.'

'What you say reminds me,' said Oisille, 'of a lady who was very beautiful, who was well married and who, because she did not live in accordance with what is honourable in love, did in fact become more carnal in her desires than swine and more cruel than the lions.'

'Madame, will you tell us this story, and bring our story-telling to a close for the day?' asked Simontaut.

'There are two reasons why I ought not to,' she replied. 'One is that it is a long story, and the other is that it is not a story of our time, and although it is by a reliable author, we have after all sworn not to tell stories from a written source.'

'That is true,' said Parlamente, 'but if it's the story I think it is, then it's written in such antiquated language, that apart from you and me, there's no one here who will have heard it. So it can be regarded as a new one.'*

Thereupon they all urged Oisille to tell the tale. She should not worry about the length, they assured her, as there was still a good hour to go before vespers. So, at their bidding, she began.

* Story 70 is in fact a transposition of the thirteenth-century poem *La chastelaine de Vergi*.

STORY SEVENTY

In the Duchy of Burgundy, there was once a Duke and a virtuous and handsome prince he was. He had married a lady whose beauty gave him such great happiness that he was blind to her true character. His only desire was to please her, and for her part she gave all the appearance of returning his affection. Now in the Duke's service there was a young nobleman, endowed with all the perfections a man should have, and greatly loved by all around him. The Duke himself, who had brought up the young man in his own household, was especially fond of him. Indeed, so fond of him was he, and so impressed by his excellent qualities, that he entrusted to him all the affairs that a young man of his age and experience could reasonably undertake.

The Duchess's heart was not the heart of a virtuous wife and princess, and neither the love her husband bore her nor the gentle way he treated her brought her satisfaction. Often she would cast glances at the young nobleman. The sight of him pleased her, and she began to feel a love for him beyond all reason. She strove continually to make this known to him, casting tender, doleful glances at him, sighing heavily, and putting on impassioned airs. But he, who had been schooled in virtue and in virtue alone, could see no vice in a lady who had no cause to turn to vice, so that for all her glances and her airs the poor, impassioned creature reaped no reward but wild desperation. One day her desperation drove her to forget that she was a wife, whose duty was to receive advances and reject them, to forget that she was a princess who ought to receive the adoration of her servants while disdaining them, until, with the reckless courage of one beside herself, she sought to quench the unbearable flames within her. It was a day when the Duke had gone to Council. The young man, because of his age, was not admitted, and the Duchess summoned him to her side. Thinking that she had some order to give him, he came at once. But she led him into a gallery, and strolled with him there, leaning on his arm, and sighing like a woman weary of a life of too much ease:

'I am amazed by you,' she said to him. 'You are young, handsome and so full of every grace. You have lived in our household where you meet many beautiful women. And yet you have never been in love with any of them. You have never been devoted to the service of a single one.' And, looking at him with as steady an eye as she could, she said no more, giving him time to reply.

'Madame,' he began, 'if your grace would deign to consider my position, it might appear more amazing if a man such as I, unworthy as I am of love, were seen to offer service and devotion to some lady, only to be rejected or ridiculed.'

Hearing this modest reply, the Duchess loved him more than ever, and swore to him that there was not a woman at her court who would not be overjoyed to have such a man devoted to her service. Nor should he fear to take his chance in love, for he would risk nothing, and would surely acquit himself with honour. The heat of a passion hot enough to melt the hardest ice was written in her face, and the young man looked down at the ground, not daring to meet her eyes. He was about to take his leave, when the Duke called his wife to the Council about a matter that concerned her. So it was she who, with great reluctance, took her leave of him.

The young man gave no sign that he had understood a single word of what she had been trying to say to him. This so puzzled and annoyed her that she did not know what to blame for her difficulty, unless it be the foolish fear by which she believed the young man was beset. Some days later, since he seemed still not to have understood her words, she made up her mind to have no thought for shame or fear and make her passion plain to him. She was certain that beauty such as hers could not but be welcomed, and though she would have preferred to have had the honour of a servant's supplications, she put honour aside to favour pleasure. She tried a few more times to convey her meaning, as on the first occasion, but still did not receive the response that she desired. So one day she took the young gentleman aside on the pretext of having some important piece of business to discuss with him. He, with due respect and humility, followed her as she went over to a window recess, where no one else in the room could see them. Torn between apprehension and desire, she began, with tremulous voice, by addressing him in the same terms as before. She reproached him for not having yet chosen a lady in her court, and again assured him that, whoever he might choose, she would herself help to ensure that he would be favourably received. He was taken aback and distressed at this, and replied:

'Madame, my heart is true, and if the lady of my choice were to refuse me, I could never know happiness again in this world. I know that there is no lady in this court who would ever deign to admit a person such as myself to her service.'

The Duchess blushed deeply, for she believed that there was nothing now which could prevent the conquest. She swore to him that the most beautiful lady in the court would, if he so desired, be overcome with joy to receive him and he would have perfect contentment from her.

'Alas! Madame,' he said, 'I cannot believe that there is any woman in this court so unfortunate and so blind as to make me the object of her affections.'

Seeing that still he was refusing to understand what she was saying to him, she lifted a little the veil that hid her passionate desires, and, fearful of the young man's virtue, she phrased her declaration as a question, saying:

'Suppose that Fortune had so favoured you that it was I myself who bore you such goodwill – then what would you say?'

He thought he must be dreaming to hear such words, and went down on one knee, saying:

'Madame, if by the grace of God I am granted the favour of the Duke my master and of yourself, then I shall consider myself the happiest man in the world, for I would ask no greater reward for my loyal service, being above all other men bound to lay down my life to serve you, and being sure, Madame, that the love you bear my lord is deep and chaste – so deep and chaste that no one, not even the greatest prince and most perfect man on earth, far less I, a mere worm, could ever mar the union that joins your grace with my sovereign lord. He has cared for me since I was a child, and has made me what I have become. Therefore, I could never entertain thoughts about his wife, daughter, sister or mother, other than those that a loyal and faithful servant owes to his master, and I would sooner die than do so . . .'

The Duchess would not let him continue. Seeing that she was in danger of suffering a dishonourable defeat, she interrupted his words abruptly, saying:

'Oh, wicked, vainglorious and foolish young man! Who has invited you to entertain such thoughts? Do you believe yourself so handsome that the very flies are enamoured of you? If by any chance you were presumptuous enough to make advances to me, I would soon show you that I love no one but my husband and have no desire to do otherwise. And when I spoke to you as I did, I did so for my own amusement, to find out about you, and laugh at you as I laugh at all amorous young fools!'

'Madame,' he replied, 'that is what I thought, and I believe what you say.'

Without waiting to hear more, she made off in haste towards her room, but seeing that her ladies-in-waiting were following, she slipped into her private chamber, there to pour forth her woe. Her affliction was indescribable, for, on the one hand, she had failed in love and felt mortally wounded, while on the other, she was angry both with herself for speaking so rashly and with him for replying in such a virtuous manner. This drove her to such fury that at one moment she wanted to do away with herself, and at the next wanted to live to wreak revenge on the man whom she now saw as her mortal enemy.

After weeping for a long time, she decided to pretend to be ill, in order to avoid being present at supper, during which the young man customarily attended the Duke. But the Duke, who loved his wife more than he loved himself, came to see her. And she, the better to achieve her ends, told him that she believed herself to be pregnant and that the pregnancy had brought on a most painful cold in the eyes. For the next two or three days she remained in bed, in such a melancholic state that the Duke guessed that something other than pregnancy was the cause. So the next night he came to sleep in her bed. But in spite of his kind words and caresses he could not stop her continual sighing.

'My love,' he began, 'you know that I love you more than life itself. If I were to lose you, I could not continue to live. If you care for my health, then I beg you to tell me what it is that makes you sigh so much. I cannot believe that such suffering comes from pregnancy alone.'

The Duchess could not have found him better disposed towards her for her purposes, and judged the time ripe to take revenge for the affront she had received. Putting her arms about her husband's neck, she began to weep, saying: 'Alas! The greatest grief I have is to see you deceived by people whose duty it ought to be to protect your honour and all that you have.'

Hearing these words, the Duke desired greatly to know what lay behind them, and he urged her not to be afraid to tell the truth. She refused, and refused again to tell him, but then at last she said:

'In the future, Monsieur, I shall not be surprised to hear of foreigners making war on princes, when those who are most beholden to their lords dare undertake such cruel deeds that loss of land and loss of wealth are as nothing to compare. I speak, Monsieur, of a certain gentleman . . .' And she named the young man she had now come to hate so much, and went on: 'a man whom you yourself have reared, a man who has been treated more as a relative and son than as a servant, and who has now committed so mean and cruel an act as to seek to sully the honour of your wife upon which the honour of your family and your children rests. Although he has long sought to give me sign of his wicked intentions, yet my heart, which has regard for you alone, could not comprehend, and so in the end he came and declared himself openly. I gave him such reply as my estate and chastity required, but my hatred of him now is such that I cannot bear to look at him. And this it is that made me stay within my room and forgo the joy of your company. Therefore, I beg you, my lord, shun this evil man as if he were the plague. For, after such a crime and fearing lest I recount it to you, he may resort to acts far worse. And so, Monsieur, that is the cause of my sorrow, which it seems only meet and right for you to deal with in all haste.'

The Duke, who on the one hand loved his wife dearly and felt that he had been gravely insulted, on the other hand so loved his loyal servant that he could scarcely believe these lies to be the truth. In deep distress and filled with anger, he retired to his room, and sent command that the young man was not to appear before him again, but was to retire to his lodgings for a period of time. The young man, not knowing the reason, was more deeply mortified than anyone could be, knowing that he had deserved the very opposite of such treatment. Sure of his innocence in thought and in deed, he sent a friend to speak to the Duke on his behalf and to bear a letter, saying that if it was on account of some ill report that he was banished from his master's presence, he humbly begged that he would suspend his judgement until he had heard the truth. Then the Duke would learn that he had in no way been insulted. On seeing the letter, the Duke moderated his anger a little, and sent for the young man to come secretly to see him in his room. With his rage written in his face, he said:

'I would never have thought that after caring for you so tenderly, as if you were my own son, I should ever have regretted doing so much for you. I would never have believed that you would try to cause me far greater harm than ever loss of life or property could, that you would try to stain the honour of the one who is the other half of my self, and disgrace my family and lineage for evermore. You will perfectly understand that an affront of this nature is so deeply wounding to my heart that had it not been for some doubt still lingering in my mind, I should long ago have had you drowned, to punish you in secret for the dishonour you have in secret sought to bring on me!'

But the young man was not dismayed by this speech. Unaware of what the Duchess had said, he continued to speak without any hesitation, and besought the Duke to tell him who was his accuser. For, he said, swords not words should answer in such a matter.

'Your accuser,' said the Duke, 'bears no arms but the armour of chastity. It was my wife, and no one else, who told me, and who begged me to avenge her.'

Although he saw how great were the evil intentions of the Duchess, the poor young man still held back from accusing her in his turn, but replied thus:

'Madame may speak as she pleases, my lord. You know her better than I. And you will know whether or no I have ever seen her other than in your company, except for one occasion when she said very little to me. Your judgement is as true as that of any prince [in Christendom.] Therefore, I beg of you, my lord, judge whether my behaviour has ever been such as to give you any grounds for suspicion. The fire of love cannot for long be hidden before it is recognized by those who have suffered the same disease. I would ask of you, my lord, to accept my word concerning two things. The first is that my loyalty to you is so true that even were Madame your wife the most beautiful creature in the world, still love would never have the power to stain my honour and my faith; and the second is that even were she not your wife, she of all the women in the world is the one whose love I least would seek; there are many others to whom [my fancy] would be sooner drawn.'

Hearing these truthful words, the Duke began to soften, and said:

'I assure you that I have not believed her. Therefore do not be afraid to go about your business as you have been accustomed to do, in the assurance that if I find that truth is on your side, my affection for you will be even greater than before. But, if I find that you are lying, then your life will be at my mercy!'

The young man thanked the Duke, and declared his readiness to submit to whatever punishment should be meted out to him if he were ever found guilty. When the Duchess saw the young man serving at table once again, she could not keep her patience, and, turning to her husband, said: 'It would be no more than you deserve, my lord, if you were to be poisoned, since you appear to have more confidence in your mortal enemies than in your closest friends!'

'I beg you, my love, do not torment yourself over this affair. If I find out that what you told me is true, I assure you that he will not have twenty-four hours to live. But he has sworn to me upon his oath that it is not true. Moreover, I myself have noticed nothing. Consequently, unless I am shown convincing proof I cannot believe it.'

'Truly, my lord,' she said, 'such kindness makes his wickedness the greater. What greater proof do you desire than that such a man as he should never be known to be in love? Believe me, if he had never presumed to devote himself to my service, he would not have waited so long to find himself a mistress, for no young man would go on leading such a solitary life in such a court, had he not set his heart on someone in such an exalted position that he was content to live in vain hope. And, since you are so sure that he never conceals the truth from you, I beg you, put him on his oath to tell you where his heart does lie, for if he tells you he's in love with someone else, then I'm happy for you to believe it, but if not, you must accept that what I say is the truth.'

The Duke found his wife's argument sound, and questioned the young man closely.

'My wife continues to insist on the truth of what she tells me,' he said, 'and has given a number of good reasons to support what she believes. They are reasons which give me grounds to be extremely suspicious about you. What she has pointed out to me is that it is rather astonishing that a man like you, young, and noble in every respect, should not, as far as anyone knows, have ever had an affair of the heart. This leads me to suspect that what she says about your feelings is true – that your hope that one day they may be fulfilled gives you such satisfaction that you cannot bear to think about other women. Now, I ask you as your friend, and order you as your master, to tell me whether you are devoted to the service of any lady at all.'

Although the poor young man wished as dearly as he held his life that he could have concealed his love, he was compelled, upon seeing his master's jealousy, to swear that there was in truth a lady whom he loved, a lady of such beauty that beside her the Duchess and all the ladies of her company were ugliness itself. He begged the Duke not to make him give the lady's name, for there was a bond between them and an understanding that it would be broken if one of them were to make it known. The Duke promised not to press him further and was so delighted with what he had learned that he treated him even more kindly than before. The Duchess was not slow to notice this, and with her customary cunning set about discovering the reason for it. The Duke made no secret of what he had been told. But she was not satisfied. Driven on, no longer now by desire for revenge alone, but by the violence of her jealousy, she insisted that her husband order the man to reveal the name of the lady he loved. She was certain, she declared, that what he had said was a lie, and that this was the best possible way to demonstrate the truth of what she herself had from the beginning maintained. If the young man refused to name the woman he thought so beautiful, then the Duke would, she went on, be the most stupid prince in the world to take him at his word. The unhappy Duke, whose mind could be changed just as his wife pleased, then went for a walk alone with the young gentleman. He told him that his distress was now even greater, for he was afraid that what he had been told on the previous occasion was a mere excuse to prevent him suspecting the truth. He was more tormented than ever by his doubts, he said, and therefore begged and besought the young man to reveal the name of the lady whom he loved so deeply. But the poor young man implored his master not to force him to commit so great a sin against the one he loved as to break the promise he had kept so long, and to make him lose in a single day that which he had preserved for seven whole years. He would rather endure death itself than wrong the lady who was so steadfast in her loyalty to him. The Duke saw that he was not prepared to answer. The jealousy that swept over him was so violent that his features became contorted with rage, and he said:

'Then make your choice. Either you tell me the name of this woman you love so much. Or you leave the lands under my jurisdiction for ever, and on the understanding that if I find you here after eight days have elapsed I shall have you most cruelly put to death!'

If ever a faithful servant was cast into the depths of despair, it was surely this young man. Truly could he have said *Angustiae sunt mihi undique*,* for, on the one hand, if he told the truth he would lose his lady when she learned that he had wilfully broken his promise and, on the other hand, if he did not tell the truth, he would be banished and would never again be able to see her. Thus pressed on all sides, a cold sweat broke over him, as if his sorrow brought him to the brink of death. When the Duke saw how the young man reacted, he concluded that it was indeed the Duchess, and no one else, with whom he was in love, and that

* Daniel 13:22 (Vulgate): 'I am hemmed in on all sides.

it was because he could not give another lady's name that he had been overcome by such anguish.

'If what you say were the truth,' he said harshly, 'you would hardly find it so painful to tell me, and I believe that it is your guilt which so tortures you.'

Roused by these words, and moved by his affection for his master, the young gentleman resolved to tell him the truth, reassuring himself that the Duke's sense of honour was so high, that he would not for the world ever divulge the secret. So, falling upon his knees before him, and wringing his hands, he said:

'My lord, it is my indebtedness toward you and the love I bear you, more than fear of death, that bid me speak, for I cannot endure that you should be so beset by false beliefs about me. To relieve you from your agony, I shall therefore do something that otherwise no form of torture could have forced from me, humbly beseeching you, my lord, that you will swear in the name of God, and promise upon your oath as a prince and Christian that you will never reveal this secret that you force me to tell you.'

The Duke then swore by all the oaths he knew that he would never divulge the secret to anyone in the world, either in speech, in writing or in manner. Then the young man, confident that he could place his trust in such a virtuous prince, laid the foundation stone of his own undoing, saying:

'Seven long years ago, my lord, knowing that your niece, the Lady of Vergy,* was widowed and without match, I strove to earn her favour. Since my birth was such that I could not hope to marry her, I contented myself with being accepted as her devoted servant. And it has pleased God that this alliance should be till now so prudently conducted that there is no man or woman alive who knows of it but ourselves. But now you too know of it, my lord, and in your hands I place my honour and my life, humbly beseeching you to guard this secret and to hold my lady, your niece, in no less esteem for what you now know, for I believe that there is under heaven no more perfect creature.'

If ever anyone was relieved and delighted, it was the Duke at this moment. For, knowing how beautiful his niece was, he

* Although the medieval source concerns the de Vergy family, the *Heptaméron* manuscripts have du Verg(i)er ('of the orchard').

was in no doubt that she was likely to be more attractive to the young man than was his wife. But, unable to comprehend how such a liaison could have been so mysteriously maintained, the Duke asked the young man how he had been able to see his lady. The young man explained how her room opened on to a garden, how on the days when he was expected a little door was left unlocked and how he would walk in and wait till he heard the bark of a little dog which his lady let into the garden to give the signal that her women had left. He told the Duke how he would go in and talk with her the whole night through, how she would appoint the day for his return, and how he had never once without good reason failed her.

The Duke, who was the most curious of men and who in his time had had many a love-affair, asked the young man to take him with him, not as a master but as a comrade, next time he should go to see his niece, partly in order to banish lingering doubts and partly to hear more about this extraordinary story. Having already gone as far as he had, the young man could not refuse his request, and told him that it was that very evening which was the time of his next assignation. If the Duke had gained a kingdom he could not have been more delighted. Pretending to retire to his private room, he had two horses harnessed, one for himself and one for the young man. Then they rode through the night, from the Duke's residence at Argilly all the way to Vergy.

Tethering their horses outside the castle wall, they went up to the little gate. The young man led the Duke inside, and asked him to wait behind a walnut tree, from where he would be able to see whether what he had told him was true or not. He did not have to wait in the garden for long before the little dog was heard barking, and the young man walked towards the tower, out of which came the lady to greet him. She kissed him and told him it seemed like a thousand years since she had last seen him. Then into her room they went, closing the door behind them. Now that the Duke had witnessed their secret he felt more than satisfied. He did not have to wait long for the young man to come out again, having told his lady that he had to go back earlier than usual because the Duke was intending to go hunting at four o'clock the next morning and he dared not break his word. The Lady of Vergy placed her honour above pleasure, and she did not try to delay him in the performance of his duty, for the thing that she prized most about this noble love of theirs was that it should remain secret before all men. So at one hour after midnight the young man departed, and his lady, in her cap and mantle, accompanied him into the garden, though she did not go as far as she would have liked, for, afraid lest she should see the Duke, he made her return to her room. The Duke and the young man mounted their horses and rode back to the château at Argilly, and as they rode, the Duke swore again and again that he would die sooner than reveal the secret.

After this the Duke grew to love and trust the young gentleman so much, that no one in his court stood higher in his favour, and at this the Duchess was filled with rage. But she was forbidden by her husband ever to mention the subject again to him. He told her that he knew the truth, and that he was perfectly content, for he also knew that the lady the young man loved was more worthy of his love than she. These words wounded the Duchess's heart so deeply that she succumbed to a sickness worse than the fever. The Duke went to her room to comfort her. But there was only one thing she wanted – to be told the name of the beautiful lady whom the young man loved. And she pressed him so hard that he finally walked from her room, saying, 'If you speak such words to me again, then we shall part.' The Duke's words aggravated her sickness, and she pretended that she could feel her unborn child stirring within her, and the poor Duke was so overjoyed at this that he came to her bed. But as his passion was mounting, she turned on to her side, and said:

'I implore you, my husband, since you feel no love, either for your wife or for your child, let us go to our death together!' These words were accompanied by such cries and floods of tears that the Duke was afraid she would lose the fruit of her womb. So, taking her in his arms, he begged her to tell him what she wanted, and assured her that there was nothing he would not do for her.

'Ah, my lord,' she replied, still weeping, 'how can I hope that you would do anything difficult for me, when you will not do for me the simplest and most reasonable thing in all the world, when you will not tell me who is the mistress of the wickedest servant you have ever had. Once I used to think that you and I were as one heart, one soul, one flesh. But now I know that you regard me as a stranger, for those secrets which you ought not to hide from me you conceal from me as if I were a stranger. Oh, how many times in the past have you confided in me over secret matters of far greater importance! Have you ever heard that I have given them away? You have tried my will and found it so equal to your own that you cannot doubt that I am more yourself than I am myself. And even if you have sworn to tell this man's secret to no one, yet you can tell it to me without breaking your word, for I am and cannot be other than you, my lord. I have you in my heart, I hold you in my arms, I carry a child within me in whom you live, and I cannot have your heart though you have mine! The more loving and faithful I am, the harsher, the more cruel you become. A thousand times a day I wish that I might die and deliver my child from such a father, yes, and deliver myself from such a husband! I hope death will come upon me soon now, for now I know that you prefer your faithless servant to your own wife, your loving wife and the mother of a child who is your own and who now will perish also because I cannot have of you that which I desire to know above all else!'

So saying, she put her arms around him and kissed him, sprinkling his face with her tears, and uttering such doleful cries that the good Duke, terrified lest he lose both wife and child, decided to tell her the whole truth. But first he swore that if ever she should reveal it to any soul alive, it would be by his own hand that she would die, and to this judgement and sentence she submitted herself. Then the poor deceived husband proceeded to tell her from beginning to end everything that he had heard and seen. She listened quietly, and pretended to be satisfied, while in her heart she had quite different thoughts. But she covered up her passion as best she could, for she feared the Duke.

The day came round when the Duke held his court, a day of great feasting when all the ladies in the land were invited, and amongst them the Duke's niece. After the banquet the dancing began, and each and every one performed their part. But the

Duchess, tortured by the sight of the Lady of Vergy in all her grace and beauty, could not rejoice, and even less could she keep her bitterness from showing itself. For, summoning all the ladies to sit around her, she began to turn their talk to matters of love, and when she saw that the Lady of Vergy did not speak, she said, her heart swollen with jealousy: 'And you, fair niece, is it possible that with your beauty you have no lover or gentleman devoted to your service?'

'Madame,' replied the Lady of Vergy, 'my beauty has brought me no such benefits, for since my husband's death I have desired no one's love but that of his children, and I am content that it should be so.'

'Fair niece, fair niece,' answered the Duchess with terrible bitterness in her voice, 'there is no love so secret that it is not known, and no little dog so tamed, so trained that his yapping is not heard!'

I leave you to imagine, Ladies, the suffering that was caused the Lady of Vergy when she saw that what had been kept hidden for so long was now to her great dishonour openly declared. Her honour, so carefully guarded, yet now so ignominiously lost, tortured her; but even more tortured was she by the suspicion that her lover had broken his promise. She believed that he could never have done such a thing unless he had fallen in love with a lady who was more beautiful than she, and to whom the overpowering force of passion must have led him to declare their secret. But the virtue of the Lady of Vergy was so great that she gave no indication of her feelings, but merely laughed, replying to the Duchess that she did not understand the language of the beasts. Yet beneath this virtuous dissimulation her heart was so heavy with grief that she rose, and walked through the Duchess's room into a dressing-room. The Duke, who was strolling nearby, saw her go in. There the poor lady, thinking herself quite alone, fell so heavily in her weakness upon the bed that a young woman, who had been sleeping on the floor, got up and looked through the curtains to see who it could be. Seeing that it was the Lady of Vergy and that she believed herself alone, the girl dared not say anything, but listened quietly, as the lady began in deathly tones to lament her lot:

'O unhappy woman, what are these words that assail my ears? What is this sentence of death that I have heard pronounced? Is this the judgement that will end my life? O most beloved of men, is this the reward for my chaste, noble and most virtuous love? O my heart, have you chosen so perilously as to choose for a faithful servant a faithless wretch, for a man of truth the most dissembling knave, for a guardian of a secret one who has an evil tongue? Alas! How can it be that a secret kept so well hidden from all of humankind should yet be revealed to the Duchess? Alas! my little dog, so obedient, you who were my only messenger throughout this long and virtuous love of mine, it was not you who betrayed me! It was this man, whose voice has carried farther than the bark of any dog! It was this man, who has less gratitude than any beast! It was this man, who broke his vow, who exposed the happy life which harming no one, we led together for so long! Oh my dear love! No one else's love but yours found a place in my heart, and with your love my life was perserved. Now must I declare you my mortal enemy? Now must I throw my honour to the winds, my body into the earth, and my soul to its eternal resting-place? Is the beauty of the Duchess so supreme that like that of Circe it has transmuted you? Has she turned you from virtue to vice, from goodness to evil, from a man into a ferocious beast? O my love, you have broken your promise to me, but I shall not break mine. I gave my word that I should never see you again, if our love should ever be divulged. Yet since without seeing you I cannot live, gladly I embrace the extremity of pain that now I feel, seeking no remedy from medicine or reason, for death alone can bring it to an end, death, which is more dear to me than life without my love, without my honour, without my happiness. It is not war or death that have stolen my love from me, it is not any sin of mine that has stripped me of my honour, it is not my weakness and failures that have made me lose everything that gave me joy, but cruel Fortune, who has made him who should have been most grateful an ingrate traitor; it is cruel Fortune who has meted out to me the very contrary of my deserts. Ah! my Duchess, what pleasure it gave you to mock me, when you spoke of my little dog! Then rejoice in that which belongs by right to me alone! Mock her, then, who thought she would be free of mockery by loving secretly and virtuously! Oh! How those words wrung my heart! How they made me blush for shame, how they made me pale with jealousy! Alas! my heart, I feel the end is nigh! You burn, my heart, for the [love that is now laid bare], you are turned to cold, hard ice, wearied unto death by jealousy and grievous wrongs! For bitter grief I cannot now, my heart, console you! Alas! poor soul, you who have adored too much the creature and forgotten his Creator, must now return to Him from whose hands you have been torn by the vanity of human love. Be assured, my soul, that the Father you will find will be better far than the lover for whose sake you so many times forsook Him. Ah my God, my Creator, who art true and perfect love, by whose grace the love I bore this man remained unstained by sin, unless it be the sin of loving him too much, I humbly pray that in thy mercy thou wilt receive the soul and spirit of her who now repents of breaking thy first and just Commandment. By the merit of Him whose love is beyond all understanding, forgive the sin which I through loving too much and too well have committed. I thee alone do I place my trust. Adieu, my lover and my friend – alas, this word, this empty word doth pierce my heart!'

So saying, she collapsed on the bed. Her face became pale, her lips blue, her extremities cold. At that very instant the man whom she loved came into the hall. He had seen the Duchess dancing with the others, and looked all round for his lady. He could see her nowhere and went into the Duchess's room, where he found the Duke, who, guessing who he was looking for, whispered in his ear, 'She went into this dressing-room, and appeared unwell'. The young man then asked if he might enter, and the Duke replied that he might. There he found the Lady of Vergy, bidding farewell to her mortal life. He took her up in his arms, saying, 'What is this, my love? Do you desire to leave me?' Hearing the voice she knew so well, the poor lady regained a little strength, and opened her eyes to look at the man who was the cause of her death. But as she gazed, love and grief welled so vehemently within her that with a piteous sigh she gave up her soul to God. The young man, more dead, if it were possible, than she who was already dead, demanded of the young woman how this sickness had overcome his lady. Every word that she had overheard she retold to him. Now he knew that the Duke had revealed his secret to his wife, and so overwhelmed was he with the fury of despair that he took his beloved's body in his arms and washed her face with his tears, saying:

'O traitor, base and wretched lover that I am! Why has not the punishment for my treachery fallen upon my head? Why upon her who is innocent? Why did not heaven strike me down the day my tongue revealed our secret, virtuous love? Why did not the earth open and swallow me up, false and faithless as I am? O my tongue, may you burn like Dives' tongue in Hell! O my heart, too afraid of death and banishment, may you ever more be torn apart by eagles, as was the heart of Ixion!* Alas! my love, the sorrow of sorrows, the most sorrowful of sorrows, is upon me! Thinking to hold you fast, I have lost you. Thinking to see you live a long, a happy and a virtuous life, I hold you dead in my arms displeased in the last extremity with me, my heart and my tongue! O you who were the most faithful and most loyal woman in all the world, myself I denounce as the most unfaithful, most disloyal man of all the men who ever lived! Would that I could blame the Duke, whose word I trusted, hoping that I could prolong our happy life. But, alas! I should have known that no one could keep my secret better than myself. The Duke had more reason to tell his wife than I had to tell him. Myself alone I accuse of the greatest crime ever committed between lovers and friends! I should have submitted myself to the sentence he threatened me with, I should have been thrown in the river. Then, at least, my love, you would have lived a widow, and I should have gone to a glorious death as the law of true love commands. But I, who have broken the law of true love, live, while you, who have loved truly, lie here dead! For your pure and innocent heart could not bear to live and know the vice with which your lover is tainted. My God, why did you create me a man, a man whose heart knows nothing and whose love is light? Why was I not created to be her little dog, who served his mistress faithfully? Alas, my little friend, the joy I used to feel when I heard your bark is turned to sorrow, for

* Ixion is being confused with Prometheus.

I let another hear your voice! And yet, my love, it was not the Duchess, though many a time she assailed me with her base solicitations, who made me waver, nor was it any other woman in this world. It was ignorance that brought me down, for in my ignorance I thought that I could secure our love for evermore. But ignorance makes my guilt no less, for I have revealed my lady's secret, I have broken my solemn promise. And it is for that alone that she now lies dead before my eyes! Alas! my love, death would be less cruel to me than it has been to you – you who have ended your own innocent life because you have truly loved. Yet I think death will not deign to touch my faithless, wretched heart, for ten thousand deaths would be easier to bear than the life I shall lead, dishonoured, and tormented by the memory of a loss caused by none other than myself. Alas! my love, had it been that someone in hatred or by mischance had dared to kill you, then I would at once have taken up my sword to avenge you. Reason demands therefore that I do not pardon the murderer who has caused your death by a deed more vile than any thrust of any sword. If I knew an executioner more odious than I, I would surely plead with him to put to death your treacherous lover. O Love! you too have I offended in loving so imperfectly, and so the succour that you gave to her who kept your laws you rightly now refuse to me. What reason could I have to expect an end so noble? No, reason demands that I die by my own hand! And now that I have bathed your face with tears, now that with my tongue I have asked you for forgiveness, it remains only that my arm stretch out my body even as your own and send my soul whither yours will fly, in the knowledge that true and virtuous love shall never end, in this world or the next!'

He raised himself over the corpse like a man deranged and, bereft of all sense, drew his dagger, and with tremendous force stabbed himself through the heart. Then he took her in his arms again, kissing her so fondly, that one would have thought these were the throes of love not death. Seeing what had happened, the young woman ran out shouting for help. The Duke, hearing the cries and guessing that some disaster had overtaken those whom he loved so dearly, was the first to enter. He did his best to separate the piteous couple in the hope of saving the young man at least. But the young man held so fast to his lady's body that it was impossible to pull him off until he was dead. Yet he had heard the Duke, who had cried out, 'Alas! Who is the cause of all this?', for he had stared back at him like a madman, and replied, 'The cause, my lord, is my tongue, and yours!' And it was as he uttered those words that he died, with his cheek pressed firmly against his beloved's face.

The Duke, desiring to know more, ordered the young woman to tell him everything that she had heard and seen, and she told her tale from start to finish, leaving nothing out. The Duke, realizing that it was he who was the cause of this calamity, threw himself on top of the two dead lovers. He wept and cried out in anguish, he covered their faces with kisses, he called upon them to pardon his sin. Then in a frenzied rage he rose, drew the dagger from the young man's body, and like the wild boar which, wounded by a spear, runs headlong at the hunter who has thrown it, he ran from the room in pursuit of the woman who had wounded him to the depths of his soul. She was dancing in the hall, gayer than usual, content in the thought that she had taken revenge on the Lady of Vergy. Storming into the midst of the dancers, the Duke seized hold of her. 'You swore on your life to keep the secret, and with your life you shall pay for what you have done!' As he spoke he pulled her head back by her veil, and stuck the dagger in her breast. The whole company, overcome with horror, thought he must have lost his reason. But his deed done, the Duke called all his liegemen round him in the hall to recount the piteous and noble story of his niece, and the cruel action of his wife. It was a tale that did not fail to call forth the tears of those who listened to it. Later he ordered an abbey to be founded to atone in part for the murder of his wife, and in it he ordered her to be buried. In it too he ordered a magnificent tomb to be built where his niece and the young nobleman might rest together, with an epitaph telling of their tragedy. Then he made an expedition against the Turks, and God granted him such success that he returned a wealthy and much honoured man. Finding that in the meantime his eldest son had grown and learned to govern his father's lands, the Duke left all he had to him, and withdrew to the religious life in the very abbey where his wife and the two lovers were buried.

There, in the sight of God, he peacefully passed away his old age.

*

'That, Ladies, is the story you asked me to tell you. I can tell from the looks in your eyes that it hasn't left you unmoved. I think you should let it stand as an example to you not to fix your affection on men, for, however pure and virtuous your affection may be, it will always lead to some disastrous conclusion. You will remember that Saint Paul preferred love such as this not to exist even between husband and wife. For, the more one fixes one's affection on earthly things, the further one is from heavenly affection. And the more one's love is virtuous and noble, the more difficult it is to break the bond. And so, Ladies, I beg you to pray to God [at all times] to grant you His Holy Spirit, that your hearts may be so inflamed with love of Him that at the hour of your death you will be spared the suffering that comes from loving too dearly things that must be left behind on earth.'

'If their love was as virtuous and noble as your account depicts it,' said [Hircan], 'then why did it have to be kept so secret?'

'Because,' replied Parlamente, 'men are so malicious that they can never believe that great love and virtue can be joined together, for they make judgements about vice in men and women in accordance with their own passions. And that is why any woman who has a close male friend other than her nearest relatives, needs to talk with him in secret, if she wishes to talk with him for any length of time at all. Whether a lady's love is virtuous or vicious, doubt may be cast on her honour, because people only judge by what they see.'

'But,' said Geburon, 'people think even worse things about women when secrets like this are eventually disclosed.'

'You are right, I admit,' said Longarine. 'And it follows that the best thing is not to love at all!'

'That is a sentence against which we beg leave to appeal,' said Dagoucin. 'If we thought that ladies were really without love, we should prefer to be without life. I'm referring to those men who live only for the sake of the love of a lady. Though they may never reach their goal, they are sustained by hope, and by it are led on to accomplish countless honourable deeds until in old age their noble and virtuous passions turn into sufferings of another kind. If it were generally believed that ladies were incapable of love, then, instead of following the profession of arms, we should all turn into mere merchants, and instead of winning honour, seek only to pile up wealth!'

'You mean to say then,' said Hircan, 'that if there were no ladies, we would all be [merchants]? As if we only had any courage at all because it was bestowed on us by women! I take quite the contrary view. Nothing debases a man's courage more than frequenting women and getting too fond of them. That's why the Hebrews forbade their men to go to war during the first year of their marriage – for fear they would shrink from taking the kind of risks expected of them, because they were still too fond of their wives!'

'If you ask me,' said Saffredent, 'that was not a very sensible law, because there's nothing more likely to make a man want to get away from home than being married! War abroad is certainly no harder to endure than strife at home! In my opinion, if you want to persuade men to stop sitting at home and go to foreign parts, you should make them marry.'

'It is quite true,' said Ennasuite, 'that marriage removes from them the burden of care for their house and home, because they rely on their wives to do that job for them and think only of winning honour, confidently leaving it to the wives to look after their domestic interests in an adequate fashion.'

'Be that as it may,' replied Saffredent, 'I'm glad that there's at least some agreement between us!'

'But,' intervened Parlamente, 'what you're discussing now isn t really the most important point. The most important question is why the gentleman, who was the cause of the whole disaster, did not immediately die of sorrow himself, like the lady, who was completely innocent.'

'It's because women love more deeply than men,' said Nomerfide.

'No,' said Simontaut, 'it's because when women become bitter and jealous, they give up the ghost without knowing why. Men, on the other hand, are more prudent, and like to find out the truth of the matter first. Once the truth is known, thanks to their good sense, they will demonstrate the greatness of their hearts. This was how the young man in the story acted. Once he had realized that he was the cause of his lady's suffering, he showed the extent of his love for her, and took his own life.'

'All the same,' said Ennasuite, 'she died for true love, because her steadfast, loyal heart could not endure the pain of being so treacherously deceived.'

'The fact was,' said Simontaut, 'that her jealousy gave her no room to use her reason. She was convinced, wrongly, that her lover had acted in a base manner, and being so convinced, she had no choice but to die. There was nothing she could do. But her lover's death, once he'd recognized that he'd done wrong, was voluntary.'

'Yet to cause such mortal grief, her love must have been very deep,' said Nomerfide.

'Then you've no need to worry,' said Hircan. 'You're not likely to succumb to that particular fever!'

'No more than you're likely to shorten *your* life because you realize what wrongs you've committed!' she retorted.

Suspecting that this argument might turn out not to be in her own best interests, Parlamente intervened, laughing, and said: 'I think two people dying for love is quite enough, without having two more coming to blows for the same cause. Anyway, there's the last bell for vespers, and that will break up our gathering, whether you like it or not.'

At her bidding, the whole company rose, and went to hear vespers. In their prayers they did not forget to pray for the souls of the true lovers, and the monks agreed of their own free will to say a *De profundis* for them. Throughout supper, too, they talked of nothing but the Lady of Vergy. After talking thus a while together, they each retired to their rooms. And so the seventh day came to a close.

END OF THE SEVENTH DAY

EIGHTH DAY

PROLOGUE

When morning came they inquired how work on their bridge was progressing, and learned that it might be completed within two or three days. Some of them were rather sorry to hear this, for they would have liked it to take longer, so that they might continue to enjoy the happy life they were leading. But, recognizing that there were only two or three days left, they made up their minds to make the most of them. Oisille was asked to administer her spiritual nourishment, as was her wont, and this she did, though she kept them longer than usual, being anxious that they should reach the end of the canonical epistles of Saint John before leaving. So well did she deliver the reading that the Holy Spirit, full of sweetness and love, seemed to be speaking through her mouth. Inflamed with this fire they went off to hear high mass. After that they dined together, still talking about the previous day's story-telling and challenging one another to make the new day its equal. And to ensure that it should be so, they each withdrew for a while to their rooms in order to prepare their stories. At the appointed hour, they came to present their accounts in the meadow, where the grass stretched out like green baize across a table top. The monks had already arrived and taken their places. When everyone was seated, they asked who should begin.

'You have done me the honour,' said Saffredent, 'of letting me begin two days. I think it would be unfair to the ladies if one of them also did not begin two days.'

'In that case,' replied Oisille, 'we must either stay here longer, or else one of you and one of us must go without starting a second day.'

'As far as I'm concerned,' said Dagoucin, 'I would have given my place to Saffredent, had I been chosen.'

'And as for me,' said Nomerfide, 'I would have given mine to Parlamente, for accustomed as I am to serve, I could not command.'

With this everyone agreed, and Parlamente began to speak.

'Ladies, every day so far has been taken up with so many wise tales that I would like to propose that today should be taken up with stories which are the most foolish and the most true we can think of. So, to start you going, I shall begin.'

STORY SEVENTY-ONE

In the town of Amboise there was once a saddler by the name of Brimbaudier. He was saddle-maker to the Queen of Navarre, and as for his character, you could tell from the colour of his face that he was a servant of Bacchus, rather than a servant of the priests of Diana. He had married a good woman, who managed his home [and children] very capably, and he was very contented. One day word was brought to him that his wife was dangerously ill. He was greatly afflicted at this, and set off as fast as he could to see what he could do for her. But he found the poor woman so far gone that a confessor rather than a doctor was what was required. His distress was piteous to behold. To report it really truthfully, I ought to put on a throaty voice like his, and it'd be even better if I could imitate the expression on his face. When he had done for her everything he possibly could, she asked to be given a cross, and he had one brought for her. This spectacle was too much for the poor fellow. He threw himself in desperation on to a bed, bellowing away in his funny thick voice: 'Woe is me! I'm going to lose my wife! What'll I do? Woe is me!'* and the like. Eventually he looked up and realized there was no one else in the room, apart from a little chambermaid – a pretty lass, and shapely too. He called her across to him and said, 'My dear, I'm going to die, no, it's worse than if I was already dead and gone, seeing your mistress dying like that. I don't know what to do, I don't know what to say, except I need you to help me. Take the keys I've got hanging at my side. Look after the house and children for me. Do the housekeeping, because I can't manage any more!'

The poor girl felt sorry for him. She pleaded with him not to despair, and not to make her lose her kind master as well as her mistress. He replied: 'My dear, it cannot be. I'm dying. Look how cold my face is. Come a bit nearer with your cheeks and warm me up a bit!' So saying, he thrust his hand into her

* The spelling of the de Thou manuscripts represents regional pronunciation.

bosom! She did get a little bit difficult, but he told her not to be alarmed. They must get to know one another a bit better, he said. At this point he grabbed her in his arms and threw her on to the bed. The wife had been left on her own with the cross and a drop of holy water. She had not spoken a word for two whole days. But now she started to shout as loud as her feeble voice allowed her to.

'Aaah! I'm not dead yet! I'm not dead yet!' she cried shaking her fist at the pair. 'Swine! Brute! I'm not dead yet!'

The husband and the serving girl jumped up. The wife was so enraged that her anger burnt up the catarrhal humours that had prevented her speaking, and she was able to hurl at them all the abuse she could devise. Indeed, from that moment on she began to get better, and for ever after nagged her husband for not loving her enough!

*

'There you are, Ladies. That just shows what hypocrites men are. It doesn't take much to console them when they're mourning the loss of their wives, does it?'

'How do you know he hadn't heard that that was the best way to cure his wife?' asked Hircan. 'He'd been treating her very considerately, and that didn't cure her, so he thought he'd see if the opposite would work any better. And he discovered it worked very well. I'm surprised you women have so frankly admitted your true colours. It's not feminine sweetness, it's feminine rancour that cures them!'

'Without a doubt, that sort of thing would make me jump up from the grave, let alone from a sick-bed!' said Longarine.

'What was he doing wrong, though,' asked Saffredent, 'in seeking consolation, when he thought she was dead? Everyone knows that marriage is only supposed to be binding for life, and that afterwards one is set free.'

'Yes,' replied Oisille, 'free from your vows and obligations, but anyone with a true heart is never released from the ties of love. It didn't take *him* long to recover from his grief, for he could not even wait till his wife had breathed her last!'

'What I find most strange,' said Nomerfide, 'is the fact that even with the spectacle of death and the cross in front of his nose he wasn't deterred from offending the Lord.'

'That's a fine argument!' exclaimed Simontaut. 'Do you mean to say you're not shocked by such goings-on, provided that they don't take place anywhere near a church or a graveyard?'

'You can make fun of me as much as you like,' replied Nomerfide, 'but all the same, meditating on death is enough to chill the heart of anyone, however young.'

'I'd agree with you wholeheartedly,' said Dagoucin, 'if it weren't for the fact that a certain princess once told me that the contrary is the case.'

'In other words,' said Parlamente, 'she told you a story to that effect. Well, if so, I invite you to take my place and tell it to us.'

Dagoucin began thus.

STORY SEVENTY-TWO

It all happened in what was, after Paris, the finest town in France. There was a luxuriously endowed hospital in this town run by a prioress assisted by about fifteen nuns. In a separate wing there was a prior and about eight monks to say the offices. The nuns, being occupied with looking after the patients, only said their paternosters and the hours of Our Lady. One day a man lay dying, a poor man of the town, and all the nuns gathered round his bed. They did all they could to restore his health, then sent for one of their monks to confess him. As he was becoming weaker, they administered extreme unction, and he gradually lost the faculty of speech. However, because he lingered on [and seemed still able to hear], the nuns did what they could to give him a few words of comfort. But they grew tired of this, and when it got late and night came they retired one by one to bed, leaving one of the youngest behind to lay out the corpse. With her there remained one of the monks. He was a very austere man, both in word and deed, and the young nun was even more in awe of him than she was of the prior himself. Having cried 'Jesus! Jesus!' in the poor man's ear for a while, they concluded he was well and truly dead. So together they laid him out, and as they carried out this last act of mercy, the monk began to speak of the misery that is life, and the blessedness that is death. On and on he went. Midnight struck. The poor girl listened attentively to his pious words, and gazed at him with tears in her eyes. This gave him considerable pleasure – so much in fact that even as he spoke of the life to come, he started to put his arms round her as if he longed to transport her to Paradise! The poor girl just listened. She regarded him as the most pious man in the place, and dared not resist. Realizing this, the wicked monk, still prating about God, had his way with her. They must have been prompted to the deed by the Devil, for there had never been any question of such a thing before. He reassured her that a sin committed in secret was not counted as a sin in the eyes of God. In a case of this kind, he told her, two persons without ties did not commit any offence, provided it did not cause a public scandal. To prevent that happening, he instructed her to take care not to mention it in her confessions to anyone except himself.

Thus they separated, and went their different ways. She left first, and as she went past the chapel, she decided to go in and say her prayers as usual. As she spoke the words 'Virgin Mary', it suddenly dawned on her that she herself was no longer a virgin. And it was neither love nor violence that had brought it about, but her own foolish timidity. She wept and wept as if her heart would break. The monk, who could hear her sobbing in the distance, guessed that she had had a change of heart and was anxious lest he should not be able to enjoy the same favours again. To forestall that possibility, he followed her into the chapel, where she lay prostrate in front of the statue of the Virgin. He spoke to her sharply, telling her that if she really had a guilty conscience she should come and confess it to him, and need not repeat the act, if she did not want to, for she was at liberty to choose without sin.

The stupid nun, thinking that she would make amends to God, went to make her confession to the monk. By way of imposing penance, he swore to her that she was not really sinning at all by loving him, and assured her that a little holy water was enough to wash away a peccadillo such as that. She had more faith in him than in God, and went back after a time to do his bidding. Finally she became pregnant. This distressed her so much that she pleaded with the prioress to have the monk thrown out of the convent, for she knew that the man was so cunning that he could not fail to seduce her again. But the prior and the [prioress], who were on good terms with one another, treated her with contempt, saying that she was big enough to look after herself where men were concerned, and that in any case the monk in question was a very good man. Eventually, consumed by guilt and remorse, she passionately implored them to grant her leave to journey to Rome, for she thought that if she made her confession at the feet of the Pope, she could recover her virginity. They readily gave their consent, preferring her to go against the rule of her order and leave the convent on a pilgrimage, than have her remain enclosed and develop an even more particular conscience! What if she were to become so desperate as to [disclose] the kind of life that was being led in the convent? So they provided her with the money for the journey.

Now God so willed that [the poor nun should arrive in Lyons during the time when the Duchess of Alençon, who was later to become the Queen of Navarre, was in the town. One evening after vespers in the church of Saint John, the Duchess was on her knees in front of the crucifix in the rood-loft.] It was here that, along with three or four of her ladies, she had come discreetly to perform a novena.* While she was thus at prayer she heard somebody come up the stair, and in the lamp light she could see it was a nun. In order to listen to the nun's devotions, the Duchess moved to the corner of the altar. The nun, thinking that she was alone, knelt down, and began to beat her breast, weeping most piteously and crying out that she had sinned.

'Alas! My God, have mercy on me a poor sinner!' she sobbed over and over again.

To find out what was the matter, the Duchess approached her, saying: 'My dear, what is the matter? Where are you from? What brings you to this place?'

The poor nun did not recognize the Duchess, and said, 'Alas! I am in desperate straits, and there is no one but God to whom I can turn. I am praying that He will enable me somehow to speak to the Duchess of Alençon. She is the only one to whom I could tell my troubles, for I am sure that if there is anything anyone can do, she will do it.'

'My dear,' replied the Duchess, 'you may talk to me just as you would to her – for I am one of her closest friends?'

'Forgive me if I do not tell you,' said the nun, 'for I can only tell my secret to the Duchess herself.'

So the Duchess told her that her wish was granted and that she need have no fear to speak quite openly. The poor girl threw herself at her feet, weeping once more and crying out loud. Then she told her the sorry story which you have already heard. The Duchess so comforted her that, while not discouraging her from continuing to repent of her sin, she persuaded her to abandon her idea of going to Rome. Then she sent her back to her

* A nine-day cycle of devotions.

convent, with letters to the bishop of the diocese, instructing him to have the scandalous monk removed.

*

'This is a story that I was told by the Duchess herself, and it's a story that shows you, Ladies, that Nomerfide's precept does not apply to everybody. For the couple in the story had to handle the dead man while they were laying him out, but they were none the less affected by their wanton lusts.'

'There's an original idea,' said Hircan, 'and one, I think, which no one has tried before – to speak words of death while performing the works of life!'

'To commit a sin like that is not,' said Oisille, 'performing the works of life! For do we not know that sin engenders death?'

'But,' said Saffredent, 'these poor people would certainly not be thinking about that particular point of theology. The daughters of Lot made their father drunk in order to conserve the human race, and it was the same with this poor couple. They wanted to repair what death had destroyed, to create a new body to replace the old. For this reason I see nothing wrong in what happened, except that the poor nun was made so sad and wept and wept and continually returned to the cause of her tears.'

'I've seen plenty like her,' said Hircan. 'They weep for their sins, and at the same time laugh over the pleasures they've had.'

'I can guess who that remark is aimed at,' said Parlamente, 'and [it seems to me] that their laughter has lasted long enough, and that it is time for the tears to start to flow.'

'Be quiet!' said Hircan. 'The tragedy that began with laughter is not yet at its end!'

'To change the subject, then,' she said, 'it occurs to me that Dagoucin has departed from the decision we made only to tell stories that are amusing. The one he's just told us was too sad.'

'You did say,' replied Dagoucin, 'that [we] would only tell stories about foolish things, and I don't think that I have failed in that respect. However, for a more amusing story, I hand over to Nomerfide. I'm sure she will make up for my lapse.'

'Well, I have a story ready to tell you,' she began, 'and it's a very appropriate one after the one you've told. It's about death, and it's about a monk. So please all listen carefully.'

●●●